THE Ozarks Druid

COURTNEY LANNING

The Ozarks Druid
Book Two in the Boston Mountain Magic series © 2021 Courtney
Lanning

For more information contact:
Riverdale Avenue Books/Quest Imprint
5676 Riverdale Avenue
Riverdale, NY 10471

www.riverdaleavebooks.com

Design by www.formatting4U.com
Cover design by Scott Carpenter

Digital ISBN: 9781626016286
Trade ISBN: 9781626016293

First edition, July 2022

Chapter One

I've heard it said that peace is more than the absence of conflict. And I have to confess, I wouldn't know too much about that, because my life has always been full of conflict. But tonight might just have taken the cake.

Barb's face was reaching peak red as we screamed at each other. This kind of behavior wasn't anything new from us. But the energy we were each building was certainly hitting new levels.

The two of us each felt like the other was dead wrong, and whoever shouted the loudest for the longest was going to win this argument. When it came to fighting with my guardians, I learned early on there's wisdom in the understanding of 'you win some and you lose some.' But I wasn't going to lose tonight. Barb didn't feel like she was going to, either.

She stood behind the blue living room sofa in her white nightgown glaring at me. Barb already had her night cream in, and her short wavy graying hair bobbed with each jab of a finger she pointed in my direction. I was tempted to tune her out because I knew that whatever she was saying was pure crap. But then I heard the words "ever again."

I immediately zoned back in and hit the rewind button on the cassette recorder that was my brain. Sometimes it felt like I had that little tape recorder thing Kevin McCallister had in the second *Home Alone* flick. I mentally pushed the button next to the << arrow, and I heard the whine of plastic parts and tape. Rherherherherhe…

"You can never see Abigail ever again," I heard Barb's voice say.

Of course, in real time, she had moved onto another sentence. But I was still processing what I heard her say.

"Fuck that!" I yelled, and I saw the whites of her eyes grow wider.

"What did you just say to me?" she all but hissed, walking around the sofa and getting closer.

"You heard me the first time, Barb. I'm not going to let you tell me

1

I can't see her. She's important to me," I said, blowing some of the long red hair out of my face.

The room was about to hit a new temperature, an unmatched level of heat.

Barb's eyes grew still.

"I have told you repeatedly to call me 'mother.' And I know you know better than to use such profanity in this house, young lady! Not only are you forbidden from seeing that hussie again, but you're grounded until the end of your holiday break," Barb said.

I clenched my fists. She'd gone too far. No matter how much I'd come to resent this woman who wanted me to call her 'mother,' not 'mom,' mind you, but mother, I did my best to retain a tiny shred of respect.

Generally, I kept my cursing nonexistent around the house. And I would never physically strike her. But my patience with this woman was thinning faster than a tree trunk between two cartoon beavers.

I'd always joked that there was no way she could be my real mom, but this fight was taking that wishful thinking to a whole new level.

"Okay, 1950s language or not, let's avoid insulting my girlfriend."

"Oh, right. If sinful behavior is going to be discussed, we'd better use hip terminology. What should I call her? BAE? THOT? Maybe we just stick with a classic that's evergreen. Abigail is a whore, and what you two have been doing is an abomination," Barb said, getting her index finger about five inches from my nose.

The temptation to bite it was of the devil. My heart was pounding, and I felt warm enough to actually be sweating despite the fact Barb kept the thermostat on 68 degrees year-round. I clenched my fists tighter and tried to keep some control over my words, but it was getting nigh impossible. Actually, scratch that. It wasn't becoming impossible. That gargantuan task was already past impossible.

"Listen, bitch," I said, squaring my shoulders and taking a step forward. "You're not going to talk about her like that ever again, you hear me? I care deeply about her. And can we discuss my behavior without using the word 'abomination' just once?"

Abomination was a favorite in Barb's vocabulary. It described the music I liked, the books I read, and now the girl I was sleeping with.

Barb's hand was a blur as it came up and struck me on the face. It hardly hurt. That same cheek had been broken during a Muay Thai

2

tournament three years ago. Bump a cheek full of screws half-way healed? Now that's some pain, physical pain at least. Of course, nothing quite hurts like the woman who calls herself 'mother' inflicting intentional pain on her child.

That was a different kind of ache, no matter how much I resented her.

I let out a low growl as I stared straight into her eyes. She always hated my growling, something I'd done for as long as I can remember. Barb thought I'd outgrow the behavior, but she was wrong.

What I knew she hated more was a direct challenge to her authority, and that's exactly what I did as I moved my face closer. We locked eyes, neither of us flinching.

Neither of us spoke for a solid 30 seconds. My breathing was ragged, and hers sharp.

I wanted to threaten her to strike me again. I could break her jaw with a back elbow spin, but I wasn't going to do that even though I badly wanted to.

My coach's words echoed in my head, *I'm not just teaching you how to hurt people. I'm training you to know when it's necessary. You're strongest when you exhaust all other options before resorting to violence.*

I could tell myself all day that Barb posed no physical threat to me. The only advantage she had was about four inches of height. I had 13 years of Muay Thai on her. And while rising blood pressure screamed at me, "Do it! Nail her!" I reminded myself I was in control of this situation.

"You listen and you listen well, young lady. These feelings you have are destructive in the worst way. Romans 1:24 ring a bell? Talking about homosexual perversion and lusts?"

I tried to bite my tongue as I often did when she got into Bible thumping mode. Was that blood I tasted in my mouth? Was I biting that hard?

"Here's what's going to happen. You're going to give me your phone, you're going to take your Bible, and you're going to stay up the rest of the night writing me an essay on Sodom and Gomorrah. Then, first thing tomorrow morning, we're both making an appointment to speak with Brother Marks."

"No, Barb. Here's what's going to happen. I'm going to keep my phone because I pay for my own plan. I'm not going to open a Bible or attend church ever again. And maybe, just maybe, you'll finally read that

3

article I texted you a couple weeks ago about your pastor being arrested after sleeping with a girl a year younger than me."

Maybe it wasn't smart to combine the agnostic fight with the bisexual fight, I thought for a split second before hearing myself laughing internally and yelling, *Nahhhhh. Go for broke! The house always wins anyway*.

Barb was quick to shift gears as a tear I'd classify as 'crocodile' slid down her right cheek.

"How can you do this to me, Eve?" she asked, hitting me with eyes that were both scornful and sympathy-seeking at the same time.

I couldn't place my finger on what exactly it was about my name I hated. It never felt right. And every time someone called me by it, especially the woman who demanded I call her mother, my right eye twitched. It felt like nails on a chalkboard, only the chalkboard was my soul, if that was possible.

"I've had you in a church pew at least three times a week since the day you were born," she said. "How can you deny the existence of God after all the miracles and love you've seen?"

Laughing at your parents is never respectful. And it had never been more tempting to do in my entire life.

"My sweet daughter. It's not too late. We can fix this."

I stomped my foot.

Our old house's heater kicked on and rattled the floor vent behind my left foot.

"No, you listen to me. And hear me well. I'm 18 now. I just finished my first semester of college, and you can't ship me off to camps anymore. I'm done with all of it, end of story. You're going to respect my choices. I'm old enough to buy lottery tickets, old enough to vote, and old enough to make up my own goddamn mind about what I believe in without you cramming your bullshit down my throat," I said, shoving my finger in her face.

She was done seeking sympathy. And her brain seemed to have settled on a course of action. Hopefully that course of action was storming off to her room to pray for me or whatever would remove her from my sight. That wasn't what she'd chosen to do, though.

Instead, she walked calmly over to the couch where I'd been sitting and kissing Abi when she came out of her bedroom. The same couch she grabbed Abi by the hair and jerked her up from before throwing her at the front door while screaming.

4

Barb picked up my purple leather purse and hurled it at me with surprising accuracy, not to mention fury. It hit my shoulder, and the strap slapped my face. Still I caught it without looking like an idiot fumbling the bag. Now *that* was a miracle.

"Get out. You're not welcome in this home anymore," Barb hissed, pointing at the front door behind me.

I looked at the wooden white door and scoffed.

"You're joking, right? It's 25 degrees out. Where do you expect me to go at 10:30 on a Sunday night?"

Barb shrugged. There wasn't an ounce of concern in her stone expression and all pretense of her actually caring vanished.

"Maybe find a homeless shelter or one of those warming centers they were discussing on the news. Then you can see what other people who make bad choices look like and the consequences they deal with."

I frowned at her. There was nothing I wanted more than to knock the legs out from that high horse she was standing on.

I scowled and said, "You know what, Barb? Mom is a title you earn. It isn't the default when you pop a child out of your womb. You want to be called mother? You have to work for it. And throwing a kid out on the streets isn't very Christ-like."

Feeling somewhat satisfied, I pushed away whatever feelings of dread I had about where I was going to sleep tonight and turned toward the door. I had my wallet and ID, but my wool coat was upstairs on my bed. I doubted Barb was going to let me go up and grab it.

Just as my hand touched the doorknob, Barb injected a bit of acid into her voice and said, "There she goes, the girl I cradled in my arms. The girl I bought violin lessons for. The girl who had a safe and warm home. Traded it all away for the pleasures of sin. Maybe you can shack up with your whore tonight, Eve. Her mother is already raising one detestable child. What's one more?"

I spun and grabbed a lamp from the long table that sat under our living room's biggest window, covered in white doilies, pictures of the family, and a crucifix. The lamp was Barb's favorite, a white porcelain body covered in nesting blue jays. The brown cord jerked out of the power socket with a loud POP and a few blue sparks.

Barb jerked like I was going to smash it over her head, but I had no intention of hurting her, not on the outside at least. I hurled the lamp across the room. It smashed into an old oak clock ticking loudly on the wall.

The lamp shattered on impact, but the mounted clock didn't budge. After the echo of the lamp shattering cleared from my ears, I heard the clock's steady ticking again.

"You want to know where Abi was before she came over here to stick her tongue down my throat, Barb? She was shopping for canned goods and then dropping them off at the little food pantry by the library. What did you do today? You went to church and ate lunch before deciding to bully your 19-year old daughter for being happy. Real big of you as a 51-year-old woman. Which one of you two do you think was the better person today?"

"That lamp was my mother's."

I shrugged.

"Next time I'm at Goodwill I'll see what other tacky lamps they have."

"Get out!" she shrieked as the veins in neck bulged.

"You're a bad parent," I said and stepped outside, trying to keep my tears hidden from her.

I despised the woman. I hated the fact that she'd just thrown me out of the house I grew up in. I loathed the fact that John wasn't here to stick up for me, and then the crushing realization that even if he had been, he probably would have shrugged and said, "Listen to your mother, Eve," like he always did.

I started a growl that worked its way up into a scream and smashed part of the old wooden porch rail with a swift punch.

Looking down at my red knuckles, I sniffled a little bit. And the gusto I got from having the last word with Barb started to fade, leaving the dawning realization I had nowhere to sleep tonight and nowhere to go.

Before my brain could start with questions like "What if I'm not good enough?" and "What if I really am the villain in this fight?" I took the two steps down into the front yard. Then I rubbed my arms covered in gooseflesh and a thin long-sleeve shirt..

"Cold never bothered me anyway," I mumbled, feeling a thin tree branch snap under my boot.

There were two giant oak trees in our—sorry, my—former, front yard. I'd climbed them both several times in my life to sneak in or out of the house. Tonight they stood above me, blocking out some of the stars in an otherwise clear sky. A cold, pale moon sat off to the right of my vision.

Telling Barb to piss off was a power play. Unfortunately, as I walked to the bus stop I grew colder and colder, and quickly realized power plays don't keep you warm at night.

Fayetteville isn't a big city. I mean, it is by Arkansas standards, but 80,000 people isn't much in other parts of the country.

Sure, I could call a ride with the tap of an app, but that would eat into the $332 I had left to my name. Thankfully I'd deposited my check from work on Friday. Part-time florist didn't leave me with tons of cash, but if it came down to it, it would get me a cheap motel room for tonight.

And Sabrina would have breakfast for me tomorrow morning at work. It was a fantastic perk of working at Petal and Stem. My boss always baked breakfast and brought it to me as I opened up the store for the morning. Muffins, pancakes, cinnamon rolls, she baked them all. One less meal I'd have to worry about.

Combine that with the fact I'd already had a can of soup before Barb kicked me out, and maybe I was one iota more prepared for life on the street than I gave myself credit for. Two meals in the bag? Things were looking up, at least they were until a possum in the bushes I walked by hissed at me, making me jump and step into an ankle-deep puddle.

I turned to look at the animal and… I just didn't have any anger left for it. I'd spent all of it on Barb. Now all that was left was spite and self pity, a cocktail I didn't want to finish.

"Have a good night, ma'am," I said and lifted my boot from the puddle. Stylish? Perhaps. Soaked through to the sock? Without a doubt. But hey, you can't get hypothermia from such a small part of the body, right?

I finally came to a stop at a brown metal sign that read, "NWAU Transit Line - Route 4." Fayetteville was a college town and home to Northwest Arkansas University, population 20,000 students. The campus also operated a free bus line that ran through town. This time of the year when all the students had gone back home to Texas? The buses would be pretty much empty, except for the occasional homeless person trying to stay out of the elements for as long as they could.

Maybe I can ask one of them where to stay tonight, I thought, shivering as the wind picked up.

Checking my phone, I saw the bus would be here in about 10 minutes. I also had a text from Abi. She'd made it home and wanted to know if I was okay.

Crap, what do I tell her?

She'd come get me in a heartbeat if I told her I'd been thrown out. And her mom, Jen, was the coolest person on the planet. She'd let me crash there for a while.

I'd kill to have Jen as a mom. She was the technical director for a theater program in town and damn good at it. Jen somehow found a way to make me interested in all these plays I never would have gone to see if she hadn't sat Abi and I down in front-row reserved seats to watch them.

Unfortunately, the arts don't always pay well in Arkansas, and Jen is a single mom. She didn't need another kid under her roof eating her food and using her hot water.

I texted Abi back that I didn't want to talk about it, and I'd see her later. Hugs, kisses, sweet dreams.

I sighed and waited for what seemed like an eternity for the bus. My nose was running, but thankfully I had a napkin in my purse to use instead of my sleeve.

See, universe? One more iota prepared for being thrown out on my ass.

Thank goodness the bus finally came. Hopefully its route would include the following stops: Bittertown, Aloneville, and Hermit Junction. The way I was feeling, any one of those places seemed good enough for me.

I hopped on the long red bus as it pulled up, and yeah, as expected I was the only one riding at this time of the night. That's fine, universe. Not like I needed a kind stranger to offer me a bed or anything.

The bus driver, an older man in his 60s, avoided eye contact with me as I took the third seat back. Well, at least the vehicle was heated.

I rode the bus south into downtown Fayetteville. The bus stopped at the beginning of Dickson Street, which is what the city calls its "entertainment district." It houses lots of great bars and restaurants. It's sort of the lifeblood of the city. The road makes up the northern border of downtown and stretches all the way down to the college campus.

On a Sunday night at 11:00 p.m., it was sparsely populated. It got that way when students went home, and especially two weeks before Christmas.

Stopping outside of Quaker Coffee & Beer, I walked up the steps to a wooden patio with several tables and chairs that hadn't been used in weeks. I stepped inside just as my arms and legs were beginning to grow a bit numb.

Thank the deity I question my belief in for the invention of heaters, I thought, rubbing my arms again.

The coffee shop/bar was open for at least another hour, giving me a little time to be indoors before I had to find a new place to be. There was some sort of 80s rock song playing on the speakers, and most of the seats inside were picnic tables on a concrete floor. There were a few tables next to a really long bench seat against one wall.

Above me stood a second story with some smaller round tables and comfy chairs. That's where I sat after ordering a hot chocolate. It felt warm in my hands, and I didn't drink it for the first minute. I just left it there in my hands, feeling its heat sink into my bones. My knuckles were still a little sore from breaking part of the porch rail. My posture got sloppy when I got emotional, something my coach was still onto me for after all these years.

I took my phone charger out of my purse and plugged it in. A battery on 43 percent wasn't going to last me through the night.

Sitting there looking at motel prices and eventually puppy pictures on Reddit, I lost track of time. It was actually 12:05 a.m. when the bartender came upstairs. She had a couple of nose piercings, small silver rings, and her hair was dyed purple.

Folded over on her arm was a worn leather Third Eye Blind jacket.

"Hey… we're about to shut it down for the night. If you need this, I'm gonna leave it right here on the table next to you. If you don't, feel free to leave it there, and I'll get it before I leave," she said.

I smiled and mouthed the words "thank you."

It was all I could do to keep from crying at this complete stranger's generosity and kindness.

See, Barb? Another person who was better than you today, I thought.

She took my empty cup and left the coat. I picked it up and slid it on. It was a little big for me, but when I zipped it up, it felt warm, kind of like a hug that I really needed right now.

I walked down the stairs and waved goodbye to her before going outside. The temperature had dropped a few more degrees, and I thought I'd wander a bit to see if I could find another place that was still open.

Most of the places still open on Dickson Street I needed to be a few

9

years older to get into. So I walked down a side street, maybe made a turn or two. I didn't know where I was going, honestly.

I passed a closed pizza place called Toppings and came to a small shop with a little pink neon sign that said "Open."

Looking in the window, I couldn't see much. Reddish purple letters on the opposite window that said "Odessa's Psychic Shop."

What the hell? I figured. I'll get my fortune read or something. Anything to get out of this cold, I thought.

Chapter Two

I walked into the shop, which was smaller than I expected. Red curtains decorated the front windows. The floor was covered in a thin garnet carpet with a large dark teal rug in the center of a room. In the back corner there was a spiral staircase that led to some kind of second story. On the round teal rug, I found two couches facing each other. One was black, and the other was white. They were both made of leather.

Between the couches sat a round pine table painted with a complex design of black and white swirls. Three candles arranged in a triangle stood on top of the table. One candle was black, one white, the final gray. None were lit. The only light came from the neon sign in the window.

A back door stood in the opposite corner of the staircase with black and white beads dangling in front of it.

"Hello?" I called.

"Be right down," a woman's voice said. It was deep and even a little solemn.

Then she walked down the staircase in purple boots and a black qipao dress with white flowers embroidered on the front. Her eyes seemed to glow red in the darkness, and her long silky black hair slowly swished from side to side with each step she took.

Cool parlor trick to add to the atmosphere. I'd have to get myself some glowing contacts. That would scare the shit out of Barb, I thought.

In one hand the woman held a long blue kiseru with a tiny butterfly carved into the end. The smoke that wafted out of the end seemed to dance over her Black skin before going ahead of her and down into the shop, filling the room with a light tobacco scent. It had all the best smells of a cigar store, just dialed down several notches so as not to be overwhelming.

I looked around at the smoke and wondered if this was part of some cheesy effect for her routine. I barely had $300 to my name and no home now. Was I going to blow money on a fortune reading?

11

She reached the bottom of the stairs and said, "Welcome to my shop."

Then she motioned for me to have a seat.

"Which couch should I sit on?"

"It doesn't matter," she said. "Whichever you choose, I will take the other."

In the shop next door, I heard a higher pitched voice yell, "I want a midnight snack! Can you please warm up the sausage meatballs?"

And an angry man shouted, "No! I'm going to bed! Kitchen's closed, furball!"

I raised an eyebrow and then looked back at the woman before me. I couldn't place her age. She was somewhere between 30 and 45 maybe? It was difficult to tell. There was an age-old wisdom to her, and yet, a youthful beauty.

"I'm sorry. I don't mean to be rude. I'm just curious. If it doesn't matter which couch I sit on, why have two different colors? Is it some sort of feng shui thing?"

The woman smiled and shook her head, hair swaying back and forth.

"The colors simply represent the bi nature of conversation, a listener and a speaker," she said.

Bi? At last, furniture I can relate to, I thought.

I chuckled.

"What is it?" the woman asked, walking over to the table.

"I'm sorry. I guess I expected a crystal ball or some strobe lights or something," I said. "Maybe a smoke machine too?"

The woman smiled again.

"I'm afraid that's not quite how I do things," she said.

I nodded and sat down on the black couch, pulling my knees up to my chest. I never really found myself comfortable sitting on furniture in what others would call a "traditional fashion." Just sort of been that way since I was a teenager.

The woman sat down across from me and placed a can of Mountain Dew on a square coaster on the table between us. Then she pulled out a bottle of tea, some kind of foreign brand I didn't recognize and opened it. She produced a strange doll-size plastic teacup from her pocket and placed it on the table, filling it with a few drops of her tea before taking a drink from the bottle. I decided not to ask questions about any of it.

Almost spooky that she guessed my favorite drink, I thought.

"That's impressive. Can you tell me my name, too?" I asked.

"I intend to tell you that and more before you leave if that is your wish," she said.

I cocked my head sideways.

"I'm not so much a crystal-ball witch as I am one who grants wishes," the woman said. "And you can call me Odessa."

"Wishes huh? Well in that case…" I said, opening the Mountain Dew can, "I wish for a new family. Can you grant me that?"

Odessa said nothing until all three candles lit simultaneously.

"Let's begin, then," she said.

That's a neat effect, I thought.

"I guess I should ask about prices first. You see, my family threw me out, and I'm on a strict, 'need food to survive' budget."

"Not to worry. I don't accept money as payment anyway," Odessa said.

I raised an eyebrow.

"Why don't you tell me about the people who raised you and why you want a different family?" Odessa said.

I rolled my eyes, frustration and melancholy fighting to the surface inside of me. How long had I been homeless? Two hours?

"Where do I begin? Barb being a bitch every opportunity she gets? John kind of trying to be a fun parent but really just ending up being an absentee father who never finds the guts to openly disagree with his wife? Me getting kicked out of my house for being bi? Or was it because I renounced my parents' faith? Where would you like me to start?"

Odessa's smile disappeared.

"You start wherever you feel your story begins," the witch said.

Suddenly, I had this inexplicable feeling inside. I needed to start with my guts. The nagging feelings that had been with me my whole life.

So I took a deep breath and said, "I… don't feel like I belong with the people that raised me, Odessa. I haven't for most of my life. They put a roof over my head and food in my stomach. But I kind of feel like those are the bare necessities of being a guardian. Like… that's not what makes a mother and father, right?"

The witch said nothing, but instead took a drink of her tea and continued listening.

"And… I can't remember one honest moment where I felt loved by these people, one of whom demanded I call her mother and the other who never seemed to care when I called him Dad."

I sighed and took a drink.

"Tonight Barb caught me kissing my girlfriend in the living room. She's pretty religious, so it didn't go well. She threw Abi out of the house, then screamed at me, tried to drag me to our adulterous future felon minister for reforming, and generally demanded I pray to a God I'm not... 100% sold on. We fought, we yelled, I smashed a lamp, and then she threw me out into the cold without a second thought. Mother of the year, right?"

Odessa remained silent as I tried not to cry.

"My whole life, Barb wanted me to be exactly like her, down to my very mannerisms. And... I guess I'm just some kind of wild child who can't be tamed. I never intentionally set out to anger her. I just did it by never being good enough. So I guess I've spent my life wondering what it'd be like to have a family that just loved me for who I was, you know?"

The witch kept her focus on me, and the black candle slowly dimmed and extinguished.

"I want... a family that will look at me as a daughter, not a blob of clay to be molded. I want a family that'll value me for who I am. Is that so much to ask for?" I sniffled.

Now the gray candle extinguished.

"No... that's not too much to ask for, Odessa. It's a parent's job to love their child. I deserve that much!" I said, clenching my fists and hearing Barb's screaming in my head, "Get out!"

I gritted my teeth and felt my anger building, as were my tears.

"Doesn't everyone deserve that, Odessa?" I asked, feeling my heart beating faster and the white candle growing, flickering with each beat.

"What does everyone deserve, child?"

"That's just it, isn't it? I was their child! You wrap children in your arms because they trust you. They depend on you to protect them from all the bad things in this world. And yeah, sure, parents aren't supposed to be perfect. They're human. I get that. But they're supposed to try anyway! And maybe they all have different ways of showing love, but they're still supposed to show it, aren't they?"

"Show what?"

"How can you not see it? Everyone just wants to be shown love. You want it. I want it. I deserve to be loved, damn it!"

14

After I screamed, the white candle exploded and shot up six feet tall. It was a miracle the ceiling tile didn't catch fire.

I didn't realize it, but I was now standing with my fist over my chest. Some tears dropped onto my Mountain Dew can and the black candle.

"I just wanted to be loved," I whispered before sitting back down slowly and gazing into the white candle's light.

Odessa smiled and said, "Child, I'm going to grant your wish. But you don't need a new family. You already have one. You just don't know it yet."

I pulled the napkin out of my purse and wiped my nose.

"What are you talking about?" I asked.

Odessa reached over the side of her couch and came back with a little white box that fit neatly in the palm of her hand.

"This belongs to you. Barbara threw it out a couple days after you were adopted, but you were meant to have it," Odessa said.

My heart skipped a beat.

"What did you say?" I asked, raising an eyebrow.

"Take the box, dear."

I did as I was told, and there was a little hum to the box as it entered my hand. There was almost a kind of static shock that clicked with me the moment I made contact with it.

Looking up at Odessa, I saw her nod.

Then I opened the box and found a silver locket inside. The necklace was cool to the touch and felt so familiar. I felt like I'd worn it before, but I knew for a fact I've never, never seen it in my entire life.

The locket was covered in Celtic knots. On the back, it was all smooth, and a small inscription read, "Aoife Fey O'Connell. It was beautiful.

"Aoife?" I asked.

"That's your real name. But I'm going to give you a strong warning. If you chose to take that name and join the O'Connell legacy, your path forward will be a difficult one. It'll come with trials and hardships like you've never known. But it'll also come with great happiness and moments of joy like you've never experienced. It'll be a heavy burden, and yet I can think of no better way to grant your wish."

This was going beyond some kind of scam, right? I didn't feel like I was being scammed. But that's what the great psychics do, right? They could read you and reel you in? Is that what she was doing?

"I'm not scamming you, dear. I've met your family before, your birth family. You have your mother's long red hair and your father's green eyes. Gorgeous people."

"What were their names?" I asked, looking down at the locket and trying not to cry again.

There's no way this is real, I thought.

"Your father's name was Tristan O'Connell, and your mother's name was Iris O'Connell. They were part of a clan dating back to Ireland centuries ago. I'm afraid I can't tell you any more about them," Odessa said.

I scowled.

"Why? Oh, let me guess. This is the part where you ask for $50, and then you'll reveal the rest to me. Fine, just let me grab my debit card and..."

"Child, do not test me," Odessa said sternly. I froze, chilled to my core. "I am not after your money. When you leave this room, you'll have paid me nothing of financial value."

I didn't know what to say to that.

"I'm sorry, Odessa," I said, looking down and away from her gaze. "This is just a little too much like a soap opera or something, you know? I feel like my long lost amnesiac sister Amelia is going to walk through that back door any moment."

The witch didn't laugh at that, but I did on the inside.

Eve, there you are! I've spent the last three years in a dungeon! Quick, press our lockets together, I imagined her saying in a dramatic voice entering the room. *She'd be the straight sister.*

I sighed.

"How can I know you're telling the truth?" I asked.

"How do you think you ended up here?" Odessa asked.

I shrugged. What did she want me to say?

"You ended up here because you needed to. You'll have all the proof you want and more, but I sincerely cannot tell you any more about your family at this point."

"Why not?" I asked.

"Because it isn't my place."

I raised an eyebrow.

"Whose place is it, then?"

Odessa looked down at the locket.

"I'd leave that to your guardian. But they'll only show up if you accept the O'Connell legacy and speak their name," Odessa said.

I took a deep breath.

"Down the rabbit hole then," I muttered. "How do I accept the legacy?"

"Put on the locket. But remember my warning," Odessa said. "Once you accept your true family, there's no going back."

I snorted.

"I was explicitly told not to come back about two hours ago. Only way now is forward," I said.

My hands started to shake as I raised the locket to my neck and felt around for the clasp on the back.

This is crazy. True family? Some sort of destiny locket? What kind of scam is she running here? I thought. *But if it's a scam… one I don't believe in… why am I shaking so much? Why does this feel so real and familiar?*

As soon as I clasped the locket around my neck, a jolt of energy ran through my body, and my head started to hurt.

There was something… something rattling me on the inside. I felt a pull into the deepest reaches of my mind, my soul. My heart began to pulse, really vibrate. Through clenched teeth and strained eyes, I watched as my drink on the table rippled with the rhythm of my heart.

The pressure in my head was growing, and I fell to my knees, whimpering.

Drugs! There had to have been something in my drink. I should have known better, I thought.

Then images began to flood my brain, there was someone running. They were holding something. A crying baby wrapped in a red bed sheet or blanket of some kind. A building… maybe an office? No, a fire station. I could see glimpses of the trucks inside. My head peaked with pressure, and I let out a scream.

And then, it was over. Beads of sweat ran down my face, but the pressure in my head was gone. I stood up with a newfound sureness of a couple things, as if I had just crammed for a test overnight and actually remembered everything I studied.

First, my name was not Eve Esther Mikaelson. And second, Barb and John were not my parents.

"Who are you?" Odessa asked.

"My name is Aoife Fey O'Connell, last of my clan," I said, panting for air

17

I should have checked myself into a mental institution. This couldn't be happening to me, but… it was all there, the name and bits of knowledge. I just knew these things, like gravity or the laws of motion. They were just facts.

"I think you know the name of who can guide you from here," Odessa said. "Speak it."

"Adrienn. Come forth," I said, almost as if my lips were moving on their own. The locket glowed green.

A gleaming beam of light shot out from the locket and zipped around the room at record speed before hovering in front of my face. When I focused, I saw what appeared to be a fairly androgynous man standing at about six inches high with shaggy green hair and matching eyes. He—no, that didn't sound right… they had little gossamer dragonfly wings behind them and wore a simple green tunic.

"Oh wow! You've gotten so tall, Aoife," they said.

Embarrassment slipped over their face, and they cleared their throat.

"So sorry, where are my manners? I am Adrienn, your fey guardian. And I've been waiting for this day a long time. How may I serve you, Lady Aoife?"

I looked over at Odessa, again feeling like I should walk out the door and straight into an asylum. But that part of me was quieting rapidly as I sat back down on the couch. I'd stepped in something, and I figured this little person was going to tell me exactly what.

"Please, tell me about my family."

Chapter Three

Adrienn sat on the edge of the table in front of me, their legs dangling over the edge. Their eyes locked with mine, and I just felt overwhelmed, in every sense of the word. This little person standing before me… they don't exist to the eyes of most people. And yet they were here and so very familiar to me.

"What would you like to know about your family?" Adrienn asked, bringing my attention back to the table in front of me.

"Crap. I didn't know this was going to be a Google situation where I had to know specifically what I was looking for.," I said. "Aoife, why don't you start small," Odessa said. "Adrienn, dear, would you like some tea?" She motioned to the tiny barbie cup she placed on the table earlier, like somehow she knew this would all happen just like the mountain dew.

The fey turned toward Odessa.

"Yes please." The fey took it and bowed their head in thanks. Then they gingerly took a sip.

I nodded. Of course, that was a great place to start. I spent my entire life wishing for a different family. Now I had one… or at least did at one point. Maybe I should start with the basics.

"Adrienn, what were they like? My family," I asked, trying my best not to blurt six other questions.

I started wrapping the ends of my long red hair around my index finger.

The fey scratched the back of their shaggy green hair and nodded slowly. Then they smiled and stared off, like they were seeing them in a distant memory.

"Your father, Tristan, was a fantastic gardener. He kept one of the biggest greenhouses in the county with all manner of plants. He could grow anything in any season with his magic. You have his eyes and laugh. Your mother, Iris, was the best huntress in the clan. She could

19

track a boar for three miles with her eyes closed. And she absolutely loved cherries, could not get enough of them. Iris spoiled you rotten for the first year of your life. I never thought Tristan would have that kind of disciplinarian in him, but when he saw Iris feeding you a cupcake when you were six months old, he damn near lost his mind."

As they mentioned these names, I felt a mixture of grief and longing in my heart. Tristan and Iris sounded so familiar, and my skin almost tingled at the mentioning of their names, like it remembered their touch from years ago. I could almost hear a woman's laughter somewhere deep in a buried memory. Iris' laugh. It was accompanied by a light-hearted and sweet sensation of Tristan singing, maybe a lullaby?

And all I wanted right there and then as a tear slipped down the right side of my face was to know them. To be held by them. I ached in ways I'd forgotten how to while growing up because I'd forgotten what I lost in them.

I wiped the tear away.

I finally worked up the courage after a silent minute to ask what happened.

"Adrienn, I somehow know I'm the last O'Connell. How do I—I can't even think of how to ask this. Why do I know things like that? And what happened to my parents?"

The fey looked down at the carpet before taking another drink and raising their eyes to mine. With a deep sigh, Adienn began, "I wasn't there when it happened, Lady Aoife. I mostly stay with the locket around your neck. It's kind of my home. The locket has been around your neck since the day you were born, and your parents gave it to you."

"But you know what happened, don't you?" I asked, trying to choke back dread. Twenty minutes ago I didn't know I had different birth parents. Barb and John never told me I was adopted. And now I was nervously sweating, waiting for the truth about what happened to my birth parents.

"I only know the basics of that tragic day 16 years ago, my lady. The entire O'Connell clan was slaughtered. One of the most famous and most powerful druidic lineages just wiped out in a single night."

"How?" I asked, more of a gasp than a question. My guts felt like a knife had been thrust into them. Knowing you're the last of your line is one thing, but actually hearing that my entire family was butchered had more of a finality to it somehow.

The fey sighed, and Odessa sat silently as she listened. Her face wore no expression.

"They were at a wake, actually. Another member of the O'Connell clan, Duncan, was killed in a car crash. It was a drunk driver during a hit and run, the police said. Everyone had gathered in the wee hours of the morning to drink, eat, and remember him under the stars. Nobody expected an attack, Lady Aoife. It's an old world custom that when parties are mourning, they aren't to be touched. Everyone upholds that tradition from druids to sirens. But a necromancer attacked anyway. He used dark magic and killed them all," Adrienn said.

"Then how exactly did I survive?"

"You weren't there, my lady. You were left in the possession of a caretaker that night, a family friend because the wake was so late. When the caretaker sensed the massive outpouring of dark magic and the deaths of the entire clan, he snatched you from your crib and rushed to get you to safety. To hide you, the caretaker dropped you off at a fire station, assuming that if I was with you, you were safe. Unfortunately, your adopted parent threw out your pendent the first chance she got. That's all I know, Lady Aoife," Adrienn said, looking back up at me.

I looked over at Odessa for a moment and raised an eyebrow.

"Somehow I suppose you stumbled across the locket. I'm guessing you didn't find it yesterday," I said.

"You're correct. I've had the locket for years now."

I stood up.

"Excuse me? You've had the answer to my past for years, and you're just now telling me about it? What the hell is wrong with you?"

Odessa did not jump up as I had.

"The magic I wield to grant wishes, to see glimpses of the future… it comes with restrictions, Aoife, arcane rules I swore to uphold centuries ago. I couldn't go seek you out like some fairy godmother. I had to wait for you to find me," she said.

"Well no offense, but that sounds like some mystical bullshit. While I was living with Lady Tremaine, you had a locket with my family's history inside. Hell, maybe Adrienn could have turned Barb into a toad or something one of the times she slapped me," I snapped at Odessa.

It probably wasn't fair to lash out at Odessa, but my entire clan was dead. I was still pissed about being thrown out, elated to learn I had another family, and devastated to learn I lost them long ago thanks to Voldemort or some other asshole.

"I would just like to state for the record that it's against the Sedema Code for me to turn a human into a toad, my lady," Adrienn piped up sheepishly.

Odessa still hadn't stood up to meet me on the verbal battlefield. She remained seated on the couch across from me, a steely expression on her face.

"I have walked many worlds, Aoife, seen much suffering and joy in others. So please understand that while I'm sympathetic to your plight, your misery is far from the only concern I've carried over my lengthy existence. I did not kill your family, and I could not bring you the locket. End of debate," Odessa said, inhaling on her pipe.

When she exhaled, I asked, "And what if I hadn't come into your shop until I was 25 or 30?"

"Then I would have given the locket to you when you were 25 or 30. But that isn't what happened, Aoife. You came into my shop this evening. You took up the O'Connell heritage tonight. Both of these events were meant to happen on this very night, not before and not after. Fate has a way of arranging things in patterns even I am unable to comprehend. But I'm convinced everything is happening as it's supposed to. As it always does."

I took a deep breath to try and calm myself as best I could for someone who just heard this wild tale. There was still so much I needed to know, primarily, who the bastard was that killed my family and where I could find them now.

Sitting back down, I took another drink of my soda and crossed my legs.

"Usually I'm not a great listener. That's always been more of Abi's thing. But I'm pretty sure you've mentioned heritage a couple times tonight. What exactly are you talking about, Odessa?"

"Adrienn is probably going to be better at answering that than I am, since they're actually part of your family," Odessa said, pulling out a second bottle of tea and refilling the tiny cup.

The fey blushed and thanked her for the tea.

"I wouldn't really say I'm part of the family. I'm just sworn to serve it," they said.

I slowly lowered my hand until it was flush with the table.

Adrienn waited as my hand moved beside them. Then they slowly stood up and walked into my palm, being careful with their tea.

I moved the fey closer to my face and noticed some rather creative stitching on their form-fitting tunic. I thought it looked basic at first, but then I realized it's actually quite intricate in its pattern. It was hard for my eyes to make sense of because of the size, but it looked like a pattern of swords—no, a single repeated blade. What was the word for this one? Cutlass?

They stayed quiet while I examined them.

"Hey Adrienn?" I asked.

"Yes, my lady?" they answered.

"Any chance we could stop with the servant thing?"

A look of horror came over their face.

"Why? Are you displeased with something I've said or done? If so, I sincerely apologize and pray you will give me a chance to make up for it." And then Adrienn bowed.

I blinked for a moment.

"What? No. I'm not displeased. You've been nothing but polite. Too polite. Listen, I just feel awkward. I've never had a fey guardian before, and I don't really think it feels right to keep you as one. Couldn't we be friends without the whole 'my lady' thing?"

The fey looked down at my hands and said nothing.

"I wouldn't do that if I were you," Odessa said, inhaling on her pipe again.

"What do you mean?"

"That fey swore on their life to serve your family for the rest of their days. With such a powerful and all encompassing oath, if you released them from their bond, they would likely die."

I gasped. Had I just asked the fey to die? I really needed to learn more about this magic stuff before I opened my mouth.

"Okay, new plan. You don't die. You keep your word, and I'll just promise not to treat you like a servant, but instead like a friend, okay? How did you become indebted to my family, anyway?"

Adrienn looked up at me and said, "I was wounded and being chased through the fey home world by a predator. It almost had me until I used the last of my strength and stumbled into the human world. I just happened to hide in your father's garden. Well, the beast followed me, and your mother slew it. Afterward, your father was the one who healed me. Without them, I'd have been another creature's dinner. So I swore right there and then on my life that I would serve them for the rest of my days. And now you've inherited my service."

23

Smiling, I held the fey closer and said, "I'll make you a deal, Adrienn. Why don't you tell me your favorite thing in the world."

They thought for a moment, and I waited without making a sound. At last, they spoke up, "Your father's singing. He used to sing songs for me on occasion, and I loved his voice. There was an energy, a life to it, perhaps even a bit of magic. It always made me happy."

I raised an eyebrow and said, "Wow. Well, I can't sing. My voice makes dying cats sound like the Mormon Tabernacle Choir. But how about this? You stick with me as whatever you need to be in order to not die, but I'll call you my friend. You drop this 'my lady' stuff. And I'll never tell you to do anything. I'll always ask if I need help. You can say no anytime you like, and I'll play songs for you on my violin whenever you want. I can't promise it'll be anywhere as good as my dad's singing, but I've made the All State Symphony a few times."

Adrienn said nothing while I laid out the terms of my deal.

"Basically, you won't be my servant, except in name. You'll be my friend. How does that sound?"

Adrienn looked like they were going to cry. "Permission to accept the deal, my lady?"

I rolled my eyes.

"Oh for Pete's sake. Deal accepted then," I said.

They flew up to my right cheek and hugged it, which was maybe the strangest sensation of the night, the world's tiniest hug. And there wasn't really a way for me to return the gesture, so I just awkwardly tapped them on the shoulder with my right index finger.

"There there, friend. Glad we got that all sorted," I said, intending for them to take the hint and hop down. But they took another 30 seconds to hug, much to my dismay.

They fluttered down to my lap, and I sighed.

"Okay, I have so many more questions. What's a druid? Isn't that a chess piece or something?" I asked, feeling stupid for even needing to raise up the question in the first place.

Now Odessa shared a smile with Adrienn.

"You are in for a treat. Druids are those who revere nature and use magic to protect it. They're able to call upon great power from commanding the elements to taming creatures of the wild. The O'Connell clan was among the most famous druidic groups. With you, it can be again," Adrienn said, locking eyes with me.

24

So I'm the Lorax. Great. I speak for the trees. Litter again, and I'll shatter your knees.

After I had a moment to process what the fey on my lap had said, there was another familiar part of my mind that arose. It felt... primal..

I began to sweat again as powerful urges rattled through my entire body. This power was not something to joke about. My ancestors had used it for centuries, as an extension of the natural world. They used this magic and were part of it.

Closing my eyes, I saw them, shadows of O'Connell druids wielding great power. One held their hand aloft and called to the storm above before lightning struck and pooled in the palm of their hand. Another shadow bled and smeared it on a cave wall. Light formed, and something that looked like a roaring tiger leapt out of the blood and in front of the shadow. The final shadow put their hands together, and moments later a thorny bush began to rise, growing to 10 times its size and sharpness.

With magic, a druid could call down lightning, summon a tiger, grow plants to 20 times their normal size. And all of this was now within my reach.

"You feel it, don't you? The legacy you've inherited is coursing through you. Generations of nature priests and priestesses through the ages live on through you," the fey said.

It felt like it'd been at least five minutes since I'd last breathed, so I took in a short sharp breath. In my mind wind blew through an endless misty forest, a chunk of land that'd always been there inside of me, but I'd failed to be aware of until this moment.

And on top of everything, my inner storm of emotion was expanding to fill up every empty corner of my body. I longed for the embrace of parents I'd never see again. I longed for vengeance for what was stolen from me as a baby. I longed to regrow the clan. I longed for so many things that the room started to spin.

My hands clenched into fists, and the couch under me groaned. Odessa's neon sign in the window grew brighter as every ounce of my long hair lifted into the air, along with my body as I stood. Outside, the wind picked up. The trees that lined the streets swayed left and right.

A dumpster spilled over nearby, and trash went swirling. On the other side of the building, a fire hydrant burst and spilled all over the sidewalk.

They've all been taken from me. And I want them back, I thought. *Their blood was spilled into the very earth that feeds my strength, a strength I now claim as my own.*

Four or five blocks away, dogs began to rouse and howl in their backyards. I sensed them from even this far away.

"Their legacy," I muttered, tears falling rapidly. "The mantle falls to me."

Bits and pieces of Iris and Tristan came to my mind and added to the storm swirling around inside. I couldn't quite picture them entirely, even though I'd laid eyes on them as a baby. The earliest of memories, his singing, her laughter, were there but I couldn't remember their faces. But it didn't matter. It was all taken.

The room began to quake as I growled.

What do I have left beside their power?

My growl grew louder, and now the entire table was rattling. Odessa stood from her couch, and Adrienn flew up into the air.

"Aoife, listen to me. You've every right to be upset, but you need to ground yourself right now," Adrienn warned.

Ground myself? No, there was no time for that. I'd spent almost my entire life under the thumb of a toxic woman who denied me any resemblance of autonomy or happiness. Sixteen years of rejecting everything that made me smile and being talked down to like living my own life was some grand, personal treason. Sixteen years I could have spent with actual parents who would have loved me, held me, quieted my cries, and wiped away my tears. I would have had an actual life to grow and flourish. And I was denied that because they were slain before I was old enough to understand the concept of murder. Where was the justice? I was robbed of everything.

A small crack formed in the wall off to the side of me as I gritted my teeth and raised my clenched fists. I felt like a bomb primed and ready to explode.

Adrienn was shouting something to Odessa, but I didn't hear much of what they said. Most of it sounded like static in between the deafening sound of leaves blowing together inside my mind. Somewhere under the layers of my brain, I almost felt like I could see and endless woods blanketed in mist under a gray sky. Was I dreaming? Or was someone in the trees, watching with glistening fangs amid the shadows? I couldn't tell if I was blinking anymore, but that figure appeared now and again, sending shivers down my spine. She smiled, the woman in the woods, and I knew right there and then I never wanted to meet her.

Outside, lightning flashed in the sky above and flooded in Odessa's front windows. Then a clap of thunder shook the block. The cracks in Odessa's wall grew, inching up and widening with every second

From next door I heard a high-pitched voice scream, "It's not me, I swear!"

Then I felt a hand on my forehead, and the storm began to wind down. It wasn't being suppressed into a small space. Rather, it was gradually dissipating down into the rest of me from my shoulders down to my feet. Some part of it even emptied into the earth under my feet.

The fury of the storm shrank back, and I heard Odessa whispering something in a language I didn't understand.

There was one more quiet rumble of thunder outside, and then it was quiet.

My awareness remained, but the overburdening power to act on it was evenly spread. I fell back onto the couch, sweating and panting.

"What was that?" Adrienn asked.

Odessa took a deep breath and sighed, walking back over to her couch.

"Just an old Celtic chant," Odessa said.

Adrienn flew up in my face and placed a hand on my forehead.

"You okay my l—um, Aoife?"

I slowly nodded.

"What... happened to me?" I asked.

They hovered about a foot in front of my nose and said, "Every O'Connell druid is connected to an ancient, flowing reservoir of power. That magic and instinct you feel... it all exists in you now, the last living O'Connell."

I lowered my head. Everything was still there inside, but it was like Odessa buried the bomb's fuse in dirt.

"Holy crap. That was intense," I gasped.

Odessa brought me over a bottle of water, and I drank it all in one sitting.

"Aoife, you need to be aware that these next several days are going to bring about big changes in your mind, soul, and body. Big changes like you just experienced. And because you can't spend the rest of your life in this shop, you're going to need someone to help level you out each and every day for some time until you master your magic," Odessa said.

I put down the empty water bottle on the table and took a deep breath.

"Can Adrienn help with that?"

The fey shook their head.

"I would if I could, Aoife, but my energy is but a drop compared to yours. You'd burn me with a single burst," they said.

"Then what am I supposed to do?" I asked.

It was only now I noticed thick vines covered in thorns had grown up through the building's foundation and carpet where I'd been standing when I was overloading.

Odessa noticed it too.

"I will help pay for that," I muttered.

"On a part-time florist salary?" she asked, raising an eyebrow.

I blushed.

"If she had a familiar to link with," Odessa continued, " Some of that energy would be shared, and then dispersed.".

Adrienn shook their head.

"Sure, but not every O'Connell finds a familiar. Some simply aren't capable of linking their soul to a permanent animal companion. For someone who just awoke their power, casting the spell to find one, matching compatibility, and linking souls, assuming the beast was willing? The odds are slim to none," Adrienn said, crossing their arms.

Odessa locked eyes with the fey and said, "What if Aoife bypassed a few steps?"

"I don't know, Odessa. The binding of familiars is complex and permanent. It's an ancient rite and not one where skipping steps is really an option. Screw with the spell too much, and you could kill one or both of the participants," Adrienn said.

I raised my hand feeling like a school child.

"Um, hi? Sorry. Can we back up a step. What are you talking about? Familiar?"

"Sorry, Aoife. It's um—an animal companion that you link to your soul. You share magic, emotions, pain, thoughts, pretty much everything," Adrienn said, turning to me and uncrossing their arms.

"So what? You want to find me a black cat to go with my broomstick?"

The fey smiled and almost laughed.

"Sort of. It goes back… gosh centuries to some of the first members

28

of the clan back in Ireland. Unfortunately, when the clan was killed, all their familiars died as well," Adrienn said.

Odessa looked at him with a steady quiet stare.

"I've heard one got away," Odessa said, quietly.

I looked over at the witch.

"What are you talking about?" Adrienn asked.

"The witches of this area talk often, and several have heard the howl of a solitary wolf now and again through the years since the O'Connell massacre. Rumors spread among the witches that Tristan's wolf, Ruad, somehow escaped that night," she said.

"That's… impossible. Tristan would have had to sever their connection before he died for her to survive and even then… No, I just don't see how he'd do that. Ruad can't be alive," Adrienn said.

Odessa's lips curled up a little on the left.

"And what if she were?"

Adrienn raised both of their hands.

"Could Aoife perform the familiar rite with her father's previous wolf? Sure, it's possible, I guess. If they're compatible, and her being a descendant makes that more likely, that might be a way to bypass a few steps in the spell like you said earlier," Adrienn said. "But like I said, I don't think she's still alive."

Before I could dissect any of Adrienn's and Odessa's words, I heard a sharp howl piercing the night air. My vision spun like the room was a vinyl record being played. The howl went straight to my core reverberating through my heart for several seconds.

When I looked at Adrienn and Odessa still talking, I realized they hadn't heard the noise. The howl came again, and I cradled my head in my hands. I'd heard this call before… years ago. Closing my eyes, I tried to picture a memory, any, connected to this sound. I only got pieces and fragments, candles, the smell of lilies, the sound of spring peepers, the touch of a lake's water, and a wolf howling across the body of water.

I didn't even have to ask.

"Ruad is nearby," I said.

Odessa and Adrienn paused, listening. But they didn't hear what I did. They didn't realize as I quickly was that Ruad was in trouble.

The tone of her howl was dripping with desperation and agony.

"What would have a wolf in trouble? " I asked, looking outside as another howl filled the air.

I stepped toward the door, clenching my fist.

Odessa suddenly spoke up, and to my surprise, she didn't question why I heard something she could not.

"Aoife, listen to me. If I'd slaughtered an entire druid clan and knew one survivor got away, I wouldn't stop hunting her," she said.

"What should I do?" I asked.

"You have an answer raging inside of you," Odessa said, as a final howl echoed through downtown Fayetteville.

I had to save Ruad and protect my father's familiar. But how did I even begin to do such a thing? Where would I find her? The howl could come from anywhere. Then I remembered Adrienn's words about inheriting O'Connell instincts.

Here goes nothing, I thought, closing my eyes and trying to focus on the memory of Ruad, the familiar sound of her howl. And my mind wasted no time pinpointing its origin like some psychic Google Maps.

"She's on Mt. Sequoyah, the east slope," I muttered.

Chapter Four

I ran out the door. Odessa's shop sat not far from the corner of Block Avenue and Spring Street in downtown Fayetteville. Looking due east, I could see lights on the county courthouse and up past that stood Mount Sequoyah, a little over 1,600 feet in elevation. I could see house lights on the top ridge and knew roughly the Mount Sequoyah Cross was off a little bit to my right.

The white cross sat on an overlook where people would often park their cars and look into downtown Fayetteville. On a clear night it was a beautiful view.

The eastern slope of Mount Sequoyah was pretty much all forest and a hiking trail or two. That was where Odessa said Ruad was in danger.

It would take me too long to run over the mountain. Certainly by the time I got up there, I'd be winded, and Ruad would be long gone.

Adrienn flew beside me as I ran east down Spring Street for a few blocks. Eventually, I came to the Lesbi Inn, a giant 16-story hotel in the heart of downtown Fayetteville.

"Adrienn, I need to get up there faster. Can you... I don't know, teleport me or something with magic?"

"I don't really have the power to transport you, sorry. But there is an unattended vehicle over there on the corner of the hotel. I bet the owner would understand if you borrowed it," the fey said, winking.

I smiled.

Look at me, thrown out and already committing grand theft auto. This is your fault, Barb.

Hopping on the neon green crotch rocket motorcycle, I found the key still in the ignition.

Starting the bike and darting out into the street, I raced across College Avenue through a red light, narrowly avoiding colliding with a minivan, which I took time to flip off. Then, I raced up Spring Street to the top of Mount Sequoyah.

I gunned the engine and worked the bike, slowing down and leaning into a couple curves. I flew past the cross and kept going around Skyline Drive until I saw the woods on the backside of the mountain. I darted through someone's side yard and took the bike into the trees as far as I could.

Now I could sense Ruad, as if there was some cord binding me to her from my memories as an infant. I just kept replaying the memory of her licking my cheek, and I knew which direction she was in.

I ditched the bike and kept running down the slope for about 100 yards. Then I heard a growl far deeper than any I could make myself. It soon gave way to a yip of pain, and red hot rage filled me.

This was the last connection I had to my family. Hell, this wolf practically was my family. And something was hurting her. I was about to dart in guns blazing, and by guns, I meant my arms, but Adrienn darted in front of my face and shook their head rapidly. They put a finger over their lips, and I figured surveillance was probably smart. I was stumbling into a situation with magic and monsters, after all.

So I crept forward through the trees, trying to avoid twigs and leaves. Under a nearly full moon I saw them on a hiking trail. It looked like five humanish figures around a rather large wolf.

People see huskies and tend to think, "Oh, that's about how big wolves are." But that's not anywhere close. Wolves are massive killing machines. I gulped and reminded myself that my clan had been bonding with them for centuries.

She won't eat me... probably.

Ruad looked to be around 140 pounds of solid muscle and claws. Her vermillion fur was shaggy and ragged. She was wrapped in chains with some kind of glowing sigils on them. They weighed her to the ground.

Her full length was about five feet long and a little under three feet high at the shoulder. The memory of her licking my cheek grew clearer in my mind. Her hot breath, the slick of her tongue, the sweet smell of flowers all around, I could feel and smell it so clearly. Ruad looked through the trees, straight toward me. She must have felt something too..

Then I heard what sounded like a young man's voice and one of the figures stepped forward. "Wow, you sure did put up quite a chase, beast.

But even you grow tired, it seems. You're not so tough without a druid at your side," he said.

At this, Ruad snarled and bared a fang or two.

"Not so scary in those chains, either," the figure said.

As my eyes adjusted, I saw he appeared to be a couple years younger than me with dark spiky hair and a giant pair of black feathered wings behind him. Was he another druid?

The other four figures looked different, too. Upon closer inspection, I saw they were actually pretty scrawny. A rather pungent odor hit my nostrils, and I gagged, causing the bird man to look in my direction.

Oh shit, I thought, putting a hand over my mouth.

As the other figures turned in my direction I saw that they were more like walking skeletons. And let me say, it's nothing like the cartoons where Spooky Scary Skeletons play and they make xylophone noises on each other's ribs.

These guys were terrifying, with just a few patches of rotten flesh attached in random places. They wore no clothing, and the bones were worn and jagged. In the eye sockets, they had glowing purple orbs. I tried not to retch as some muscles hung loose from the bone, wiggling like millipedes with every movement. What joints remained in the skeleton took the appearance of moist jerky. The skin looked like thick papyrus, veins pulsing and plump while the flesh around them was pulled in like a turkey's wattle. Some things the mind just wasn't supposed to see.

The skeletons all held some sort of club. One also held a long silver knife.

I did not want to take them on. That part of me that ordered myself to check into an asylum resurfaced and screamed at me to run. Run home, beg Barb to let me inside, and go to bed. This went way beyond teenage rebellion. Now there were dead things standing about 15 feet in front of me and that was just suddenly normal to me now.

Those thoughts remained until the wolf snarled again, and one of the skeletons bashed Ruad's head with a club, drawing more blood. She yipped, but the winged boy's attention was drawn back to her.

"Easy now. The boss wants her alive and concussion free. He's got big plans for you, little doggie," he said, smiling.

The primal part of me surfaced again, and I growled. That was my last remaining family they'd just struck. I was going to tear them to pieces. There wouldn't be enough bones left for broth when I was finished. And I'd tear those wings right off the kid in front of me, with my bare teeth.

"Adrienn, can you distract them with some kind of light show? Something that looks like fireworks? I'm going to jump on one of the skeletons and drive it into the ground," I said.

The fey nodded and zipped up into the night sky.

"Now let's get you back to the boss," the boy said as three of the skeletons moved in to pick up the chained and growling wolf.

Just before they could, a flash of red light darted in front of them. Then a burst of lights shot out in every direction, blinding them and casting deep shadows along the hiking path they stood in the middle of.

"What the hell is going on?" the winged boy yelled.

I darted from the trees and leapt onto the back of the skeleton farthest from Ruad. Then I tried to wrestle it to the ground, but this wasn't some flimsy cartoon skeleton. It held firm and picked me up with its right hand, flinging me to the ground in front of it.

Okay, rescue off to a rough start, I thought.

I swept the skeleton's legs out from under it, and it went down to the forest ground. I stood up, but one of the other skeletons had already turned and raised its club. It swung, and I ducked, coming up smashing my elbow into the skeleton's jaw. It didn't even flinch.

"Aw hell," I muttered before a third skeleton smashed a club into my right shoulder. I fell to the ground in front of Ruad with a grunt of pain.

I looked into her bloodshot amber eyes, and if a wolf could come close to gasping, that's what she did. But as I looked deeper, I saw a weariness to her. I could tell she didn't get captured tonight because of any brilliant strategy on part of this bird boy and his skeletons. Ruad looked genuinely tired and devoid of hope. Her right side was covered in scratches that hadn't healed completely, and I only saw them because she was missing clumps of fur here and there. Her muscles hung with a heaviness that I could tell had built up since the O'Connell massacre.

I shuddered to think of feeling like that for 16 years.

"I'm going to get you out of this," I said to her.

And with a firm alto voice, she said, "No you aren't. You should have left me, Aoife. You would have been safe."

I flinched for a second, having never seen a talking wolf before. My mind spun trying to comprehend this impossible reality like when someone is convinced they've seen a ghost or an angel. But my mind stopped trying to rationalize the moment a brief memory unfolded.

Someone was holding me in their arms as my legs dangled over the side of a bed, and Ruad sniffed my knees before licking my toes.

"She's growing so fast," Ruad said to whoever was holding me.

My brain caught up and realized the voice was familiar, and I longed to hear her say other things. We had years of missing time and words that could've been spoken.

The skeleton I'd knocked down had stood up again, and the bird boy laughed behind me.

"Who are you supposed to be?" he asked.

I stood and felt rage stirring in me again.

"You need to let her go right now," I said.

Now that I got a better look at him, I saw he was wearing a tight black tank top and a fuzzy jacket over it. He wore cargo pants with a brown belt.

"And who are you to make such a demand?" he smirked.

"No! She's nobody, just some stupid neighbor who doesn't know any better. Let her go, Ash," Ruad said.

Locking eyes with Ash, I growled, "My name is Aoife Fey O'Connell. You will release my father's familiar this instant."

Ash's eyes filled with surprise, and I saw his smirk grow even wider.

"Did you say O'Connell? That's amazing. This night just gets luckier and luckier. First I capture the wolf and now the last O'Connell? I'm going to buy a lottery ticket when this is all over," he said, laughing. "Tie her up with chains too."

The light show had dwindled, and I saw Adrienn fly up into the night sky again.

I spun toward the skeletons and raised my fists, prepared to fight.

"You aren't anywhere near strong enough to take them," Ruad said.

"Listen, I've been getting bits and pieces of memories, time with my family, time with you. I don't know what to do with all of it yet, but I think what it spells out is we're supposed to be together. And maybe together we'd have a shot at beating them," I said.

Ruad looked off in the distance and said, "It doesn't matter anymore."

"How can you say that? You're the last piece of the clan left, Ruad!"

"The clan is dead, and you will be too now that you came out here tonight," she said, laying her head down in the dirt.

She's really giving up? What's wrong with her?

I saw a rock the size of my shoe, so I leaned down and picked it up, just in time to avoid being smashed with another club.

I smashed it into the chin of one of the skeletons, and the rock actually shattered.

"Oh you've got to be kidding me," I said.

The skeleton armed with a knife lunged forward, and I sidestepped it, taking a cut to my left arm.

I grimaced. The cut was just below my elbow toward my wrist.

While I looked down at the wound, another club smashed into my back and shoved me forward into a pile of leaves and mud next to Ruad's left paw.

"Why… why aren't you fighting back?" I gasped as the skeletons moved closer.

"I fought back for years, Aoife. I'm tired of running around these mountains without any idea of what I'm doing. I'm exhausted. Life has beat me down, and you know what? I'm done. I'm just done."

Ash chimed in, "You should take a note from your wolf and lie still. I'm pretty sure the boss wants you alive for at least a little while."

I crawled backward from the advancing skeletons and grimaced as my left arm gave out, leaving me on my back propped up on a single arm in front of Ruad.

"Ruad, I'm sorry I wasn't here sooner. I was lied to my whole life and didn't even know about the clan until an hour ago. I'm sorry you've been out here in the mountains wandering alone with nowhere to go all these years. I'm sorry my father is gone. But I'm here now! And you're all I have left of them. Please help me. I really would like to get to know you and learn more about my family."

"No, Aoife! I said I'm done," the wolf snarled at me.
"Why?! What kind of pity party are you attending right now? Because I'm pretty sure Tristan…"

"Don't speak as if you knew him!" Ruad suddenly barked.

The blast of energy and volume knocked the skeletons back a few steps and made my head ring. I felt the bark rattle my chest. Even Ash had taken a step back, surprised at the power Ruad showed off even while being bound. Apparently he didn't know the wolf could still exhibit such power with the chains on.

Ruad locked eyes with me and bared her fangs. It was at this point I noticed a deep scar on her chest.

"You were their daughter for two years, Aoife. I was with Tristan for three decades. When a druid binds themselves to a familiar, it's a closer type of connection than any you can even fathom. It's almost a merging of souls, a permanent bridge that emotions, thoughts, pain, and everything else flow across freely."

I said nothing.

"But your father severed the connection that night with a cursed blade I'd never seen before. I don't know where he got it, but it was agonizing as he severed our connection. I didn't even know such a thing was possible. Normally when a familiar dies, their druid does as well. The opposite is also true. That night, he ordered me away, and then he plunged the dagger into his chest."

Tears started to fall from Ruad's eyes. I didn't know wolves could shed tears, but learning that fact broke my heart.

"Imagine the man I'd shared my life with for more than 30 years suddenly ending our connection. It was the most terrible pain I'd ever felt, like prying apart two pieces of bolted steel. Our consciousness that had once been bridged was now shattered, and I had to deal with the emptiness where there had once been a steady voice. You can't know what that feels like. And as much as I loved Tristan, I hate him for doing this to me."

I was crying again. Ruad was right. I had no clue what she'd gone through. And I'd called it a pity party.

"I'm sorry," I said to her and reached a hand out toward her nose, stopping short an inch. "You're right, Ruad. I don't know your pain. But I can if you'll let me."

The wolf had started to look away but was now locked in my glance again as my green eyes stared down her amber eyes.

"I've spent my entire life feeling like there was a piece of me hidden, and everyone around me was lying about it, playing a massive game of keep away. That created a loneliness I can't even begin to describe. Tonight I lost my home. And then I discovered I had a family but lost them minutes later when I learned of their demise. This night has been a roller coaster from hell I don't know how I'll recover from. I've discovered magic and monsters are real, my heritage as a druid, and it all makes my head spin. But there's two things I am dead certain of, Ruad."

She didn't look away.

"First, I am not my father. I don't even know him. If I had a treasure like you linked to my soul, I would never cast you away, no matter the danger I faced. And second, you're all I have left of him. All I have left of Iris. All I have left of any true family and a sense of home, really."

Ruad started crying again.

"So I'm asking you to open your heart one last time, Ruad. Become my familiar, and I swear to you here and now on every ounce of my power and life that I will never sever our connection like my father did. I, Aoife Fey O'Connell, promise to never cast you aside, before everyone here tonight my word stands," I said, feeling my very life itself quake before those words. A wave of magic washed over me from head to toe, leaving my consciousness afloat in a sea of trees for a moment. It faded gradually like a descending tide.

I remembered how powerful Odessa said oaths were when sworn on a life or name, and I'd just made a whopper of one.

"That's really sweet. I'm going to cry. And if these skeletons still had tear ducts, I'm sure they'd cry as well," Ash said, motioning to the skeletons. "But I'm afraid the soap opera hour is over. It's canceled as a matter of fact. Seriously, where are the extra chains?"

The skeletons looked around for any left, and I felt a burst of urgency in Ruad unlike before.

"Place your dominant hand on my forehead now!" Ruad barked. "I will not become your familiar, but I will lend you some of my power."

I inched my right hand forward, and there was a spark of magic as I made contact with her. Then that spark became a roaring flame as Ruad poured her magic into me. It felt like a heat that lit my muscles and bones on fire the moment it made contact.

I was vaguely aware of Ash screaming something, but the energy inside me already began to build. Leaves and twigs swirled up around me as I felt myself changing forms.

My muscles expanded a bit, as did my jaw to accommodate new fangs. Claws extended from my larger hands and feet. They actually shredded my shoes. I heard fabric and strings tear instantly. My hair grew much longer and shaggier, and the world itself also began to change.

My sensory input was dialed up to 11, with smells, sounds, and visuals overwhelming my brain. I smelled rabbits nearby, along with a few cats. I could hear people beginning to gather on the street I'd rode my stolen bike off of. And I could see the skeletons and Ash so much more clearly now.

Somewhere in the transformation, my human ears had vanished, and a pair of triangular wolf ears appeared on the top of my head, twitching toward new sounds in several directions. Turning, I saw a bushy red tail the same size as Ruad's had torn through my pants at some point in the change. It brought a new meaning to the word balance. I leaned a little more forward than I had before. This way felt more natural now.

Evolution at work, I guess.

With my newfound strength, I ripped the chains off of my familiar, feeling her freed energy as I did so. She was feeling excited to do battle for the first time with a human partner in more than a decade. Ash did not look pleased at all.

"Take them now!" he yelled.

The skeletons approached us, but I found that now my punches were smashing them with ease. I was faster, dodging their swings at a much quicker rate. I could read their body movements. And when I slammed my elbows into their heads, they went flying backwards. This power was amazing.

We made short work of the skeletons, and when I turned to take care of Ash, there were just a few feathers remaining.

"He took off running?" I asked.

"No, look up in the sky," Ruad said.

As I looked up, I just barely caught his figure flying away in the distance.

"Coward," I muttered.

"More like genius. He knew the tables turned the moment I lent you my power," Ruad said.

I sighed. My heart was still pounding.

"How does it feel?" Ruad asked, intentionally bumping into me.

"Like I'm an extra in *Halloweentown*," I said.

She almost smiled, which is a little unnerving with her being a wolf and all. And part of me wondered if she'd actually seen the movie.

"I wish Tristan and Iris could see you in that form. You'll make a decent wolf," Ruad said.

I nodded, a new weariness coming over me.

"I have about a thousand questions, but I'm also exhausted. Do you have a cave we could crash in for the night?" I asked.

Adrienn flew down out of the sky and into my locket. I guess they were exhausted, too.

"Cave? What do I look like, some kind of wild animal?" Ruad asked.

"Well... yeah," I said.

That smile came again.

"So do you, druid. I actually know of an abandoned cabin not far from here."

"Lead the way," I said, and off we went.

Chapter Five

I felt pretty good, better than I had in the last 24 hours, anyway. Was I homeless? Sure, but so were 500,000 other people in this country. My fate wasn't uncommon. At least I was alive, and I knew that I had a family that loved me at one point, a whole clan, actually. It may have been a magic family, but it was still a family and most importantly a feeling of home.

Things were changing inside of me, though. I knew if Ruad and I eventually forged our own connection that things would change. But I had no idea just how much. Not yet at least.

My body was exhausted from the fight and first transformation. I replayed scenes of the changes my body underwent in my mind. I had a tail, right? Even after my claws and the rest of that stuff disappeared following the fight, my senses remained somewhat heightened.

As Ruad led us to this abandoned cabin, we passed a red fox. Of course, I smelled her before I saw her. And I could tell just from the scent she had just fed on a rabbit. If that wasn't strange enough, I also knew the vixen was pregnant with a litter of three.

She didn't really pay much attention to us once we spotted her. It was likely she knew Ruad wasn't in a hunting mode, whether by scent, body language, or some other means, I had no clue, but in some strange way I understood.

With all the exhaustion that came from a magical transformation and fight, I assumed I'd be able to sleep easily. But with only the scraps of torn blankets and tarps in Ruad's makeshift den, I struggled getting warm in the cold December air. I must have shivered for an hour straight before Ruad, who was about six inches from me, groaned and said, "My god, you're like a helpless pup. Come over here and share my warmth."

I looked at her balmy fur, still holding on to a twinge of red, even in the low light, and I asked, "Are you sure?"

41

"You won't find Malachos if you die of frostbite. Get over here before I change my mind."

So I slowly snuggled up close and buried my face in her fur.

Instead of smelling wet dog like a normal human, I smelled more intangible things, like home and comfort. The last time I had even looked at Ruad, I was two. So, now that my arms were wrapped around her as we slept, our being reunited went deeper than simple nostalgia. To me, it was primal comfort.

There was a noticeable tension from Ruad for the first hour of snuggling. She seemed strained, cautious. I couldn't tell if the wolf expected me to stab her as she slept or if she simply didn't want another human touching her.

Gradually, through the night, that tension seemed to fade. Her muscles loosened. Maybe she was getting used to me after all.

While my body felt safe and warm curled up against a 140-pound talking wolf, my mind bounced between dreams. Some of them were memories from Ruad and my father. Others were her wandering through the Ozarks alone.

In my final dream, I stood before a mirror. The image reflected a different me, one transformed and flowing with wolf magic again. Her eyes shifted, looking for something. Prey? Her claws extended, and she bared her fangs as she found it..

She was looking at Abi. I started to pound on the glass, but my girlfriend couldn't hear me. I watched as the wolf me rushed forward and tore into her shoulder first. Then, as Abi screamed, my mirror image started to tear deeper into her, going for her heart.

My own heart was beating like a drum, and that's when the image turned toward me. Blood dripped down her fangs, and I saw raw power and strength with each step she took toward me.

I was torn. Part of me wanted to run screaming in the opposite direction and never look back. But the other part of me was attracted to the glow of her eyes, lit with a hunger for fury and feeding. That power... I wanted it, craved it, much as it terrified me. There was a sense of control in her that I liked. That thought eventually won out and kept me anchored at the mirror.

Fleeting questions rocketed through my mind. Who is this girl in the mirror? Is she part of me?

That part of my brain screamed, while the other half smiled. And that's when the mirror image locked eyes with me. My heart practically stopped beating. In an instant, she'd leapt through the glass and fell upon me snarling.

I fell backward with a yip, and just before I hit the floor, I awoke in the cabin with some alarm chime blaring through the room.

"If you don't silence the noise box you brought in with you, I'm going to crunch it in my jaws, Aoife," Ruad warned in a low morning growl.

"Morning to you too," I said, rolling on my back and stretching out.

My fingers met the border of this little den she had built from tarps, blankets, quilts, sheets, shirts, and whatever else Ruad had scrounged from the back yards of residents of Mt. Sequoyah.

We actually hadn't walked too far from where we fought off the bird boy and his skeleton friends the previous night. The abandoned cabin sat on the northeast slope of Mt. Sequoyah about a quarter mile from the trail where I rescued Ruad. Or if those animal shelter bumper stickers were to be believed, where Ruad rescued me. Who rescued whom, huh?

My phone's alarm was some stupid xylophone going up and down scales in rapid fashion. Just the sound of it made me want to smash my screen normally, but with my heightened sensitivity it was actually giving me a headache.

Everything was still dialed up much more than before.

I swiped up on my phone's screen, and it unlocked, revealing a picture of Abi and I while on a date at a Japanese steak house. My stomach growled as I tried to go back to sleep.

Then I realized, *Shit!* I had to be at work in a couple hours! Turning on the front-facing camera, I groaned.

Without snuggling up against Ruad I was cold again, especially my feet. I was suddenly reminded transforming had torn my shoes last night.

Sunlight streamed in through the broken windows of the front door. The cabin actually faced east, I realized. It was a little after 7:00 a.m., and my phone was about dead.

"Ruad? I need to get dressed and showered for work. Are you going to hang out here until I come back, or do you wander around the mountain during the day?" I asked.

She stood up and stretched, with her rear legs curled, and her back sloped down toward her front paws. Ruad yawned as she did so, giving me a fresh view of all 42 of her razor-sharp teeth. Canines, molars,

43

incisors, and premolars that all looked like they could tear me to shreds in a hot minute.

It's okay, I told myself. *She was your father's familiar. She's not going to eat you... probably.*

Her amber eyes locked with mine as she finished stretching and stood to her full height.

"No, Aoife. I'm not going to eat you. So you can stop giving me that terrified bunny look," Ruad muttered.

Then she turned her head and asked, "What did you mean about work? Do you intend to fix up the cabin?"

I shook my head.

"I don't really want to live here. No offense. I'll have to worry about where I'm going to live later," I said, sighing and forcing that fear back down.

One problem at a time, or I'm going to go crazy. Right now, I need to find some food, get cleaned up, and get to work, I thought.

"Then by work, you meant?"

"My job. I work in a flower shop," I said, remembering I was talking to a wolf. "Um, I sell flowers to other humans is what I mean. It's what I do for money."

"I see. Well, money is a necessity for you humans. Even Tristan talked about it some. If you must attend to this work, we can leave soon," Ruad said.

It took a second for that to sink in.

"We?" I asked, trying to picture how my boss would react to me bringing a full-size wolf into her flower shop. It probably wouldn't go great. Sabrina is a cat person and nice as can be. She's flexible with my schedule and pays me every week. I get away with a lot at Petal and Stem, but bringing in Ruad was way past pushing it.

"Yes, we, Aoife. He fled last night, but Ash knows what you look like now, and he's likely reported back to Malachos. So until we've avenged the clan, and you're properly trained, wherever you go, I follow. And where I go, you follow."

I scratched the back of my head.

"I don't know how easy that's going to..." I was cut off.

"It's not easy being a druid. It takes years of studying and training, years that you've missed out on, need I remind you. It's a lot of work studying plants, magic, animals, combat, and everything else. But you

44

asked me to join you, remember? So here I am, whether I like it or not. And besides, you're a defenseless pup without me around," she said.

I put my hands on my hips and scowled at her.

"Excuse me, Ruad, but I don't think I need to remind you who saved whom last night. I am no pup."

Faster than I could anticipate, Ruad shoved me into the wall with one of her massive paws and had her jaws around my neck, canines lightly touching my skin.

"You were powerless against the skeletons and would have died had I not lent you my magic, Aoife. Do not mistake our victory last night to be some sign of your own strength," she growled.

My heart was pounding, but I clenched my fists and smirked.

"Sure, but now your belly is wide open. I have clear access to your ribs from this angle, and if you don't think I could…"

Her teeth sank about a millimeter more into my neck as I raised my fist slowly toward Ruad's ribs.

"You were saying?" she growled.

I sighed and lowered my hands against the wall.

"Pup," she muttered and let me go. "I have so much to teach you, and hopefully your first lesson sinks in quickly. I am stronger and faster than you. You need me at your side, and that is where I will be until we draw our last breath. You swore on your life to never cast me aside, Aoife. You swore."

I raised my palms toward her and sighed. She was right. I felt my heart quivering. I had suggested leaving her in the cabin, and that might as well have been a 50/50 chance of me not coming back in her mind.

"You're absolutely right, Ruad. I'm grateful for your help, and I'll… figure something out," I said, sighing.

My familiar seemed to ease up on the inner tensions just a smidge but said nothing.

For the third time this morning, I had crossed out my first goal of the day. In my mind, I saw a sheet of paper with "Find a new place to live" written on it. That had been crossed out and replaced with "Go to work." Now that had been crossed out with, "Just find somewhere to clean up and eat."

One step at a time, I thought. *I'll figure out how to get Ruad around town with me after I eat something.*

"I'll step outside for a moment," Ruad said. "Wait here."

I arched an eyebrow, but didn't argue with the wolf.

I didn't move.

Ruad returned with an entire branch of berries from... who knows where. My stomach growled some more, but I couldn't complain. I had breakfast.

"You're sure these aren't poisonous?" I joked, taking one of the little red berries.

Ruad rolled her amber eyes and went back outside. When she returned, she was holding a rabbit in her bloody jaws and eating her own breakfast.

I finished my berries quickly while trying to avoid eye contact with her and then said, "Thanks, Ruad."

It was then my mind turned toward getting myself cleaned up for the day.

Okay... I can't really bathe in the creek outside. I need soap and shampoo. A warm shower would be great, I thought.

And then an idea came to me. I could use my coach's gym. He had installed a small shower in the back, and I could use that to clean up. The gym would be locked up during the day, but I knew for a fact he kept a back window unlocked just in case he ever lost his key. I would just have to hope he wasn't there.

He really shouldn't be. By day, Coach was an insurance salesman. He only taught Muay Thai a few times a week in the evenings.

"Okay, let's get moving. I need a shower before work, and a change of clothes wouldn't hurt, either," I said.

Ruad said nothing and followed me out of the cabin. Fortunately, the gym was actually just at the base of Mt. Sequoyah back toward downtown Fayetteville. We wouldn't have to walk far.

I couldn't count the number of folks rubbernecking at the barefoot girl being followed by a wolf. It was embarrassing, but there wasn't much I could do about it. Though I was glad my enhanced senses had finally faded, so I didn't die from all the truck exhaust as folks drove by.

Sure, I was in my human form. But the way people were staring at me, I might as well have had ears on top of my head and a big bushy red tail behind me. Homeless people in Fayetteville are nothing new. Homeless people with dogs in Fayetteville are nothing new. Homeless people with wolves in Fayetteville are a little new.

Ruad and I worked our way down the mountain, which is entirely residential on the west side, and eventually came to Lafayette Street, which I knew would take us to College Avenue, the main north and south highway through Fayetteville.

Coach's gym, Quake Muay Thai, sat at the corner of Lafayette and College, in a building that used to be a gas station and then a mechanic's garage. Now it was a small Muay Thai gym with a couple dozen students throughout the week.

It sat across the street on one side from a local grocery store called T-Mart. The front of the gym faced the only gas station in downtown Fayetteville. Truth be told, it sold more beer and fried food than gas thanks to all those college kids looking for cheap drinks and snacks.

Quake Muay Thai was painted a hideous orange color on the outside. Coach never really had the money to redecorate. Most of the time I assumed he was actually losing money on the building because his classes were never huge.

From the outside, it actually looked like a catch-22. Coach didn't have the room for any larger classes in his current space. And he didn't have the money to move into a bigger space because his classes were too small to generate enough income.

But honestly, Coach didn't seem to mind it all that much. He seemed to enjoy the more intimate space so he could spend more one-on-one time teaching his students how to fight and defend themselves.

I walked down Lafayette Street and stopped short about 30 feet from College Avenue. Morning traffic wasn't as bad because all of the college students were already gone for holiday break.

Fayetteville was first and foremost a college town. For a few weeks in December and January and all of the summer, the natives got a little bit of breathing room from all those Texas students that were trucked in by the thousands from Dallas. But if you caught the town at the right time of the year, you could actually drive around without mopeds zipping in and out of traffic like little suicide missions. You might even be able to get into a restaurant without waiting an extra 20 minutes.

I waited for a blue pickup truck to drive past me, and then Ruad and I headed into a little alleyway behind the gym. Glancing across the street, I saw there were just a couple cars at Coyote Fuel Station gassing up. They didn't seem to be paying any attention to the barefoot girl and her giant wolf about to commit breaking and entering.

We came to the backside of the gym which was all cinder block walls covered in chipped white paint.

47

"Shouldn't you scout the inside of the building first to make sure whoever owns this place isn't around?"

"It's fine. Coach has a day job. And what did I say about talking out loud when we left the mountain?" I asked, turning to Ruad and putting my hands on my waist.

"I believe you gave me an order, and then I showed you how quickly I could snap an entire tree branch in my jaws. After that, you seemed to understand that you don't give me orders," Ruad said.

I gave my companion a polite smile and said, "Right. Good. I was just testing your memory, and it looks like your wolf brain is strong... almost as strong as your jaws."

I headed over to a wide window about three feet off the ground. It was about five feet wide with the inner part of the glass opening horizontally. I placed my palms on it and applied a little pressure while sliding it.

When I'd finished opening the window, the hole was about two feet tall and three feet wide. I lifted my legs and slid into a back corner of what Coach called his "personnel quarters." It was a mini living area with a tiny broom closet that contained his even tinier shower, a little coffee table covered in what looked like days-old spaghetti sauce, a tiny dorm fridge, a Goodwill couch with more than one patch on the upholstery, and a red radio with a clothes hanger for an antenna.

I quietly placed a foot on the thin carpet and lowered my head into the room. I picked up a few smells right away, a bowl of Waffle Crisp and orange juice. Those were his favorite. Coach had been here not too long ago.

Right after me, Ruad hopped through the back window with more grace than I would have imagined a 140-pound animal could. She just looked around the room and judged it to be less than impressive.

I walked to a door leading out into the main part of the gym and went through, to see if Coach was out front. Most of the overhead lights were off. About 90 percent of the floor in the main gym area was covered with black and gray foam mat tiles. The rest of the floor was covered in that same thin carpet in Coach's personnel space.

On the left half of the room were tattered old punching bags that hung from the metal ceiling. The right side of the room was open space for sparring. The room was probably 40 feet wide and had a length of 20 feet.

A thin white drywall went across the entire width of the gym separating the main area from Coach's personnel area. We were the only ones in the building.

I released all the tension I'd been holding in my shoulders and sighed, walking back to the personnel area. Ruad followed and finally spoke up, "You sure do seem worried about this Coach fellow catching you in here. I thought you said he was a friend on the way down the mountain?"

Smiling, I told her, "He's been my fighting teacher for more than a decade. I trust him, and I don't want to disappoint him by committing a misdemeanor. Coach knows I've always had trouble at home with Barb. He's patient with me and pretty understanding. If I asked him to, I'm sure he'd make up a guest bedroom for me to stay with him and his daughters tonight."

"Are you going to ask him?"

I shook my head.

"I'm not going to bother him with my problems more than I have to," I said, closing the personnel area door.

I walked over to the broom closet and found a tiny white standing shower with a glass door, along with a rack of white towels and a black foldable hamper. Reaching up above me, I pulled a little metal string and clicked on the dim bulb lighting the closet.

"Looks like a tight fit. You gonna be okay with a thin piece of wood separating us, or are you worried Malachos will attack me in the shower?"

Ruad rolled her eyes.

"As if I stayed in the same room when Tristan cleaned himself. Yes, you can bathe without me in there," the wolf said.

I smiled and closed the door behind me.

Thinking about my phone for a second, I opened the door again and went over to an old couch that Coach had bought used several years ago.

There, in the electric outlet, was a spare phone charger. Hooking mine up, I realized my battery was down to two percent. Close call.

Then I went back inside the broom closet.

Stripping out of my muddy clothes, I realized just how rank I actually smelled.

I took off everything except my locket.

Inside the shower I found some body wash and shampoo that looked like they'd never been used before.

Better than nothing.

After bathing, I got out and dried off.

Then, with a towel firmly wrapped around me, I went out into the main gym area, looking around to make sure Coach hadn't come in.

I wandered over to the corner behind the punching bags, feeling naked even though I had the towel around me. Maybe it was all the windows on the front end of the gym. I felt like all of Fayetteville was peeping through them, when in reality, most of the town didn't even know about this gym.

A row of tall lockers, each more dented than the last stood waiting for me. I found locker nine and twisted the numbered dial on my little silver lock to remove it. Inside, I had some spare clothes, along with a few other miscellaneous items.

I pulled out some Paris rose scented deodorant. I always wondered if it was actually what roses smell like in the City of Love and put it on. Then I found a pair of black jeggings with stupid little belt loops too small for any actual belt and a white Northwest Arkansas University hoodie.

There was also a very worn pair of black sneakers at the bottom of the locker. The bottoms had pretty much no traction left, but worn down shoes beat no shoes any day, especially in December.

I slipped them on after putting on a pair of thin black socks.

It's amazing how clean clothes and a hot shower really make things better after a night of homelessness. I mean... I was still homeless, but the point is I felt better.

Ruad came over and looked me up and down.

"I'll never understand why humans make such a fuss about their fake fur," she said.

"Because not all of us can grow a fur coat like you," I said, putting my hair up into a ponytail.

"Adrienn, please come forth," I said.

The green-haired fey shot out of the necklace in a ball of glowing green light.

"How can I help you, my la- Um, Aoife?"

I smirked. They were working on it at least.

"I just wanted to check and see if you needed food before I headed to work. I mean, I had some berries, and Ruad ate Little Bunny Foo Foo for breakfast, but it occurs to me you haven't eaten."

They shook their head and smiled.

"Fey don't have to eat as often as humans. I'm actually fine," they said.

"Oh… okay. Well if you ever need anything, you can let me know, okay? I've never been one to let others suffer in silence, ya know?"

"Aoife, I'm supposed to serve you, not the other way around," they said.

I sighed.

"You're my friend now, not my servant. You really helped out last night, and I want to make sure you're taken care of."

Adrienn made a pouty face almost like they were going to cry.

"You're too kind, Aoife."

I put my hands on my hips and said, "Yeah, basic human compassion. I'm a regular Mother Teresa."

The fey smiled, and I looked over at Ruad.

"I would appreciate it if you two would try to keep a low profile today. Adrienn can hide in my necklace, but I'm still not sure how you're going to blend in, Ruad," I said. "Somehow, I doubt everyone in Fayetteville is going to be cool with a wolf just walking around on the sidewalk. Hell, we're just lucky Arkansas doesn't have laws against wolf dogs. That's what I'll have to pass you off as."

Ruad said nothing.

I racked my brain. People in Fayetteville love their dogs. You walk around downtown, even in the Entertainment District on Dickson Street, and you'll see tons of dogs on leashes. But Ruad was a wolf, and she obviously looked like one. I couldn't just pass her off as a husky with some wolf in her. She was freaking huge.

Sighing, I looked around the room as if the answer to my problems might be hiding behind a punching bag.

I went and got my phone, seeing it was fully charged. Coach must have had some high-speed charger or something. I smiled and went back out into the gym area.

I turned to look at the storage space again, and my eyes settled on locker number 2, belonging to one Lily Anne. She attended class once a week, and came in with her service dog, Parsa. Everyone loved when Parsa came because Lily Anne would take her dog's vest off and put it in her locker.

Then people could play with the German shepherd to their heart's content. Parsa was a sweetheart and loved everyone in class. It was then I realized what I could do.

Lily Anne's locker didn't have a lock, so I opened it and found the spare service dog vest she kept in case something happened to Parsa's main one. It was black Velcro and had several straps across it with metal clips. Across the top was a large red mesh portion that had some sewn patches on the left and right side. They read, "Service dog. Do not pet."

I pulled out the straps as far as they would go and walked over to Ruad.

"Would you care to wear this vest whenever we're out in public? It'll make it to where no one gives me any trouble about having a wolf traveling with them."

"Why, what sort of enchantment does it hold? I don't sense any magic from this item," Ruad said.

I laughed.

"In the human world, some people have disabilities and need the help of a trained dog to make it through the day. The dogs are called service animals, and they wear vests just like this to let people know they're more than pets. And it's law that service animals have to be allowed everywhere normal humans are. They're considered medical equipment."

"I see. You want to deceive everyone with this vest and trick them into thinking I'm some kind of trained animal," Ruad said, studying the vest as she twisted and turned her head.

I nodded.

She sighed and lowered her head as I carefully fastened the vest on her. It fit well enough. I made a note to stop by a medical supply store and pick up my own service dog vest before Lily Anne came to class on Thursday night.

"I know you'll hate this, but you're also going to have to wear a leash connected to me if you're outside. It's kind of the local law, and we'll get in trouble if you aren't."

Ruad sighed even deeper and then nodded.

I pulled out a purple leash that was about eight feet long and clipped it to Ruad's vest.

She did not look pleased.

"As long as we are indoors, I only have to wear the stupid vest, right?"

I nodded, and she relented.

Adrienn flew over in front of Ruad's face and said, "I think you look fantastic with it. It makes you look more official."

The wolf snapped her jaws forward at the fey with a little snarl, and Adrienn flew back up into my necklace with a yip.

I smirked.

"Okay, you two. Let's get to work. Day one of being a druid. Here we go," I said and headed toward Pedal and Stem.

Chapter Six

Ruad and I walked along College Avenue for nearly a mile to the north toward a shopping plaza that contained Petal and Stem. I pulled tighter on my leather Third Eye Blind coat the bartender gave me whenever the cold wind would blow.

Ruad's purple leash was clipped to one of those flimsy belt loops on the right side of my jeggings.

Fortunately, downtown Fayetteville and the section immediately north was very accessible to pedestrians. The sidewalks along College Avenue had been widened and painted with murals ranging from vines and fruits to people doing yoga. To outsiders, Fayetteville was a bit of a hippie town.

It was a little city of about 80,000 people that served as the intersection of college town—arts scene, hippie city, and rapidly growing entrepreneurial businesses. There was a lot of startup capital moving into the area, and some crazy developers had dreams to turn this region into the Silicon South.

Flowerbeds in the road median were filled with winter-resistant bushes that looked the same all year. I could swear the plants were made of steel and resilient to everything except the rabbits, squirrels and birds that made their home inside of them.

On either side of College Avenue stood these short little black and white streetlights. They were cute and actually serviced the road with a decent amount of light after the sun went down.

Fayetteville taxpayers will happily provide funding to artsy up an area of town, but by golly, they want it to be practical, too.

Ruad and I made good use of the sidewalks as we headed north about a mile and eventually came to the Evelyn Hills shopping plaza. It was a good-sized center just northwest of Sequoyah Mountain. The plaza contained all sorts of businesses from a popular natural food store and co-op that people in this town would probably defend to the death if the need arose, to a fancy taco restaurant, one of the last functioning arcades in 2019, a dollar store, and more.

My employer, Petal and Stem, sat right smack dab in the middle of the shopping plaza next to a nail salon.

As Ruad and I cut across the grass, we were yelled at by a homeless man who frequents the traffic signal in front of the shopping plaza.

"Hey! Go get me a soda!" he yelled.

The man continued to shout orders at people walking by, as though they were his royal subjects, and he was king of the shopping plaza.

I just ignored him. He'd already rejected a bottle of water I brought him once.

It was probably one of my worst habits, but I scorned easy. If I tried to do something nice for someone or worked to make a situation better, and it blew up in my face, that would be the last time I would try to help. Some days bitterness just comes quick. I'm only human.

Maybe now that I was homeless I should start shouting at people.

Hey! I shouted in my mind. *Bring me some Thai food!*

Strangely enough… nobody did. And I looked left and right to check.

The shopping plaza was already seeing some traffic, no surprise given the bagel shop and the hippie grocery store opened at the buttcrack of dawn. Some people that drove by looked away when they saw the service vest and leash. Others continued to stare because Ruad is huge.

"I forgot how much I hate vehicles," Ruad muttered.

We approached the flower shop, and I pulled my work keys out of my purse. The front door was glass and metal, with a single keyhole above the handle. I unlocked the door and went into the dark flower shop.

Sunlight filtered in through the front windows. I checked my phone and saw it was 8:42 a.m. The store had to be opened by 9:00 a.m., and Sabrina would usually show up around 9:30 a.m. on mornings she knew I was working.

Ruad and I were greeted by the scent of several different kinds of flowers, both cut and potted. The front of the flower shop had about enough room to comfortably hold between five and eight customers. Tall coolers sat off to the left with fresh-cut flowers stored at 33 degrees exactly.

Sabrina was very particular about keeping floral arrangements at that temperature. It ensured they would last longer before drooping over and showing increased signs of decay.

I locked the door behind me and walked over to the wall opposite of the coolers to find a long row of four light switches. I turned them all on, bringing even more light to the room.

The carpet in the front of the store was an earthy green. There was a rocking chair with a small table and a few magazines to the right of the front door when customers came in and needed to wait a few more minutes for me or Sabrina to finish their arrangement.

I walked behind the wooden counter where our iPad and cash register box sat on a little swivel. It came up to my chest.

Turning on the iPad and plugging in the charging cable, I opened our cash register app and made sure the card swiper was connected for the day.

Ruad followed me through the doorway behind the register and into the back room, which was a lengthy narrow space about 25 feet long and ten feet wide.

A number of different potted plants sat along the concrete floor with little metal drains every seven feet. There was a green hose coiled up in one corner attached to an indoor faucet.

In the center of the room sat a 10-foot long table with cushioned benches on both sides. Tools for trimming the plants and arranging bouquets sat at the back end of the table.

And behind that was a door leading outside.

Looking up, I saw a pigeon walking across the skylight that made up most of the ceiling of the shop's backroom.

Taking a deep breath, I felt a little easier because I loved this job. I'd been working here part-time since I was 14, and it was one of the few things Barb actually approved of.

"Even for a normal human, your boss sure does keep a solid selection of flowers during the cold season," Ruad said, interrupting my grumpy Barb thoughts.

"Before I knew what druids were, I wondered if she might have been akin to Professor Sprout," I said, looking up at a sunflower clock on the wall and noting I had to have the store open in 10 minutes.

I stopped for a moment and looked at Ruad.

"You aren't going to ask who Professor Sprout is?"

The wolf looked at me and without missing a beat, said, "The herbology professor at Hogwarts."

I raised an eyebrow and froze.

"Don't look so surprised. Your mother and father took turns reading the *Harry Potter* books to you every night before bed. Before you were even a year old, you'd heard them all, even if you don't remember them. I had to listen to all those books multiple times," Ruad said.

She didn't sound annoyed. The wolf just stated matter of fact that she'd heard all the *Harry Potter* books read to me as a child. I whistled.

"Druid magic and huntress abilities aside, your parents were kind of dorks," Ruad said.

The mental image of real, caring parents reading to me every night left me tearing up. Barb had forbidden me to read *Harry Potter* like any of the other thousands of crazy church mothers who paid too much attention to the Bible's mention of witchcraft. That was initially what I thought got me into the series, childhood rebellion.

But now I found out my parents had read it to me every night before bed, trying to fill my early childhood with a sense of wonder and awe. I was filled with longing to sit on a couch between Tristan and Iris, cuddled up under a fuzzy blanket, cup of cocoa in my hands, to hear them read me *Harry Potter* out loud like I was a child again, before Barb tried to knock all that childhood amazement and curiosity out of me.

I lost it and just let tears flow down my cheeks as I realized I'd never have that again. And then my thoughts turned bitterly to Barb, who, if I asked to read me a bedtime story as a little girl, would pull out her Bible and flip to Revelation, as if the world burning in a religious war was as fascinating and wondrous as a boy and his friends trying to defeat a dark wizard.

Abi said her mom would read Maurice Sendak stories to her as a child. She even loaned me a book once after a sleepover when I was seven. And when I asked Barb to read it to me, the cruel woman said the stories wouldn't nourish my spirit at all. That night, I got a story from the book of Exodus and felt particularly malnourished in the motherly love department.

I found a roll of paper towels and blew my nose. I tore off a second one to wipe my eyes, and Ruad sat down in front of me, looking at me with a knowing look, well, as much as a talking wolf can give such a face.

When I stopped crying, she said, "Those were their happiest nights, you know? I remember the warmth from Tristan's emotions in my chest. When the temperature fell outside, Tristan would build a fire, Iris would make hot chocolate, and they'd sit on the sofa and read to you."

That brought more tears, and I cried until 8:59 a.m. I kneeled down and hugged Ruad. She seemed a little apprehensive at first, and then her head lowered onto my left shoulder.

Then I stood up, took a deep breath, wiped my tears and grabbed a clipboard hanging on the wall.

"Okay," I said aloud, trying to get myself ready for opening.

I took it back to the front and unlocked the door, turned on a little red and blue light up "open" sign that hung above the entrance, and went back to the counter.

"So you don't freak out customers, maybe you should lie down or sit behind the counter next to me," I said.

Ruad did as I asked and came around, sitting and leaning on my hip.

Feeling the weight of her on my hip, I thought, for the 1,000th time, *Geez, she's huge.*

I scanned the list of orders for the day. There was an arrangement for a funeral this morning that had been called in late Saturday just before Sabrina closed up the afternoon. I didn't work that day.

She'd started it and got about half finished before placing the order in the cooler. I spotted it, went over, grabbed the arrangement, and took it into the back room.

The order was relatively simple. It was a heart-shaped collection of about 30 yellow button poms. Sabrina had the outline done. All I needed to do was fill out the center and tie the top of the heart with a white lace ribbon. It would then be placed on the casket of a Lt. Roger Belkin.

Simple enough, I thought, and set to work.

I reached under the table and pulled out the large box of ribbons and ties we used for arrangements. Ruad sat behind me.

About three or four minutes into my work, I started humming the tune to the *Harry Potter* movies. Ruad lay behind me as I worked.

I finished up and placed the arrangement back in the cooler just before a Black woman who appeared to be in her 30s with short-cut hair came into the store.

"Welcome to Petal and Stem," I said, turning to face her behind the counter.

She smiled and walked over to me. The woman was wearing a poofy red coat with a small black backpack slung behind one shoulder.

"Hi, I'm here to pick up an order," she said.

"Sure thing. Name?" I asked.

"Mary Belkin."

I nodded and walked over to the cooler. Ruad stayed behind the counter. When I came back with the arrangement, Mary nodded.

"Your total comes to $75.43," I said.

Mary reached into her backpack and pulled out a money clip. She counted me off four $20's and then put it back in her purse.

"You can keep the change," she said.

I smiled and thanked her.

The customer turned to leave just as Sabrina opened the door and came in with a small white box in one hand. Mary looked at her, saw her manager tag, and said, "Your flowers are impressive. When my uncle passed away last week, and we started planning out the funeral, I asked friends who should do flowers for the casket. They all agreed on Petal and Stem. It was kind of shocking, actually. Because my friends can't even agree on where to go to lunch, but it seems they know who sells the best flowers in town."

Damn right this is the best flower shop in Fayetteville, I thought, listening to them talk.

"Well that's very sweet of you to say," Sabrina said. And with that, Mary left.

Sabrina is a tall woman in her 50s. My boss wears her hair long, down past the middle of her back. It's a fairly light brown, and she brushes it straight every morning.

Today she had a red ribbon in her hair and was wearing black leather pants with a flowery red top under a matching red coat. Her nails were painted green, and she wore red lipstick for the ultimate Christmas combo.

Sabrina wore a little makeup and usually had a thin layer of eyeliner on, which she was also wearing now.

It didn't seem to matter to Sabrina that she was approaching 60. The woman had a youthful heart and a real zest for life.. In her spare time, I knew Sabrina liked to do yoga and work on genealogy projects.

She's a true icon of cheery goodness and joy.

"Hey boss," I said, walking around the counter.

"Good morning, Eve," she said, smiling. I twitched. That was the wrong name.

Sabrina had this eye thing where when she smiled, her brown eyes opened a little wider as her grin grew. She said that came as an unexplained habit when she was a ballet dancer back in L.A. Just before the curtain would go up, her nerves would fire, and she would widen her eyes and smile to calm them. She'd supposedly always done it since.

My nose detected banana muffins in the white box Sabrina was holding, and while that took some of my attention, I managed to keep enough wits about me to put up both of my palms and say, "Okay, don't freak out."

Sabrina set the box down in the rocking chair and crossed her arms. But she kept a smile on her face. She was ready for whatever news I had for her.

"There's a... dog behind your counter. She's my new service animal, okay? Her name is Ruad, and she's completely house trained. My animal is big, but she's very quiet and friendly, I promise," I said.

Sabrina raised an eyebrow.

"You got a service dog?" she asked.

Now came the part I hated. I was going to have to lie to my boss, a woman I dearly cared for and respected.

"Yes. On Saturday, I went to the hospital after a small epileptic episode," I said, going through my brain for lines I rehearsed on the way here. "It wasn't anything too crazy, but John freaked out, and we got this service dog from a veteran at church who owns a dog training company out near Siloam Springs. She, uh, detects seizures and will warn me if I'm about to have an episode."

My heart sank, and I did everything I could to keep my jaw from clenching. I hated this. But what else could I have done?

Sabrina told me when she lived in California she used to be Wiccan, before she became a "good Catholic girl" as she put it now. So maybe she'd understand the whole pagan nature thing, but I had no way of knowing that.

I mean, she was cool when she found out I was dating Abi. But a talking wolf was an entirely different thing to accept.

"Oh my goodness! A seizure sounds really bad. Are you sure you should be working today?" Sabrina asked, walking over to place the back of her hand on my forehead, as if a fever and seizures were the same thing.

"I'm good, really. John really overreacted and insisted on the dog. I promise she won't cause any trouble," I said.

Sabrina's smile returned.

"May I see her?"

I nodded and asked Ruad to come around the counter. Soon a wolf with thick red fur was sitting next to me, leaning on my hip with her weight again.

I'm going to have joint problems before I'm 20 at this rate, I thought.

My boss gasped when she saw her, though apparently not out of fear.

"I didn't know wolf dogs could be service animals!" she said, slowly placing her hand toward Ruad's nose.

She didn't know Ruad was an intelligent animal. My boss thought she was dealing with a normal dog, and it clearly needed to smell her hand to know she wasn't a threat.

Ruad looked up at me. I could practically feel her annoyance at being treated like a pet. She sniffed Sabrina's hand twice. I detected warm vanilla sugar lotion wafting into my nose from where I was standing. Then Ruad lightly licked the tip of Sabrina's extended hand. That was as close to a friendly greeting as my boss was going to get.

Sabrina slowly leaned forward and started lightly patting Ruad's head. The wolf stood still as a statue.

When Sabrina finally rose and fetched her box again, she said, "Ruad is welcome here, but I'd keep her behind the counter. A wolf dog might frighten some of the customers."

"Yes ma'am," I said.

My boss went into the back room and placed the box on the long table, opening it.

"I brought in some banana muffins if you and Ruad want some," she said, walking over to some red and white poinsettias and looking closely at the leaves.

"Thanks," I said, walking over to the box and finding four large banana muffins wrapped in blue paper.

As I took one out, I asked, "Hey Sabrina?"

"Yes?"

"Another small request, but could you start calling me Aoife from now on? It's just something I'm trying out, and I think it makes me more comfortable than Eve," I said, flinching.

Sabrina looked over at me and said, "Oh shoot. I really liked Eve... but sure. I'll work on the new name. Just be patient with me for the first week or two, okay?"

I smiled and nodded.

"Thank you."

I leaned over to Ruad and whispered, "I know you're not a house pet. Sorry you might have to endure a few pets in public. But generally, that vest should keep people away from you."

Ruad let out a small groan from her chest.

"Do you want a muffin?"

My familiar thought for a moment and said, "Do you think she'd consider it rude if I didn't eat one? She did mention my name."

I smiled. This wolf had manners. Eat your heart out Little Red Riding Hood.

"I don't think she'll mind one way or another. It's your call," I said.

Ruad sighed and nodded.

I peeled off the paper and gave her a muffin. I didn't dare toss it in the air for her to catch it, or she might have taken my arm off in frustration for the disrespect. Instead, I calmly laid it flat on my palm.

She took it gently with her teeth and set it on the ground, where she tore the top half off and chewed it.

"Should you ever meet Tristan's ghost, don't tell him I said this, but his banana bread was always burned. These aren't half bad," she said, before taking the rest of it in her mouth and chewing.

"These are great, Sabrina," I said, after tearing into mine. It didn't take long to finish.

I ate a second muffin, and then got to work on filling orders the rest of the morning. When I finished everything in the queue, a teen not too much younger than myself came in. He looked to be about 16 and had been growing out every ounce of mustache his body could possibly produce. It was still thinner than those worn by stereotypical French waiters at fancy restaurants.

He wore a full suit with a black trilby and some kind of cane that looked like a prop from *The Great Gatsby*. I tried not to gag at the overpowering cologne he was wearing.

Oh boy, I thought.

The teen walked over and eyed my wolf. He then looked at me and in as deep of a voice he could muster up, he said, "Good lady. I'm looking for a dozen red roses. Tout de suite, please."

Nodding, and trying not to laugh, I went into the back and got his requested flowers. Upon my return, I saw him trying to reach over the counter and pet Ruad, who was growling. I scowled and scolded immediately.

"Her vest should inform you she is not a pet for anyone to touch," I said.

The teen looked like he'd been caught with his hand in the cookie jar.

"What is she, an emotional support animal or some garbage like that?"

I bared my fangs, well, where my fangs would be if I still had them, and let out a growl. A voice inside of me was just screaming at top volume to murder the bastard that insulted my father's familiar.

Come on, Aoife. Calm. If Ruad really felt threatened or insulted, she'd have killed him in two seconds flat. She doesn't need you to fight her battles, I thought.

I shook my head and took a deep breath.

The customer gave me a weird look like my intense stare was freaking him out. When I finally managed to grab control back from that inner voice, I said, "She's a working service animal trained to detect my seizures."

He looked at Ruad and raised an eyebrow.

"People will do anything to bring their pets with them," he said, sighing and handing me his debit card.

I bit my tongue so hard I might have tasted blood. But I took his debit card, swiped it, flipped the iPad around so he could sign with his finger, and said a silent prayer to the gods for whomever these flowers were for. Then, he left.

Around 1:00 p.m., I went over to the fancy taco place with Ruad. We got our tacos to go because some of the customers kept trying to pet my father's familiar, despite me scolding them for ignoring her vest.

Parents need to do a better job teaching their crotch gremlins about service animal rules.

Ruad's tacos were just beef, lettuce, and tortillas. She seemed to enjoy them well enough.

About an hour later, Sabrina said she had to run some errands and left the store in my care, while I worked on another order.

A black pot with a batch of inch plant growing inside sat in front of me. I'd wrapped the pot in a pink ribbon. This was going to a grandmother for her birthday. Apparently, the purple heart flowers were among her favorites.

Becky was turning 88, and I'd placed a nice big label with her name and "Happy Birthday!" written on it just above the purple leaves. It was nestled tightly in the grip of a wooden stand with three fingers.

I was working on pinning a big yellow smiley face button to the front when I slipped and sent the pin into my right thumb. I jerked the thumb up sharply and looked at it while cursing.

Ruad looked up at me.

A small bead of blood inflated on my thumb at the prick site and then dropped down into the leaves below.

"Damn it!" I hissed.

And before I could look for where it landed to clean it off, my whole world pulsed. It was like I could hear the blood inside my skull, and every few seconds, it would vibrate, like a second heartbeat keeping time to no one source. With these vibrations came an extreme smell of vegetation that filled my nostrils until all I could taste, smell, and feel was the color green.

A wave of that emerald energy splashed over my mind, drowning it in all the intense nature that came with it. Suddenly, all my attention and being was drawn down to this plant before me.

Strange thing was, I didn't question these strange thoughts. My only worry was the plant, which I could sense at once had root damage from overwatering. I couldn't look away from the plant, which began to rattle in front of me.

Inside my mind, I felt two lines of parallel roots about to touch. One set of roots came from the plant in front of me. The other set of roots was my own being. And the moment the roots touched, they began dancing with each other, threading themselves together like the plant was trying to become a part of me.

The plant needed more sunlight, and I desperately felt my own skin crying out for more sunlight, as though my flesh were made of leaves.

And speaking of leaves, the leaves on the inch plant started to shake slowly. The speed built up until every leaf was convulsing and pointing straight at me.

I gripped the countertop, unable to break my attention away from the plant.

"A… Ad…" I tried to get my mouth to form, but all I could focus on was the shaking plant in front of me. It needed so much care and attention, or it would die in a couple weeks. My legs began to ache, as though they craved fertilizer, and I realized the soil didn't contain enough nutrients.

Ruad looked up at me and said, "Adrienn, get out here! Aoife needs you!"

With a spark of green light, the fey flew up in front of my face.

"Oh boy... I was worried about this. I knew I should have said something earlier. But I was worried you would think I was a worrywart. And that's not really how I wanted you to view me and-"

"Adrienn!" Ruad yelled.

My hands gripped the counter so hard, it began to groan.

"Okay, Aoife, listen to me. The magical energy in your blood has linked with a plant for the first time. Linking with a plant for the first time through a blood connection is always a system shock because you're a mammal linking with a completely different type of lifeform. This isn't like linking with a wolf."

I wanted to say, "Gee, thanks. That explanation really makes me feel better," but I couldn't get out any words as hard as I was shaking. By the GODS I needed nutrients! I was starving here. Didn't they see that?

"I don't think your magical theory explanation is helping, fey!" my wolf growled.

"S... sssss," I managed.

"Yes?" Adrienn asked.

"SUN!" I screamed at the top of my lungs.

This was a tough season for inch plants, and the creeping plant felt that. It should be dormant, and with the cold air that occasionally came in through the back door, it very much wanted to be dormant as it should. But here I was, forcing it to grow against its will.

I'm a monster, I shouted in my head.

The countertop began to crack a little from my grip.

"Aoife, I know you want to overpower this plant, but you can't, not like you're used to. This isn't a match of muscles. This is a match of energy and will. You're going to have to channel more magic into the plant. Imagine drowning it in your own energy."

I shook my head. I didn't know what magic felt like. How was I supposed to drown the plant in it?

"That's enough! I'll just flood my own energy into the plant and tear it away from Aoife," Ruad barked.

Adrienn flew down in front of the wolf and said, "No! Don't! This is the first time Aoife's magical energy has awakened and connected to a plant. If you drown out her own energy with yours and sever the connection, you'll stunt her druidic growth and connection to plants forever."

Ruad powered down and grunted.

"What do you suggest, then?"

Adrienn thought for a moment and said, "She doesn't know what her own magic feels like. She needs to recognize her own energy and take control. But that's difficult since she doesn't really know who she is."

I tried to tear my brain away from the shouting needs of this plant, but it kept pulling my attention in like a vacuum. Adrienn was saying something, but their voice was starting to sound distant and muffled.

It was then I felt Ruad sink her teeth into my right arm, and I yelped. She drew more blood than the pinprick, and I was about to curse again. But then I realized my mind had been jerked free a little more than before.

Then I could feel Ruad's will in my mind, almost like a whisper. It grew in volume.

"Close your eyes, and feel it, Aoife. Feel your magic. Ever since you put Adrienn's locket on and became who you were meant to be, it's been there, an extra vibration in your blood. It's constant. It's ancient. It's your magic. Sense it, Aoife. Take hold of it," Ruad said.

I pulled a little further from the plant and slowly reached into my blood, all five quarts of it. Trying to quiet the screaming tension from the plant yanking at my attention, I took a deep breath. My magic was here. Furrowing my brow, I searched until I barely felt it, like brushing your hand over the very edge of a spider web only this spiderweb was a string of energy through my body.

That's it, I thought. The feeling grew stronger as I grabbed at that web's thread.

When I identified where the inch plant's roots intertwined with my own, I closed my eyes and let my magic carry me away. The sensation didn't feel like I was being pulled up or down, but rather inward by a familiar source, one I should have known for years of my life now. But I was just getting acquainted with my inheritance.

I started to feel ethereal as the magic pulled me inward, and I couldn't place a time limit on this process any more than a botanist could rush the blossoming of a flower. It just had to happen.

At last, I felt my feet on solid ground again, and a damp, clammy air ran across my skin. Opening my eyes, I found myself in a misty forest.

This looks like the one I saw briefly back in Odessa's shop, I thought. Endless gray skies above, trees and shrubs as far as my eyes could see. Familiarity blanketed my senses as I wandered here, even if I had no memory of ever setting foot in these woods before.

My magic flowed and echoed all around me in this forest, like a primal call, dancing through the hairs on my head and down between my toes.

It was difficult to put into words how I felt standing here. The best I could come up with was this place made me feel like the truest version of myself. There were no lies here, just the rawest platform of my inner being. Place and distance didn't seem to have much meaning here. Regardless, I moved amongst the oaks and evergreens of this forest for an unknown length and time.

Suddenly, I turned, and there before me was an inch plant, having taken root in the forest. But this one was huge. It was the size of a small house and still growing.

This forest is inside me, I thought, an epiphany settling on my brain. *Adrienn said I'd linked with the plant when my blood dropped onto it, so if it's here, then this place is like a forest inside my own subconscious.*

That explained why my magic felt so clear and present here. These woods existed solely within my noggin. And now the inch plant did too, I realized. I scowled and remembered how moments earlier this plant had tried to hijack my drive and desires when we linked.

"Oh hell no. You want to live in my mind forest then you pay some goddamn rent, plant!" I yelled running forward to the purple leaves.

I stepped between the stems, each one as dense as my arm and growing even thicker. I grabbed one of the stems, barely wrapping both my hands around it and felt its own energy and will invading my mind forest.

Then I started to shake and reach for my own energy that was currently all around me.

"Aoife! Drown the plant in your own magic!" I heard Adrienn shout somewhere echoing in the woods.

I felt pins and needles on my fingers as my hands glowed green. I pulled the magic in the air around me inside and sent every piece of it into the stem I held.

I began to sweat, and a light-headed feeling overtook me , but I pushed forward anyway. I wondered if this was the opposite of how appliances felt when they were plugged into a socket. The inch plant didn't seem to know how to react. Fortunately, it didn't have much time to decide as I overtook it with my energy. It felt like throwing a bucket of water on a single sprout.

And when the plant began to glow green with my own magic, I willed it to shrink, picturing a potted piece of vegetation once more.

At first, nothing happened, and my heart skipped a beat, worried that I had let this thing grow too much.

Then gradually, the inch plant began to shrink before my eyes. After what seemed like several minutes, it was back in a pot and smaller than my right hand.

I sighed, and sweat dripped off my forehead. I could still feel myself linked with the plant, only now it was an extension of me, like a third arm. I took a deep breath.

Closing my eyes, I pictured myself leaving the forest behind and returning to the real world. Once more, I felt my consciousness pulled, this time, outward.

When I opened my eyes again, I saw Ruad licking my arm where she'd drawn a little blood. The bleeding stopped, and my right arm was covered partially in wolf saliva.

I almost muttered something about it being gross, but there was another familiar emotion that began to rise in me, the most vague memory on the fringe of my mind.

I'd fallen and skinned my knee when I was between one and two years old. She came over as I cried and licked the knee clean. As soon as I saw Ruad, there was a sense of comfort. I immediately calmed down. Then my parents came over and tied some kind of yellow leaf to my knee. The next day, any markings were gone.

There's a healing property to saliva. It's where the phrase, "licking your wounds," comes from. Lots of mammals do it. But humans and dogs have been bonded for centuries. And dogs licking human wounds isn't as strange an act as modern folk would believe. They lick their own wounds. Why would they not do the same for their human family whom they loved and bonded with?

With my father and Ruad, that bond was much deeper, so its healing effect had been too. "Thanks," I muttered, finally letting go of the counter and popping my wrists.

I looked up at Adrienn and gave them my thanks as well. They bowed and flew back into my necklace in case anyone came in.

As if on cue, a woman did come into the shop. She was wearing scraggly clothing and smelled like vinegar and mud. One of her eyes was swollen shut, and she appeared distressed with ragged breathing. Her pale skin was mostly hidden by a blue hoodie and torn jeans.

"Open your goddamned register and give me all the money inside right now!" she yelled.

Ruad looked up at her and growled.

My chest tightened, my heartbeat sped up, and I felt like I'd hopped right out of one frying pan and into another.

My father's familiar would undoubtedly protect me. But if she was seen biting someone that came into the store, even a robber, that could cause other nearby business owners to get kind of nervous about her. And if word spread there was a wolf biting people at this store, it wouldn't matter if it was self defense. It might spook customers. And Sabrina didn't need that.

"Did you hear me?" the woman yelled.

She limped over to the counter. The would-be robber was not very tall, maybe about five feet. She looked scrawny, and her brown hair was filled with what looked like dried mud.

Petal and Stem had never been robbed before as far as I knew. This was a safe area, not that Fayetteville itself was dangerous.

I noticed a few bruises on the woman's neck, especially on her left side. She was in rough shape. But a quiet voice inside of me whispered, "She's trying to rob you! Be a wolf again, and rip her throat out."

I growled, and Ruad stood ready, just waiting for the word. I wagered with Ruad's help I could once more assume a wolf form and end this woman's life. A piece of my subconscious wanted to smash her face into the counter for daring to make demands of me. Fighting hard, I swallowed that urge, but it wasn't easy, and it didn't entirely go away. In fact, most of it came back when the woman lifted the right side of her hoodie and revealed a small pistol inside her waistband.

"You see that, yeah? If you don't open the register right now, I'm going to pull this out and kill you. How does that sound?"

That urge to hurt the woman in front of me skyrocketed, but I fought it as best I could. Someone else could walk by at any moment, and I didn't want them to see me changing into a different form.

For the next few seconds, I fought a volatile mixture of rage and fear. I wanted to kill her. No, I just needed to hurt her. Maybe just enough to make her run away.

Kill her! the voice inside screamed, far from a whisper.

I fought to maintain some semblance of logic, talk down the voice. Sabrina didn't need a dead body at her shop. This was a busy season for her, and having a death investigation would be terrible for the shop as a whole. I might even get fired. Then I'd be homeless and jobless.

Sabrina had been nothing but kind to me since the day I walked in and asked for a job application. She was always baking me breakfast treats, asking how Abi was doing, letting me vent about Barb, and generally providing a very safe space for me to work.

As the urge to maim and murder grew louder, my hands quivered. And still, I fought the urge to end her. I could just hurt her or chase her out of the store.

The two ideas clashed, and I drowned out the internal murder screaming with a specific, almost surgical urge to cause harm. I honed that desire into a narrow point, like the tip of a spear, and aimed it straight toward her.

The attacker's hand reached for her gun, and I heard her say, "This is your last…" Then she suddenly stopped speaking right about the time I felt something release, some magic perhaps? A subconscious trigger?

We both happened to look down, and there was a growing red spot in the center of her torso. And sticking out of her body was a long leafy vine of some sort. I followed it back to the source and realized the inch plant had grown. Three strands of leaves had rocketed forward in a triangular spear tip and pierced the would-be robber's body, probably just to the left of the stomach. The smell of blood hit my nostrils instantly, raising the primal shout of violence inside of me.

"Oh my god…" I muttered, putting my hands up to my mouth.

Did I do that? I thought.

The woman's hands dropped to her wound, and she tried to pull the plant out of her. I didn't know how far it'd penetrated. Was it sticking out her back side right now?

I looked at the plant and willed it to withdraw. It did, pulling out some more blood as the leaves and vines left her wound. Her torso made an awful squelching noise as the plant left.

The woman put both her hands over the wound, turned, and shuffled out the door with a deep grimace and moan. Out of all the things she probably expected to happen in the course of a simple robbery, that likely wasn't one of them.

She wandered off down the sidewalk somewhere out of sight. I wanted to stop her, and part of me thought about calling an ambulance, but the other part of me just froze, trying to process what had just happened.

What did I just do? I thought.

My heart felt like it sank to the floor below, next to a few pools of that woman's blood. Ruad seemed to sense my shock, and even Adrienn flew back out of the locket. Both asked if I was okay, but all I could hear was my own breathing.

"I did that," I muttered. "That blood… I spilled it. I said yes to the voice inside."

Panic seemed to snap me back to reality as I stared at the blood trail going out of the store. I had to get rid of it.

Putting my body to a mundane task would free up my mind to do some deep thinking, if that was even possible anymore.

But somehow, that's what I did.

I got out a few rags, some multi-surface cleaner, and wiped up all the blood. With time, I got the store back in tip top shape, but I couldn't stop shaking. To get some air, I took Ruad outside the door, and she licked up any bigger blood spots from the sidewalk. There wasn't much, and it looked like the attacker wandered off around the shopping plaza and out toward College Avenue.

If she went south a little ways, she'd come upon a walk-in clinic. If her thinking was clear enough, maybe she'd get help.

Oh well, them's the breaks, that inner voice said, back for more. I tensed up at that thought, mounting guilt and fear inflating inside my chest.

If someone seeks to hurt others, their life is forfeit, the voice reasoned. I clenched my fists. That logic was enough to follow until it came time for life to become forfeit. Everything's easy until it's time.

My body was shaking from the magic I'd used today. I just wanted to sleep and to stop feeling this emotional culpability.

I'd just finished rinsing off any remaining blood on the inch plant when a customer came in to take it home. Apparently, it was a birthday gift for some lucky guy named Harold.

Normally, I'd have started a new order, but that was literally our last inch plant. So, I just had to do the best I could. And "the best I could" seemed like something I imagined I'd be doing a lot more of in the near future.

Sabrina returned, and I had to spend the rest of the afternoon pretending like nothing had happened. When I said everything was fine, I lied to her twice, and that just left me feeling like I needed two showers. There was something icky on my conscience, and it left me nauseous.

She doesn't deserve to be lied to, I thought, frowning.

Ruad stayed quiet for the rest of the day. She could probably sense my growing discomfort.

Eventually, 5:00 p.m. rolled around, and we closed up shop. I left, locking the door and leaving Sabrina in the back doing some more paperwork.

I started walking back toward the cabin, which I really didn't want to sleep in again. But that was the least of my concerns as guilt continued to inflate like a hot air balloon in my chest. Actually, my whole chest seemed like it was going to burst, and I was seconds away from collapsing into tears. Nothing felt right anymore!

Ruad spoke up at last and said, "This is weighing pretty heavily on you, isn't it, Pup? Your heartbeat has been erratic all afternoon."

I just shook my head until I found a quiet voice that said, "Magic was fine until it got scary. Now I'm not sure I want it anymore, not if it comes coupled with murderous instincts I constantly have to fight."

My father's familiar walked in front of me and stopped.

"Aoife, you need to understand that what you did today was perfectly justified. It was self defense. That woman had a weapon."

Now I lost it. Stupid emotions.

"But she wasn't the one who used a weapon today, Ruad. I was! My weapon could have her bleeding to death in a ditch right now. And I didn't know accepting a fucking druidic legacy could lead to that outcome. Odessa, you, and Adrienn forgot to include that in the list of possible side effects," I hissed, tears streaking down my cheeks.

Adrienn flew out of my necklace and up into my hair, out of sight, but not out of earshot.

"It's okay, Aoife. You didn't do anything wrong today. Tristan and Iris have defended themselves just as you did on countless occasions," they said.

I shook my head as a few tears fell to the ground.

"Neither of you understand."

"Help us, then," Adrienn said, gently.

I tried to summon the words.

"I'm... scared," I whimpered. "There was a voice inside of me that wanted blood. And I gave in. I gave in, you guys. I don't know what kind of monster that makes me."

My fey guardian and my father's familiar exchanged glances. For a moment, they were speechless. But then Adrienn found the words.

"Being the alpha of a druid clan isn't easy, Aoife. Neither of us expect you to get it right on your first try. Gods know Tristan didn't always get it right. But he learned, as you did today, that these magical gifts come with responsibility. Your father didn't have that lesson down perfect on day one," Adrienn said. "Iris told me plenty of stories about his impulsiveness."

I stopped crying. And Ruad spoke, a few inches from my face.

"Pup, Tristan was a bit of a screwup when he became alpha. Sometimes I questioned if he even really wanted to lead. On one of his first missions defending our territory, he got cocky against an invading griffin. Another member of the pack had to save Tristan that day and lost his arm for it. Your father was every bit as distraught then as you are today. But he learned about responsibility, as you will with our help."

I hugged Ruad, and though I could tell she wanted to flinch from the sudden contact, she kept it together and even stifled a sigh.

Adrienn just patted me on the side of the head while I reassembled myself. Responsibility, sure, I might be able to do that. Maybe. With assistance.

"You know, speaking of Tristan, I think I know something that might help you, Aoife," Adrienn said.

* * *

After a long bus ride southeast of Fayetteville, I stepped out at Lake Sequoyah Park. We walked down into a forested area, and Adrienn flew out of my locket to lead the way and provide a little glowing green light. Around 10-15 minutes later, we came to a part of Lake Sequoyah that consisted of a series of small islands and waterways covered with deep trees. The terrain was soft and muddy in some areas and rocky in other parts.

"Come on, Adrienn. What are we doing here? It's cold, windy, and wet."

"We're almost there," they said, as we came to the water's edge.

The inlet was about 20 feet across, and Adrienn flew over. I found a nearby fallen tree and crossed walking on that, as did Ruad.

We walked through another patch of elms and came to a building of some kind.

I stopped to stare at it.

"What is this?" I muttered.

We came to what looked like… an all glass structure. What was it doing out here in the middle of the woods? On an island in Lake Sequoyah?

Surrounding the building on the ground outside were glowing green runes carved into pieces of stone. They stopped glowing after we all stepped over them.

Adrienn led us to a door, and I opened it, slowly going inside. They flew up toward the ceiling about nine feet above me and lit a few lanterns with green fire.

As light filled the room, I realized I was standing in a greenhouse. There were pots of several plants that were still very much alive… somehow. All sorts of flowers, bushes, little trees, and more sat in long rectangular flower beds.

The greenhouse was probably about the size of the backroom at Petal and Stem.

"Holy crap. Look at this place," I said. "Where are we?"

Adrienn flew down, and I held out my hand flat. They landed on it and gestured around.

"Welcome to Tristan's secret greenhouse."

I gasped, and Ruad sort of smiled.

"Well done, fey," I could have sworn I heard her mutter.

"My… father? This was his space?"

Adrienn nodded and smiled.

"Aoife, you're going through some rough changes, things that make puberty look like a walk in the park. There's an animal inside you, fighting to take over. And I recognize it because your father wrestled with the same bloodlust. It's the nature of the beast, pun not intended. But you know how your father balanced all that out?" Adrienn asked.

I shook my head.

"Tristan studied every plant he could and buried himself in a relentless pursuit of nature magic to balance everything inside. You're scared now because you feel a pull toward unchecked anger and violence.

It's new and terrifying. But you're not alone. Ruad and I will be here for you every step of the way, just like we were for your father," my fey guardian said.

I looked around at the various work benches and plants, picturing my father tinkering in here. Maybe there were even memories of Tristan and Ruad buried some of these plants. But for now, I finally felt some measure of peace at Adrienn's words. And the next thing I wanted was rest.

"Thank you both for this," I said, hugging Ruad and Adrienn.

As I dug for bedding of some kind, I heard Adrienn and Ruad talking about me.

"What made you think of this place, fey?"

Adrienn shook their head smiling. Then they said, "She's his daughter in every way, you know? Remember how he dealt with these same problems? He built this greenhouse, and we helped him manage all those killer instincts. I just felt like this was a good place for us to start doing the same for Aoife."

Ruad said nothing after that.

I found an old humongous brown blanket, a truly hideous and scratchy thing my father had brought here for some reason, and I walked over to a corner of the greenhouse surrounded by a few different shrubs.

I sat down, and Ruad walked a little circle around the stone floor before curling up and leaving me an opening. I laid down on my side, face buried in her red fur. And Adrienn started to head back into my necklace.

Catching them with my hand, I heard a small gasp of surprise from Adrienn.

Then I slowly moved the fey over and buried them in my hair and Ruad's fur. The wolf let out a little huff of air at that.

I snuggled in closer and felt Adrienn finally stretch out before placing their head on the bridge of my nose and falling asleep.

Under the ugly blanket and buried in all that wolf fur, I dozed off picturing my father and mother standing over me smiling. It felt good to finally have a home.

Chapter Seven

I picked up the small pin and held it in my right hand before glancing down at the small black seed in my left palm.

"Are you sure about this, Adrienn?" I asked the fey as they hovered in the air about a foot in front of my face.

A pile of branches sat strewn behind me, picked clean of the berries I'd eaten for breakfast. They did the job, but I made the mistake of grumbling about missing real breakfast.

Ruad gave me a lecture about how fortunate I was to be able to live eating off the land while living in my father's greenhouse for free. Was she right? Sure. Two expenses gone, rent and groceries. But I missed waffles and bacon for breakfast.

I could hate on Barb for lots of things, lying to me about my heritage, trying to dominate my life choices, working hard to mold me into a Barb Jr., throwing me out onto the street in the dead of winter and so, *so* much more. But I had to admit, she could cook some truly delicious and unhealthy food when we had a truce going.

Even now I could still hear sausage and fried potatoes popping in skillets on her stove, the smell of flaky homemade biscuits baking in the oven and the sight of a giant white pot of gravy being stirred next to the skillets.

My options were different now… ranging from wild berries to a bird Ruad had taught me how to pluck, cook, and eat. It wasn't exactly fried chicken.

"Aoife? Are you still with me?" the fey asked, scratching their shaggy green hair.

I shook my head and looked down at the pin again. My heart started to beat a little faster.

"Sorry, I'm just remembering the incident at Petal and Stem yesterday. It's kind of stressing me out. I don't want to have to fight a plant trying to dominate my consciousness again," I said, taking a breath.

The fey nodded their head.

"I get it, Aoife. This is typically the scariest part of druids who start training to master nature manipulation. Every plant has a will of its own. And yesterday, you had to fight against one when your blood came in contact with it," Adrienn said.

I set the pin down on the floor and rubbed my forehead.

"Can you run me through that again? I'm still not quite sure I understand what happened," I said.

Adrienn smiled.

"You're waking up to druidic magic for the first time. And you don't really have a feel for your own magical energy. So for now, until you learn how to call upon your own power, the most effective way to access your magic is through your blood, where it resides. When your blood fell on the inch plant, it threw some of your magic into the plant. And the plant, taking you for a hostile invader, latched onto your consciousness, trying to take you over and fulfill its own needs, namely, soil nutrients and increased sunlight."

I sighed.

"And that won't happen this time because...?" I asked.

"Because you're going to grow a plant from seed. Seeds have no will of their own, and when you grow plants rapidly that are infused with your own magic, they automatically become extensions of your will, as the inch plant did when you finally took control yesterday. Only this time, you'll start with that control because you're growing the plant from scratch with a seed," Adrienn said.

This made sense in theory. But here's the thing about theories. They're not great at vanquishing fear. If I tell my brain a theory, it responds, "Oh, neat. I'm still scared. But that's neat." And that's how my brain was responding now.

Ruad was lying on her side about a few feet behind me and finally spoke up. She'd been quiet since fetching her squirrelly breakfast about half an hour ago.

"Oh for crying out loud, Pup. If you aren't going to practice using the plants, we might as well be working on your transformation. You still haven't mastered doing it on your own yet," Ruad said.

Adrienn said nothing as I made eye contact with them. They seemed to be much gentler with the training, whereas Ruad threw me into walls and sank her fangs into my neck, then had Adrienn heal me up. Good fey/bad wolf? Who knows?

"I am going to. I just need a second to get my nerves up, okay?" I said.

Ruad said, "I know we agreed to trade off on plant days and wolf days with your training, but one lesson that's applicable to both? Your enemy won't wait for you to get your nerves up. So snap to it."

Adrienn gave me a sympathetic glance. They were probably much more likely to say things like, "That's okay! You got really close, sport. Try again."

I looked down at the seed again.

What I'm really saying to my fey guardian is, 'I don't trust you' I thought.

Adrienn was sworn to serve me, and I know they had my best interest at heart.

If they say it'll be okay, then it'll have to be okay, I thought.

I picked up the pin again, dipped the tip in a little jar of alcohol to my right, and then pricked my left index finger, noting a slight sting.

Without looking at Adrienn, I folded my finger down onto the seed and covered it in a drop of blood. There was a slight feeling, almost like a static shock for a moment, and then my blood was gone.

"Whoa. Did the seed drink my blood like water? That's kind of alarming," I muttered.

"It absorbed that along with your magical energy. Can you not sense a link with the seed now?" Adrienn asked.

Closing my eyes, I did feel something like a small thread connecting me to the seed. It wasn't anywhere near as powerful as the inch plant. Now that the link was made, I felt like I understood what Adrienn had told me. This seed really was a blank slate, waiting for instructions from me via my druidic energy.

"I feel it. It's like an invisible shoestring tied around my hand. What do I do now?"

"Feed the seed more energy and grow it into a full plant," Adrienn said.

I looked at them in disbelief.

"You're joking, right? It takes months for these to grow. You want me to just wham, bam, make a flower?" I asked.

The fey nodded and pointed to the seed.

"This is one of the first things most druidic children learn to do when they awaken their power. Sprout the seed, and make it grow. But you're no druidic child. Although untrained, you have raw power. So, in theory, this should be easier for you," Adrienn said.

There they go again with their theories, I thought.

I shook my head. This was nuts. Then again, so was growing a tail, claws, and ears a couple nights ago. Growing a flower in a few seconds probably wasn't the weirdest thing.

So I grabbed hold of that invisible shoe string with my energy and began to replicate how I felt feeding magic into the inch plant within my mind forest.

This is just pushing your energy into the plant, like at the shop, I told myself. *Your father used to do the same thing right here in this greenhouse.*

I dialed my own magic back when I felt a second energy on this seed. It was older, faint. So I closed my eyes and searched for its origin. It felt like walking into a dark room I'd been in before. I knew where the furniture was. I just had to take it slow and feel along the walls. The magic on this seed felt familiar in a way I'd long forgotten, a fingerprint I hadn't seen since I was a baby.

Dad, I thought, picturing him in my mind's eye. I saw him in the greenhouse, wearing a green satchel at his side. He reached into it with his left hand and pulled out a few seeds. Gently closing his hand around them, he smiled. I watched as a green aura, his aura, glowed. Then it faded, and vines crawled from inside his enclosed fist and wrapped around his hand.

I watched him move the seeds into some nearby pots, and then it hit me. The seed I now held came from a plant Tristan grew. And my heart stirred a little. I was slowly learning how to recognize the inheritance he'd left me through my own magic. And that thought left me breathless.

Opening my eyes, I gently made a fist around the seed. My father had done multiple seeds, but I was going to try just one. Focusing on my hand, I pulled magic to it and then passed it along into the seed. I started to feel a little light headed as I tried my best to focus, and I wondered if anything was happening.

Then the moment of validation came. I watched with amazement as tiny white roots formed and wrapped around between my fingers. I grew dizzier, my vision blurred for a moment, but I also increased the amount of energy I was feeding into the seed, giving it all I could without shattering the living thing.

Rotating my fist sideways, I watched a green stem poke between my thumb and index finger. It rose as my hand glowed a faded green, quite a bit more faint than my father's had in the memory of him.

I was sweating now, and my legs were growing unsteady. But the stem kept rising, and I saw the seed split and unfurl into green leaves. I was watching life happen before my very eyes. Something that should take days and weeks was happening almost instantly.

No way, I thought. *This is insane.*

I had no intention of stopping. So I sank to my knees to keep from falling and gripped my left wrist with my right hand.

"You're doing great, Aoife!" Adrienn said, hovering over the plant. "If you feel strong enough, keep going!"

I gritted my teeth. Throwing magic into the seed was getting harder. Now I felt like I was scraping internally, like trying to get the last spoon or two of soup from the side of the bowl.

Still, the stem continued to rise and sprout more leaves. The leaves unfurled at the bottom of the stem closer to my fist..

The roots wrapped tighter around my fingers, thinned, and became fine, almost like hair. They now covered most of my hand.

After all the lower leaves were finished growing to their full size, a head appeared at the top of the stem. When the plant was about six feet tall, a cluster of smaller leaves formed and became the bulb. It pushed outward into the air, widening until tiny yellow petals formed. Those spread out, and the yellow-green center started to rise, almost as if they were inflating.

Sweat fell from my forehead as I realized the plant was done growing. I'd just used magic to grow a sunflower from seed to full plant in under a minute.

I closed my right eye, trying not to pass out from the exertion, and Adrienn flew a little closer, asking if I was okay.

"I'm fine," I muttered, opening both my eyes again. "Just need... to breathe. Oh boy, that takes it out of you."

Ruad walked around to my left as the first sunflower scent hit my nostrils.

"Not bad, Pup. Not bad," she said, eyeing the flower.

Adrienn got my attention again.

"This is the counterweight to your wolf instincts, Aoife. Magic can transform you, but you can also use it to eventually master the nature element. One day, you'll be able to grow these plants in a matter of seconds and manipulate them equally as fast."

"How do you mean?" I asked.

"Do you remember that robber you stabbed yesterday with the inch plant? Like that. Once you've gained mastery over a plant, you can manipulate it in all kinds of ways, so long as you have the energy," they said.

I raised an eyebrow. I remembered wanting to stab the criminal, and the plant kind of reacted on its own, growing instantly and piercing the woman's body.

Now Adrienn was telling me I could do the same stuff and more with this sunflower?

I went to the bridge between this sunflower and myself, the thin shoelace thread, and I began to think about it wrapping around the closest table leg roughly five feet to my left. To my amazement, the sunflower's stem grew even longer, and its head moved over to the wooden table. It then proceeded to wrap around the leg four times with the bulb coming to a rest and facing me.

"That's seriously cool," I muttered.

As I willed the plant to return, it unwound itself and shrank back to its normal six feet.

Next I thought about the bottom leaves growing to be three times larger than they were. And the base leaves expanded, taking a little more energy. They kept their same ratio but grew until they were bigger than my head.

For a final test, I imagined a saw blade spinning and cutting into a piece of wood. I focused that sharpness on one of the leaves as I shrank it back down to about the size of my hand. Its edges hardened and became so sharp, I pricked my right index finger.

Son of a bitch, I thought, sticking that finger in my mouth for a second. Then I took it back out and plucked the razor leaf carefully with my right hand.

With a flick of my wrist, I hurled the leaf at the same table I'd had the sunflower wrap around. It sank into the wood about half an inch with a hollow sound.

Then I could feel the leaf in the table, like that shoestring had extended across the room. When I started getting dizzy again, I stopped feeding energy into the leaf, and it started to fold over, becoming normal and soft again.

"This is… amazing," I said.

Ruad gave me a wolfish grin, realizing one of my first instincts for the plant was to weaponize a piece of it. Adrienn just beamed at me, looking down like a proud teacher.

My cell phone alarm chirped, and I realized it was time to leave, shower in Coach's gym, and get to work.

"What do I do now?" I asked, looking at the roots still very firmly wrapped around my fist. "I can't really go to work like this."

Adrienn pointed over to an empty flower pot with some soil they'd had me add before we even began training this morning. I walked over to the brown terracotta pot about as long as my foot.

"Place your fist over the soil and manipulate the plant like you did when it wrapped around the table," Adrienn said.

I took a breath and did as I was instructed, imagining the roots unfolding and moving down into the moist soil. It took a second, but eventually, the roots unraveled and made their way down into the dirt, one strand at a time until my hand was free.

I watched the sunflower's base sink until it was firmly rooted in the pot.

Then I sat on my rump and caught my breath for a moment.

"So you're telling me Dad could do that with several plants at once?" I asked Ruad and Adrienn.

They both nodded, and Ruad said, "I've watched your father go into battle against monsters and pull out seeds like a human draws a gun. Then he grew them into several different forms to attack, to protect himself or others, to slay his target. He was a master of this particular druid craft."

I nodded and sighed. One day I'd be that skilled. "Okay, I'm all sweaty, so let's hop on a bus and head to the gym so I can shower," I said.

Adrienn flew back into my necklace, and Ruad sighed as I placed her service dog vest on again, tightening the Velcro loops.

On the bus ride back into Fayetteville, my phone buzzed with a good morning text from Abi. She also asked if she could buy me lunch.

My girlfriend and actual food? Sign me up.

And with that, I smiled. The last couple days had been so wild, that I could use a piece of normalcy again. Seeing Abi would bring that.

Ruad and I were the only ones on the bus, not that they were usually crowded.

As I watched us head toward the bus depot on campus, I leaned my head on Ruad, who was sitting up in the seat next to me. Surprisingly, she didn't move. So I sighed, content. At that point, a realization hit me.

How could I have possibly lived without her before now? I thought.

"Hey, Ruad? When I touched that seed earlier, it had a small bit of Tristan's magic in it. And I almost saw a little memory inside it."

"That doesn't surprise me, Pup. Magic is a pretty all-encompassing energy. It can contain things like emotions and memories," she said.

"So… when our magic touched as I transformed, did you see any memories of my home life with Barb?"

My father's familiar did not speak for a time, and then she said, "I did. Your adopted guardians were poor substitutes for Tristan and Iris."

I scoffed and said, "That's an understatement."

The wolf continued to think and then sighed.

"Honestly, I'm not sure which is worse, family that makes you miserable or no family at all. These last 16 years have been shit for both of us. When I saw you with Barb and John, it was just one more dagger in my chest after being separated from Tristan and the rest of the clan. There were nights the feeling of abandonment was so thick I thought about throwing myself off Hawksbill Crag."

That thought made me twinge, and I threw my arms around her instinctively.

"I'm so sorry, Ruad. I wish we knew each other sooner."

To my surprise, Ruad actually smirked and said, "I know, Pup. I don't blame you for forgetting me anymore. I have to admit… over the last few days, I've felt my pain of being forgotten fade a little. It feels nice to have a family again."

That warmed my heart, and I kissed the top of Ruad's head. Adrienn chose that moment to fly out of the pendant and hug Ruad's paw, saying, "I'm so happy to be part of your family, Ruad."

She growled lightly and hissed, "So help me, fey, I will devour you whole."

I giggled as Adrienn gasped and flew back into their pendant.

After another couple minutes, Ruad spoke up and said, "One of the most potent memories I saw was what happened when your adopted caretaker tried to keep you from your mate. I won't make that mistake. But I will warn you to be careful, Aoife. The necromancer that murdered our clan is still looking for us. They'll use any weakness they can exploit to finish us off, including loved ones."

I pictured some nameless enemy attacking Abi, and a growl rose from deep in my chest.

"I won't let that happen," I muttered.

Ruad nodded and said, "I know. I won't either. I'll defend your mate like she was part of the clan. One day, she may very well be."

I raised an eyebrow, and Ruad seemed to sense my confusion.

"This may be my ignorance talking, but doesn't the clan have rules against that kind of thing?"

Ruad scoffed.

"Epona help me, no. The O'Connell clan has welcomed all pairings across centuries. Your heart can belong to anyone, so long as you're happy and treated well, Pup."

My eyes widened, and all I could say was, "Huh. Cool." But then I squinted and said, "Hang on. If I'm supposed to rebuild the clan, shouldn't you push me toward an eligible bachelor so I can start popping out babies and growing our numbers?"

Ruad locked eyes with me and said, "You misunderstand, Pup. O'Connells are bound by Earth and its magical history. The planet's very roots bind us, beyond time, beyond blood. You don't need offspring to rebuild the clan."

I sat there in awe for a moment.

"Now THAT'S inclusive. Sounds like these Pagans got a good thing going," I muttered.

"WE Pagans," Ruad corrected me.

I still wasn't sure what to think about that. I had been raised in a church my entire life, and I came to hate it all because of how Barb treated me and my forced involvement. So now that she'd kicked me out, what did I believe in? I sat in silence for a moment before leaning my head on Ruad and feeling a flood of oxytocin wash over my brain.

Knowing we were family had become like a drug to me, helping keep me stable in the recent storm of my life over the last couple days.

"What do I believe in? I guess I believe in us," I said, smiling, my head still on Ruad.

"That's so sweet," Ruad teased as I rolled my eyes.

We hopped off at the bus depot and walked about a mile to Coach's gym, where I showered and changed into my last spare clothes, a gray long sleeve shirt with a small yellow butterfly on the left side and blue jeggings.

I put my hair in a ponytail and headed to work with Ruad in tow.

We arrived early and opened the shop. There wasn't a single customer until after Sabrina arrived and brought us homemade croissants. I didn't even need to ask Ruad if she wanted one before her nose was in the container sniffing one out.

I texted Abi that I was going on break at 1:00 p.m. She agreed, and we decided to meet at the bagel shop in the same shopping plaza as Petal and Stem. If it was warm enough, we'd go eat in the park behind the hippy grocery store. That setting would work best for me to show her Ruad and maybe even my new magic.

My pulse quickened when I began to wonder how much I would tell her. I mean, Ruad would be there, so I had to tell her something to explain the giant dog following me around everywhere. Sabrina might have bought the seizure explanation, but there's no way Abi would. She'd know I wasn't in the hospital last weekend.

And sure, having Ruad speak to her would be easy enough proof. Summoning Adrienn would be even more. Transforming would be the final nail in the coffin for any disbelief Abi had left.

So if I had all the proof, what was I so scared of? I wasn't embarrassed about all of this. What was driving my fear?

And then it clicked with me. I didn't know how she'd react.

When the very first magical thing happened to me in Odessa's shop, I had a potent reaction. A repressed history of the O'Connell clan shot forth in my mind when I touched my locket and awakened as Aoife.

It was like reality was rewritten for me on the fly to understand I was a druid and magic existed. Abi wasn't going to get that. She would see, at most, a talking wolf, a six-inch-tall fey with green hair and her girlfriend warping plants. Then she'd have to try and process all of that.

Now I was beginning to wonder if it was fair to reveal all of this to her. What other choice did I have? It wasn't as though I could reveal part of my story to her without the rest. I couldn't *just* show her Ruad or *only* Adrienn. The whole story would have to be dished out. And what if she decided my freaky ass wasn't worth keeping around after that?

I was trying to tie a ribbon to a vase in the back as that last thought rocketed through my skull, and my hands began to shake. I couldn't focus well after that. Thankfully, Sabrina was at the front of the store with a customer, or she might have thought I was having a seizure.

Ruad walked over and said, "Pup, you look pale and stressed. What's bothering you?"

Shaking my head, I redoubled my efforts to finish this vase decoration before the customer showed up.

"Nothing's bothering me. I'm fine," I said, not wanting my father's familiar to go all Dr. Phil on me.

"Please, I don't need a bridge between us to sense when my friend is sick with anxiety. Adrienn, you might want to come out and help with the human emotions part. I think the pup needs you," she said.

My locket glowed green, and out flew Adrienn. They looked around to make sure Sabrina and the customer were busy.

Then Adrienn flew up to my face as a tear raced down my right cheek.

I wiped my tear and held out the opposite hand for Adrienn to land on.

"What's wrong, Aoife?"

When I failed to speak any coherent sentence, Ruad thought for a moment and said, "I'd wager the pup is afraid her mate won't accept her druidic nature and will leave. It's probably stressing her out, especially after being thrown out of her home."

"Can you please stop calling Abi my mate? It's kind of weird. We're people, not animals," I said, scowling at Ruad. "The word you're to use from now on is girlfriend."

Adrienn spoke up and said, "I once heard Odessa describe female human pairings as gals being pals."

I sighed and tried to stifle a giggle.

Then my fey guardian turned their attention back to my problem at hand.

"Aoife, it's natural for normal humans to have a strong reaction to seeing magic for the first time. They're witnessing something previously defined as impossible. So you're right to worry a tad for your gal pal's reaction."

"Okay, for the record, gal pal is an entirely different thing from a girlfriend," I said.

"My point is, there's no way to know how Abi will react until she hears Ruad speak or sees you perform magic. But from what I've picked up as you've talked about her over the last couple days, it seems like you two have a strong relationship. And I'd wager it's sturdy enough to weather this new truth. You just have to be patient and give her some grace. She's a normal human, after all."

I smiled and held the fey up to my cheek. Then I asked, "Will you please stay out to keep me company until my lunch break?"

The fey nodded and flew up to my shoulder as I let my hair down. They hid inside as I felt Adrienn leaning on my neck.

I just wish I had some way to ease her into this druid stuff, I thought.

And then an idea came to me as I walked over to the wall and found a small file cabinet. Opening it, I sorted through dozens of folders, each with a tiny pack of seeds inside. Eventually, I found the seeds I was looking for and put one in my pocket.

Then, I went back to the vase and worked steadily until my stomach began to growl shortly before 1:00 p.m.

I left Sabrina to take care of her shop while I wandered out for a long lunch break. She said it'd be fine if I was gone for an hour, especially after she learned I was meeting Abi.

As I walked into the bagel shop parking lot, I heard a familiar voice yell, "Hey! Get me a Coke!"

Ignoring the voice, I walked into the restaurant and was greeted with smells ranging from chocolate chip to onion. Ruad leaned against my hip while I looked at all the bagels.

One of the employees behind the counter was cutting a bagel, and when he saw my wolf he yelled, "badass!" Then he walked around the counter and froze dead in his tracks when he saw the service dog vest.

He looked up at me and said, "Ma'am, that's a truly beautiful creature."

Then he went back around the counter as I let out a sigh of relief. An older couple was sitting in one of the back booths, drinking coffee. The woman stared at me, continually looking from me to Ruad. And I caught her several times. In fact, I'm pretty sure it was one long continuous stare on her part. Boy, do I despise people who stare.

I can understand stealing a quick glance or two from the corner of your eye. I've been known to do it when I see someone who looks like Chris Pine. But to continually look at someone is just rude.

Taking a look around the restaurant, I noted Abi wasn't there yet. And that old woman in the purple sweater continued to stare. Her husband didn't seem to pay much attention. He was reading the newspaper in front of him.

But after another 30 seconds of staring, I finally had enough. So I faced the woman and stared right back. She didn't back down. Usually, when you catch someone staring, they look away. It's called shame, and even rude humans are supposed to possess a modicum of it.

She just kept looking, though, even after we made eye contact.

So I waltzed over to her table, much to her chagrin and said, "Excuse me, is there something I can help you with?"

The husband looked up from his newspaper confused. Then he saw Ruad and raised an eyebrow. The woman just shook her head without saying anything.

"Okay, good. Well I just noticed you were staring at me and my service animal pretty hard, and I wanted to let you know I find that behavior rude. So stop it," I said with a firm smile.

The woman did not apologize, and man, did it remind me of how much I hated people that couldn't be shamed for their bad behavior. I wasn't after an apology specifically. I just wanted her to look in any of the other 359 angles that were available to her.

At last, the woman turned away and pulled out her phone to play some kind of card game. Her husband sighed and apologized on her behalf, muttering something about how "Debbie" forgot her glasses this morning and was having trouble seeing things.

Nodding, I walked back to the front just as a tall Black woman with short curly dark hair and a white jacket came into the restaurant. My girlfriend had arrived. Abi had tawny skin and brown eyes, with her nails painted caramel.

Her wool jacket was unbuttoned, and I saw Abi was wearing a red T-shirt with the words "theatre brat" written in the center.

She wore a pair of low-rise jeans under the shirt that left a small bit of her belly exposed.

I smiled at her, and she returned the look before glancing down at Ruad. She raised an eyebrow and looked up at me for an explanation.

"We have some catching up to do," I said.

Her smile returned as she walked over and placed her lips on mine. She was quick to check and make sure Ruad wasn't alarmed by her approach before she did so. But the wolf seemed to sense from my body language or the pheromones I was putting out that the girl who walked over to kiss me wasn't a threat.

When my girlfriend pulled away, she said, "Went and got yourself a wolf, did ya, Eve? Are you going to change your name from Eve to Little Red Riding Hood?"

I twitched, and she seemed to notice.

"Not quite, but speaking of name changes, I am seriously going by Aoife now if you're cool with that."

Abi shrugged her shoulders and said, "Aoife it is. I'm gonna stick with Abigail if you don't mind."

I smirked until I caught that old woman staring at us again, and I glared at Debbie. Like before, she didn't budge. I started to growl and walk over to the table again, but Abi caught my arm.

"Hey, don't. She's not worth it," Abi said.

"That bitch needs to learn some manners," I muttered.

"Stop thinking about her, and think about this," Abi said, pulling my chin toward her and kissing me again.

I felt my anger fade immediately and kissed her back. Then we parted, and she said, "Bagels?"

"Bagels," I said, smiling again.

The cashier looked about our age and was wearing a black apron. He had short orange hair and looked a little flushed when we stopped kissing.

"Ho-how can I help you today?" he asked.

Abi stared at the menu board and said, "You go on ahead. I don't know what I want yet."

The second man behind the counter who called Ruad "badass" had started up a loud mixer for someone's coffee order at the drive-thru window. I waited for him to stop before ordering a pizza bagel.

Abi got a hummus and veggie bagel, and while we were waiting, the older couple from earlier shuffled by us. The old lady muttered, "faggots" as she walked by. I grabbed Debbie by the jaw and smashed her face into the glass bagel display, shattering it. She went down hard, screaming.

At least, that's what happened in my head.

In reality, I caught Debbie's elbow and leaned in close, growling, "If I ever hear you speak to me or my girlfriend like that again, you'll regret it."

Then I let the bigot go before her husband, who was opening the door, was any the wiser. The old woman's face went pale, and her husband had to call a couple times before she shuffled toward him again.

Hopefully that's the last time I see Debbie. She's a bitch when she's not in snack cake form, I thought.

The wolf admirer handed us our bagels to go, and we walked back outside.

"So… what's the wolf's name?" Abi asked.

"Ruad. And I'll just warn you now. She doesn't like to be touched."

Abi took my free hand with her own and said, "That's fine. As long as her owner doesn't mind being touched."

I scoffed and muttered, "Oh my goodness. You're terrible. And right here in front of *my* bagel."

Abi's own grin grew, and she asked, "Seems like it's warming up. Wanna head to the park and eat?"

"Sounds like a good idea to me," I said.

We walked over behind the hippy food store. Directly behind the shopping plaza on Hillcrest Avenue is a line of modest older houses. We walked north a little bit to the last house in the row, a brick home with faded gray shingles.

Next to this house was a little trail that'd been damaged with fallen debris in a huge ice storm back in 2011. The trail had never really been repaired since. But it was easy enough to find if you were familiar with the area.

Ruad, Abi and I walked down it and past the private property back into a patch of forest called the Brooks-Hummel Nature Park, just north of Lake Lucille.

It's one of the great things about Fayetteville, really. You've got a decent-sized town to provide for good shopping and dining options, but if you ever really just need to get away for a hot minute and duck into some trees to feel isolated, you can.

That's what the park was like, no playground equipment, just trails to hike.

We found our way to a center clearing and sat down along the side of the trail to eat. The sunlight was directly above us, and it was about 55 degrees out today.

Arkansas winters were like that. You'd get some really cold days at the start, then some warmer ones around Christmas, and the cold would likely return for a longer stay in January and February before the tornadoes started popping up.

As we ate, Abi poked my shoulder and said, "Okay, Jackie London. Let's hear it. Where'd Ruad come from, and why do you have a service dog now?"

I sighed and finished the last bite of my pepperoni bagel. Half a pepperoni had fallen to the ground, so I tossed it in the air over to Ruad. She let it fall about two inches to her left, a low growl escaping her chest.

"Oh, so I can eat the berries and nuts you bring me, but you're too good for a pepperoni?"

She just stared at me with a scowl, and I suddenly realized it was how I tossed it. She did not want to catch things in mid-air like some kind of pet, and I should have known that. I should have just handed it to her, unnerving as it is sticking one's hand near a mouth of 42 razor-sharp teeth. But those teeth belonged to my father's familiar, and I knew she would never harm me.

"Your wolf sure is picky about pizza toppings. Guess you should have gone with pupperoni," she said, laughing.

I did my best not to roll my eyes. Abi had some of the worst jokes on the planet. Some were so bad, they would melt the ears off of an elephant. And no matter how many times I chose to avoid laughing at her dumb punchlines, she found amusement enough to laugh at herself.

"But seriously. Storytime or what?" she asked, taking another bite of her veggie bagel. Abi was one of the slowest eaters in the world. Meanwhile, I was scarfing food a million miles per hour before I ever met her.

Looking over at Abi, I reached across and put a hand on her thigh.

"Gay," she said, still laughing. That finally got a chuckle out of me.

"The first thing I need to tell you is Barb kicked me out on the night you left," I said.

Anger flashed across Abi's face.

"That bitch did what?"

"After she caught us and ordered you out, she called you some unflattering Old Testament names, and I fought with her. So she kicked me out."

"That's an evil thing to do. It's gotta be illegal. Why didn't you call me? Where have you been staying?"

"First, it's not illegal. I'm 18. She can and did kick my ass to the curb. Second, I… didn't want to bother you and your mother by giving y'all one more mouth to feed," I said, looking down at a nearby tree trunk.

Abi crossed her arms and just stared angrily at me. She was really more upset with Barb, but I understood how she felt that I'd kept the truth from her.

"Oh my god. Did you seriously choose to live on the street because you thought crashing for a couple nights at my place would leave Mom and I destitute? Aoife, you're ridiculous! We would have taken you in if you'd just called me, no hesitation. We are not that bad off. You've crashed at my place plenty of times, quite a few nights I recall vividly," she said.

I sighed again and nodded.

"In my defense… there was also a lot going on that night. And I'm not on the street. I've had a roof over my head the past two nights."

I just won't mention that the first roof was that of an abandoned cabin, I thought.

Abi put a hand over her face and sighed.

"I'm gonna kill your Mom."

"Yeah, about that. she's… not really my mother," I said, still looking over at that tree trunk.

My girlfriend slowly lowered her hand and squinted. "Come again?"

Taking a deep breath, I said, "Okay, the next few minutes of this story are going to get really weird. But I want you to promise not to interrupt and to know that I will provide proof when everything is said and done."

Abi raised an eyebrow and asked, "Are you sure you don't need to be taken to the doctor or something? Because that sounds a little weird."

"I'm fine. But you need to promise me you'll let me tell this story without interruption. Afterward, I'll answer any questions you have."

She looked at me with a little concern but finally said, "I promise," and finished her bagel.

"Okay… Barb and John are not my real parents. They adopted me at the age of two and never told me. My real parents are named Tristan and Iris."

"That's insane! How did you find out? Did you meet them?"

I rolled my eyes.

Good promise keeping, I thought.

"No, they're dead. And you promised not to interrupt, remember?"

"Sorry! That's just ridiculous and hard to... Okay, I'm gonna be quiet now."

Scratching my hair, I was careful not to reveal Adrienn. "Um… where was I? Right. My parents are dead. It turns out they were part of a pack," I said.

Abi raised an eyebrow.

"A… group of people, nature worshippers who, um…" I trailed off. Scratching my head, I thought of the best way to try and explain this.

"This is going badly. Maybe I should start in chronological order. So as I wandered downtown after Barb threw me out, I stumbled upon a fortune teller shop belonging to a witch named Odessa. She gave me this locket," I said, pulling out the piece of jewelry and showing it to Abi. I ran my fingers over the Celtic knotwork.

"My name was on the back, Aoife Fay O'Connell. I'd worn it since I was a baby, and when Barb and John adopted me, she tossed it, renamed me, and never spoke a word of any of this."

Abi's eyes widened quite a bit at that.

"Here's where things get really weird. Remember your promise. So the highlights are, magic is real, and a fey lives inside this locket. They look like a little man about six inches tall with shaggy green hair and wings. Their name is Adrienn."

Abi's eyes found a way to widen even more at that.

"Hang on. There's more. Adrienn is my fey protector given to me by my parents before they were slaughtered by a necromancer with the rest of my pack."

Now my girlfriend was crossing her arms and looked like she was debating calling 911 to have some men in white scrubs put me in a rubber room. But she kept her promise.

"Adrienn taught me about how I'm a druid, a user of nature magic, and the last of my pack. Then together, we went and rescued my father's wolf, Ruad, from a boy with dark wings and several skeletons. And the last couple days they've been teaching me how to use nature magic after I sort of turned into a partial wolf once. So… yeah. I've been a little busy to tell you about everything, but those are the bullet points."

While Abi had wanted to interject at least four or five times, I now watched as she was silent and unsure of what to ask first.

"When you're ready to see proof or ask a question, let me know," I said, my throat tightening up. Honestly, I was kind of surprised to get all of those words out.

My pulse quickened, and I felt butterflies return to my stomach for about the 50th time today. I'd just placed all my cards on the table. Now I had to hope Abi didn't get spooked and dump my ass thinking I was a crazy person.

I've already lost my home. Please don't take the love of my life, too, I thought, trying not to cry, as if that would be the feather that broke the crazy camel's back.

I have proof, I thought, silently, another thing that should work in theory. But I'd already gone over how well theories work on fear.

Abi finally raised a finger and said, "Okay, that all sounded bonkers. But, you promised me proof. So before I call the guys with butterfly nets to come capture you, I'm going to give you a shot at proving this craziness. You want to try to turn into a werewolf or something?"

A bit of nervous giggling escaped my lips.

"I'm not a werewolf. I'm just a druid."

"Isn't that a chess piece?" she asked.

Some more nervous laughter escaped, and I took a deep breath.

"Proof... right, sure. I promised that. I can deliver that. Ruad," I asked nervously, "Would you please introduce yourself?"

Abi raised an eyebrow, but before she could open her mouth, Ruad thankfully spoke up, "Hello, Abigail. My name is Ruad. I was her father's familiar. I assure you, my druid companion is telling the truth."

My girlfriend's jaw dropped to the ground at twice the speed of my pepperoni. She just stared at Ruad without saying anything.

Before her brain could put together a logical conclusion like puppetry or ventriloquism, I said, "Adrienn, would you mind introducing yourself, please?"

Abi looked up at me in time to see the fey climb out of my hair above my shoulder and fly over to her. She held up her hands flat, unsure of what else to do.

Adrienn landed and bowed, "Hello, Abigail. It's a pleasure to meet you. Aoife has said some lovely things about you. My name is Adrienn, fey guardian, and most recently, friend to Lady Aoife."

I gave the fey a flat expression.

"Oh... sorry. Just Aoife," they said, laughing a little.

Taking a breath, Abi nodded slowly.

"It's... nice to meet you both," she said, tensing up, as if Adrienn would suddenly snarl and bite a finger off.

"How are you doing over there, Abi?"

"Like the park is spinning, and I want off before I pass out," she said, quietly.

Adrienn flew back up into the air again.

"Apologies if I startled you. Shall I return to the locket until the park stops spinning?"

Abi didn't know how to respond to that and just sat there, so Adrienn did it anyway, vanishing with a little green flash in my locket.

I moved slowly in front of Abi, my worst fears coming true as I could see a load of confusion and disbelief crushing her. Now she wasn't just wanting to have me committed, but possibly herself as well.

Getting in front of where her vision had migrated a few inches to the right, I said, "Hey, you're not crazy. I'm just going through some changes. But it's going to be okay. I'm still your..." and I sighed before I said it because it was embarrassing. "Your... sweet cinnamon."

The "theatre brat," as her shirt read, had chosen that term of endearment a couple weeks after we started dating. It came from a line she liked in *The Canterbury Tales*, "My fair bird, my sweet cinnamon? Awake, sweetheart mine, and speak to me!"

Abi's eyes met mine, and she muttered, "Your fair bird is having some trouble. This is... absolutely nuts. The new name I could handle. I've got friends that change their name each birthday, trying out different ones. The wolf? Fine. It's just a big puppy dog. But it talks? And then there's Tinkerbell's punk rock cousin with green hair? I just..." Her voice trailed off.

I tried to keep from crying as I reached into my pocket for one last play.

Holding the seed gently in my left hand, I held it out in front of Abi. Her eyes slowly moved over to it.

And I began to send energy into the seed as my hand glowed with a light green aura. I guided the seed as it slowly grew, wrapping around my index and middle fingers. Up and up a stem grew a little quicker than the sunflower this morning.

Abi was transfixed on my little magic show now. Slowly, the tiny leaves unfolded. Then the bulb formed, and out grew purple and yellow petals. I put a little more energy into it, and the pansy grew about twice as big up toward Abi.

She gasped and put a hand over her mouth.

"I'm still me, Abi."

Reaching forward, she picked the flower from my hand, severing the stem and causing a little pop in my head.

Ow. I should have seen that coming, what with it being her favorite flower and all, I thought.

95

She smelled the flower, and a tear formed in her right eye.

Then Abi shook her head and took a deep breath as I put my hand over the ground and moved the roots down into the soil.

"Okay then," I muttered. "What now?"

She glanced over at me and sighed. Then we both stood up slowly. I could hear the joints in my knees popping.

Off in the distance, I could have sworn I heard a raven cry. I looked around but couldn't spot it. Ruad was looking around too.

"Have you seen too much? Did I break you?" I asked, flinching.

Abi smiled, which I took to be a good sign.

"I think I'll be okay. There's just one last thing I might as well see while my brain is overloading."

"Name it."

"Did you say you turned into a wolf? What was that like?"

Scratching my head, I chuckled.

"Yeah, it was just the one time. It was… partial, powerful, and kind of weird," I said.

"Can I see?"

I shrugged and said, "I don't even know if I can do it again. What do you think, Ruad? Is it possible?"

The wolf sighed and said, "I suppose I could loan you a small bit of my magic to keep you from losing your mate."

She walked over and bit my hand. I felt her begin to push some of her magic into my body, and like that night, my senses enhanced. Leaves and wind swirled around me as she let go. Things happened like the first night we fought together.

Seconds later, my transformation was complete. It was at that point I realized I'd shredded my shoes again and put a hole in the back of my pants. Thankfully, my shirt didn't shred because it was stretchy.

"Son of a bitch," I muttered.

Abi just stood there before walking over and grabbing a strand of my thickened red hair, now the exact same shade as Ruad's fur. Then she grabbed my left ear, and I flinched.

"Ow! Be gentle with those. They're not a piece of cosplay," I hissed.

She hopped back and put her palms up.

"I'm sorry! This is just so… wild. So you're going to fight monsters and stuff like this? I mean…you've got claws," she said, gently grabbing my right hand and looking over it. "And a tail," she said, turning me around and grabbing it lighter than she did my ear.

"Yeah, theoretically, I'll rebuild the pack and… I dunno, raid the Tombs of Atuan or something."

Abi took that all in for a moment and then smirked.

"Honestly, Aoife. I thought we left all that furry stuff behind in tenth grade."

I blushed.

"That's not what this is! This is a serious druidic legacy I've got to protect here!"

"Of course," she said. "Uwu and all that."

I rolled my eyes as Ruad's energy faded, and I changed back.

When Abi finally stopped giggling, she said, "Come on back to my car. I've got a spare pair of sneakers you can borrow in the trunk."

As we walked to her little economy car, I chucked my torn shoes into a nearby trash can, placing my feet on cold asphalt.

She handed me a pair of black converse, and I slipped them on, thanking the gods that we had the same shoe size. Abi had drawn little dragons on the white parts of the shoe. Though that was a while ago, so the marker was a little faded. Part of the dragon's wing on the left shoe had vanished.

I smiled, and she took my hands.

"Thank you," I said. Then my face turned serious. "Are we going to be okay?"

She flashed me a smirk and said, "Are you asking if I'm going to dump my girlfriend because she has magic powers now?"

I rolled my eyes.

"I think we'll be fine. I'm just going to need a day or two to wrap my head around all this. But I'm not upset or anything," she said, kissing me.

I returned the kiss, feeling the butterflies in my stomach finally fluttering off. I wasn't going to lose her after all.

"You get back to work, and I'll head home to Mom to help with some chores. You sure you don't need a place to crash?"

"Nah, I'm good. I've got my own place now," I said.

"Wow. One of these days you'll have to show me how you quickly mastered apartment hunting," she said. "I can't believe you found a place in two days."

I gave her a dry chuckle.

"Well technically Adrienn found it."

"Oh! Is it like… apartment magic?"

I gave her a flat look.

"Right… when I get this headache gone, you're going to have to tell me more about the little guy. He was pretty cool looking."

"Uh… they. They're pretty cool looking," I said, looking down at my locket.

"Oh, right! Sorry about that."

She gave me a quick peck on the cheek and then hopped in her car.

"Text me when you get off work?" she asked.

I nodded.

"Oh yeah, here," she said, handing me a gray sweat jacket from her back seat." I can see your red panties through that hole above your butt."

I blushed and took the jacket, tying it around my waist.

I'm going to get some more clothes tonight after work, I vowed in my head.

I waved after Abi drove off and walked back over to Petal and Stem.

"That seemed to go well," Ruad said.

"You're telling me," I said.

"One question."

"Shoot."

"What's a furry?" she asked.

I just sighed and held the door open for her before saying, "I don't want to talk about it right now."

* * *

The rest of the work day passed by well enough. After work, I walked across the street to a thrift store and bought some extra clothes to get me through the week.

The bus ride back to Lake Sequoyah was quiet as I thought back on the events of the afternoon, namely, how close I'd come to losing Abi.

It was definitely the flower thing that kept her around, I thought. We walked back through the woods to the greenhouse, and I was greeted with a scent I placed from a couple nights ago. Ruad sensed it, too.

Tensing up, we rounded the corner of the path and found a raven perched on the doorknob attached to our greenhouse. It held a small folded piece of paper in its beak. When we spotted it, the bird dropped the note and flew up into the night sky.

Running over to the piece of paper, I picked it up and read it. The message wasn't long, but it painted the situation perfectly.

"What is it, Aoife?"

I clutched my right fist crumpling the paper.

She seemed to sense the anger brewing in my chest and reaching a fever pitch.

"Aoife?"

"It's bird boy. He's found me and taken Abi prisoner."

Ruad said nothing for a moment and then asked, "What do you want to do?"

As I felt my magic building, I let loose a heavy growl, "Kill him."

Chapter Eight

I started to storm back toward the bus route, but Ruad ran in front of me.

"We need a plan," she said.

"I have a plan. I choke the bird boy until he coughs up my girlfriend," I said, turning to walk around Ruad.

The vermillion wolf again blocked my path and said, "Aoife, I know you're upset. We don't need to be magically connected to feel it. But I've also seen what happens when someone rushes into a trap without a plan. Hell, I've seen what happens when people rush into a trap with a plan. You're just going to get captured and turned over to the necromancer."

My blood pressure was rising, and I was beginning to lose the words Ruad spoke. I cared about her warning less and less. All that mattered was ripping that bird to pieces with my claws. I wanted blood, and I would have blood.

"Aoife," Ruad shouted, "Aoife! Focus on my voice!"

With my chest tightening, I again tried to go around her, ignoring the wolf's words. Abi was in danger. I must save her. Those eight words were the only ones I could hear.

My father's familiar then resorted to one of her favorite tactics. Ruad slammed me into a thick oak tree, and the whole trunk rattled as she forced her paw dead center on my throat.

"Pup's all grown up and ready to rush into battle, is she?"

"Move," I growled, and she pressed her paws harder on my throat.

"You need to listen to me, Aoife. I've been impressed at how quickly you've taken to training with your magic, but you're not ready for something like this."

"I have to rescue Abi! We don't have time for..."

Ruad's sudden bark was so loud my ears felt like they'd been beaten with an aluminum baseball bat. She let me sink to my knees as I held my ears and whimpered.

"Glad I got your attention. That, my anxious pup, is the Alpha's Command," Ruad said.

I was still clenching my ears, though I'd stopped whimpering now… mostly. She was right. That rage I'd been building toward Abi's abductor had all but vanished. It was as if her bark had shattered the feeling's foundation, and it all came crashing down.

Looking down at the crumpled note on the ground, I suddenly felt the urge to pick it up and stick it in my pocket.

Perfect time for my druidic anti-litter instincts to kick in, I thought.

Ruad stuck her snout under my chin and lifted my gaze. Then she moved and looked directly into my eyes. Her amber irises were inches from my own. When they finally stopped aching, my ears came to focus on whatever Ruad was about to say next.

"Pup, listen to me. This is a dangerous situation, and not just for Abi, but for us as well. Ash clearly intends to use her as bait for a trap. If you rush in there, you'll just wind up captured. So let's come up with a plan," Ruad said.

"I love her, Ruad. She was already on the fence about all this magic stuff this afternoon. What she needed was time to adjust, and now? If I lose her, I don't know what I'll do," I said.

Ruad inched a little closer and said, "Aoife, I understand how important she is to you. She's your mate, and we're going to get her back."

She's really just gonna keep using that word, isn't she? I thought

But I smiled and hugged Ruad. She wiggled uncomfortably, but then settled into my arms.

"Easy does it, Pup."

"Ruad… I'm sorry. When I get going, I feel this rage inside of me. It's fierce. It demands blood and violence, and I'm powerless to stop the urge. The feeling scares me," I said, burying my face in her fur, inhaling her scent to calm down.

The vermillion wolf made no move to free herself from my grasp. Instead, she just thought for a moment. At last, she said, "Like Adrienn said, Aoife. You're coming into a lot of power in a short span of time. You know, Tristan had problems just like this with his temper."

My eyes widened. "Really?"

"Sure. Your father was a lot like you, especially when he was younger. Between his impatience and your short temper, you're

101

definitely his child. Of course, he knew how to make those feelings work for him, to build determination, and do what was best for the pack," Ruad said.

I said nothing. Just listened.

"Tristan channeled his anger into passion to protect his loved ones. But he also knew not to be reckless, because if he died, he'd be leaving behind his wife, and his clan. And I'd die alongside him," Ruad said, as her voice quieted.

I clung to Ruad, trying to soak up every word about my father.

"But hear me, Pup. Tristan, no matter how strong, couldn't do anything alone. If we lived in a perfect world, you would have bonded to another pup when you were about 10. And you'd have been learning nature magic years before that. But you were robbed of those opportunities by the man Ash works for."

My grip on Ruad tightened at the mention of my clan's killer.

"It's okay to be scared. It's okay to be angry. Just remember you're not alone anymore. *We're* not alone. I'm here. And Adrienn is always with you as well," Ruad said with her best attempt at a soothing voice. But a wolf's voice is a wolf's voice. My familiar isn't going to win any sweet talking contests.

Still, I greatly appreciated her words. She was infinitely more calm than I was in this scenario. I also felt like there was a determination in Ruad to fulfill her word. We'd get Abi back.

"How long did it take Tristan to tame his inner wolf?" I asked.

Ruad pulled free of my hug and once again stood inches from my own eyes.

"You don't tame your inner wolf, Pup. It's not a dog to put on a leash and go for a walk. You make your peace with it just like you do any other part of yourself."

I sighed.

Of course there would be a complicated answer like that. How silly of me to not know I had to make peace with my inner wolf, I thought.

Ruad seemed to sense my inner thoughts and scoffed.

"So sassy. Geez you got a big dose of Iris, you know that? Tristan was the quieter of your parents. But Iris... oof. She always had something to say, whether she kept it in her head or on her tongue," Ruad said.

I smiled. I would never get tired of Ruad telling me more about my parents.

"How long do we have until we meet with Ash?" Ruad asked.

"He said to meet him on that same Mount Sequoyah trail at 10:00 p.m.," I said.

The wolf nodded.

"Okay, that should give us enough time to come up with something," Ruad said. "I just wish we didn't have to waste so much time riding that bus back into town."

My pendent glowed green, and out shot Adrienn in all their little light.

"I actually might be able to help with that," the fey said.

The wolf and I exchanged glances.

* * *

Adrienn led us to another little island behind the one that contained Tristan's greenhouse.

In a clearing between three or four evergreen trees was a small fairy ring of little white mushrooms, maybe nine in total. The circle might have been 10 feet wide.

As we approached, I felt a trace of energy and familiarity to this place. Ruad walked over and sniffed at one of the mushrooms.

"I don't think this works anymore, Adrienn," Ruad said.

"Can someone please explain what I'm looking at? I mean… mushrooms, sure. But what do they do?" I asked.

Adrienn and Ruad looked at one another.

"I'll take this one," the fey said. "This is a fairy ring. It's a basic druid spell that allows for instant movement between moderate distances."

"How does it work?"

"This spell is a Tristan special," Adrienn said. "Our alpha planted this circle of mushrooms and grew them slowly, allowing them to soak up his magic like a ring of organic sponges. When they had all the energy they could hold, Tristan plucked one up and took it to a second spot to start a new fairy ring. Same routine there. For weeks he allowed the roots to grow deep and tight with his energy until they became like an anchor deep in the Earth. Far under Fayetteville the roots of each fairy circle connected, and he figured out that to travel quickly between fairy circles became as simple as opening a doorway and stepping through to the other side."

I looked down at the little white toadstools again and nodded. Two locations connected by druidic energy that would allow for teleportation as long as the connection was regularly fed by my father infusing his energy.

Wow, I'm surprised my brain put all that together so quickly, I thought.

"Okay, so where does this circle connect to?" I asked.

Adrienn smiled and zipped up to my face.

"That's the great part! Tristan made this spell when he was younger, so over the next several years, he was able to make more circles all through the Ozark Mountains. He must have made about a dozen of them," Adrienn said.

I nodded my head.

"That's amazing!"

"But what Adrienn seems to keep forgetting is these circles all needed Tristan's energy to maintain their connections. Without that weekly feeding, they died a long time ago," Ruad said. "So we're wasting time here."

The fey shook their head and held their index finger up.

"Not quite, Balto. The connection isn't designed to die, but go dormant. That's the benefit of your father growing them in real time. If he'd accelerated the growth, then it'd die much faster without his magical input. Since he took the time, it's a much more stable connection. As long as the fairy rings elsewhere are intact, we just have to jumpstart the circle," Adrienn said.

"You may not remember since we haven't really seen each other in almost two decades, but do you recall what I said would happen if you called me that name again?" Ruad growled.

The fey grew a few shades paler and zipped up into my hair behind my left ear.

"You can't possibly expect me to remember every threat you've made over the course of our time together. There are so many!" Adrienn shouted.

I sighed.

"How do we reactivate the rings, Adienn?" I asked.

My patience shattered, and I snapped at them.

"We don't have time for this bullshit. How do we activate the ring, Adrienn?" I snarled. Ruad and Adrienn just looked at me in silence.

After a beat, Adrienn flew down to the middle of the circle and placed their palms on the ground, closing their eyes.

For a moment, nobody said anything. Then Adrienn spoke up and opened their eyes again.

"I think I can relink the circles, but I'm going to need a drop of your blood, and for you to be inside the circle," Adrienn said.

I took a step back toward Ruad, clutching my hand and thinking back to the incident at work with the inch plant.

"I didn't grow these mushrooms, Adrienn."

"Your father did," they said, flying over toward me and landing in my right hand as I held it out. "And because you're his offspring, the circle will respond to you with favor. I promise."

"Your father designed this spell. His magic powered it. Tristan's blood and magic flow through your veins, and that's why you can reactivate this spell. I promise, the spell will respond to you as the daughter of Tristan," they said.

"Is there any way you can do it?" I asked.

Adrienn sighed and turned around toward the fairy ring.

"I don't have a lot of energy inside of me, especially not in this form or world. But you have plenty, so I can guide your energy to relink the rings and get us to Abi a lot faster. I promise, I'll be with you every step of the way. I won't let what took place at the shop happen again," the fey said, turning back to me.

I looked into their little green eyes and sighed. Nodding, I moved us both into the fairy ring. They flew down into the center and once again placed their palms onto the earth.

"When I say go, place a drop of blood on one of the mushrooms, Aoife," they said.

Taking a deep breath, I watched them close their eyes. My nerves began to fire as I struggled to shove past memories aside.

I eventually exhaled and felt a sense of calm enter me.

It'll be okay, I thought. *Adrienn and Ruad are both here. They won't let anything bad happen to me.*

"Okay," Adrienn said. "I need you to place your blood on a mushroom, and just before you do, invite me into your mind forest. A fey can't enter without an invitation."

Reaching up to my teeth, I bit into my thumb, grunting a little as a drop of blood pooled to the surface. Then I held the red tip of my wounded finger over a mushroom by my right foot and said, "Adrienn, I invite you into my mind forest. Be welcomed."

With that, I saw a drop of blood fall down onto the mushroom. It splattered close to the edge, and I fell to my knees. As I knelt, I saw Lake Sequoyah Park and Ruad around me, normal. But the world felt like it inverted horizontally as my knee touched the dirt. And when I slowly stood, I became aware of my changed surroundings. Ruad and the park were gone. Now I stood surrounded by mist and trees.

The air was damp, and I was alone in a space I once again knew to be my mind forest. I took shallow breaths, looking around and feeling clammy. I kept waiting for something to happen, some huge mental struggle.

Inside my mind forest, the ground shook. All around me, the sound of splitting earth rattled through the trees, and giant white mushrooms burst from the ground. They were identical to the ones I bled on back in Lake Sequoyah Park, except here they were three times my size.

Looking down, three white roots snaked out of the ground and overtook my right foot, which was now bare. Somehow in coming to my mind forest, I'd lost my shoes.

Fuck, I'm tired of losing shoes, I thought.

I shrieked as the roots began to wrap around my foot.

"Adrienn! Where are you?"

The roots stopped at my ankle, and I caught my breath. And instead of fear, another emotion traveled up my leg and into my core, longing.

My heart rate slowed, and I looked at the nine mushrooms that had sprouted around me.

"You're not trying to fight for control. You just want to know me," I muttered. "And that's fair, because I'm the one that came knocking and woke you from your slumber after all these years."

The roots on my right foot tightened just a tad, like a little hug. It didn't hurt, just felt a little snug.

These fungi had been planted, raised, and regularly nourished by my father. And they hadn't seen him in years. Now they wanted to know who had woken them up and why.

People are quick to assign thoughts and feelings to animals, while at the same time ripping up the grass or cutting down a forest of trees. In this meeting of soul and earth, I found a deep intimacy that taught me plants are every bit as alive as their bleeding counterparts. Their roots store a consciousness that stretches across the ages. They speak a language few humans listen to, but I hear now and understand. I am a druid as my parents were druids. My father grew these mushrooms, and now they speak to me.

"My name is Aoife Fay O'Connell. I am the daughter of Tristan O'Connell. And I call you to reawaken, to once more forge your connections across these mountains and forests. Will you help me, please?" I asked.

For a moment, there was no response, and then each of the mushrooms began to sway back and forth, as if dancing.

"You're happy to see me again?" I asked, feeling more connection through my leg and the roots. "My father took me through the fairy rings before, didn't he?"

The dancing mushrooms wiggled and shook again. And I smiled.

I guess it's probably safer than hooking me in a car seat and driving up Interstate 49. No risk of a crash when you travel via magic fungi, I thought.

"Okay, then. How do I reconnect all the rings?" I asked.

"I can help with that," Adrienn said, flying down between the trees of my mind forest and landing in the circle of giant mushrooms.

"I need you to come over here to repair the connection," Adrienn said.

I pointed down at my foot.

"Try moving and see what happens," Adrienn said.

"I don't want to hurt the mushrooms," I said.

"Just trust me," they said.

I did just that and slowly started walking to the center of the circle. As soon as I expected the roots to snag, they provided some more slack and moved easily with me. So I took another few steps, and they just continued to grow out of the ground following me.

When I reached Adrienn, they motioned for me to kneel, and I did. They had me place my hands on the root foot, and the stretching required for that made me feel like I was back in P.E. class again.

I hope muscle strain doesn't carry over to this inner realm, I thought.

With both of my hands on the root foot, Adrienn placed a hand on the top of the roots and the other on the ground.

They took a deep breath and closed their eyes. Then, they asked me to do the same.

"You're going to feel a little light headed as I pull the energy out of you to reconnect these rings, okay? Maybe for starters, we just reconnect this one to the one on Mount Sequoyah?"

I nodded.

"Okay. Here we go."

And I did begin to feel a little dizzy as Adrienn pulled out my magic and guided it down into the roots.

I heard a small pop in my ears, and when I opened my eyes, I found my hands, the roots and the mushrooms all glowing green.

And before my eyes, little golden orbs of light began to form. The one on my left was glowing brighter than the others.

These lights must be this fairy ring, I thought.

There must have been a dozen orbs representing different rings across the Ozarks from our area, all the way over toward Eureka Springs and even one or two down in the River Valley around what I guessed were Mountainburg and Cedarville.

Looking at the different lights, I realized my father traversed a wide territory, keeping a balance between people and nature. And since he'd been killed, along with the rest of the pack, these different places had likely fallen into magical dormancy.

I frowned thinking about all my pack's work being undone like this, but as I clenched my fists I realized something.

I survived, I thought. *And now Ruad, Adrienn and I will rebuild it all, across every inch of territory.*

After Adrienn drew more magic from within of me, the orb closest to us began to light up. It was west of our current fairy ring, and I assumed that meant it was the one on top of Mount Sequoyah.

"Okay. It's live again," Adrienn said.

I sighed in relief and looked at the mushrooms around us.

"I'll take care of you as my father did, by feeding you my magical energy every week," I said.

They danced and waved even more. Once more, I closed my eyes and kneeled.

"Aoife?" Ruad called.

"I'm alright," I said. I opened my eyes and stood, in reality again.

Adrienn emerged from their pendant and hovered above the fairy ring.

"We good to go?" I asked.

They nodded.

"Then let's go get Abi back," I said, looking down at my feet, half expecting to find roots tangled around them. I only found the shoes Abi gave me, with the faded dragon sketch looking up at me.

Ruad walked into the fairy ring, sniffing at another mushroom.

"It really does feel more alive. Whatever you two did in there, it worked," she said.

"Looks like I'm growing up. You'll probably have to stop calling me 'pup' now. It's not really accurate anymore, right?"

Ruad flashed me a grin. "Down, Pup. Save that energy for getting your mate back."

"Did you call my father 'Pup'?" I asked, putting my hands on my hips.

The vermillion wolf locked eyes with me and said, "I wasn't there to see Tristan's birth. I was there when you came into the world, Pup. Four people watched you come into existence, screaming loud and sporting a little blood. I was one of them, along with Tristan and the midwife. And, of course, your mother."

I realized I hadn't been breathing, so I let out my breath and inhaled again.

"Wait, did you say midwife?" I asked, raising an eyebrow.

The vermillion wolf nodded and said, "You were born like all the other children in the pack, in a purified spring under the moon and stars. I watched you take your first breath. And that is why you will always be 'Pup' to me."

Dammit, I wanted to sass her, but she's so rarely this open with me that I didn't want to ruin the moment.

So I bit my tongue, and we stood there in the feeling while I took in her words. And I decided being "Pup" wasn't all that bad. It was a privilege.

Once the moment was over, I turned to Adrienn and asked what was next.

Adrienn looked up at the two of us and said, "To use the fairy ring, you'll move to the center, place your hand onto the dirt like this, and picture the Mount Sequoyah ring in your mind. You'll almost feel a mental trigger you have to pull in order to kick the process off. Then you'll appear in the other ring."

I nodded, and the fey flew back into their spot within my pendant.

Doing as they instructed, I kneeled and placed a palm on the earth. But my connection didn't feel automatic or solid. So I used two hands and gathered my focus, feeling the ring take some of my magic.

Not sure how much more of that I have to give away, but I did my best to ignore it for Abi's sake.

I felt Ruad lightly place her jaws around my right arm, as she had with Tristan so many times, I was sure.

Picturing the other fairy ring in my mind, I saw the image of a slightly smaller ring behind a couple boulders and a mulberry bush. And Adrienn was right, I did feel a sort of mental trigger of energy appear. I pulled it, and we disappeared in a poof of gray dust.

Chapter Nine

Being displaced and reappearing suddenly felt like one of those dreams where I was falling. But then I felt solid ground underneath me again.

Ruad let go of my arm and looked around at the bush and boulders. "Not bad, Pup."

I smiled. Even with Pup tacked on the end, a compliment was a compliment.

"What time is it?" Ruad asked.

I pulled out my phone and saw it was around 9:30 p.m.

"Looks like we have half an hour to make our plan, Balto," I said.

"I know Adrienn thinks they're too quick for me to snap my jaws around, but if you call me that again, you're definitely slow enough to lose a limb," Ruad growled.

Looking around and ignoring the threat simultaneously, I realized we were just a minute or two from the hiking trail where I freed Ruad the first time.

"Okay, we're close. Do you have a plan?" I asked my father's familiar.

She said nothing for a moment and then looked up at the night sky.

"I think a bait and switch should work fine. Ash has been chasing me for the better part of a year. You approach him and the minions that are likely to be around. I'll wait nearby. When I see an opportunity, I'll move forward and seize him by the throat, ending this in one swift move," Ruad said. "I'm going to kill him and end this. If you can't handle seeing that, shut your eyes the moment you see me."

Looking down at the grass beneath me, I sighed. I had watched a man die in the ring before during a Muay Thai tournament. It was an unsettling sight knowing I had been fighting in the same ring just minutes before. Would I be able to watch Ruad tear this raven boy's throat open? It was what I intended to do when my inner wolf thirsted for blood right

111

after I read the letter. Was this the right thing to do, and could I deal with it?

No, I have to be able to handle this, especially if I intend to do the same to the necromancer who took my family, I thought, grimacing.

Ruad and I took a few steps toward the path where I'd initially encountered her. And then she was gone from my side. I looked around but didn't hear her anywhere, nor could I see where she went.

Damn. No wonder she was able to stay one step ahead of capture all these years, I thought.

I arrived in the clearing and stopped about 20 feet short of the enemies before me. Ash stood with his stupid spiky black hair and large wings resting behind him. He wore a black long sleeve shirt with jeans and brown boots.

To his left and right were eight skeletons, four on each side. They were a little more decomposed than the last undead I'd seen with him, but the stench was just as awful. Decaying flesh hung from their bones in strips like the world's most disgusting party streamers. Ants were actively crawling on at least two, and I shivered whenever I saw red orbs filling their otherwise dark eye sockets.

Then I looked beyond Ash and saw Abi quite literally chained to an oak tree about four or five inches off the ground. Her arms and legs hung limp. She faced the ground and did not stir.

"You arrived early, Aoife," Ash said. "I like that. It means I can get out of this damned cold even sooner."

I stood before Ash and felt a growl stir deep within me.

Ash smiled and clapped his hands together.

"Alright, then. Let's get this done and over with," he said, holding up a pair of handcuffs. "You just slide these on, call out your wolf, and I'll hand you over to the boss. Easy peasy."

I shook my head.

"Here's how this goes. You have one person to trade, while I'm surrendering two, counting myself," I said.

"Okay..." he said.

"So I'll surrender myself, you'll let Abi go, and then I'll call out Ruad for surrender," I said.

Where are you, Ruad? I thought, trying to avoid looking around.

I noticed each skeleton was holding a machete, except for one which was holding a really big stick.

Poor guy must feel so left out, I thought.

My humor faded when I looked at Abi again.

"For your sake, I hope you didn't hurt her," I said, my gaze drilling into Ash's own brown eyes.

And for a second, I watched Ash's smile fade. He took a moment to look back at his chained prisoner, and I even caught sight of a quick frown on his face. Ash crossed his arms before looking back at me, sans cockiness, and I started to wonder about his motivations. His body language almost seemed to imply he wasn't enjoying this, and that left me confused.

"She's fine," was all he said.

I didn't trust him, but there was something in his demeanor that had shifted a little bit. It got me wondering if there was some way to… I dunno… talk him down? At the very least, I had to keep him talking until Ruad made her move.

The undead minions made no move, and a cold wind blew through the trees around us. I shivered a little but didn't budge an inch to rub my arms.

"You don't seem to be happy about this situation anymore, Ash. What happened? Realize that kidnapping a girl is a felony? Wondering what they'll do to your wings in prison?"

He did not smile.

"I don't exactly revel in snatching a girl off the streets. I'm just fulfilling an obligation here. It's nothing personal," he said, crossing his arms.

His hair blew up with the wind, as did mine.

I growled again.

"Abducting my girlfriend feels pretty goddamn personal to me, you giant pigeon."

"They're raven wings, actually," he said.

I raised an eyebrow.

"You don't actually think I care, do you?" I asked.

He shrugged.

"Okay, let's get this over with," he said, tossing the handcuffs at my feet. They landed in the dirt before me with a single clinking sound.

They looked a little heavier than something a police officer would carry with them.

"I accept your deal, Aoife. You slap those on, and I'll release your girlfriend. Once she's free, you call out the wolf," Ash said.

I picked up the handcuffs slowly, noting Ruad still hadn't made her move.

I guess this is where that trust thing comes into play, I thought. My heart was thumping almost out of my chest, faster and faster with every second that passed.

So, I cuffed myself and wondered where my familiar was and what was taking her so long.

Feeling the metal on my wrists, I looked up at Ash and asked, "Now you've got two girls taken captive. How does that feel?"

I gave him my deepest scowl, and he said nothing at first. Then he took a step forward and muttered, "Like I said, it's nothing personal. I'm paying a debt I owe. Once I help the necromancer capture you and Ruad, I'm home free. Don't think I take any pleasure in the events to follow."

My scowl deepened before I asked, "What does he have on you?"

Ash shook his head as he took another step.

"It's complicated. Suffice it to say I was sold to the necromancer without any say in the matter," he said.

Magic really ain't all Hogwarts and hippogriffs, is it? I thought.

And why would it all be some wonderful fantasy? Real life is complicated and messy. If magic was part of real life, and it clearly was, then why would it be any different? Seems bird boy was backed into a corner like I was. Furious as I was that he involved Abi, I wondered how much of this was really his fault.

"The necromancer you work for killed my parents, my whole clan."

Ash locked eyes with me and said, "I know. And I'm sorry. I didn't pick my boss."

When he was about half-way to me, I heard a snarl from above and Ruad leaped from one of the trees overhead. My smile grew as she landed on Ash and... went right through him, landing on the ground.

Then, before my smile could even fade a little, the winged boy vanished from sight, and pale boney fingers pierced the earth beneath my father's familiar. In quick order, I saw fingers become palms, then wrists, then arms. As the top of the skull emerged, I saw empty eye sockets with a millipede dangling from one. My focus shifted back to the hands, and I saw them holding a large metal ring. It was like *Night of the Living Dead* sped up 50x.

Ruad realized what was happening right as the skeleton clamped the ring closed over her, and I watched her surprise, her horror.

Runes carved into the metal ring glowed black as the skeleton skittered away. Then Ruad collapsed to the ground and let out a rough exhale as if someone had knocked the air out from her lungs.

"Ruad!"

She tried to get up, but even using all her strength, she was powerless to rise from the dirt. Meanwhile, the skeleton that ensnared Ruad walked over toward the others, its boney feet scraping across mud and stones.

I watched one of the undead in the back move toward us. As it approached, the air around it began to blur and shimmer. Slowly, from the ground up, the bones and dripping flesh disappeared, and a man with large black wings took their place. My foe had been hiding in the back disguised as a skeleton.

He stepped forward and looked down at his new prizes.

"Must feel like you're being crushed under about half a ton, Ruad. That brace you're ensnared in was made by my boss for when you tried the old bait and switch. It also puts a muzzle on your magic, making it almost impossible for you to share with Aoife."

I couldn't believe what had just happened in the span of five seconds. Had we really lost so quickly? Did we ever have a real chance?

I clenched my fists and grinded my teeth.

"I think that's about it. Let's wrap this up," Ash said, again walking towards me.

My heart rate began to skyrocket. I'd lost my clan. They'd taken Abi, and I wasn't going to lose my father's familiar. I just wasn't.

With my mind wandering, grasping for anything I could use, it found Coach's words.

"Necessity breeds innovation," he'd told a 13-year-old me before a tournament.

I still wasn't great at reading my opponent's moves, but what Coach taught me was when you're in the ring, your options are to lose or figure it out.

I sure as hell wasn't about to lose Ruad, so I had to figure it out. Adrienn was pretty well tapped from linking the fairy rings earlier. There wasn't much they'd be able to do. So it was down to me.

I stole another glance at Ruad as Ash walked closer. She was still struggling in the dirt, her legs clearly outmatched by the enchanted weight thrown on her. What could I do to help her? Then I thought: What would Tristan do to help her?

My father would change into his wolf form and tear Ash to pieces. I couldn't do that because I wasn't bound to Ruad as he was. We didn't share the same link.

Before I could focus much more on what separated us, Ruad's words came back to my head, "You'll always be 'Pup' to me." This wolf had watched me come into this world, and she was here now. Ruad may have been my father's familiar. But that didn't mean we lacked a connection of our own. We were family. We were pack mates. We were O'Connells, dammit.

It was upon that realization I felt something stirring deep inside me, a scent... hers. Shaggy red fur that smelled of dry leaves and pine needles. Following my gut instinct, I closed my eyes and felt the world around me disappear. I traveled inside to my mind forest, endless mist and trees surrounding me again.

Ruad's scent was stronger than ever before. I gasped when I saw her, hunched over and shivering in front of me. This wasn't the vermillion wolf I'd known and loved. Her fur was patchy, muddied and stuck with crumbled leaves and dirt, and an eye was partially faded

"Ruad..." I gasped again, taking in the sight of her.

"What do you see, Pup?" her ragged voice asked me.

I found myself speechless. What did I see? I mean... I knew, but I was in denial. If the mind forest is a glimpse inward, then this was Ruad's inner self. Her heart was broken. On the outside, she looked healthy and strong. But on the inside? This is what remained of my father's familiar after he severed his connection with her.

This is what months and years of loneliness and Sisyphean struggles to avoid capture had left her with. My eyes started to water.

"I see you, Ruad. All of you, ravaged by isolation and hopelessness," I said, standing still.

Inner Ruad scoffed, years past being able to chuckle. Then she said, "Now you see why asking me to bind myself to you a few nights ago was such a ridiculous request. You don't want a broken familiar, and I don't want to trust anyone with that kind of control over my fate ever again."

Listening to her voice, I realized this was Ruad preparing to throw in the towel. And that made me angry. Irrationally angry. Now I was back to speaking without thinking.

"What a bunch of fucking trash," I said.

Her eyes widened, and then the fangs came out.

116

"What did you say to me, Pup?"

"I said that's a bunch of fucking garbage, Ruad. You think I wouldn't want you because of the emotional and mental damage you've suffered? How dare you assume to know what I want? And that line you tried to feed me about wanting to be alone for the rest of your life? Absolute bullshit."

Ruad's amber eyes began to glow, and she took a step forward, baring all her fangs now.

"You looking for me to kill you in mercy before Ash takes us?" she asked.

I tapped into my own anger at her willingness to once more give up, and I showed her my own less-impressive fangs.

"Tell yourself whatever lies you want, but I'm not buying it! I know how badly I want you in my life, and you know how badly you want the pain of isolation to come to an end. So how about we act like fucking adults and lay our cards on the table? Become my familiar, Ruad. And we just might make it out of this alive," I proposed.

She body slammed me into a tree before I could react and had her fangs over my throat.

"You don't know what you're asking!" she roared.

"I'm asking you to trust me…"

"Tristan plunged a dagger into my heart and tore our connection to shreds. How can you possibly sit there and ask that I form a new one with you?!"

Now I raised my voice as loud as it would go.

"I am not my father's failure. I am his goddamn redemption, Ruad! And yours too if you'll just give me a chance. Hear me. I want you, all of you. Your scars, your torn fur, your years of loneliness, your wisdom, your memories, your love, and your loyalty. I fucking want it all!"

The vermillion wolf froze. So, I continued.

"Tristan left you alone, but I'm swearing to you now. If it comes to it, I'll die with you. But only after I fight to my last breath protecting you. Preferably not tonight to Ash, but whenever fate says your number is up, mine will be too. Give my family one more chance to be the perfect partner for your soul, and bind us together for as long as the path runs ahead, Ruad. Please."

We sat there in silence for several seconds before Ruad whispered, "Promise I'll never be alone?"

Without hesitation, I whispered back, "I promise."

The ground around us suddenly cracked apart, a sweeping wind flew over the trees, and the mist around me grew so thin it almost vanished. My heart began to feel like it was beating 1,000 times per minute, and I suddenly knew Ruad's heart was doing the same thing.

She leaned her forehead down on mine and said, "If you really want this scrappy sack of fur and teeth, Pup, say the words that'll bind our souls together."

Before I could ask about the words, they appeared in my mind, like growing letters spelling out a phrase in the darkness.

"Ceangail ár n-anamacha!" we yelled in unison.

The ground in my mind forest quaked underneath us as a second shockwave flew out, rattling the trees.

There was an energy between us, as though we were opposite charges being pulled together.

"Take my paw," she said, and I did so.

I grabbed her right paw.

"Close your eyes, and do not hold anything back. For the connection to forge, we have to be completely open to each other," she said.

I closed my eyes, not knowing entirely what that meant. But I felt a bridge begin to build between us on a deeper level.

Memories began to pop into my mind's eye, her licking my cheek, being picked up by firefighters, my adoption by Barb and John, my first violin recital, my first Muay Thai victory, and on and on my life replayed before my eyes like a flickering strobe light. Then those memories turned into a golden electrical current and flew across the bridge building between Ruad and I.

Likewise, her own memories came rushing into my mind, her own mother's silver eyes, the singing of my father, running after deer in these very mountains, and even a deep piercing pain that must have been the cursed dagger Tristan used.

I screeched from the pain radiating in my chest and jerked forward, but Ruad barked, "Do not let go! We are not finished!"

I felt the pain grow through each bone and muscle to an unbearable point. I wept with the deepest of tears, plunged into an isolating shadow that swallowed every attempt to escape and rejoin the light. Now I'd lost my father twice. Then I heard Tristan's voice, "Go! Find Aoife!" Aimlessness, loneliness, sadness, all consuming Ruad for nearly two decades. It tore my insides apart as it had her for years, like a knife and fork being run through my chest in every direction. And just when I thought I'd break into a million pieces, a reassurance whispered inside of me.

"But I'm here now," I said softly, gripping her paw tighter, "And I'm never leaving. I have sworn it."

Was there some shred of hope or relief coming across the bridge now? It was hard to tell, but at least it was something. We exchanged emotions, memories, desires, and everything I refused to hold back. And then it was there, a solid link between our hearts, souls, and minds.

"You saw the memory of how Tristan transformed?" Ruad asked.

I nodded.

"Say the words," she said, a stream of steady magic pouring forth from her body into mine. I took a deep breath and left my mind forest, the mist and trees around me blurring into blackness before being replaced with the woods on Mount Sequoyah, a platoon of skeletal warriors, and an approaching Ash.

Ruad paid him no mind as the raven walked toward her. My familiar's amber eyes were locked with mine. Her emotions were synced with my own. Our desires were bound tighter than the strands of a rope. She nodded.

With a confident voice, I yelled, "Athrú mac tíre!"

My magic surged, backed by energy from Ruad, and the transformation raced forward as the leaves and sticks nearby spun in a vortex, encapsulating me.

My claws and fangs deepened. My tail returned, and my hair shot up, taking me a few steps closer to feral.

I snapped the handcuffs like they were toothpicks and rocketed toward Ash. My fist met his face with a crunching sound, and he flew back into a skeleton, knocking it to the ground.

"Nice job, Pup!" Ruad said.

But the compliment had no time to sink in because the skeletons all charged forward. And I couldn't move, or they'd have an open shot at my familiar still trapped on the ground. So I raised my claws and held my ground the best I could.

For the next few minutes, I exhausted myself defending Ruad. I smashed bones, clawed weapons from skeletal grasps, and did my best to avoid being decapitated. My opponents managed to get one solid gash on my right shoulder and nicked my left side a couple times between my ribs.

At last, I smashed the skull of the last remaining skeleton and sank to my knees, panting. Breaking bones was hard work. Breaking bones filled with dark magic? No wonder I was whipped. I looked up hoping Ash had flown the coop as he had the first time we fought.

But he stood before a still unconscious Abi. Bird boy's expression was uneasy as he shifted from leg to leg, as if weighing his remaining options. I could only guess what was going through his mind at this point, but the bantering raven was no longer here. Present now? One increasingly-nervous necromancer pawn who somehow seemed angry and scared at the same time. He squinted and bit his tongue when ·glancing at the piles of bones I'd smashed on my left and right.

And that… it just stirred a deep rage inside of me. I ground my teeth realizing he wasn't about to throw in the towel. Something was keeping Ash in a fight that he didn't seem to be as enthused about anymore.

A primal quivering started somewhere deep in my chest and rippled outward. And whereas I'd felt excitement from Ruad since my transformation. Now I felt a twinge of unease.

I assumed her anxiety came from my growing rage at Ash, who also seemed to look increasingly unsteady. Could he feel my animosity from here? A deep growl filled my throat, and I became consumed with the idea of physically killing Ash with my own claws. I wanted nothing more than to kill him for putting Abi through this. My hesitation from earlier was nowhere to be found. And as that rage consumed me, I felt a claw from inside grab onto my consciousness and yank hard.

Once more the world faded to black, and when I opened my eyes, I was standing in my mind forest.

Geez, I'm really getting some frequent flier miles visiting this place, I thought.

A twig snapped from behind, and I looked to see a girl who looked like me emerge from behind a pine tree surrounded in fog. The copy looked like me in my wolf form, just… several years more feral. She was covered in dirt, blood, and her hair was thick with mange. Bruises and cuts littered her arms and legs, wounds that never healed properly.

When my inner self spoke, every word was like hearing iron growl.

"Kill him now," she hissed.

I stood in silence as the trees around me glowed a deep crimson. I felt a steady beat of rage pulsing in the woods around me. My chest tightened, and thoughts of tearing open Ash's jugular with my fangs flooded my mind.

With a small voice, I said, "That's not who I am."

"It's who you are now!" the other me screamed, rattling leaves on every tree in the area.

I shivered but held my ground.

"No, I am not some mindless beast to be controlled by primal impulses like whatever you are," I said.

The other me hissed and raced forward yelling, "You're a fucking wolf. Act like it!"

I shook my head, trying to raise my claws and defend myself, but she was too quick.

"You think you're better than me? You think I'm just some new side effect of you bonding with Ruad? I'm 100% you. I've always been here, waiting. Every time you sank into fury, every time you felt alone. If I'm a mindless beast, so are you. And I can't wait for you to show the world what an unbound monster can do. Now go kill that fucking bird, Aoife Fey O'Connell," she said before sinking her fangs into my neck and catapulting my consciousness back out into the real world.

My fingers traced my neck as I found myself back on Mount Sequoyah once more. I found no visible wounds, but what I did notice was a pile of raw hatred and energy boiling in my chest and waiting to burst in a fit of rage. They were accompanied by an insatiable desire for raven blood, and one happened to be standing in front of me.

I heard Ruad call my name, but I couldn't focus on it over the sound of Ash's panicking, beating heart. Running at Ash with a speed I'd never matched before in my life, I saw him try to throw up some sort of illusion. But I was too quick. I grabbed him by the throat and slammed him down into the ground.

That's when the pounding began. I went to town, bashing his face several times, letting out each and every ounce of frustration I felt for what he'd done to Ruad and Abi.

Ruad's voice couldn't stop me. Ash's whimpering couldn't stop me. I could tell as I hit him that bird boy wasn't used to such direct combat. He was more comfortable being tricky and casting his illusions while striking opponents from behind or the side.

Well that's not happening now is it? I thought, continuing to pound away at him.

I only stopped when I detected the unfamiliar scent of a girl I hadn't noticed before. And my fists paused. Why did I smell another woman here in this battle? A realization hit me as my rage slowly drained. Ash wasn't who I saw him as.

I looked down at him, and suddenly before my eyes was a younger girl where Ash had been on the ground. She had all the same wounds I'd just given bird boy, but her hair was longer, more sleek. She was shorter. And she wasn't wearing a tank top but a gray T-shirt with a Nike logo on the front.

She slowly sat up as I gazed at her. Then the raven looked down at her appearance and cursed.

"Fuck," she muttered with a much different voice than I'd heard before.

Slowly, I stood up.

She still had wings, but this new person was smaller. And I was just now realizing Ash never quite smelled like a man did, especially not when sweating and involved in combat.

Women and men obviously smell different, but it's especially clear when it comes to things like sweat and body odor. That was made even more apparent to me with my heightened sense of smell. "Is… Ash short for Ashley?" I stammered, raising an eyebrow.

She looked down and out, but what if this was another kind of illusion or trick from my opponent?

The raven snapped quickly. "Don't call me that!"

I flinched when I heard her scream and said, "Um, sorry… Ash."

I was beginning to put a few pieces together in my brain about who my opponent really was, but before I could ask more questions, I detected another odor, or lack thereof. I couldn't smell Abi anywhere.

When I looked over at the tree with the chains, I realized she wasn't there.

Then I turned my attention back to Ash.

"Did you really abduct Abi?" I asked.

Ash looked down at the ground and said nothing.

"You just wrote the note and hoped I'd go apeshit, didn't you?" I asked.

Silence again.

"That sounds about like something the wretched girl would do," a man said, walking out of the trees to the right of Ash.

She looked up and gasped as I turned my attention to this man wrapped in a black and silver cloak and hood. The only bit of his face I could see was a glimpse at his cut up, scarred lips and chin.

Around his neck hung a long beaded charm with a smooth black orb at the end. The orb appeared to have a hog carved into it.

"Master, I've got the wolf and…"

"Shut your mouth!" he yelled and raised his right hand.

Ash began to float off the ground and groan. The cloaked man slowly closed his hand, and Ash began to scream.

"You've never been able to do anything right! For months you've been chasing this wolf, and you wind up getting beaten by a newly-awakened druid who knows little to nothing about magic?"

Ash continued to scream, her wings violently beating as the cloaked man closed his fist ever so slowly.

"You know, when Morrigu told me she would loan me a raven servant to satisfy her debt to me, I was excited. Ravens are known for illusions and thunder magic. But when she handed me you, this wretched human girl who had bargained her body away for parlor tricks, I was furious. A Raven who could barely do illusion magic. You've had far too long to prove your worth, and your time to impress me is at an end."

"You… can't. Morrigu still needs me," Ash managed to choke out.

"Oh you stupid little abomination. You never seemed to quite understand how your bargain worked. Morrigu never needed you. You were simply kept around to fulfill the debt from your wish. And when you were given to me, your obligation to Morrigu was over with. You were mine to use as I pleased. And here we are at the end of your usefulness," he said, thrusting his fist forward and sending the winged girl crashing through tree limbs and into a sycamore trunk.

He pinned the girl there, and then his hand started to glow blue.

"I'll show you the thunder magic you never had the talent to learn," he hissed.

A clap of thunder echoed through the forest as a bolt of lightning raced from his glowing hand toward her. In an instant I reached over and picked up a large log, lugging it in front of Ash. The lightning struck the log, splintering it into a thousand tiny burning pieces. My arms rattled from the impact, and I coughed from the smoke.

When the dust cleared, I saw the necromancer still standing with his hand raised. It was steaming.

"Well now this is a surprise. The druid leaping to save the raven that hunted her familiar to the brink of death. Why?" the necromancer asked.

"I'm still putting the pieces together, but it sounds like Ash made a desperate bargain, and it went awry," I said. "What I hate the most is it seems like the raven was taken advantage of. And now that they're of no further use to you, you're just gonna kill them? Fuck that."

The necromancer sneered as renewed silence fell over the forest around us.

"You both have something in common, you know?" he said. "Each of you fight to be something you're not, leaping after your wishes and fantasies like mindless animals driven only by your instincts."

I scowled and popped my neck in a couple places.

"Her life is meaningless to me. I gave her a chance to be useful. She failed. Now move out of the way, druid. I'll get to you soon enough."

I picked up a rock the size of my hand and hurled it at the necromancer with all my strength. He blasted it with lightning, and with his attention focused elsewhere, I snatched Ash and raced behind another tree to set her down.

She was severely beaten and bleeding from her nose and eyes.

"Why?" she asked.

"I just have this sense that you're not actually a bad person. You just got wrapped up in terrible circumstances," I said. "Is he the person that killed my parents?"

She softly nodded.

"You chill here. I'm going to walk over and kill him. Then we'll sort this out, little miss," I said.

Ash grabbed my hand as I turned, and I saw fear on her face.

"His power is greater than you can possibly know. You don't stand a chance," the raven said.

I was about to come face-to-face with my clan's killer, and while my inner self was bringing about a second wind for my magic, I considered Ash's words.

Ruad was still bound. I was exhausted, and so was Ash.

Maybe fighting him now would be suicide, I thought. *I barely took out his underling.*

Still, I had to do something. I doubt he was going to just let us all leave. He'd been after Ruad for years. Now that he'd seen me, the last O'Connell, the bastard would be after me, too.

I looked down at Ash's hand grasping mine with a quiet fear and desperation. She knew what the wizard was capable of. I would defer to her wisdom.

"Okay, then. Leave it to me," I said. "No fighting."

Before Ash let my hand go, she said, "Oh, and don't call me miss."

I looked down at the raven.

"Mister?" I asked, raising an eyebrow.

He nodded.

"You got it, Mr. Raven," I said and turned to face the necromancer, who was now walking toward us.

What am I going to do? I thought, looking around the trail we'd been fighting on.

I still felt a great deal of anger and apprehension coming from Ruad. She continued to struggle with the brace weighing her to the ground. My familiar had my same urge to tear this bastard's head off. And yet, there was hesitation in her heart. Ruad also seemed to know what this man was capable of and understood we weren't equipped to face him.

Looking at Ruad, an idea came to me. I didn't have much magic left, but I remember how she'd barked at me earlier and shattered my focus. What did she call it? The alpha's command?

Something like that probably wouldn't have much effect on the necromancer. But if I tweaked it…

"Cover your ears," I hissed at Ash.

The raven did as he was told, and then I summoned every ounce of magic I had left and pushed it up into my throat. Then I threw back my jaw, looked directly at the moon overhead and let forth the loudest, shrieking howl I could manage.

It was a savage, ear-bursting noise that cracked into the necromancer's head like a whip made of sound waves. My throat burned at the output, and I could see Ruad flinching, her paws over her ears.

Tree bark around the cloaked man peeled, and I saw him sink to his knees with his hands over his ears. I could smell blood dripping out from beneath his hands.

Without warning, I snatched Ash and threw him over my uninjured shoulder. Then I appeared above Ruad and brought my full strength to bear on the brace holding her with my right fist. It cracked. Then, it fully broke when I followed up with a swift kick.

Suddenly Ruad was up, and we took off running for the fairy ring. Nobody had to ask what the plan was.

When I stole a glance at the necromancer, I saw jaw face twisted in pain. He was still on his knees. We left the clearing behind us as I heard him growl. A bolt of lightning flew wildly into the trees above me.

Goddamn that was close, I thought.

My strength was fading fast as my lungs worked to take in enough air with each step. I smelled the necromancer as he left the clearing and gave chase, but we had a little lead on him.

When we came to a familiar boulder, I flopped down into the fairy ring with Ruad and Ash.

I was dead tired and unable to move another inch.

"Now what?" Ash nearly shrieked.

"Adrienne, please!" I gasped, and a familiar green light darted out of my pendant.

I closed my eyes when I felt us leaving Mount Sequoyah and did not open them again for quite some time. A memory of Tristan using the fairy circles to make quick escapes played through my mind, and I realized it had come from my familiar over our new bridge.

My familiar... that felt good to say.

Chapter Ten

I floated somewhere between consciousness and sleep. It's that space of time people usually hit about half an hour before their alarm clock goes off. I definitely wasn't awake to process things from my five senses, enhanced as they were. But I wasn't dead to the world, either.

Floating in this void, I knew my body was still exhausted from the fight with Ash and the necromancer. It wasn't quite ready to wake up, but my mind had random flashes of thought.

I found myself peering into the bridge between Ruad and I. A few days ago, I didn't know she existed. And now? I'd die for her. Literally. If one of us died, the other was toast, too.

She'd been there at the start of my life, and I wanted to be at her side until the end of my life.

As I processed feelings from my connection with Ruad, the first thing I sorted out was the word "mine." That's not to say the emotion I picked up was my own. It's just the word that immediately came to mind. Mine. This is mine. What is it? A nickel? A piece of gum? What is mine?

Swimming in the darkness of my sort of sleeping mind, I finally realized mine was Ruad's emotion. "This is mine." So mine was really hers. And what exactly was hers?

As if on cue, a memory came forward associated with this feeling of possession. It was a recent memory, too.

Ruad was lying on the floor of Tristan's greenhouse. She was on something. It was her "mine." She finally glanced down at it, and I saw me. Oh, that's what she was feeling possessive of. I was hers. And not in a cute, "Hehe, this is my human," way but a, "If you move a finger in this general direction, I'll murder you and everyone you've ever loved," kind of way.

My familiar was being protective of my unconscious body, lying over my stomach and staring hard at something. The thing she was declaring "mine" to.

Her eyes glanced up at a certain raven, still looking rough, but otherwise conscious. He was sitting against a wall.

"I'll warn you one final time, raven. Make no moves, lest I get nervous and tear open your throat," Ruad growled.

Ash looked too tired to smirk and said, "I didn't ask you to bring me back to your little clubhouse, wolf."

Ruad scoffed and said, "It wasn't my first plan upon being freed from the brace you slapped on me. I intended to let the necromancer kill you, but for reasons I can't even begin to understand, Pup chose to save your ass."

Ash didn't say anything for a moment.

"Why did she do that?" he finally asked.

The wolf looked down at me again and muttered, "I've been combing through her memories and emotions during the battle, hoping to better understand her decision. But I can't make any sense of what I feel or see."

"Did she pity me?"

"Best I can guess, she just had an overwhelming urge to protect you, a complete turn from when she initially read your note," Ruad said, looking up at Ash again.

I continued to float through the memory, smirking at the fact that Ruad was literally staying on top of me to keep me safe.

"So what? I'm your prisoner now?" Ash asked.

Ruad's eyes burned into the raven that had spent months trying to capture her.

"That's probably better than you deserve given what you've put me through, but let's be pragmatic. Do you have the strength and energy to best me in combat and escape here while injured? No. You're still hurt from the beating my Pup gave you. So it's probably just best for you to rest until she wakes up, and I can ask her what the hell she was thinking by bringing you here. Am I going to kill you before she wakes up? I'd like to, raven. But I think that would upset Pup since she went through all the trouble to save you. So let's just sit tight for now. You regain your strength. And I'll let Pup do the same."

Ash raised an eyebrow.

"You keep referring to her as 'Pup,' but you didn't... like... give birth to her, right? She's human?" He asked.

"It's a pet name. She is human, yes. But also a druid from the same clan as me," Ruad said.

"Ironic, the pet giving the human a pet name," Ash muttered.

Ruad barked at him, "I'm not her pet! I'm her familiar. There is a grand difference. Our link is pure, unlike the bastardized magical process that made you what you are."

Ash's eyes burned into Ruad's.

"I'm fully aware of what I am, wolf. No need to be disrespectful about it."

Ruad said nothing. And then the memory ended.

As I floated away from my bridge with Ruad, I noted her feeling of protectiveness did not fade. She was metaphorically growling "Mine" just as loud now as she had whenever the memory took place.

It felt... nice, having someone be possessive of me. And it wasn't in a creepy stalker or abusive way. Just, having someone that saw value in me, someone that treasured me. Ruad was a little hard on me sometimes, but she'd also shown I was precious to her.

Abi was previously the only one who really showed me I meant something. And I loved her for it. But there was also something to be said for having that affection from a different type of relationship... family.

Barb and John had certainly never shown that kind of adoration for me. Barb was too busy trying to stave off my "disruptive" behavior and make me into her little clone. And John was barely around enough to show me any affection.

But Ruad... actually cared about me. She threw herself on top of me to keep me safe, even if it made it a little harder to breathe. The way that made me feel, I wanted to just bottle it up and stick it somewhere for a rainy day. I felt stupid happy, and a little melancholy for all the wasted time I could've had Ruad by my side in life if only Barb hadn't tossed my locket after the adoption. The bitch.

I thought back to all the fights we had that ended up with me in my bedroom crying at the foot of my bed, just praying to the stars for someone to come into my life and show me they cared, instead of trying to mold me into something I wasn't meant to be.

Now I had that, and it was almost too good to be true.

Another half hour went by, and slowly, I opened my eyes. Things were a little blurry for a moment, but when I rubbed my eyes, that cleared up. Ruad looked over at me and said, "There's the Pup. How are you feeling?"

I sneezed and then looked at her.

"I feel like I have a 120 pounds of wolf on my stomach," I said.

"I'm closer to 140, Pup. Magically-enhanced muscles and bones. Typical familiar stuff," she said.

She stood up, and I took in some extra air before throwing my arms around her and breathing in her scent again. I was sore, but Ruad was with me. Lifting my shirt, I saw all of my cuts were covered with greenish-brown leaves and some kind of aloe. Reaching behind me, I found the same on my back, over the large slash where a blade had cut me good.

I lifted one of the leaves, and where a skeleton had previously cut me, a small mark remained. But it wasn't bleeding. I put the leaf back on. A week ago, I think this gooey leaf stuff would have felt icky. Now? It felt natural as hydrogen peroxide and a fresh bandage.

The leaves were perfectly round, something I'd never seen before.

"What kind of plant dropped these?" I asked.

Ruad looked at me and said, "You'll have to ask Adrienn. They just remembered your father kept a few stored away. I remember Tristan growing plenty of them, but I don't know what they're called, or where they come from."

"I'm guessing Adrienn is the one who applied these and unhooked my bra to get at the back wound?" I asked.

Ruad nodded.

I looked down at my necklace and said, "Hey Adrienn. Got a minute?"

A flash of green light appeared, and the little fey flew up in front of my face.

"Aoife! Glad to see you're up!"

I held out my right hand flat, and they landed. I lightly kissed Adrienn's head and smiled.

"Thank you for helping get us all back here safely." I said.

They looked down at my hand and sort of lightly kicked their right foot.

"I uh… had to borrow some of your magic to activate the circle. I hope you don't mind. There wasn't really time to ask," they said.

Shaking my head, I said, "Whatever you and Ruad did to get me back safely, I'm grateful."

Adrienn smiled real big after that.

"And thanks for patching me up," I said.

The fey blushed a little and said, "For the record, I had my eyes closed when I… with your undergarments. I mean, I opened them to look at the wounds and see where the leaves needed to go, but I didn't…"

"Adrienn," I said, interrupting them. "It's fine. Thanks for your help."

They flew up into the air a few inches and then took their usual spot on my shoulder.

"This is a touching reunion and all, but if it's okay, can I leave now?" Ash spoke up.

It took me a moment to process hearing a feminine voice coming from the person I once considered my enemy. I coughed and slowly stood up, with Ruad helping to keep me steady.

As I walked toward the raven, Ruad put herself between us.

"Watch the wings," she growled.

I put a hand on Ruad's head and said, "It's okay. He's not going to hurt me."

Ash said nothing as I slowly walked around Ruad and held out my hand. He looked at my gesture and then sighed, gripping tight. I wasn't watching his wings, but Ruad was, like a hawk. Ironic.

I helped Ash up slowly, and he grimaced in pain, groaning quite a bit. After a few seconds, he finally stood up straight.

Long black hair fell around him as he averted his eyes from me.

"Ash, you're free to leave any time you want. I just want to make sure you're safe and healthy before you do," I said.

The raven looked at the door and then back at me. The sun had been up for about three or four hours now.

"Are you hurt?" I asked.

He said nothing.

"You can drop the macho act. I really am just trying to help."

"Why?" He suddenly asked. There was pain in his voice, and it sounded like he was fighting back tears. I slowly held up my hands and backed a step away, motioning for Ruad to do the same. She reluctantly did.

Speaking softly, I said, "I'm not going to hurt you, Ash. You really can walk out that door any time you want. I just want to help because… you were wronged in such a devastating way. I've known a few transgender folks through high school, and I imagine most of them would jump at the chance to use magic and fix their problems, winding up with a horrible bargain in the process."

Ash's fists rattled a little, and the feathers on his wings ruffled.

"Am I wrong?" I asked.

Ash hesitated for a moment and then shook his head.

"Okay. So we're not enemies. Now, if I ask Adrienn for more of those leaves, will you let me patch you up?" I asked.

The raven slowly sat back down where he had been. There was no affirmation, but I guess that was as close to an answer as I was going to get.

"Adrienn?" I asked.

The fey flew up.

"Can you show me where those leaves you used on me last night are?"

The fey led me over to a corner of the room where a wooden box sat. Two painted red lines intersected to form what looked like a medical symbol on top.

I removed the lid from the box and found some thin rope made of vines, some powders inside folded envelopes, and three different kinds of leaves.

The left side of the box held the leaves used for my cuts. The center had a little section of red leaves with jagged edges. And to the right sat a single orange triangular leaf.

"Since most of Ash's injuries are from blunt impacts to his body, you'll want the red leaves. They reduce swelling and muffle pain. Put the leaf between your flattened palms and push a little magic into it. It'll heat up and sweat a little slime. Stick it over the wound, and Ash should feel better right away," Adrienn said.

I smiled at the fey and thanked them. As I reached for the leaves, Adrienn landed back on my shoulder.

Walking back over to Ash, I asked him if he was okay raising his shirt for me to examine where I'd punched him. His chin was swollen from where I slugged him. That much I could see. He grimaced, slowly moving his right arm and raising the Nirvana shirt. His stomach was covered in bruises, splotches of purple, red, and yellow mixed together.

I didn't think I'd hit hard enough to break anything.

Placing a red leaf between my hands, I pushed a little energy into it until it felt warm. When it started to sweat, I pulled it off my right hand.

"These leaves are going to feel a little slimy, but it will reduce the pain and heal your bruises faster," I said.

"Within 24 hours," Adrienn added.

The raven made no reply. So I covered his stomach with about four leaves, until the bruises hidden beneath vegetation.

Then I handed one last leaf to him and said, "for your chin."

He sighed and took it, before applying the leaf to the bottom of his swollen jaw.

For a minute, there was silence in the greenhouse. Then I heard a barely audible sigh of relief come from the raven. He slumped down an inch or two, and I turned toward Ruad, stifling a stupid grin.

He's like the toddler who screams they don't need a nap, and then five seconds later they're asleep, I thought.

Turning back toward Ash, I asked, "Since you're free to go at any time, would you trust me enough to talk about your former boss a little?"

The raven looked up at me with glassy eyes and a worn out frown.

"He's just the latest consequence in a series of bad choices, Aoife. I'm sorry for everything I did to you and the wolf," Ash said, looking at a pile of soil against the wall across from him.

"Thanks for saying so," I said.

Ruad said nothing. And I sensed quite a bit of hatred inside my wolf's heart for Ash. I couldn't ask Ruad to make those feelings disappear. Ash had been trying to capture my familiar for months, pushing her to the brink of hopelessness. Still, I didn't sense any immediate desire to tear the raven's throat out coming from Ruad. Maybe that was a start?

"His name is Malachos. He's a necromancer with an intense interest in your clan, but I never knew why. I just know he wanted you and Ruad."

I took a breath. Ash did the same.

"He's crazy strong and has spent years looking for something. He never said what. Malachos' magic is stronger than you and Ruad put together and multiplied by 10," Ash said. "That's about all I know."

Looking down at the softwood floor, I waited, feeling like the raven had more to say. When he said nothing, I gently nudged him.

"Do you want to tell me how you got involved with Malachos... or maybe who Morrigu is?" I asked.

Ash's eyes flared.

I sensed a tension in the raven. But I could both sympathize with Ash for his fate and seek out clues about Malachos' plans.

We sat there for a few minutes in silence, Ash growing more tense.

Ruad coughed, and I kind of pawed at a clump of hair on the ground next to my left leg.

"Morrigu started all of this. Or I guess I did. She just let me jump out of the plane without a parachute," Ash said.

Cocking my head, I asked, "Can't you fly?"

Ash glared at me.

"Oh, sorry. Symbolic parachute. I'll shut up now."

After another 30 seconds, Ash took a deep breath and said, "She's a goddess."

I said nothing, but the look on my face seemed to send a message to Ash anyway. Stupid expressions always betrayed me.

"What? You rest with a talking wolf, but a goddess is too weird for you? I've watched you use druidic magic twice now. You grew ears and a tail last night. But a goddess? That's just too much?"

I threw my hands up flat.

"Hold on there. I didn't say it was too much. I just—need a minute for my brain to process magic things. You've had your wings for months, right? Well I just woke up to my druidic heritage a few days ago."

Ash whistled.

"And you still kicked my ass. That's depressing."

"Well... I thought you had my girlfriend. And you did actually have my wolf. Desperation breeds innovation, or something like that," I said.

The raven gave me a flat expression.

"I think you might have just butchered two or three analogies," he said.

Looking up at my ceiling, I sighed and said, "So... a goddess?"

Any humor left Ash's face. "Yeah, a goddess of fate, omens, wars, things like that. Her name means queen of phantoms or some such."

I glanced at Ash's wings but looked back down at his face when he caught me.

"Yeah, that's her handiwork. The result of an overeager trans boy just wanting to grow up and be a man. In a rush to fix his dysphoria, the boy made a regrettable bargain."

Ruad sat down next to me, maybe finally accepting Ash wasn't going to attack us again. At least not tonight. My familiar stifled a yawn, though I don't know if it was out of respect or wanting to appear still fully alert.

"I was 15 and hurting something fierce with each day puberty advanced. I felt like a never-ending glass shard was being stabbed into my heart each time someone at school called me 'Ashley' or 'young lady' or 'she.' Throw in a forced subscription to Lucifer's Waterfall Monthly, and you've got my living Hell."

When he fell silent, I heard nothing in the room but our heartbeats.

"I didn't want to be any of the Disney princesses, growing up. But I really did like Mulan. I watched the DVD so often that I had 'Make a Man Out of You' memorized. I sang it every day from the ages of 7-12. I think that might have just added to the pain I'd feel later. I can remember one night several months ago just sitting out back on the swing set, wondering if I could swing high enough that I'd get seriously hurt if I jumped off. I was about to try it until Mom called me in for dinner," Ash said. "It's a special kind of pain fostered in your heart that Morrigu takes advantage of."

Now Ash locked eyes with me.

"Morrigu appeared to me one day when I was out hiking alone on Mount Kessler. She took the form of a crow and flew right out of the sky, landing in front of me and changing into this tall woman in a long black feather dress, her eyes crimson as the evening sun. And Morrigu strolled right up to me, asked if I was interested in making a deal.

"What else could I do but stand there with my mouth agape. But eventually, my brain began to tick and thought, 'Well at least hear this magical being out. What's the harm?'

"The goddess said she had her eye on me for weeks. I carried such a unique and potent hurt in my chest, and that's when we're most susceptible to change. Morrigu said she understood and longed to help me. Stupid teenage me thought she actually cared. Maybe it was her tone or the sad look in her eyes, like an adult who actually saw my pain. I guess I wished for that too, and she must have been listening."

Ash stopped speaking and sighed, looking around at some of the flowers in the greenhouse. It took him a minute to continue.

"Morrigu promised the whole world would see a man when they looked at me. And my stupid brain should have picked up on the wording right there and then. All it would cost me was a single favor afterward, to be named at a later time. This is why you don't give teenagers a credit card. 'Pay for it later' equals 'free' in our mind."

I winced at that analogy.

"So I took the deal, and she used a powerful spell to turn me into the raven you see before you. And she kept her word, because ravens are masters of illusionary magic. With a little practice, I could make anyone see me as a man, hear me as a man. The side effect of being a raven? These giant-ass wings and talons."

He moved his wings, allowing me to actually see his feet for the first time, sans illusions. And there they were, a pale yellow color and about the size of an average man's foot. Each talon had three prongs on the front, complete with a large black claw. There was a shorter prong on the back of each talon.

Those are raven feet, all right, I thought.

I didn't stare long. I didn't want to be rude, so I returned my gaze to Ash's face and listened.

"When she cast her spell over me, I was in such terrible pain, having bones shift and being metamorphosed. Things were breaking, cracking, tearing, and being remade. I passed out for a bit, and when I woke up, she was gone. I was abandoned in this cursed form, and she left me a parchment explaining the basics of illusionary magic.

"It took me two nights of lying to my parents and saying I was sleeping at a friend's house before my practice paid off, and I could master a basic enough illusion to resume my normal life. But it's exhausting, maintaining illusions all day, making sure my parents and everyone else just see a normal human teenager.

"These wings... it's almost like they need energy of their own, and they drain me considerably," he said.

Looking left and right, I eyed his wings and tried to imagine what it would be like carrying them with me all the time. Pile on the fact they seemed to devour his stamina, and I could understand how that alone would drive someone batty.

"Are there benefits? Sure. When I'm out and about, I can make people see Ash, just the normal man I've always wanted to be. And flying? It's one of the most amazing feelings in the world. But having someone prey on my vulnerabilities and then tricking me into such a twisted bargain where I didn't get the immediate transition I asked for left me bitter. I'm still a fucking girl under all this magic," Ash said, clenching his fists.

He was probably seconds away from crying, and I could tell the raven was using every bit of strength he had to hide that fact.

"I'm guessing that favor Morrigu came to reclaim was to loan you out to Malachos?" I asked, quietly.

136

Ash nodded, and then the dam broke. He looked away as the first tears formed. Then, a whimper escaped. And another. Before long, he was on his feet and turned toward the door.

Something stopped him, and without turning to face me, he said, "Tricked me and then loaned me out like a lawn mower, Aoife. I don't know why I'm telling you all this, and I'm sorry. I just... just..."

Now he turned, eyes red and puffy, tears running down each cheek. I slowly stood and cautiously walked over to him. The last thing I wanted was to startle him. But seeing the raven cry like this broke my heart.

From my understanding, Ash had been in pain for years. And Morrigu had somehow found a way to make it worse, while selling this bargain as the ultimate solution.

I moved closer, arms opened wide. Ruad was on her feet and watching closely.

And with no hesitation Ash fell forward, crying into my shoulder, his arms and wings slowly wrapping around me.

Prior to now, two people on the planet knew how Ash felt, Morrigu and Malachos. Neither cared. I was probably the first person to offer him a shoulder to cry on over all this. He'd been through a lot, more than a lot. And there was a piece of me that knew how he felt, steeped in loneliness and feeling unseen.

There was always a piece of my heart that felt invisible to Barb and John, wishing on star after star for a fresh start with a family that loved me and understood the itch I felt for magic.

He continued to sob for another few minutes, and then we sat back down again, only this time he was curled up next to me, with his knees up to his chin.

"Adrienn? Is there anything you know of that might be able to reverse Morrigu's spell? Do you know what she did to Ash?" I asked.

The fey hovered in front of us, looking Ash over with an eye that could see magic so much better than I ever could. It almost looked like the fey was scanning Ash's body, like some kind of barcode laser.

"I'm afraid not, Aoife," Adrienn said.

"Are there no other ravens like Ash? Any that could help him?" I asked.

The fey looked at Ash again and said, "Yes and no. There are other ravens like Ash, part animal, part human. They're called hybrida and are usually the descendants of humans who take on animal forms or animals

137

who take on human forms and… well, you know. They're rare and usually form flocks with others in similar forms. But they're born naturally, not through a spell like Ash. Granted, Morrigu is a goddess, so she certainly has the power to change people if she wishes. Since she laid the spell, she'd be one of the only beings who could remove it."

Ash gave me a look that said he'd accepted his fate long ago, probably the first time Malachos hurt him for failing to capture Ruad.

We sat there for a while, still rebuilding our strength. And after an hour or two, Ash stood up and walked toward the door.

"Ash, wait," I said.

"What?" He asked, his voice sounding a bit raw, not at me, I hoped.

Yeah, Aoife. What? I mocked myself inside. *What are you going to say to this suffering boy?*

"You're not alone, Ash," I said.

"What do you mean?"

I sighed and said, "I've been alone for most of my life. I didn't have many friends in school aside from Abi. At home, Barb and John never really tried to connect with me. So I know it sucks to feel alone. Then I learned about my clan and how I'd lost them before I was old enough to remember them. If… if they were still alive today, I believe they would take you in.

I don't know if you'll ever meet another hybrida. And I know I only look like an animal some of the time. But if you ever find yourself without a place to go or someone to talk to about all this magic stuff, you can come back here anytime you want. I'll be a friend, someone you can count on, I promise."

With that, I took out his hostage letter and wrote my phone number on the back.

"Call or text me anytime you need something, even if it's just an ear to bend. I won't let you suffer alone," I said.

Ash took the paper and folded it up, putting it in his pants pocket. Then I watched his face blur as he struggled and started to grimace. After another try or two, he looked like the same man I fought last night, sans injuries. And to his parents, I'm sure he'd look like their child, sans wings and talons.

"Who knows? Maybe one day you could help me rebuild my clan or take down Malachos or something?" I asked.

He gave me a slight smirk, which quickly faded and said, "I don't know, Aoife. I have a lot to process right now. I think based on what Malachos said last night, I fulfilled my debt to Morrigu. But if she comes calling, it doesn't sound like there's much I can do. I just need to stew. Thank you for saving my life and listening earlier. But I don't know if I'm exactly eager to form the Wolf/Bird Club and hunt down Malachos."

Then he turned, opened the wooden door, and took off into the sky, albeit a little slower than I'd seen him fly before.

As I watched him fly off, I understood. He needed time. His boss had just tried to kill him, and his previous enemy had saved his life. Anyone would need time to process that.

All I could really think about was what I'd told him about my clan. And the more I thought about it, the more I agreed with my initial assessment. The O'Connell clan would absolutely have given him a place to call home, even if it was just a home away from home.

Maybe that realization was the first step I needed toward rebuilding my clan.

I hoped Ash would find some modicum of peace in the coming days. And I also dreamed that he'd come back to fight by my side when I needed him most. But the former was more important to me than the latter.

Chapter Eleven

We got off the bus in my old neighborhood. Old neighborhood? Didn't I used to live here until just a matter of days ago? It felt like an eternity since Barb had thrown me out of the house on a cold winter night.

The sun was out today, and it was in the 60s. Arkansas winters, you gotta love them. Some days it might be winter. Or maybe it was going to be a few days of spring. And just when you were getting comfortable, tornado! Good times.

"So we're going back to your old house to get supplies? And you're sure you want to see your adopted mother again? I've seen your last memory with her. It left a scar on your heart," Ruad said, quietly.

I spent a moment trying to figure out how Ruad could have seen that memory before my brain caught up and realized.

Oh yeah... inner bridge thing, I thought. She must have seen it when we made our bond last night.

After another pause, a new thought dawned on me. Maybe more important than what Ruad saw during our bond was who she saw. Did she see me as I am now? Or maybe a broken version of myself under Barb's thumb? What was the worst case scenario? Maybe she saw a feral version of me.

One of the neighbors was out washing his car in the driveway, an accountant named Roy. He was scrubbing his red Mustang with a large yellow sponge as my familiar and I walked by. He just gave me a look after staring at the wolf.

"She's trained," I hollered at him.

He said nothing and went back to washing his car.

Prick, I thought, as he stole glances at me from the corner of his eyes.

I placed my left hand on Ruad's head, which wasn't too far below my own. If Ruad stood on her hind legs, she'd be taller than me. And it constantly amused me how she went from teddy bear I needed to fall asleep at night to killing machine that would murder anyone who hurt me.

Looking down at her, I smiled and said, "If I'm going to live in Dad's greenhouse permanently, then I'll need to get a few things. And that's why I timed our approach for 2:15 p.m. sharp today. Barb has a women's Bible study every Thursday at 2:30 p.m. She never misses, even if she's sick and spreads it to her entire group."

"If the other humans are old like she is, that seems like a considerable risk for a religious gathering," Ruad said.

"They're convinced God will protect them. I've tried multiple times to explain that God gave her common sense for a reason, but I can't possibly know anything because I'm a hellion," I said.

My familiar cocked her head to the side.

"You're still conflicted about your religious beliefs, aren't you?" she said.

I sighed. It was something that did still pop up in my mind occasionally. Having a religion forced upon me my entire life and then discovering my heritage as a druid and user of nature magic... it changed things.

"Magic? Goddesses like Morrigu? Talking wolves? Necromancers? What am I supposed to believe, Ruad?" I asked as we continued down my old street past some green and yellow trash bins.

"You'll learn as you grow older, Pup, that beliefs are not always set in stone. Life situations open your eyes to new things all the time. To shut your mind to different experiences stunts growth. Based on your memories, it's what your adopted mother did long ago," Ruad said.

"Barb? That woman wouldn't know a new experience if it bit her on the ass. The only time she experienced something new was when her favorite Mexican restaurant in town closed, and she moved to the one across the street. Even that took three months," I said.

I clenched my fists thinking about her again. The woman who had left me with nothing. Who knows what would have happened to me that night if I hadn't stumbled into Odessa's shop and learned about Adrienn and Ruad?

"How do I feel about religion? I dunno, Ruad. I just don't know what I believe in anymore when it comes to higher powers. How do I feel about Barb? I hate her. So let's get inside, grab my shit, and go," I said.

We walked across the lawn and up to the front door. Next door behind a six-foot privacy fence I heard our neighbor's two Scottie dogs barking at Ruad. Without really thinking, I snapped my head toward them and let out a deep bark of my own, telling them to shut up. I hated those dogs.

They went quiet.

Upon realizing what I'd done, I took a moment to reflect and ask, "What did I just do?"

Ruad looked up at me and said, "I've been a familiar to your father for years, Aoife. Without bragging, I'm pretty powerful. You're a newly-awakened druid. Our souls are bonded, and we have an internal bridge now, remember?"

Fumbling in my purse for my old house key, I said, "I get all that. But what does that have to do with me barking at the neighbor's dogs?"

"It's our bridge. Since I'm the dominant force between us, a lot of things are flowing from me internally over into you. Energy, memories, and even some behavioral habits. Yapping little dogs are annoying, and I would have silenced them with my own command. But you beat me to it."

I sighed and put the little brass key in the lock, turning it left. I opened the door and motioned for Ruad to head in first. She did so as I processed her explanation.

"So… basically, I'm starting to act like you because your instincts and behavior are so dominant and overpowering?"

The more I thought about Ruad's behavior soaking into my psyche, the more I wondered what else had leaked over into my subconscious.

Maybe I'll start howling at the moon, I thought, chuckling, brushing deeper thoughts or concerns off with dry humor. Typical me.

Closing the door behind me, I looked at the vermillion wolf standing behind Barb's favorite blue recliner. Part of me wanted to have her sit in the chair and maybe even roll around on it, as if her size wouldn't break the thing. Barb is allergic to dogs. I smirked at that thought before returning to the previous discussion with Ruad.

"Geez, it's almost like I'm *your* familiar with how powerful you are in this pairing," I said, putting my hands on my hips.

"Being a familiar doesn't imply a ranking or weakness, Pup. A familiar is considered an equal with its caller, the one who begins the pact and bonding process. Tristan and I were equals in every way. You and I are not equals at the moment. You're practically a…"

142

"A pup," I sighed.

My familiar flashed a wolfish grin and said, "Now you're getting it."

After a second sigh, I heard Barb's loud ticking clock on the wall. In the kitchen, I listened to her crockpot bubbling. It smelled like she was making a chicken stew for tonight. If there was anything I missed about the woman who adopted me, it was her cooking. She was damn good at it.

Looking around the living room, I saw she still hadn't replaced the lamp I shattered. Good. For once, I should be the one to take something from her life, instead of the other way around.

White doilies still covered a long brown table by the door. Though without the lamp I'd smashed, they seemed a little odd and out of place.

I noticed Ruad looking down at the thin gray carpet her paws stood on top of.

"That carpeting is older than I am," I said.

I felt this squeezing sensation coming into my chest with every breath I took in this house. Maybe it was the potpourri Barb seemed to think came straight from the garden of Eden. Either way, my chest was getting tighter.

"Aoife?" Ruad said.

Taking shallow breaths, I struggled between a fiery rage and hate for Barb and anxiety over what'd happen if Barb walked around the kitchen corner. My pulse quickened, picturing her staring us down, the word 'vermin' racing from her lips. Then she'd look at Ruad with eyes of disgust, imagining my familiar as some sort of begging beast.

Right then I almost heard Barb call Abi a whore again. I began to grind my teeth, fear and rage bouncing back and forth like a metronome. Tick tick tick tick, fear, hate, fear, hate.

Perhaps the most worrying part of this thought chain was I didn't know how I'd react with all of Ruad's wolfish instincts coursing through me. I doubted I'd be able to stand here and take Barb's verbal and emotional abuse.

"Let's just get this over with," I muttered.

Ruad nudged me, trying to bring me back into reality. It sort of worked, enough for me to walk steadily toward the stairs in the living room corner.

My bedroom was the only one upstairs, and man did it get hot up there. We arrived at the top of the stairs and were greeted with a little landing that had three doors. To my right was a locked bathroom nobody used anymore. It used to be mine until Barb caught me having a little too much fun inside. So she locked it and told me to use the downstairs facilities from now on.

Joke's on her. I just started having sex with Abi.

The next door on the right led to my bedroom. Well, my old bedroom. And the only door on the left side had a narrow staircase inside that led up to the attic.

I spent a lot of time in this part of the house. It was either in my room of my own accord, or in the attic because I was being punished for some minute offense. It didn't matter if I told Barb I didn't want to get up and go to church on Sunday morning, or I got busted for putting a bag of shit in Jason Parker's locker at school for bullying Abi. Into the attic I went.

Staring at the silver attic doorknob, I began to sweat, just like eight-year-old me did when I was being punished during the summer. If the wasps didn't stress that kid out enough, being trapped in an unventilated room with no water for an hour would kick anxiety into overdrive.

Even now, I could hear her pounding on the door, crying and begging Barb to let her out.

"I'm sorry! I'm sorry! Please just open the door. I can't breathe!" she would scream.

Barb always seemed to know just when she was about to pass out and opened the door, letting cool air conditioning wash over her sweat-covered face.

My chest started to tighten again. That little girl was still in here somewhere. That little girl who was afraid of a frail, aging, and bitter woman. If the little girl was still inside, was the fear? Surely it was, right? Fear doesn't just vanish.

It doesn't matter that I've got all this raw nature magic coursing through me. I'm still afraid, I thought, staring at the wall for several seconds as dread filled me again.

A light chomp on my left hand.

"Aoife," Ruad called.

She hadn't hurt me, not really. As my pulse came back down, I shook my head.

Goddamn this house and that woman, I thought. I rubbed some sweat off my forehead.

"This woman who raised you... she was cruel," Ruad said.

144

She thumped into my thigh again and said, "Let's go into your bedroom to gather what you need so we can get out of here."

I just stood there for a moment, the sweat dripping down my brow and a wave of sadness washing over me.

"I had Tristan and Iris. I *had* a loving mother and father."

"Aoife, this isn't the time to go down this road," Ruad said.

"And, and… then they were taken away from me by Malachos. After that, I wound up with Barb and John. Mrs. Do As You're Told and Mr. Absentee. What did I do to deserve that, Ruad?" I asked, already starting to cry. "Was there some terrible thing I did as a two-year-old to…"

"Stop it," Ruad growled. "Nothing that happened to Tristan and Iris was your fault. Getting stuck with Barb and John wasn't your fault. I think the human expression is you were dealt a bad hand. Some people are in life. I'm sorry you've gone through so much, but the moment you start blaming yourself for what happened, Malachos wins. Do you understand?"

When I said nothing, Ruad nosed my chin up and looked me in the eyes.

"Do you understand?"

I slowly nodded, feeling like my insides had been replaced with a bag of dog shit.

Putting my arms around Ruad, I buried my face in her fur for what must have been the 100th time. It was beginning to be the only place I wanted to be anymore. After a minute, I took one last deep breath and stood up.

"Sorry, Ruad. I guess there's just a lot more pain in this place than I remembered," I muttered.

Ruad stood close and said, "I shouldn't be surprised, but, just like in nature, a place like this can hold tight a memory's essence, so long as the person who made the memory has deep enough emotional scarring. Do you want to come back later?"

"The trauma will still be here. My stuff might not be. In fact, I wouldn't be surprised if Barb already had my room gutted and turned it into a prayer den."

I opened the white door into my room and saw it was still as I left it. My wool coat was spread across the bed. Barb hadn't set one foot in here since I'd been thrown out. I couldn't even smell her in here.

There wasn't much to my room. I had a sliding closet door with a mirror on it. My bed was a twin with a simple purple comforter. No posters or wall decorations because they were a constant fight between Barb and I.

She was always hanging crucifixes in here, which I tore down. She wanted a cross in every room of the house, but I insisted this was my room, and I should have a say over what hung on my walls.

Yet whenever I tried to put posters up, one of Nightwish, another of *The Hunger Games,* Barb tore them down. So it ended up being a stalemate. Nothing would go on the walls.

Everything was a fight. Barb had given me a bunch of her old dresses to wear growing up, really awful gaudy things, mostly in beige. I tried to wear band T-shirts through high school, a real Hot Topic poster child. Abi had bought me a Lacuna Coil shirt for Christmas once. Barb confiscated it. No jeans with holes in them, either.

I eventually learned to leave most of my clothes at Abi's house and change there before school in the morning. I had to get up earlier, but it was also more time I was away from Barb. Always a plus.

Still, I had a few things here I wanted to take to the greenhouse. There was my Within Temptation backpack. I'm not sure why Barb hadn't thrown this out. Oh, that's right. She tried. I threatened to break her arm. Heh. Good times.

I had some socks with black cats on them, my lucky thong, and a couple Eluveitie shirts I'd managed to hide from Barb in the back corner of my closet shelf, all gifts from Abi. I had a couple bras, one red and the other black I tossed in the backpack.

And then my eyes came to rest on my brown dresser. Sitting on top of it was a cloth violin case, black on the outside and gray on the inside.

Walking over, I put my hand on it and smiled. Abi had worked an entire summer waiting tables at Big Jimmy's Grill on Dickson Street to buy this for me. She hated the job so much, and I kept asking her why she stayed.

On our second anniversary I found out why. She'd been making good tip money there and saved all of it to buy me a violin of my own.

I'd been using a hand-me-down from Barb. And although it was in perfectly fine condition, I hated it because it was hers.

"What's in there?" Ruad asked.

"My violin," I said.

"I didn't know you played," Ruad said.

"I never really wanted to. Should you be forced to do something just because you're good at it?"

"Barb forced you to play?"

I nodded.

"She learned to play as a girl. And though she hasn't played in decades, Barb wanted me to learn so she could show me off to her friends at church. Look at the civilized little Eve. See? She isn't the monstrous brat I act like she is. No, she's refined, a good little girl just like her mother," I said, gagging.

"Did you ever try to quit?" Ruad asked.

I opened the case and stared at Abi's gift.

"Sure I did. But Barb found me an instructor that was somehow more cruel than she was. If I acted out, that was more time I got to spend in the attic. And unfortunately for myself, I had great ears and nimble fingers. Maybe even a little bit of talent. Once Barb found that out, there was no way she was going to let me quit," I said. "And it wasn't enough that I played the violin, I had to play it her way, always with the church hymns. I wanted to be more Emilie Autumn or Lindsey Stirling if I had to play. But Barb wanted someone to accompany the pianist each Sunday morning. How I came to hate songs like 'As The Deer' and 'It Is Well.'"

The violin was a place where Barb had control, and there wasn't anything I could really do about it. I played on her violin with lessons she paid for.

"I just hate seeing you despise something you have such a talent for," Abi had told me on so many occasions when I'd stayed the night at her house.

Then she found a loophole. She worked all summer getting her ass slapped and called everything from "honey" to "sweet cheeks," so she could save up and buy me my own violin.

I looked at it, the Alessandro Verona Master Art violin, staring right back at me with its heavily shaded varnish. I cried when she gave it to me. I almost didn't accept it until I remembered an important lesson Barb's father had once taught me. You never deprive someone the opportunity to give you a gift. When it comes to gift giving, there's a unique joy in handing someone a present and watching them unwrap it.

Watching their eyes light up as they mouth the words, "No way." There's just nothing like it. So what did I do? I just cried. It took me two days before I could finally work up enough nerve to play the thing.

147

One night under the full moon, I had Abi meet me at one of the local parks. When she showed up, I had candles lit, and I played for her, to really show my gratitude. What else could you do for someone who bought you a $2,000 violin?

I played the hell out of it for her, every non-church song I knew, even a rendition of "Be Our Guest," from her favorite movie of all time. That really made her smile.

"Aoife?" Ruad asked, probably another couple seconds away from nibbling on my fingers again.

I didn't answer right away. Seeing the violin brought Abi to the forefront of my mind. And she was doing her thing, lifting me back to the surface.

I smiled as I reached down to pack up the violin and bow.

"I'm okay, Ruad. I've got everything I need."

The wolf nodded. "Okay. Ready to go?"

Just as I was about to answer, I heard a car pull up outside.

"Dammit," I said, checking the time on my phone. "She's not supposed to be back for another hour. There's no way her group would cut their Bible study short."

And she'd never miss the gossip session with her friends afterward. That'd eat up another 20 minutes, otherwise known as the southern goodbye. Inch closer to the door, but keep facing your friends and chatting about what Cathy did last week and how disappointed everyone was with her moral failing.

I didn't want to face Barb in the house. No, I couldn't, so I slung the violin case strap over my right shoulder. It sat on top of my Within Temptation backpack as I walked down the stairs and exited to the porch.

Barb was standing on the front lawn about five feet from me as I leaned against the rail I'd broken last time I left here.

She was wearing a red and gold quarter length shirt with a matching red skirt that went down to her ankles. The black heels she sported looked like they'd be a pain in the ass to stand in the grass with, but Barb managed okay with her cloven hooves.

I wanted to pretend like I was cool enough to say things like that in front of her, but attic Aoife was back. That terrified little girl locked in the suffocating crawlspace had returned, and she didn't have magic, a talking wolf, or a fey guardian. All she could do was cower.

Barb glanced down at Ruad, her eyes widening at the shaggy

vermillion wolf. Still, she kept her calm. If she didn't consider it such a sinful vice, she'd have made an excellent poker player.

"Do I want to know what you and that animal were doing in my house, Eve?" she asked, taking the first shot.

My chest tightened again, and I felt a volatile mix of rage and fear wash over me. I tightened my right fist until I thought my fingers would snap. I was starting to sweat. I didn't think it was possible to simultaneously want to tear her limb from limb and run away screaming as loud as I could out of fear. The polarity of those emotions was tearing me in two.

But I could feel feral Aoife start to exert some influence from my mind forest as well. So I was left with a growing rage fed by loathing and fear of this oppressive woman before me, the one who dared to call herself my mother.

"Her name is Ruad. And while we're on names," I said, holding up my locket as high as it would go while still attached to my neck. "My name isn't Eve. It's Aoife Fey O'Connell. Surely you remember this?"

"Where in the world did you find that thing?" she asked.

"Not important. What is important is how you lied to me my whole life. I'm not your daughter, Barb, never have been. My parents are Tristan and Iris O'Connell. My necklace has my name carved into it, but you threw this away before I could find out about them," I said, jabbing a finger at her.

Barb stood motionless on the lawn. She said nothing. Then she said, "What are you doing breaking into my house, Eve?"

"Don't call me that, hag. It's Aoife. The previous name was your first attempt at erasing my past and making me your obedient little clone. Your house is fine. I just came to grab a few things and be on my way. Honestly, I'm surprised you'd leave your Bible meeting to come back and heckle me," I said.

"Well when I got a notification from the new security system that someone was breaking in, I didn't really have much choice. I didn't think I'd find my daughter-turned-robber when I showed up," Barb said.

I crossed my arms, trying to swallow the rage that built every time she called me her daughter.

"But I'm not your daughter, Barb. You saying I am doesn't make it any more true," I said.

"You've been my daughter since that social worker called to tell me about a baby that was dropped off at a fire station," Barb said.

Shaking my head, I realized maybe this was a final opportunity to do something other than be enraged or saddened at Barb. Perhaps I needed to learn more about what led up to my adoption before I found closure. Glossing over my adoption wasn't doing me any good.

"What happened when you got that call?" I asked, trying to soften my voice a little bit. I don't know if I succeeded.

Barb squinted at me, probably trying to figure out if I was stalling for some reason. But that didn't make any sense because I already had everything I wanted. So she sighed and relented, which surprised me.

"Your father and I weren't able to have children, and I always wanted to be a mother. The truth is, with John on the road so much playing his music, the house was pretty quiet. So when I got the call about taking you in, I figured it was a gift from God. I'd finally have the child I always wanted, and I figured that surely your father would sense his newfound responsibilities and stay home," Barb said.

I didn't know how to respond to what she was telling me. So I just kept listening. And the more she talked, the more bitter Barb seemed to grow. It was as though she regretted revisiting these memories again after so many years, regretted bringing them up to me now. Her voice grew lower and more terse.

"When I saw you and learned we were finally getting a daughter, I was ecstatic. I felt like Sarah, finally getting the child I'd prayed for all those years. I had plans to nurture you. As you grew, John chose to continue traveling with his band. But that was okay because I finally had a friend in this big empty house. I spent hours dreaming of the days you'd start talking so I could teach you to grow into the perfect girl," she said, taking her eyes off me and looking at the lawn, dead and brown as our relationship.

"Your definition of perfect is what ruined us, Barb. You were so damn busy daydreaming about what you wanted me to be that you didn't pause for one moment to see who I actually was. You started scraping away pieces of me you didn't like on day one, throwing away my locket and name," I said.

Barb's eyes found mine again, and she loaded a dart of poison into her glare.

"Having high expectations isn't a sin, Eve. But you actively choosing to disappoint me again and again sure is. I'm so frustrated in what you've become," she said.

I scoffed and shook my head as a new epiphany dawned on me. I'd spent so much of my life trying to balance this impossible equation, not giving up my identity while trying to keep Barb happy. And that brought endless stress, guilt, and fear into my life.

But I didn't have to worry about those expectations anymore. I wasn't Barb's daughter that had to strive for perfection. And she wasn't my mother that could demand it. In a sense, that was more freeing than I imagined.

"The name's Aoife, Barb. Try to keep up. And you know what? I think I see you for who you really are. You're not some scary boogeyman. You're just a bitter, lonely woman," I said.

The woman who adopted me let loose as dirty a frown as she could muster and said, "Are you any different?"

I might have started that way the night she kicked me out, but I realized something. Looking down at my pendant and then Ruad, I smiled.

"I'm not alone, Barb. I have a family. And I've got a girlfriend who loves and accepts me for who I am. Abi's mother was always better to me than you were. You spent all those years trying to emotionally pound me into becoming like you. In spite of all that, I've learned who I was, who I am now, and who I want to become."

Barb was silent now, still glowering at me.

"But you, Barb? You'll always be alone, entombed in that big empty house, and married to a man who never really wanted to share his life with you. You'll never change," I said.

I thought I saw a tear forming in her left eye, but if it was really there, it was of the crocodile variety. Besides, it wasn't my responsibility to care about how she felt or what she expected of me anymore. I was free. Barb made no move to stop me as I walked past her. I could hear her teeth grinding, but my former guardian said not a word, just continued to stare a hole into the back of my head.

It wasn't that I wanted Barb to say something, but the lack of words surprised me. This was our closure, no? Would I come to regret her lack of goodbye or achieving an epiphany?

Fuck it, I thought. *That's another problem for another day. I've done enough emotional exploration today.*

So I walked down the driveway, over to the bus stop, and went back to the greenhouse with Ruad in tow.

* * *

When I got inside and set my stuff down, I sat down on the floor and sighed. Today had been emotionally exhausting, and I was relieved it was over. I was glad to be home with my family.

My pendant glowed green, and Adrienn flew out. They hovered in front of my face just smiling, so I giggled and said, "What?"

The fey spoke up, saying, "I just wanted you to know how proud I am of you for finally confronting Barb over all the abuse. And you did it without screaming or punching her. You did great."

I looked down at the dirt against the greenhouse wall, and a small smile spread across my smile. It hadn't occurred to me just how big a thing it was to have closure. But there was relief growing in my chest.

"The fey's right, Pup. You did do good today," Ruad said.

I smiled even bigger now. Maybe I was getting ready to tear up just a little bit. Who knows?

"The truth is, Pup, hearing you talk to Barb about the pain you've endured made me take a second look at my own history after the clan was killed. When I finally tracked you down and saw you'd been taken in by that woman, I was heartbroken. I thought my last chance to avoid a life of isolation had been taken from me. And that bitterness weighed me down for the next 17 years. I got used to running from my feelings and accepted that I'd be alone forever.

"But you changed that, Pup. You came back into my life and made me realize how much I missed Tristan and Iris and how badly I needed you.

"I was in bad shape. But now? I realize I was so lonely I might have even come close to missing Adrienn," Ruad said, chuckling at that last part.

The fey just shook their head and landed on the edge of Ruad's snout.

"Maybe I came close to missing you, too, living with Odessa all those years," they said.

Before Ruad could scoff, I brought all of us in for a tight hug. This was my family now, and I was more than happy with that.

I closed my eyes and cherished this moment.

Things might not be the same as they would have been with Tristan and Iris, but after all these years, I think I can feel their love through Adrienn and Ruad, I thought, closing my eyes.

When I finally broke the hug, I saw the violin again.

"Hey, Adrienn?"

"What can I do for you, Aoife?" they asked, hovering in front of my eyes.

I smiled and said, "Actually, it's the other way around. You once said Tristan's singing made you really happy. And while I can't sing to save my life, I did promise to play the violin for you anytime you wanted."

Adrienn smiled and flew down onto Ruad's head, sitting on top of my familiar. Ruad growled but to my astonishment, the fey shushed her and said the show was about to begin.

"This one is called Silver Spring. It was one of the first songs I wrote after Abi gave me this violin," I said quietly.

And then I played for them, as best I could. It'd been a couple weeks since my fingers had held a bow, but about 30 seconds in, they found their groove. I made the violin my own again.

As my fingers grew more nimble, I swam through the complex melody and brought the violin's brilliant tone into focus.

I closed my eyes and finished the last repeat of the melody.

When I was done, Adrienn flew up into the air and clapped. They seemed legitimately happy with my performance that, in any other setting, would have just been a warm-up.

The fey actually scolded Ruad and said, "Compliment her playing, wolf! I know you're an animal, but surely can appreciate…"

Adrienn didn't get to finish that sentence because Ruad ate them. She wasn't taking any shit from a creature the size of a butterfly.

I giggled and put the violin back, zipping up my case.

"Ruad, would you spit out my fey guardian, please?"

"They aren't much of a guardian if they get caught so easily," Ruad said without parting her teeth. That wolfish grin returned to her.

"You made your point," I said, holding my left hand just under her chin. "Please."

Ruad rolled her eyes and spit the fey into my hand. They looked miserable and powerless, covered in saliva.

After I dried them off with my shirt, Adrienn turned and stuck their tongue out at Ruad. And while I would have continued watching their antics, something in the window drew my eye.

The window was covered in vines that I knew for a fact hadn't been there before. Furthermore, the vines looked like they were about to flower.

Adrienn must have realized I'd gone silent and followed my gaze.

"Wow. You know, when Tristan used to sing in this greenhouse, some of the plants would grow to twice their size. Others would dance their leaves with his beat. It was really amusing to watch," the fey said.

I shook my head.

"I don't understand. I didn't actively expend any magic. I didn't say any special words. There was none of my blood on the window. What happened?" I asked.

"There's lots more to magic than blood and words, Pup."

"You might not have felt any magic leave your body, but it went into the music, some at least. And the vines responded to that because you're a druid. Magic can pop into any act of passion, cooking, writing, music, etc. It's all an expression of the divine part of the human soul," Adrienn said.

"Open a window, and get some air, Adrienn. Good grief," Ruad said. I snickered.

We sat around talking for the rest of the night until sleep eventually took us. And man did I feel like I'd earned the sleep I was about to enjoy after all the emotional damage I'd worked through today. It didn't take me even five minutes for me to drift off into slumber.

Chapter Twelve

Ruad and I were snuggled up together enjoying a peaceful morning. It was my favorite part about having a familiar so far. Yeah sure, the magic was neat. Transforming felt like nothing I'd ever experienced before. Having the raw power and strength flow through me, the heightened senses, all of it was amazing.

But being curled up in a ball with Ruad for eight hours a night and recharging my batteries? Smelling like dog the next morning was worth it, and if I was being entirely honest, I'd grown to love that smell.

Since Ruad was a freaking giant compared to me, I wondered how big of a bed Tristan and Iris had to share with her. Did my dad sleep curled up with his familiar like I did? I suppose I could just ask her, but I was just so comfy, that is until I heard a small pop and a cry of pain outside my greenhouse.

I bolted awake and was on my feet with Ruad somehow ahead of me.

"You're like twice my size. How did you jump up ahead of me and get out front?"

"I'm running out of ways to say, 'I'm better than you at this,' Pup," Ruad said.

We both then turned our attention outside, where someone was crying for help. It sounded like a man around my age.

A few days ago, Ruad and I would have been able to just look out the glass wall since this was a greenhouse. But I'd brought in some wild trees and shrubs, replanted them inside and used my magic to grow them up so their large leaves and branches covered all the windows.

I left openings at the top so I could stare at the stars with Ruad and Adrienn.

Walking toward the front door, I opened it and found a few scattered glowing runes on the ground around the greenhouse. These were ones my father had installed for protection. They were glowing red.

155

Beyond the runes, I saw a man with short black hair struggling in the dirt tangled in white and brown roots that had shot out of the cracked earth.

"Help me! Please!" He yelled.

His olive eyes showed panic, and I didn't blame him. I was just a tad more used to this druidic magic than he was.

I walked over by him. The runes glowed green and then slowly died as I walked over them. The roots didn't attack me.

Putting my hands on my hips, I stood over the man and said, "What do we have here?"

He looked me over in my hastily-thrown on green robe, and I saw he was some kind of park ranger judging by his uniform. Crap. Did he come to evict me from my home? Because losing one was traumatic enough for a college girl.

"The more you try to free yourself, the tighter they'll grow." I said.

"Can you please get me out of here?" he shrieked.

"Let's start with who you are and why you're here first, because the last person to show up at my home kidnapped my girlfriend," I said, crossing my arms.

Ruad looked over at me and said, "Actually, that was an illusion, remember?"

"Whose side are you on? He didn't have to know that!" I said.

Then I did a double take and said, "And why are you talking in front of another person? Ignore her. I've just been throwing my voice to make it look like my wolf is talking."

The park ranger gave me a frustrated look because he was still obviously tangled in roots on the ground and a talking wolf was the least of his concerns.

"Richard has been here before, Pup. You can let him go," my familiar said, calmly.

I looked over at her and raised an eyebrow.

This man was here before? I thought.

"His name is Richard Choi. His father was friends with Iris," Ruad said.

She wasn't lying. This man knew my mother? Somehow I'd forgotten that my parents were actual human beings who had social contact with other people across the region. Why did it shock me that other people would have met them and remembered them? Iris and

Tristan were memories to me, but other people would recall them if asked, I'm sure. It wasn't like Malachos had killed everyone they'd ever spoken with.

I walked over, touched one of the roots and closed my eyes to concentrate. I sent my magic down into the earth around them, and they started to unravel, letting Richard loose.

He exhaled a sigh of relief, and for the first time I got a good look at him when he wasn't thrashing about on the ground. Richard was a lean man, very tall, with a warm fawn skin tone. His brown eyes swept the ground for more roots around him. The park ranger was clean shaven and had a small burn on the right side of his neck.

I offered him a hand and helped him up. He took it and thanked me.

As he brushed some of the dirt off his outfit, I crossed my arms again.

"So... Richard Choi. You knew Iris?" I asked.

"Yes. My father brought me here once when I was about four or five. I remember her riding back to the park with us and helping my father with a problem. I remembered seeing your wolf here, but I didn't know she could talk," Richard said, kneeling and holding a hand out to pet Ruad.

I lightly kicked his hand to the side with my knee and said, "Hey, my familiar, not a family dog. And nobody touches her but me."

"Of course. I apologize," he said, standing back up.

The park ranger didn't look to be more than a few years older than me. Maybe he was fresh out of college.

"What are you doing here, Richard?" I asked.

"I have a problem, and it's the kind my father told me Iris always solved for him," Richard said.

What kind of problem would Mom solve for his father? I thought.

"Why don't you come inside and explain it to me?" I said, and we walked into the greenhouse.

Richard stepped over the runes with some caution, looking down at the ground.

We went inside and sat down on some patio furniture I had snatched from Goodwill. I had a little round metal table with a glass top and two green metal folding chairs.

"Wait here," I said as he sat down.

Then I walked over toward the bedroomish corner of the greenhouse, where I'd brought in a couple room dividers from the local

Salvation Army. They were simple brown dividers, wood and a thin white paper to create the illusion of little opaque windows.

I went behind the dividers and put on a pair of black jeans and a red hoodie with a cardinal on the front.

Then I took my toothbrush, some toothpaste, a rag and walked toward the front door.

"I'll be right back," I said, walking out to the lake.

Ruad followed me and sat down next to a bush while I performed a very minor water purification spell on the lake's surface. It would clear the water from anything harmful to my system for around a 10-12 foot radius around my little island.

Then I brushed my teeth, spitting into the bush next to Ruad.

"Watch it, Pup," she said, showing a little fang.

"Oops, sorry," I said, grinning.

Before I could react, she had body slammed me, and I was falling backward into the lake. The frigid December lake.

Then at the last second, she sank her teeth into my hoodie and pulled me back up.

"Oops, sorry," she said, grinning.

I didn't even dignify her actions with a reply.

I washed my face with a rag that was cold enough I'd swear I now knew what the surface of Neptune felt like.

Then, Ruad and I headed back inside.

We walked in, and I tossed the rag into a little black foldable hamper by my bed. I'd snagged all sorts of goodies from local thrift stores.

Then I walked over to a little green card table I'd set up and placed a metal percolator on top of a little butane stove, turning a nozzle until a little blue flame appeared on the bottom. Inside the percolator I dumped some coffee grounds and water I'd fetched from the lake.

I pulled out a couple coffee mugs, one with Minnie Mouse on it and another with an X-Wing fighter. Who says this greenhouse lacked class?

Richard glanced around the greenhouse and asked, "How do you keep it so warm in here? I assume you don't have power out here."

I pointed to a white stone birdbath in the corner opposite my bed. I'd filled it with water a few days ago and used my magic (along with a seed Sabrina let me steal from the shop) to grow a sacred lotus extra big. Adrienn had also shown me how to use my magic to tweak the plant a little bit.

Richard looked over the plant with its upward purple leaves surrounding a yellow stamen.

"A flower is making it warm in here?" he asked.

"Nelumbo nucifera to be exact. And yes, it's warming the whole room. You see, the sacred lotus is a pretty neat plant. It already has the ability to produce some heat. Well, I just used some magic to dial its heat producing ability up quite a bit and warm the room. Boom. Biodiverse thermostat," I said.

He looked at the plant in disbelief for a moment before glancing back at me.

"Wow. You really are a druid, aren't you?" he asked.

"I'm figuring it out," I said.

Richard looked down at the table and asked, "So... how did you know Iris?"

Glancing over at Ruad, I sighed. How did I know her? Well she'd brought me into the world. Was there any more intimate way to know a person?

"She was my mother," I said, getting up to pour us both some coffee. Hope Richard liked his black.

Was... as in, she's not around anymore because some bastard killed my entire clan, I thought, bitterly. Oh good. My mental process was already off to a positive start for the day.

Richard looked down at the ground and said, "I'm sorry for your loss. My father went to the funeral for your parents and I think the other clan members."

A funeral I didn't know about because Barb snatched my necklace away and didn't even try to find out who my parents were, I thought.

This wasn't the conversation I wanted to have about Iris. So I changed the topic.

"If you knew my mother and father were dead, why did you come here today?" I asked.

The park ranger met my eyes again and took a deep breath. Then he threw his hands up in the air and said, "I'm out of options. Iris always helped my father if there was a supernatural predator in the park that was endangering folks. For decades, dad said, the O'Connell pack kept monsters in the woods under control. I guess I hoped one of them might still be around to help this next generation park ranger."

After I took a drink of my coffee, I looked over at Ruad, and thanks

159

to our shared connection, she knew exactly what I wanted from her... verification.

"He's telling the truth. His father was a park ranger who met with Iris multiple times. And he's also right about the O'Connell clan keeping people safe in the woods. It's part of what we did."

Nodding, I returned my gaze to Richard. He took a sip of his drink, and to his credit, didn't grimace.

"Your father sent you to this place?" I asked.

"No, he's retired. He came here from South Korea with my mother in the '60s and got a job as a park ranger at Hobbs State Park. He put in almost 50 years, so I think he's earned an easy retirement. But I always remembered the stories he told about Iris and the rest of your clan, especially when your mom slaughtered the griffin that killed a camper," he said.

Ruad smiled.

"Oh yeah, that's a pretty good one, actually."

I wished I could have been there to see Mom in action taking the beast down. Maybe Ruad could tell me about it sometime.

"So my parents... they were, what? Monster hunters?"

Ruad shook her head.

"Not at all. Tristan and Iris were druids, Pup. Their job was all about balance, balance of nature and folks in nature. They helped out mythical creatures and regular humans whenever the two would come into conflict. And they did that for a pretty good chunk of the Ozark Natural Forest in Arkansas. The whole clan did. It was kind of a sacred duty of sorts for the couple dozen of us."

I smiled at that. There was a small sense of pride in my heart. I was part of something bigger than myself, people who worked to protect something. And Malachos had taken that protection away from the people of Northwest Arkansas. Now someone had gotten hurt or killed because of it.

"Tristan and Iris managed this place like a territory, Pup. Mythical creatures that caused trouble out here in the wilderness answered to them. And when Iris brought forth judgment on a creature, it was beautiful, like a work of art," Ruad said.

I clenched my fist and looked over at Richard.

"What did you need help with? As Iris' daughter, it's my duty to assist in any way I can."

Richard smiled for the first time since he arrived and took a longer drink. Ruad said nothing and stared at me. If she was opposed to this, she would have said so outright instead of staring.

I began to feel pressure building in my heart. Was this what O'Connell pride felt like? The fact there was a unique need my parents and clan filled, and it was necessary now more than ever?

Of course, there was fury, too. Whatever situation Richard needed help with was partially on Malachos for taking the forest protectors away. I closed my eyes and took a deep breath, trying to push feral Aoife back down, my fingers twitching a little. She'd kill anything that could remotely be connected to Malachos, no matter how thin the thread.

Richard reached into his coat pocket and pulled out a little Polaroid square photo. I'd be a little more surprised he had one of these, but they'd come back in popularity lately. Retro is always cool sooner or later, I suppose.

Looking down in the center of the photo, I saw a little boy who looked to be about 11 or 12. He had a little fauxhawk with dirty blond hair and wore a blue soccer jersey. In a few more years, I wagered he'd grow up to be a real heartbreaker. His eyes were the same shade of aqua blue as his jersey.

The way he was holding the camera, I could tell it was a selfie. He was up high in a tree and had the photo angled down to show how far up he'd climbed. Adventurous scamp.

Oh yeah, people are going to love him, I thought.

"Who is this?" I asked.

Richard looked down at the photo and said, "Ashton Bizbee. Friends called him Abz for short. He and his father went camping three days ago up north of War Eagle. It was supposed to be an overnight thing.

When they didn't check in, Mrs. Bizbee called it in as a missing persons case. I was part of a search party that just yesterday found Mr. Bizbee's body.

Now Richard pulled out his smartphone and showed me a photograph that almost made me want to spit out the coffee I'd just finished.

It looked like a shriveled up husk of a man. The skin was translucent, and he was curled into a little ball without any hair or nails.

"We found him in some bushes surrounded by a ball of webbing. The coroner has no idea what happened. That's why he's delayed a report. Same with the Benton County sheriff. The local television stations and newspapers have no idea the body was found.

Staring at the photograph, I began to wonder about what horrible thing could have done this. I had a feeling Richard was about to tell me.

"We haven't found a body for Ashton, which makes me think he's still alive. They wouldn't discard food," he said.

"What wouldn't discard food?" I asked, scowling.

Richard looked at Ruad and then to me.

"I don't know the name for them," the park ranger said.

Ruad spoke up and said, "They're spiders, just not like the ones of this world. They're from the Fey Realm. Adrienn should know about them."

With a flash of green light, Adrienn flew out of my pendant and appeared on the table. Richard flinched at the appearance of my guardian.

"Hey there, Adrienn. What can you tell us about spiders from the Fey Realm?"

They looked down at the corpse photo on the phone and then up at me with eyes of fear.

"Aoife, you're not ready," they said. "Not for something like this."

I sighed and said, "Ruad will have my back. And there's not really any choice here. They've got a little boy."

Adrienn looked down at the table, over to the picture of the boy.

"Damn it," they said. It was the first time I'd ever heard them swear. I raised an eyebrow.

"Please," I said.

The fey shook their head and said, "Ruad, you really want her to go up against these things? They're big, and they're nasty. And it won't just be one. Spiders of my realm always hunt in swarms of three."

The wolf looked over at the photograph and said, "Pup isn't going to stop now that she knows this is what Iris and Tristan did. So either she'll go alone without our permission, or she'll go with us at her side. I like her odds better if I'm by her side. Don't you?"

The green-haired fey shook their head.

"I don't like any kind of odds when Aoife is dealing with those," Adrienn said, crossing their arms. "But you both seem determined, and being a few inches tall, my options to restrict you are practically nonexistent."

Richard hadn't said a word. The park ranger was surprised by

Adrienn's sudden appearance, yet respectful enough to wait for an introduction.

I caught his glance and said, "Oh. Should have done this after I pulled those roots off you. I'm Aoife. My familiar is Ruad. And this is my fey guardian Adrienn."

The park ranger looked down at Adrienn and said, "I'm Richard. Nice to meet you."

The fey looked up at him for a moment and said, "My, you have gotten taller. It's been a long time. I don't think you saw me when you came out here with your father."

"I guess not," Richard said. "But I'm grateful for whatever information you can provide. I'm sure Ashton's mother would be, too."

Looking down at the corpse photo on Richard's phone once again, Adrienn nodded and said, "Spiders from my realm are six to eight feet tall and weigh around 300 pounds. Their bodies are a mix of brown and orange. Their fangs allow them to spit acid that they usually inject into their victims when draining."

"Webs?" Ruad asked.

"Not as much as you'd think. These things prefer to wait inside the tops of trees and drop down on their victims to attack. The webbing is usually just for food storage. It's typically not used offensively," Adrienn said.

Richard took his phone back and finished his coffee.

"How do we find the kid?" Ruad asked.

Looking up at the park ranger, I asked, "Do you have something of Ashton's?"

"We found his camera at their campsite," he said.

I nodded.

"You got it with you?"

"Back at my jeep in a plastic bag," he said.

Ruad put two and two together.

"Sniff him out. Not a bad idea, Pup. And that was your first instinct, too. You're getting more wolf in you every day. I love it."

I smiled.

"Enough for you to stop calling me Pup?"

Ruad laughed and said, "Oh no, Pup. That's not determined by how much wolf you have in you. It's about how long you've had wolf in you. You're just days in. It's going to be a while."

That brought a frown and a quick eye roll.

"Hey Adrienn, how did these spiders even get here if they're from the Fey Realm?" I asked.

The fey flew up toward me and hovered in front of my eyes.

"My guess? Some sort of gateway up near Eureka Springs," they said.

I frowned.

"Gateway?"

Ruad nodded and said, "Eureka is famous for its mystical water, dozens of springs scattered all through those mountains and even under the city itself. If the conditions are right, some of those springs act as gateways to other worlds. It could be a portal opens for a whole season, under a meteor shower, all sorts of stuff. Eureka Springs is a funny place."

I shook my head. I was learning something new about this magical world that hid in plain sight every day.

"Eureka Springs sounds like it needs somebody watching it at all times if that's the case," I muttered.

Adrienn shrugged and went back into my necklace. Then I turned toward Richard.

"Okay, let's get going. I assume you'll drive us up to the park?" I asked.

Richard nodded as I pulled out my phone and sent a quick text message. Then we were off, heading to Hobbs State Park.

We parked near the beginning of the Pigeon Roost trail, and Richard hopped out acting like he was going with us. I put my hand up and said, "Where do you think you're going?"

He frowned and pulled out a handgun.

"To kill giant spiders," he said, making sure the safety was on.

I shook my head as Ruad came around the vehicle next to us.

"Richard, I can't protect you and rescue Ashton," I said.

He frowned.

"This is my park, and I brought you the case. I won't need protecting," he said. "You'll just get lost without me."

I crossed my arms.

"Can you use nature magic or move at superhuman speeds, Richard?" I asked.

His frown deepened.

"Can you do this?" I asked before uttering, "Athrú mac tíre."

Energy swirled around me, sending dust and rocks scattering everywhere. Richard's jacket fluttered about while he covered his face. When he put his hands down, I was in my wolf form, enhanced senses telling me all kinds of things about the surrounding park.

I could hear people hiking a quarter mile east of us. To our north, three, no four doe walked through some bushes, feeding. Richard's heartbeat was above average, and I could tell he was still angry at the thought of being left behind. Though, to be honest, I should have been able to tell that without enhanced senses.

He looked me up and down as I placed my shoes in his vehicle.

"I'll be back for those," I said, feeling cold dirt under my feet.

"So I can't do any of those. I still know the entire park better than either of you," he said.

I shook my head.

"I doubt that. Ruad's been wandering the Boston Mountains since my parents died. I'd be willing to bet she's spent plenty of time around Beaver Lake," I said, looking down at her.

Suddenly I felt Ruad's annoyance beginning to peak. She was tired of our bickering.

"Richard, I can't protect both you and Pup. You're staying here. We'll go fetch the boy," she said.

"Exactly… Wait, no. That's not what I meant," I said, putting my claws on my hips and scowling at her.

Richard smirked and said, "I'll be waiting here then. Call if he needs medical attention."

The park ranger then reached into his jeep and pulled out one of those Polaroid camera newer models they'd released in the last year or two. It was colorful, with plenty of blue and red on it. The camera was in a Ziplock bag. He opened it and held it down to Ruad to sniff. She did so, memorizing Ashton's scent.

He started to put the camera away when I cleared my throat and frowned at him.

"Oh… right. Sorry, Aoife. I guess I didn't take into account you being a werewolf and…"

Both Ruad and I barked at him, "Druid, not a werewolf!"

He flinched and pushed his back to the jeep, zipping the baggie after I'd finished sniffing it.

It was strange realizing each human had their own individualized scent. Most folks just smell like… whatever they're wearing, deodorant, perfume, cologne, etc. But underneath that, each body has an intrinsic odor I couldn't really put into words.

When I had Ashton's scent memorized, which was really cool to experience, I couldn't compare it to other smells. It wasn't like I was smelling walnuts or cedar chips. It was just a human scent. What do humans smell like? Other humans, I guess. They don't smell like those doe from earlier, nor the badger to our south. I had a scent, and it was Ashton's. Nobody else's.

My eyes met with Richard's, and he said, "It's unreal, Aoife. The girl that rode in my jeep on the way here is gone. Now there's a wolf in girl's clothing standing before me. And you look ready to hunt. It's unnerving."

Without giving his words much thought, I nodded, and then Ruad and I took off running north through the trees at a speed that showed Richard he wouldn't have been able to keep up with us. Once we were pretty deep into the trees, we stopped and sniffed the air. Some hikers were nearby, but they wouldn't see us. We were careful.

Ruad looked over at me, and then we took off running again, chasing a scent to the north. There weren't any words that needed to be spoken between us. She was the leader. I matched her pace. Later, it would occur to me just how in sync we were, both on a scent tracing through trees and hills at a brisk pace.

I knew she would turn left before she did it. So I was ready when the turn came. We stopped to sniff at a mushroom or two that Ashton must have lingered over. And then we came to the campsite.

We leapt out of the trees and into a clearing, only to be greeted by two green tents with blue rain tarps above them. One tent was still standing, and the other was torn up a bit. The spiders were not mindless beasts. They appeared to have a scary amount of accuracy to their movements based on the tracks and minor campsite damage.

I walked over to where their fire had been and found some foil and ash, even some sticks they'd cooked hot dogs on a couple nights ago.

"They were awake when they were attacked," Ruad said.

I nodded as she pieced together the scene. Richard's scent was intermingled with the campsite, as well as other humans that I assumed made up a small search party.

Sniffing some moss on a nearby fallen log, I realized Ashton's trail headed further north, while what I assumed was his father's headed south.

They split up? No, that can't be right, I thought. Then it hit me.

"Ruad, I think Ashton's father told him to run while he tried to hold the spiders off. The boy's trail heads north."

My familiar locked eyes with me and said, "All that's north is Beaver Lake."

"What if he didn't know that?" I asked.

The wolf nodded, and we were off again. She paused to sniff at a patch of clovers. He definitely came this way.

And then we arrived at the lake's edge. Murky grayish surface water greeted us. The water reflected a cloudy sky above. It was about 500 feet across to the next shore and nowhere the boy could run.

We looked around, and I found a small shoe print in the mud partially underwater. Sniffing a few smooth stones around me, I noted it was Ashton's. But I also smelled the spiders.

"He hesitated here when he got to the water's edge, unsure of whether to go left or right," Ruad said, looking around.

The red wolf came upon a large broken branch, still partially connected to an oak tree. She sniffed it.

"One of the spiders got the boy here, came down out of this tree to snatch him."

I looked over at her and then at the broken branch.

"Where did it take him, though? It would have carried him up into the trees, right? Should we shift our search up about 20 feet?" I asked.

Ruad shook her head.

"We'll be right where the spiders want us then. They'll feel our vibrations in the trees before we see them and have the advantage," Ruad said.

I rubbed my chin for a moment looking out over the water where a largemouth bass jumped a few inches out of the lake before splashing back down.

"If we can't smell the boy along the ground anymore, then we need to change up our game. He's up in a tree somewhere in a spider nest. Most of the trees are bare this time of year, except for one kind," I said.

Ruad nodded.

"Good thinking, Pup. We need to scour the area for the biggest patch of evergreen trees and then flush the spiders out. On the ride over here,

Adrienn said the Fey Realm spiders were nocturnal. So they shouldn't see us coming," Ruad said.

It suddenly made sense why the search party didn't find Ashton. He's up in a tree somewhere, I thought.

We moved west searching through the trees, trying to find a probable nesting site. It took us another half hour of back and forth, but half a mile southwest, we finally came upon a big collection of evergreens right next to each other, branches intermingled and everything.

They were about 50 feet tall at their highest point and 30 at their shortest. Blue-green needles obscured our vision. We cautiously sniffed around lower parts of the surrounding trees until we caught an odor that smelled a little like old truck tires. It was simultaneously earthy and oily, and it took some real restraint not to gag. The odor undoubtedly came from fey arachnids.

"Just like Adrienn told us. I'm detecting three odors for the spiders," Ruad said.

I looked at the clump of trees. It really was a perfect hiding spot. Though fortunately for us, winter really narrowed down their choices. If it were July, we'd be in big trouble.

"Have any ideas, Aoife?" Ruad asked.

I thought for a moment. Part of me wanted to set a fire and literally smoke them out, but my problem was they had Ashton up there. If the nest went up in flames, would they take their food and run? Or would they leave it? If they left Ashton, would we have enough time to get him out before the fire got to him? No, that was too risky.

Continuing to rack my brain, I looked around at the other elms, oaks, and sycamores surrounding us. If we brought the spiders down here, how much of an advantage would we really have? Being closed in with all these trees wouldn't leave anyone a lot of room to maneuver. Of course, given how big these creatures were, or rather how wide, we'd have the advantage of moving through the trees on the ground level. That was why they stayed up in the trees.

But how were we going to flush them out? I didn't want to use Ruad as bait, And I certainly didn't want to be bait.

Besides, if we went the bait route, we'd be giving up the element of surprise.

"Ruad, I'm stumped. We've got about three hours until sunset. At night, they'll have the advantage. Every plan I think of to flush them out ruins our surprise advantage or endangers Ashton's life."

The wolf looked at me thoughtfully. But I sensed she was running into all the same problems I was.

"What would my mother have done in a situation like this?"

Ruad smiled. I sensed a bit of warm sentimentality in her at the mention of Iris, not only coming through our bond, but in the way she perked up and... smiled?

"Your mother would have sauntered up to the tree and called her opponent out. She was very sportsmanlike. She always wanted to win on fair terms, even if her opponent was dishonest as the year is long," Ruad said.

That stirred some more O'Connell pride in me. My mother was a brave and honorable huntress, a formidable warrior. And that ran in my blood. We weren't going to get the drop on these spiders, even if we knew where they were.

Okay, we'll do it like Mom did, I thought.

Walking over toward the pine trees, Ruad was about to scold me, I could feel it. And then, out of nowhere, she didn't. It didn't matter if this was the best strategy we could come up with. She knew I was feeling out what it would be like to walk in my mother's footsteps. I needed that, but I also needed to figure this out on my own.

I stopped about 15 feet short of the evergreen nest and shouted up, "Hey spiders! Listen up! My name is Aoife Fey O'Connell, protector of the Ozarks. You're trespassing and guilty of murdering a human and kidnapping another. We need to settle this."

Wind rushed through the evergreen trees, rustling the branches around us. I tried to peek through the needles and see if the spiders were moving. But they were perfectly camouflaged in their nest, exactly as they wanted to be.

Ruad stepped up next to me, and I heard some branches shifting about inside the nest. They heard me just fine.

A hissing voice that made my ears itch rattled out of the nest.

"Can't be. Can't be. O'Connells are dead. Woods are ours now," came a shrieking hiss.

"There's still a few left, spiders. We're right here. You're in my territory, and I aim to drive you out, either through some portal back into the Fey Realm or death's door. Hand over the boy, and I'll let you leave. Cause trouble, and we'll kill all three of you, O'Connell style."

I had no idea what O'Connell style was, but as head of the clan, I supposed I could just make it up later.

There was more movement inside the trees. I tried to listen closely for a human heartbeat, closing my eyes to focus.

Be there. Come on, Ashton, I thought.

And there it was, light as all get-out, but I heard a tiny human heartbeat at a slow rhythm.

"Bing pot," I muttered.

"Isn't the human expression... bingo?" Ruad asked, turning her head to the side.

"It's a... look I don't have time to explain it right now," I muttered.

A different spider hissed out of the trees, "Don't fear. Don't fear you, wolfkin. Stay long and die soon."

I frowned. My patience was done, so I walked over to a rock sticking out of the ground. It was about four feet long and three feet tall. I groaned and pulled it out of the earth.

Ask most folks what our state's number one natural resource is, and they might guess timber. They'd be wrong. The real answer is rocks. Arkansas soil grows more rocks than rice and soybeans combined. Makes it stupid hard to plant a garden here.

It also makes it difficult to give houses a basement, something they tend to need since we're in Tornado Alley.

With the small boulder in my right hand, I saw a few worms hanging from the bottom. And in the dirt some twitchy centipedes ran for new shelter.

"Aoife, what are you doing?"

"Warning shot," I muttered, holding my right hand back and then hurling the rock up into the tree with all my might.

It snapped several branches and missed where I could sense Ashton's heartbeat by a few comfortable feet. Moments later a spider came crashing down on its back. I had hit it spot on, apparently. It really was about eight feet long, and all of its legs were thick as branches. The rust-colored spider kicked about as the stone I threw came falling down and hit it again under one of its fangs. The spider hissed, and Ruad was on the move.

Each of the spider's legs was sharp and pointed, except for the front two, which appeared to have two small toes on them. Ruad dodged the kicking legs and found an opening.

170

"They're really only weak on the underside, Pup. Don't waste an opening with these things," she yelled.

Talk about a lucky shot, I thought.

Ruad was on the spider and ripping into its underside as the monster hissed all the more. The wolf thrashed and tore at the spider until it finally died. It twitched for a moment, curled up its legs and fell motionless.

One down, I thought.

But before I could react, I saw tree branches just above Ruad shift, and another spider leapt down, snatching my wolf with four of its legs. Before my familiar could react, it jumped back up into the tree with blinding speed.

I heard Ruad yip and then felt a burning sensation on my left side just under the ribs. It felt like acid was eating into my flesh as I sank to my knees. It was biting her.

"Fuck this noise," I yelled and ran toward the tree nest. "Hey assholes! Offer withdrawn about letting you leave alive. You fuck with my wolf, it's straight to the electric chair. And here comes the chair!"

Drawing all my strength into my right arm, I smashed through two of the trees in the cluster. Then I summoned all my strength to my left leg and shattered the remaining trees.

"Say goodbye to your goddamn nest!" I yelled as the whole mess of trees came tumbling down.

Dad probably wouldn't have approved of destroying trees in most circumstances. But with my familiar's life on the line, I think he'd make an exception. As the trees fell, the branches clumped together, and I could make out shapes of shadows flickering around. Two of the larger shadows had to be spiders, and one of them had Ruad biting its rearmost left leg.

I ran forward and leapt into the mess of evergreen branches, ignoring the pinpricks from hundreds of needles. The spider not fighting Ruad made a sweep for me with its fangs, but I ducked, and it bit into a branch.

Moving upward, I snatched Ruad into my arms and then leapt out of the mess of brush, landing on the ground and rolling about 10 feet away.

My side still felt like it burned something fierce, but I wasn't concerned about it. I smelled Ruad's blood dripping down her side combined with the acid.

Without thinking, I buried my face in the wound and started licking away any external bits of acid, spitting it onto the nearby ground. A small patch of her fur was missing where she'd been bitten.

For the next few seconds, I licked the wound clean and then came to my senses, wiping blood off my chin.

Ruad stood as I spit onto the ground again.

"It's not gross, Pup. Your human mind might think that, but in the wild, wolves lick their wounds all the time. Helps with the healing," she said, wincing as she stood.

Nodding, I found myself strangely agreeing with Ruad. It was like how I'd adapted to smelling like a dog for most of the morning. My human brain thought that was gross initially, and I wanted to bathe constantly. Now? I didn't care. My familiar was hurt, and I was going to do whatever I could to help, no questions asked.

I accepted what I'd done as an instinctual necessity, and the growing wolf part of my brain said this was normal behavior. My human brain didn't have the capacity to argue, but it did make me wonder what I was becoming, and if these instincts that seemed to be growing stronger each day would eventually plateau or turn into something more. I'm not sure whether that excited me or scared me, but for now I needed to use it to save Ashton.

Wiping the last of the blood from around my mouth, I looked over at the mass of evergreen branches and saw two spiders emerge.

One was bigger than the other by far. It was probably nine or 10 feet long. Sixteen eyes stared at us as the monsters angrily hissed at one another. They'd hurt Ruad, but they'd also seen I was no slouch.

"You want the big one?" I offered, smirking.

Ruad didn't see any humor in the situation and said, "I can't run, Aoife. My side hurts too much. We need a plan."

"Want me to throw another rock and see if we get lucky again?"

She scoffed at that. Okay, maybe there was a little humor between us. Ruad couldn't help it around me.

The bigger spider moved forward first, about 30 feet from us.

Somewhere buried in that mess of tree branches and pine needles is Ashton, wrapped up in a ball of webbing, I thought.

Another loud hiss from the big spider drew my attention.

"Indeed O'Connell, die all the same," it hissed.

I shook my head.

"You fucked with my wolf. So it doesn't matter who attacks first. I'm killing both of you," I said popping a few joints in my left hand as I stretched my claws.

Looking back at Ruad, I said, "You stay here. I'm still good on my feet, so I'll move quick, weaving in and out of attacks and luring it closer. When it's close enough, I'll attack from above and draw its attention upward. Then you'll move in and shred its soft underbelly."

"Be careful, Pup," Ruad said.

I nodded and then launched myself at the spider, about five feet away. I stopped short and dodged left as its front left leg smashed into the ground where I was previously.

I rolled to dodge another attack and swiped my claws at one of the legs. It felt like scratching tree bark.

"Gee grandma, what a thick exoskeleton you have," I said.

We continued our song and dance, but when we were halfway to Ruad, the big spider changed tunes on me, shooting a splotch of acid that ate through the sleeve on my left arm and down to the flesh instantly.

I screamed and ducked just in time to avoid another swipe from its front left leg. The burning was almost unbearable. As the acid ate away at my skin, it hissed, almost like it was sizzling.

The next swipe broke skin on my left side. Blood began to drip down my hoodie, so I tore its remains off, along with my shirt and bra.

"Come on, Shelob!" I yelled, dodging again and clawing its underside before leaping away.

When we were finally close enough to Ruad, I was exhausted. Keeping a body moving at such high speeds and tension while reading attacks was draining. Leaping to the left, I pushed off a sycamore stump and flew up into the air over the spider.

It started to rear up on its hind legs to snatch the seemingly easy prey, and that's when Ruad went to town, sinking her fangs into the spider's underbelly.

The creature buzzed with pain, but before I could smile at the success of my plan, the other spider came out of nowhere and snatched my right arm with its fangs. It threw me back down into an oak tree and slammed my whole body into it.

My vision spun from the impact as the smaller spider, which was still six feet long, mind you, pushed me back into the tree with overwhelming strength. At first I expected acid to burn through on my uninjured arm, but the spider had other ideas. It decided to snap my arm like a twig with its fangs between the elbow and shoulder.

The pain was immense, easily the worst I'd ever felt in my life. I let out a scream, my body twitching in agony, but the spider did not let up. In that moment something snapped deep within me, something primal and raw. Feral Aoife came out to play now with claws out and a rush of adrenaline pulsing through my whole body.

"Eat shit, you asshole," I roared, digging my claws into the mouth as far as they would go and tearing whatever I could outward. I tore half the bastard's mouth open, with blue blood soaking my claws.

It hissed in fury and backed off, but not before splattering my body with a thick web, sticking me to the tree. It was warm but solidified quickly, trapping my good arm underneath.

I looked over and saw Ruad still tearing into the bigger spider, trying to strike a killing blow. My right arm wasn't going to do me any good, and I was pinned to this stupid tree. Feral Aoife retreated as I struggled to break through the webbing. It was no good. I only had one arm trying to tear through.

The smaller spider came back toward me and raised its front right leg, probably aiming to pierce my skull or throat.

"Dammit," I muttered as the spider looked onward with victory assured in its eyes. It jabbed its leg forward about two feet to my left hitting nothing but the edge of the tree as I raised an eyebrow.

Before I could say, "You missed, buddy," I heard a sudden flutter, and then I was cut free and hoisted to the right.

I looked over to see a man in a black tank top with spiky locks carrying me away from the spider. His long dark wings resumed a softer form after cutting me free with razor-like feathers.

When he put me down again, I sighed in relief.

"Perfect timing, Ash," I said.

"Yeah well, I would have been here sooner, but your text wasn't very specific. It just said, 'Giant spiders, kidnapped boy, Hobbs Park.' And with all due respect, it's a big ass park, Aoife."

"Okay, okay, geesh. Sorry. Thank you for coming. You saved my bacon," I said, hugging him with my good arm.

He looked taken back at my expression of gratitude. Poor kid still wasn't used to working with someone who valued him as a teammate.

When I let him go, Ash was blushing a little.

"Um… well, you're welcome. I figured I owed you for saving my life," he muttered.

I touched the side of his face and said, "Ash, friends don't have to worry about owing each other, okay? We can just have each other's backs when needed."

He said nothing and nodded.

"What now?" he asked.

The smaller spider started to approach us again.

"I need an illusion," I said.

"Name the play," he said.

And I smiled at the instant kinship that'd formed between us, like we were always meant to be a team.

"Just make about four or five of me, cloak yourself, and follow behind. When I scream now, you have all the copies of me jump into the air. Then we're going to nail this spider's underbelly."

He nodded as four Aoifes appeared, three on my left and one on my right. Ash wasn't visible anymore.

I rushed forward, hissing at the pain in my right arm.

I'm not going to last much longer, I thought, feeling a dizziness creeping into my legs and gut.

The spider widened its four front legs as we charged. On my command with a simple shout, Ash had the copies leap into the air, diverting the spider's attention. It reared up on its hind legs and stabbed a fake Aoife with its front right leg.

I stretched my left claws and dug into the spider as Ash reappeared on my right side and slashed into the creature with his left wing's now razor-like feathers.

We pushed forward, tearing into more and more of the spider until we got to its hind legs.

"Shred, you eight legged bastard! Shred!" I yelled as my claw emerged covered in pale blue blood.

The spider shrieked in shock and agony, convulsed and then collapsed on us, dead. I lifted what I could with my left arm, but the stupid thing was 250 pounds of dead weight. Ash scooped me up and flew me out from under the creature before we were crushed.

I hissed as my right arm flapped a bit from the movement.

"Sorry!" Ash said, setting me down.

"It's fine. Thanks for everything, Ash."

He smirked a little.

"You can pay me back by helping me clean this blue blood out of my feathers. I like my wings black and sleek," he said.

I looked at his left wing, partially soaked with fey spider blood.

"Can't you just make an illusion so it looks normal again?"

Ash raised an eyebrow.

"That's not the point! I'd still know the blood was there, and I can feel it on my feathers. It's nasty!"

Now I was smirking.

"Hey, once I get this arm in a sling, I'll help clean your wing," I said, walking over to the mess of tree branches. I felt an overwhelming sense of relief in my familiar as the big spider took its last breath.

She limped over to the former tree nest with blue blood dripping from her jaw. It was also splattered on her chest.

With a little digging, we found a smaller ball of webbing. Ash slashed it open, and I held little Ashton comatose in my good arm. I placed one of my wolf ears to his chest. He was still breathing... enough anyway.

I handed the kid to Ash and said, "Please take him to the park ranger at the start of the Pigeon Hole trail back on the highway. His name is Richard. He'll take Ashton here to the hospital."

"What about you?" he asked, looking over my broken arm.

"Ashton is more important. Ruad and I will be fine. We'll start making our way back to the highway."

My pendant glowed, and Adrienn shot out.

"Holy crap! Your arm!" they said, hovering over my shoulder.

I held out my hand and said, "It's okay. We got them. I'll get to a hospital later and have this taken care of with my lack of health insurance."

The fey landed on my palm and shook their head.

"There's actually a fairy circle a little north of here we can use to get back home. And Tristan's medical kit still has a few healing plants we can use to take care of these injuries," Adrienn said.

I smiled.

"You've always got the best solutions, my little guardian. Thank you," I said.

With a bow and smile, they flew up into the air and pointed the way to the fairy circle.

"Want me to pop in and check on you after I get the kid to Richard?" Ash asked.

Nodding, I said, "Thank you so much, Ash. I'm grateful. We did good work today."

Ruad scoffed. I could tell there were still strong feelings of hatred for the raven in her heart. I couldn't blame her given what Ash had put her through, even if it was under Malachos' orders.

Ash didn't look at Ruad. He just popped up into the sky and flew away.

"You good to hike a bit north?" I asked.

Ruad nodded.

We started north with Adrienn leading the way. The clouds parted, and a bit of sunlight came out, reflecting on the lake's gray water when it came into view.

"Ruad, thanks for your help today," I said.

The wolf looked up at me as she limped along and said, "This is what O'Connells do, Aoife. Iris and Tristan would be proud of you."

I looked at my broken arm and then back to Ruad.

"Could Iris have taken all three of those spiders on by herself?"

"She would have killed them all."

Sighing, I stopped. Then Ruad stopped.

"Ruad, I need to get stronger and fast. I bet Malachos could have killed all three of those spiders instantly. If he attacks us again... I won't be ready."

My familiar looked up at the sky as the sun hid behind the clouds again.

"You were robbed of the ability to learn a lot of the basics, Pup. But there just might be something we can do about catching you up."

Adrienn suddenly looked nervous.

"You want to use the cavern?" they asked.

Ruad met their green eyes and nodded.

"Oh boy," Adrienn muttered, slapping their face.

I raised an eyebrow.

"What are you two talking about?"

Ruad exchanged another glance with Adrienn and said, "Let's just get home and patched up. We can talk about it later."

I nodded, and we started north again. Whatever they had in mind caused some nerves to spike in my gut. Clenching my good fist, I realized

I would do whatever it took to get stronger. If Ash hadn't shown up, I'd be dead now. I can't put myself in this position again.

Still, first things first. I needed to get this arm fixed.

The last thoughts I had before we made it to the fairy circle were about rebuilding the clan. My mind turned to Ash again. Ruad clearly hated his guts, but I couldn't deny the exhilarating feeling that echoed through my chest as the two of us fought side-by-side today. When you feel stuff like that, it's impossible to forget about it. It was an instinctual bond, one I knew I couldn't ignore regardless of what it meant for mine and Ash's future.

We did make a pretty good team.

Chapter Thirteen

The moon and stars shone high in the sky through a clear and crisp night as Abi and I carried in a couple pies from Toppings. I pretended to forget Ruad in the back seat, and the wolf called out, "Pup, do you really want your mate to lose a car door?"

Abi turned around and gave Ruad a look that said, "Excuse me?"

I laughed and pointed at my familiar.

"Haha, you got the evil stare."

Ruad turned toward my girlfriend and said, "Consider that I do not fear your scowl. Now consider who would really be at fault for your vehicle damage, myself, or Aoife for leaving me in here."

Now the evil stare turned toward me, sending a chill down my spine. Girlfriend or not, she'd murder me.

"I don't like how quickly that shifted," I muttered.

"Then I'd walk over and let your wolf out of my back seat before she does something to get you into trouble."

Scooting backward, I reached over for the door handle and opened it. Ruad walked onto the grass and said, "Eh, she's more my Pup than I am her wolf at this point."

We walked toward the front door, and I rolled my eyes.

Abi and her mother lived in a two-bedroom townhouse in the west part of town, which had been growing like a weed because it was one of the cheaper areas to live in.

Their home was one of those long and skinny houses that had been built in the last few years as new neighborhoods sprang up almost overnight. Fayetteville continued to crawl out in every direction it could, absorbing what had once just been empty country. Some folks liked that and continued to move here.

Others, primarily families that had inherited their country plots from two or three generations, probably weren't too interested in watching town (and higher property taxes) inching towards them. I'm guessing my pack would have been in the latter if they were still around today.

Fortunately for me, Fayetteville didn't seem to be expanding southeast in any hurry. So my little greenhouse was probably safe.

We walked into the house, vinyl flooring under our feet. Abi shut the front door as soon as my familiar was inside. A gas fireplace in the living room greeted us to the left. Two little stockings were hung above it, one red and one green. Abi's name was stitched into hers, while Jen was stitched into the other.

Jen was sitting in the living room on a blue couch watching a *Law and Order* rerun, her long braids tied back. She wore a red bathrobe, standard after 8:00 p.m. attire for her.

When Jen's eyes spotted our pizza, she hopped up and walked into the entryway. Of course, she pretended to be more interested in me.

"Aoife! I'm glad to see you, honey," she said, throwing her arms around me. "I was so sorry to hear about Barb behaving like she did. You didn't deserve that."

I smiled and returned the hug.

"Thanks, Jen."

When we parted, she looked down at my familiar and said, "So you must be Ruad, the vermillion wolf. Tell me, what does it sound like when a wolf speaks?"

My eyes grew wide, and I looked at Abi, trying to reproduce the glare she gave me earlier. She didn't seem impressed or apologetic.

"I don't keep secrets from Mom, Aoife. You know that. Strangely enough, she seems to believe me about how crazy your life has gotten," Abi said.

She walked into her kitchen, shoes clicking on the linoleum floor. Abi was wearing a blue sweater decorated with a fiddler playing on top of a roof and some black jeans.

Ruad didn't exactly wait for permission to speak. She looked right at Jen and said, "Your daughter seems to make an excellent mate for my Pup."

I just put my face in my hands. I know she intended that to be a compliment, but my wolf was a little socially inept. I guess there's a line to just how human a familiar can get. Or did she continue to say stuff like this just to embarrass me?

To Jen's credit, she didn't freak out at Ruad's voice. She looked a bit shocked, but that was about it. Instead, she bowed a little and said, "Thank you. I think I did a pretty good job with Abi. And I think she makes an adorable pair with Aoife. You know, when Abi first realized she had feelings for Aoife, she came home and asked if girls kissed each other differently than they kissed guys."

Jen started laughing, and Abi flashed a color of crimson I'd only seen once or twice. "Mom! Not cool!" she shrieked.

I laughed, and Abi brought out that glare again. I stopped laughing and quickly looked down at Ruad.

"What are you laughing at, my sweet cinnamon?"

Now I blushed. I hated that nickname, no matter how much Abi loved it. Part of what I think she enjoyed about it was how much it embarrassed me.

"Can we just... eat pizza please?" I managed to choke out.

"As soon as you introduce me to Adrienn," Jen said, turning to me.

I blinked for a second and then looked down at my necklace.

"Sure, of course," I said.

"The concept of a fey guardian is so fascinating to me," Jen said. "Can I ask how they came to be your guardian?"

I took a breath and said, "They were hurt and running away from a monster in their world. Using the last of their energy, Adrienn escaped into the human world and hid in my father's garden. But before they could close their portal, the monster followed them through. My mother ended up slaying it, and in gratitude, they swore to serve my family for the rest of their days. When I was born, Adrienn passed to me."

They flashed out of the pendant with green light and flew up into the air doing a little spin.

"Tada!" they said, bowing.

Jen smiled and started to clap.

"Now that is something else. You're astounding, really. Both of you are. Aoife, you've made some amazing friends here."

Adrienn flew onto my left shoulder and sat down.

"They're all the family I have left," I said, placing a hand on Ruad.

We were silent for a moment until Abi brought in some paper plates. Something twitched inside of me, and I said, "Honey, those are really wasteful. Can we just use regular plates?"

Again, such a nice time for inner druid to pop up, I thought.

"Aw come on, Aoife. I don't want to do dishes tonight. I'm tired."

"I'll do them," I said, taking the paper plates back into the kitchen and pulling out a few red plates from the cabinet above the toaster.

I pulled out a few slices of sausage pizza, my stomach rumbling.

Then I handed Ruad a slice of sausage pizza. She took it from my hand, and it vanished almost as quickly as I'd pulled it out of the box.

Jen and Abi each took a few slices on their plates from the other pie, which was green peppers and onions. I cut one of those into quarters and handed Adrienn a piece.

We each grabbed a Pepsi from the fridge and sat down in the living room. Jen and Abi over on the couch, me in the matching blue recliner.

Commercial ended right as we sat down, and suddenly Sam Waterston was back on the screen.

"So what happens in this one?" I asked, Ruad lying down to the left of my chair.

"Oh, it's a good one. A teacher gets murdered, and there's a clue left inside of a yearbook," Jen said.

I'd almost forgotten Jen had most of these episodes committed to memory. It blows my mind how a theater director could work with drama students all day and then come home and watch a few reruns of a police drama. Maybe it's like Doritos for her brain.

The next commercial came, and Jen looked over my way.

"So, I never did ask. How did you finish up the semester?"

I smiled. It seemed like an eternity since I'd talked about normal life with anyone. With all that'd happened over the last couple weeks, I'd almost forgotten I was a freshman studying mythology.

"My finals were great, except for college algebra. Math can go fuck itself. I ended up with something like a 69.7 in that class, which fortunately for me rounded up to a 70. I'm happy to scrape by with a C- and never go without a calculator again," I said.

Abi made a face and said, "That's how I felt about my biology lab. Who cares if I can't name all the parts of a plant cell. I'm majoring in drama for crying out loud."

Jen smiled at us and said, "Now now. Gen eds have a role to play in your college education."

We rolled our eyes at the same moment. Is that still a jynx? Did Abi owe me a coke?

"You're right, Jen. They do play a role. How else would bloodthirsty universities make money from us if they didn't shackle us with all sorts of classes unrelated to our majors?" I asked.

The technical director was a strong proponent of higher education. Most of her friends worked at Northwest Arkansas University, some even teaching Abi.

Jen pointed a finger at me and said, "Now you listen here. Those classes you dislike? They're the ones that help make you both well-rounded students. And you'd best learn to take advantage of them."

We rolled our eyes again, and I could have sworn we thought in unison, "What a load."

Abi's mother looked us both over, analyzed our expressions, and scolded us further, "Let me guess. You were both just thinking, 'what a load,' right?"

I exchanged glances with my girlfriend.

"No more pizza for either of you!" Jen scolded.

And when *Law and Order* came back on, it was like Abi and I ceased to exist anymore. At the next commercial break, we picked up our conversation right where it left off.

"So are you going to be able to keep up with college classes and druid stuff next semester?" Jen asked.

I didn't have an answer for that. Looking down at the floor and Ruad, I considered what my future would look like, something I hadn't done very much these last weeks. Did I want to be on monster patrol in the forest while trying to study for classes like Introduction to Celtic Folklore? Would I be able to even if I wanted to?

What would happen if I was in the middle of class and I got a call from a certain park ranger asking for help again? I know Buffy went to school and fought monsters at the same time, but I didn't think I could handle that. So what were my options? Drop out of college and work at the flower shop for the rest of my life while trying to rebuild my pack?

Jen's voice snapped me out of my thoughts.

"Aoife?"

I shook my head and said, "I honestly haven't thought that far ahead. Right now, I just want to rebuild my clan and try to be more like Tristan and Iris."

Abi looked over at me and smiled.

"I'm sure you'll do great at both," she said. "I've got your back."

Now Jen stood up and smiled. She carried our plates into the kitchen and said, "Well, if you ever want to talk about it all, just let me know."

She came over and ruffled my hair.

"You're welcome to stay here tonight, or really anytime at all. All of you are," Jen said, looking down at Ruad.

Nodding, I looked up into Jen's brown eyes and knew she meant every word. She was a wonderful mother, and I appreciated how great she'd been with Abi and I.

"Thank you, Jen," I said, standing up and hugging her.

She returned the gesture and then walked over to Abi, kissing her on the cheek.

"Okay, ladies. I'm going to bed. Ruad, if these two get busy later, I'll leave my door cracked. You are more than welcome to come sleep in my bed. It's big, and I have the world's softest comforter."

My brain went somewhere different than Abi's. And I knew it. There was an immediate pang of jealousy. Ruad was mine, and she would sleep at my side until the day I died. How dare Jen try to steal her away, even for one night? I worked hard to keep from growling at the thought.

My girlfriend, on the other hand, blushed and stood up, pushing her mother toward the hallway, "Good night, Mother!"

When she was gone, Ruad looked up at me and said, "I don't care how busy you get in your work with Abi. I can wait patiently until you're finished. When Tristan got busy with his garden, I would just lie around waiting for him to be done."

I flinched.

"Ruad. That's not what she—we'll figure it out," I said, sighing.

Abi gave me a look of concern.

"We'll… figure it out? What exactly does that mean?" she asked, glancing at Ruad with eyes the size of dinner plates.

Adrienn nearly fell off my shoulder because they were laughing so hard.

After a moment of silence, I slumped and realized how tired I was. My body still hadn't recovered fully from the fey spider fight.

My girlfriend came over and gently wrapped her arms around me shortly after I heard Jen's bedroom door close.

I flinched as she touched my right arm and bit my tongue to keep from crying out. Ruad growled a little bit.

"Felt that too, did ya?" I asked, looking at my familiar. She did a better job of hiding her pain after the battle, but we both limped back into the greenhouse and collapsed while Adrienn fetched some different healing plants for us.

Abi gently let me go and raised an eyebrow.

"How badly hurt were you in that spider fight yesterday?" she asked.

I started to sweat and looked down at Ruad.

I don't want to lie to her, but I also don't want to worry her, I thought.

She walked over and slowly lifted the sleeve on my right arm. I was wearing a Northwest Arkansas University long sleeve shirt. It was very loose and flowy, a few sizes too big for me. Abi pushed the sleeve all the way up to my shoulder and gasped, putting a hand over her mouth.

Where the spider's fangs had snapped my arm was a crimson scar and a deep purple splotchy bruise that covered the bottom of my tricep.

Had the bone healed? Sure, thanks to the last pieces of something Adrienn called manuka root they'd found in my father's first aid kit. Wrap the limb tight, and it heals overnight, Adrienn said, while I cried at how tight the bandage was wrapped and bound around my arm.

Of course, my arm still hurt like hell this morning. But at least I could move it some.

"They, uh, broke my arm. But Adrienn dug up some magical plants to heal me... mostly," I said.

I pushed my sleeve down while Abi tried not to cry. I could see the tears collect at the edges of her eyes, and it pained me to see her so scared for me.

"But we saved a little boy and anyone else they might have killed, Abi. Ruad and I are the only ones who could have dealt with that situation. You can't send cops in to handle stuff like this," I said, looking down. I was doing that a lot tonight.

Abi wiped an eye and asked, "And... are you going to keep doing stuff like this?"

My heart tore a little at that question, almost like a literal fissure had appeared on the beating muscle in my chest. Was she going to ask me to stop doing this kind of stuff? I mean, it wasn't like I was eager to run headfirst into more danger, but... at the same time, we'd saved a young boy. I felt more pride in what we'd done than pain in my broken arm. That made it all worth it.

All I could do was nod while picturing a rope bridge in my head. The rope was slowly tearing, and on one side stood Abi holding out her hand. The other side had my parents with their hands extended.

Abi sighed. Then she walked over, leaned down, and placed her lips

185

on mine. When she slid away, almost reluctantly, she must have read the confusion on my face. I always had a hard time hiding what I was thinking around her, even when I tried.

"Oh my sweet cinnamon," she said, touching the left side of my face with her hand. "I know so much is changing for you right now, and you're eager to fill some role left by your parents. I can't even begin to imagine how much this weighs on your heart. I know it's important, maybe the most important thing right now."

I slowly added my own hand to hers and felt myself easing into her touch. "Nothing is more important to me than you. But this is... I don't know, destiny? Fate? Responsibility? No word feels right. It's epic, and it's fulfilling. Odessa told me once I accepted my true family there'd be no turning back. That sinks in more every day. It's frightening at times, thinking how far I might go. Yet still exciting."

She sighed and closed her eyes. When she opened them again, they were tearing up. My chest tightened up, and I couldn't help but ask myself, *God, what was I doing to Abi?*

"I'm not going to be one of those cliché girlfriends who says you can't take these kinds of risks. But I also won't lie about how much this scares me. I mean, giant spiders, Aoife? Do you know how insane that sounds? What are you going to fight next? Cthulhu?"

I did a little shrug of my shoulders. "Could be?"

She gave me that same face again, the scolding one that she did when I had left Ruad in the car. Only this time there was a softness to it, and I swore I could see a quick little smile come and go. She continued, "It was an arm this time. What next time? A punctured lung? Shattered spine? It's terrifying."

I lowered my head some but kept her gaze.

When she regained her composure, she choked out, "But you can't stop. I can't make you. If you hadn't gone in there, a little boy would be dead. I get it. It paralyzes me, but I get it, Aoife. Just promise me something."

"Name it," I said, doing my best to hold back tears.

"Promise me that no matter how dangerous it gets, no matter how strong the monsters are, that you'll always come back to me."

Now I was crying.

"Okay, my fair bird. I'll always come back to you," I said, pulling her in tight with my good arm.

186

We stood there like that for a few minutes, her head hanging over my shoulder as we sobbed together. Then Abi looked down at Ruad. The wolf wore a softened expression, one I rarely get to see.

"Promise me you'll always drag her back to me," Abi whispered. "No matter how banged up she gets."

Ruad nodded.

The expression may not have looked like much in reality, but in my chest, I felt my familiar doubling down on an ironclad promise. My familiar would drag her Pup back no matter what.

Ruad went through so much with Tristan, and I sensed an oath was 20 times more important to her than the average person who made one. Her word wasn't just her bond, but an essence of her being at this point. Tristan and Ruad made an oath to live side by side as druid and familiar until the day they died, and my father broke that promise. I flinched thinking of the pain radiating through Ruad's heart, still lingering from the worst day of her life.

It was the greatest oath he could have taken, and Ruad had everything invested in their bond. Deep in my mind forest were the buried feelings of betrayal I sensed in my familiar. They would rise and torment her from time to time. Tristan had made his promise worthless, and that was a stain on more than just his honor.

Then, just days ago, against all instincts, Ruad chose to trust my own oath to her when our souls bonded. Knowing how deep her previous pain went, she opened her heart once more, showing a greater trust in my oath than I could even process. I would swear a thousand times to love and treasure her presence each day she stood breathing by my side.

So when she made a promise to drag my ass back from any fight, I knew how much that oath was worth. It wasn't just something I'd take to the bank. It was a deed that no one on this entire planet could refute.

Abi looked at me. "Do you want to go lie down?" The tightness in my chest unraveled. For once in a long while I felt at peace. I nodded. Then she smiled, slipped her fingers into mine and led me by the hand into her bedroom.

We walked upstairs with Ruad in tow. Adrienn retired to my locket for the night.

Upstairs was a bathroom and Abi's bedroom. Her walls were painted blue and had little glow-in-the-dark stars on the walls and ceiling. On one wall hung a Broadway poster of Rent, one of Abi's favorite musicals.

As I looked back over those little plastic stars, a more nostalgic part of my brain thought back to all our sleepovers where I needed to cool down after a blow-out with Barb.

I would lie on my back long after Abi fell asleep on my chest. And as her head slowly rose up and down with each of my breaths, I smiled, counting those stars over and over. There were exactly nine-and-a-half. Half, because I'd broken one by throwing a pencil really hard at the ceiling after a frustrating homework assignment.

But over the last couple years, I always knew if I looked up at the ceiling and saw those stars, I was safe. Nobody was going to barge into my room unannounced and yell at me for some perceived rule violation. It was a warm and welcome feeling of knowing I was secure, happy, and had Abi nearby. I could breathe freely under these stars.

Opposite of the bed, she had a desk with a laptop and some textbooks scattered around it. Next to it was a bookshelf filled with a 50/50 mix of screenplays and manga Abi swears she hasn't read in years, *Vampire Knight* looking the most worn.

On top of the bookshelf sat a couple of Funko dolls, one of Sweeney Todd and another of Erik, the Phantom. They'd been birthday presents from me.

Abi had a long birch dresser also painted blue. On top of it sat a little mirror and her makeup box.

We sat down on the bed holding hands, and Abi said, "So tell me more about this mystic cavern you mentioned in your text."

I sighed. This wasn't something I was sure I could do.

Looking up into Abi's eyes and running a few fingers lightly over her tawny skin, I answered, "Ruad says it's a cavern that was carved over thousands of years by water from a magic spring near Eureka Springs. The spring has some kind of ability to alter time, slow it down, even freeze it. Something about certain places in nature being literally timeliness. Some of that magic remains in the cavern, leftover from when the water shaped it. So when we enter the cave, it seals us away for a year. At least, that's how time flows on the inside. Outside? It moves normally. One year inside the cave is one night out here."

She thought that over for a moment.

"And why do you need to go there?"

"Because I need to get a whole lot stronger as fast as possible. Sweetie, most druids my age would have had years of training under their belts by now in nature magic and syncing with their familiars if they had one. Thanks to Malachos, I never got that. And it's costing lives. The lack of O'Connells in the area has already led to those fey spiders moving in and feeding on humans. I'm sure other monsters have encroached on my pack's territory over the last decade-and-a-half. I need to be stronger to rebuild my clan and protect the area," I said.

Abi put a hand on mine, which, without me realizing, was clenched into a fist.

"And this is the only way?" she asked.

I nodded.

"Ruad and Adrienn are going to put me through a druid boot camp in there, to master the basics of my wolf form and druidic magic. It's going to be more intense than anything Coach ever put me through," I said.

My girlfriend smiled and kissed my lips lightly.

"I've watched you train for tournaments and matches for a few years now. Training doesn't scare you, Aoife. This might be magic training, but it's still making yourself stronger. That's something you're already good at. So what's really eating you up inside?"

Fighting the temptation to look away, I took a deep breath and tried not to cry again. I thought about the words I needed to speak, but my mouth was suffering some sort of disconnect. My bottom lip began to tremble.

"For you, I'm gone for only a day. You get a text when I go in and when I come out. But me? I'm gone for an entire year, Abi. I... I don't want to be away from you for that long. I don't think I can do it," I said, more tears falling from my eyes.

Abi was silent as I stopped rubbing her arm.

"I'm not strong enough... to be apart from you that long. I don't think there's any amount of training I could do to become that strong."

We sat there on the bed. My left leg was falling asleep, but I didn't care. Ruad looked surprised to hear my confession, but she remained silent.

Abi broke the silence wiping away a tear with her thumb and said, "Honey, downstairs you showed me just how determined you were to follow your parents' legacy," she said, breaking the silence. She ran her thumb over my face, wiping away a tear. "I know you didn't tell my mom this, but I can see it in your eyes. College? Studies? Getting a job teaching mythology? That's all out the window. And do you know why?"

I shook my head slowly.

"Because you've found your destiny. It's sudden, dangerous, and powerful. But it calls to you all the same. I watched your eyes when you told me about saving Ashton, Aoife. Through the magic, through the danger, through the pain, you knew what you had to do, and you did it."

She wiped another tear from my face.

"You know what you have to do here, too. And you'll do it. I'll be here before you go into that cave, and I'll be here when you come out. My sweet cinnamon, you're going to become the most powerful druid, rebuild the clan that was stolen from you, and this will just be a stepping stone along the way."

That last part brought a smile to my face. She didn't know anything about magic, wasn't a mind reader, didn't have any special bond like Ruad and I or anything, and yet she knew exactly what to say to reassure me

After I had that thought, Ruad raised her head and spoke up, "Because she's your mate, Pup. And she knows you better than anyone. Abi knows your truth, and she speaks it."

She pulled her hand from my face and started to rub the top of my head furiously.

"Who's a strong girl? Huh? Who's a strong girl? Is it you? Is it you?" she said in a mocking voice one would use to speak to a pet.

I started laughing. I couldn't help it. She was so ridiculous.

"Okay, you made your point. Stop it," I said, seizing her wrist.

Ruad chuckled and said, "Your mate is hilarious, Pup."

Abi grabbed the collar of my shirt and pulled me closer to her.

"Speaking of mate…" she said, letting her sentence trail off as she lightly kissed the tip of my nose. I felt my blood begin to warm, my heart all aflutter. God. Tonight had been an emotional roller coaster.

Ah yes, the opening move, I thought.

Kissing her back lightly on the lips, I closed my eyes. Then, I reopened my right eye and looked over at Ruad. Did I dare motion for her to leave the room? Would she be insulted by that? Surely not. But she couldn't stay in here.

I know she's supposed to stay by my side at all times, but… I thought.

"Don't worry, Pup. I can smell your teen hormones from here. I remember when Iris and Tristan smelled like this. So I'll just make myself scarce," she said, exiting the room.

A pang of jealousy re-entered my system. But I heard her plop down at the top of the stairs. She wasn't going into Jen's room.

Phew.

Now back to business at hand. Jen tossed a pillow at the door, slamming it shut.

"She's coming back in when we go to sleep," I whispered, before kissing my girlfriend on the neck. "We're kind of a package deal now."

"I don't care what she does when we're done. I care about what we're doing now," she said as she lifted my shirt off.

I ran my hands through her hair and kissed her as she started to undo my black bra.

"Don't worry, my sweet cinnamon. I've got big plans for the next hour. I'll give you something to think about for the next year," she said as I took her sweater off.

My heart was in the fast lane, and I could begin to feel heat building.

Looking toward the cave, the road ahead of me would be rough. But the approaching stretch I was about to traverse would give me something to remember for the next few hundred miles. Tomorrow's problems would still be there, but for now, I had other stuff to focus on, like getting this leather belt off my girlfriend.

Chapter Fourteen

Day Three

I stared at a vermillion wolf that was poised to tear me to shreds, ready to put me through the wringer for the third time this week. Week? How many days had passed since we'd entered this damn cave?

The blue glowing lights from the cavern ceiling cast an eerie glow to the sweat dripping off my forehead and arms. I was already sick of looking at the lights, and, according to Ruad, I still had another 362 days underneath them. Adrienn told me right after we entered that previous druid occupants had spent some of their time here infusing rocks up there with magic that created light. It made sense, given that some druids would spend years here, meditating and listening to the earth. I wouldn't want to be sealed in the darkness for a year.

Damp air filled a massive cavern I now got to call home. Centuries of water shaping stone left a space filled with jagged limestone stalactites that glittered in blue luminescence. It'd take 40 Ruads lined up in a line to reach from one cavern wall to another. Wolf measuring units probably weren't scientific, but what was when dealing with nature magic and druidic legacies?

"Pup! Pay attention. You're not going to break your time limit by staring at me," Ruad barked. Her teeth glistened under the cavern glow.

I tensed up. She was right.

"Come on! The time to beat is five minutes. Tristan could hold his wolf form for 12 hours. Before you leave this cave, I want you to be able to do it for at least one hour," Ruad said.

I took a deep breath and looked Ruad in the eyes.

"My father was amazing," I said.

That O'Connell pride started to build inside me again, like a proud fire in my gut. My father was strong, a powerful leader for the entire clan.

And here I was, trying to rebuild that legacy. I wasn't even a fraction of what he and my mother were. But I would be, soon enough.

The problem isn't just staying transformed for five minutes. That's the easy part. Not only did I have to maintain my form, but I had to maintain my form while sparring Ruad. That was the real challenge. And if I eventually want to defeat Malachos, there's no telling how long I'd have to keep up my energy. I'd need to surpass even my father. A strange twist of nerves and pride bundled up in my stomach.

"Well?" Ruad asked.

Speaking the words, wind swirled around me, sending my expanding hair flying in every direction. Skin on my fingers slid and adjusted to account for claws growing a few inches. My jaw expanded to account for larger canines, and with a few cracks and pops my spine extended into a bushy tail the same shade as my hair. The flustering hair covered my human ears vanishing. And triangular wolf ears emerged on the top of my skull with an itchy and now familiar sensitivity.

"Will you please start the clock, Adrienn?" I said.

They'd been up in the air observing our spars.

"You got it," they said. "Begin!"

In our other spars, rushing straight at Ruad had resulted more teeth marks around my throat. I wasn't fast enough to surprise my familiar head-on, so this time I flanked her, charging her from the right.

She turned to face me, but I ran a full circle around her. When she realized what I was doing, Ruad crouched down low, patiently waiting for an opening.

She watched and analyzed for a minute or two before realizing I wasn't going to attack her. Then she ran forward at a speed I didn't anticipate.

Coach told me once that I would encounter people faster than me in the ring. Their kicks would be devastating. His advice? Stop being a scared kitten and get in closer. Speed only counts when you're in the right range bracket.

So far I had tried to keep my distance because Ruad's fangs and claws scared me. Getting torn open by them had not been a pleasant experience, even with Adrienn's quick heals from the plants I grew for us.

Taking a breath, I tried to shove that fear aside. Then I stopped. Fear should be addressed head on instead. Trying to avoid it just allows it to jump you from behind.

Fine. Let's go get bit, I thought, charging forward to meet Ruad. This seemed to surprise her, as until now if she'd come directly at me, I'd tried to dodge her. I was never fast enough, though, and she always snagged my shoulder or one of my legs.

But this time was different. This time, I charged right at her fangs and threw my left arm into her jaws. She didn't expect this, either. I felt her teeth dig in, and I grimaced. But this was also part of our training, increasing my pain tolerance.

With her jaws fastened tightly on my left arm, I knew she'd try to throw me, so I planted my feet firmly on the ground.

Then I pulled my left arm down, shredding my flesh on her teeth like getting a finger caught in a cheese grater. Despite the pain, my move allowed me to bring my left knee up into her jaw, getting in a solid hit. She seemed dazed for a moment, so I slid underneath her. Even stunned for a moment she was quick to recover and took a slash at my shoulder.

I grunted at the pain but still I moved forward with my attack. With my uninjured arm, I hoisted Ruad up into the air. The wolf was instantly furious. She did not like to be picked up. It made her antsy.

Ruad let go of my arm, and as soon as she did, I went to town on her ribs with my fists, pounding her higher into the air.

"I'm going to show you I'm not a pup anymore, Ruad! I'm going to show you I can reach Tristan's potential and rebuild this clan!"

My familiar grabbed my right fist with her jaw and used it to pull herself out of the air, breaking a few of my knuckles in the process. She hit the ground, planted her feet, and immediately body slammed me into the cave wall.

"Words are meaningless, Pup. Shut up and let your battle speak for you," she said.

As rock started to fall around me, I felt my power fading away. I was letting it go because of my injuries, I realized. I didn't want to continue this pain anymore. It was more than any normal human could endure.

My blood fell to the floor. I was sure I'd at least bruised a good portion of my back slamming into the cave wall like that. Three of my right knuckles were broken. Ruad might have even pulled my arm out of socket when she came back down to the ground. I wanted this to be over.

Before I could let go of my form, voices and whispers spoke to me in a wave of echoes. I looked around, trying to find the source, but the noise came from everywhere and nowhere. So I did something I wasn't used to. I shut up and listened until I heard a familiar voice… Tristan's.

I heard blood dripping from his body and hitting the earth under him. I heard whimpering children behind him, terrified by whatever had hurt my father so bad. And at last I heard his reassuring tone, "Don't worry. Everything is going to be okay. You're going home safe. I swear it."

How am I hearing my father? Did this already happen? How long ago?

Suddenly, it wasn't just noise. His pain traveled from the past and became my own.

Tristan's left arm was broken, along with a couple toes. A few of his ribs were bruised, and he couldn't see out of one eye.

But the one thing I didn't hear or feel from my father? Fear. A growl built from his chest, and as I listened, I felt his power expanding, feeding off the pain. I imagined whatever threat stood before him, and Tristan and Ruad had one basic understanding. Without them in the way, the children they protected would die. That too likely added to my father's rising strength. This echo from the past taught me of my father's endurance, everything Tristan carried as alpha of the pack. I needed to tap into that now.

Through the echo, it felt like my father was right within my grasp. Maybe if I reached out to him, I could speak with him? Connect with either his past self or maybe even his spirit in the afterlife? So I reached out with my inner voice, crying for him.

"Dad! Can you hear me? Dad! Please, I want to hear your voice, even if it's to give me a few words of reassurance. Just… please, Dad. Are you there?"

And despite my heart crying out for him, there was no response. The cave had provided all the time magic it was going to for now, and I had to live with that. The important thing was I could live with that. Maybe someday I'd speak with my father again, but right now I had to endure.

As I finished listening to this echo from the past, I smiled, feeling almost like Tristan was watching me train and get stronger just like he must have at some point. And I also noticed Ruad frozen, as if she was hearing her own memory from the past. Was it the same as mine? Or something else entirely?

Inside, I grabbed onto that fleeting energy with my claws and dug in deep. We weren't done yet. Not by a long shot.

I'm an O'Connell, dammit. I can take anything Ruad dishes out, I thought.

Climbing out of the cave wall, I turned and slammed my right shoulder into the stone, setting it back in place. More pain. More fuel for the fire.

Turning to face Ruad, I realized we were about to enter the drop-down knockout portion of the fight. Magic swirled around me. As the energy built up, a thick red aura slid over my body like a lumpy second skin. The ground rumbled under me. Pebbles rattled away. Call it a second wind. Maybe even a third.

Ruad smirked. She knew what was coming, and maybe was even a little proud of how long I'd held on thus far. She hadn't seen shit yet.

I raised my left fist and slammed it down into the cave floor with such a heavy impact that it sent dust flying up everywhere around me for several feet. I was completely engulfed.

"Clever, Pup."

What I really needed was an opening. In a head-on charge she would win. My familiar would close the gap between us and get me with a mid-range slash or bite every time. There wasn't anything I could do about that. So I was going to make an opening.

I picked up a boulder that was a little taller than me, and groaned under the weight. With my claws dug into the boulder, I tossed it. As it flew, I rushed and leapt out of the dust to Ruad's left, completely hiding myself behind the thrown rock so she couldn't see.

When my wolf noticed the boulder, she threw her head to her right side, prepared for an attack.

"Nice try, Pup. A good distraction is almost always worth attempting. Throw the rock one way and attack from the opposite," Ruad said, lowering herself to the ground for a right-side strike.

The dust where I'd previously been standing was starting to dissipate.

I used noise from the boulder crashing to the ground to my advantage. The rumbling covered my own sounds as I stepped around the rock and charged for Ruad's unprotected side.

She must have sensed a change in air current with her whiskers because her head whipped back around just before my knee made contact with her ribs. Even Ruad let out a yip.

So she's mortal after all, was all I had time to think before she slashed me across the stomach with one of her claws.

"That was damn clever, Pup. But you shouldn't put all your effort into one-hit blows. I'm still standing."

"Did I say I was finished?" I asked. She stopped speaking as I slashed down her front left leg with my own claws. She wouldn't be raising it to nick me again.

Ruad understood at once. I was here. This was it. I wasn't going down or backing off until she was unable to fight. I would endure any pain from her fangs and claws to see this through. It wasn't about shattering a time limit anymore. It was about shattering a pain limit.

"Come on!" I yelled.

My familiar answered by charging forward and sinking her teeth into my left thigh. I snarled and got a horizontal slash across her back, opening up the fur and letting more blood out. But she did not let go.

Ruad actually picked me up a few inches by the thigh and drove me back at record speed, slamming me into the cave wall. Part of the cavern shook, and I coughed up a good splatter of blood that doused Ruad's vermillion coat.

"That's enough, Pup. You've taken enough damage," she said, letting go of my thigh.

Feral Aoife wasn't through, and neither was I.

I snarled and muttered, "You haven't, though. Damage is something you look at when the fight's finished. And last I checked... I'm still standing!"

With that, I put my fists together in the air and brought them down, bashing into Ruad's head. I buried her face into the ground and picked her up with both hands.

Then I slammed my familiar into the floor on her back. She yipped and snarled, slashing me across the abdomen with her rear claws.

"You're teaching me so much, Ruad. But after so many lessons, it's time for me to show you what I'm capable of. And what I'm showing you at this moment is I can take it. You're going to acknowledge that, goddamnit."

Holding her down with my right arm on her neck, I finally took a breath. I could use pain for fuel, but I was learning my consciousness would only stick around for so long. Things were starting to get hazy.

With another couple slashes across my stomach from her rear claws, Ruad managed to free herself and maneuvered back toward the center of the cavern. It was the first time I'd been able to make her retreat.

Small victories where I can take them, I thought.

Looking down at my left thigh, I saw the puncture holes from her teeth. I wasn't going to be moving around on this thing for the rest of the fight. It hurt too much. She'd turned my thigh into Swiss cheese.

So I put my remaining energy into my right leg and knelt down low to the ground, front arms out forward like Ruad had been earlier.

I felt the wolf instincts growing even stronger inside of me. Hurt as I was, that thin red aura around me kept building.

"I'm ending this, Ruad!" I yelled, launching myself forward fast as I could go, claws extended. I didn't have the strength left for fancy tricks anymore. But maybe she didn't have the strength to counter a direct assault either. It was a risk I had to take.

When I was about halfway to Ruad, I felt the temperature around me drop immediately. And Ruad began to glow a light blue. This was the first time I felt her energy being used for something like this.

What is she doing? I thought, rocketing toward her.

Her eyes glowed a brilliant shade of maya, and I saw my familiar open her jaw.

I extended my claws as far as they would go and prepared to meet whatever this was. I was about 10 feet from my familiar when a beam of blue light shot from her mouth and slammed into me, instantly encasing the left side of my body in a thick layer of ice. I lost all my momentum and actually reversed course from the sheer power of her magic.

Hitting the ground now about 20 feet from Ruad, I couldn't feel my left side at all, my leg and arm encased in ice, ribs, too. The ice stopped a few inches from my face. Dust kicked up as I scraped along backward until I came to rest a few feet from the cave wall Ruad had smashed me into a few seconds ago.

I had nothing left. My left eye closed, and I saw Ruad limp over to me.

"Good job, Pup."

"You… didn't tell me you could… do that," I muttered with a weak tone, returning to my human form.

Ruad smiled.

"We're going to see just how far you can go over the next year. And as I rise to meet your new limits, you'll learn things about me you didn't know before," she said.

"Will you teach me ice magic?" I asked.

The wolf just stared at me for a moment before smashing the ice on my left side with her right paw. That half of my body immediately fell down to the dirt for me to lie entirely flat.

"I'm going to teach you a lot of things. Adrienn too."

I closed my good eye and started to drift off into sleep.

"Speaking of Adrienn. You wanna come down here and bandage your druid friend?"

I heard them fly down to the ground next to me and gasp.

"Don't you think you overdid it a little, Ruad?" They asked. "She's been bitten, slashed, and broken to pieces in some parts of her body."

Ruad said nothing for a minute. I could feel pain inside of her at the fey's words. She wanted to come over and lick my wounds, then kill the person responsible for inflicting them. But in addition to the pain, she felt resolve, a will to make me stronger so something worse than her didn't do this to me in the future. Malachos wouldn't wait for Adrienn to bandage me up.

"I'm going to overdo it several more times in the months ahead, Adrienn. I expect you to as well. It's the only way she'll grow stronger. She has a lot of training to make up for. As for her injuries, that's what the plants are for. Now get her patched up."

The fey didn't move.

"To what end?" they asked.

"How long did she maintain her wolf form?"

There was a pause, and Adrienn said, "Twelve minutes."

A little pride surged in Ruad, though she didn't admit it.

While she felt delighted, I couldn't feel much of anything. The room was starting to spin, and my vision eventually sank beneath a tide of darkness, muscles loosening all over my body. My eyes finally closed. And just before I lost realization of everything around me, Ruad said, "That's a grand improvement. Damn fine job, Pup."

Day 45

"Okay, you've brought up your speed on growing plants from seeds with your magic, but now we need to build that skill for when you're in a tough spot," Adrienn said.

I looked down at the five seeds in my right hand. They were all Boston ivy vine seeds, tiny, pointed, and black. Taking four in my left hand, I held the remaining seed in my right.

"How do you want to do this?" I asked, looking up at my fey guardian. They glowed green and hovered about three feet above my face.

Holding out their tiny hands, I saw each palm begin to glow, one red, one blue.

"I'm going to fly around and throw small bits of energy at you that'll glow different colors. If you get hit once, you lose. You win by growing a vine from those seeds and capturing me," they said.

Nodding, I took a deep breath. Something like this was to help me keep my focus. I'd spent the last two days learning how to grow all manner of plants in just a few seconds by manipulating them with my magic. The focus required was difficult to obtain.

But that's what the training was for. Could I dodge, focus, and aim at the same time? I guess we were about to find out.

"Go!" Adrienn yelled and started darting around in wild zigs and zags.

I summoned magic to my right hand and tried to sprout the seed, but a flash of yellow light flew down at me. Breaking my focus from the energy I was gathering, I jumped to the left, only to be struck by a blue orb of light.

Adrienn flew down. "Bang. You lose, Aoife."

Watching the light Adrienn hit me with fade, I took a deep breath. This was going to be more difficult than I thought.

We tried again, and I dodged about three or four flashes of light before getting hit again.

A third try saw me struck after four flashes again.

"Dammit! You're too fast!" I yelled, sweating.

The fey hovered in front of my face. They said nothing, offering no hints or tricks to pass at the training. I needed silence and focus to grow these seeds quickly. How was I supposed to do it in battle?

I thought I was impressive when I finally learned how to channel my magical energy into a seed without needing to draw blood, but this felt like jumping from pre-K to high school.

"Ready to go again?" They asked.

It's just going to be the same as last time. I'm not fast enough to dodge their light, I thought.

And then it came to me. Adrienn said I had to use these vines to capture them, but they didn't say I was forbidden from using all tools at my disposal.

With a shout of the words and drawing of energy, dust and wind swirled around me, transforming me into my wolf form.

Adrienn smiled.

We resumed, and I was finally fast enough to dodge their light bolts. Agility and speed were covered, but now I was eating energy to stay in this form, and I still needed to manipulate my plants.

Was this how Tristan did things? I thought, trying to remember stories Ruad told me about my father using nature magic. Did she ever say if he was in his wolf form? I didn't exactly have time to sit and think about it.

Focusing on the seed in my hand, I grew the vine, stripped off the leaves, and extended it long enough that it would have been a lasso.

Tying a knot, I swung the lasso around at Adrienn.

"Get along, little doggie!" I yelled, smiling, and tossing the vine up at where they were.

They zigged past my lasso easily. The next few tries saw me trying to use my energy to manipulate my vine to close around the fey, but it wasn't fast enough.

Dodging more light blasts, I eventually grew frustrated and decided the vine lasso wasn't going to work. Taking another seed in my right claw, I grew the vine into a baseball size cluster and hurled it up at the fey. Adrienn narrowly dodged the ball, and when it hit the cave wall, the vines snatched up a nearby spider, wrapping around it.

When the fey saw this, they smiled and called down, "Wow. Manipulating the vine's behavior as you grow it, giving it instructions like that. You're impressive, Aoife."

"Not impressive enough, apparently," I said, sweating to manipulate another vine ball and hurling it at the fey.

They zigged around it with ease and hurled more light bolts at me.

This might just be the worst game of dodgeball in the history of ever, I thought.

"Maybe I need a bigger net," I said, picking up two stones. I used my remaining two seeds to grow a net of vines and used the rocks as weights until I had a rather large net with holes too small for even Adrienn to easily squeeze through.

I put energy into my legs and ran up the cave wall, throwing my net. It doubled in size as it flew through the air, and to my credit, Adrienn did look a little surprised to see it. But it missed them by about four or five inches.

"That's all your seeds, isn't it?" They asked.

I nodded.

"We'll try again when you're ready," Adrienn said.

They offered no critique, just a patient understanding that I needed a second to catch my breath, and we'd try again later.

We sat there for a while until my strength returned. But the next three attempts I made at capturing Adrienn were less than stellar.

I collapsed next to an underground spring we'd been using for our water and splashed my face. It was cold, and my red bangs hung damp like a rag on my forehead.

Adrienn flew into the water, making a tiny cannonball. When they came out, little droplets flew off their wings. This cavern where time selectively stood still had some awfully strange qualities. We didn't have to eat here, but staying hydrated was still a necessity. Not sure how that worked. Though not having my monthly cycles was a plus.

As my fey guardian flew over me, water droplets fell down onto my forehead from their wings. I sighed and relaxed my shoulders. They flew down and stood on top of my head before sitting down cross-legged.

I snickered. "Excuse me. Can I help you?"

They said, "What? My butt is still wet from diving into the water. You want me to sit it on the cold cave floor? I think not. Your hair is nice and warm as I wait for it to dry off."

I swatted them away and stuck my tongue out.

"Gross! Fey booty germs! I can't believe you did this to me," I screamed while both Adrienn and Ruad laughed.

My next two attempts to capture Adrienn were unsuccessful, and I realized raw speed, strength, and aim wasn't going to get me through this. I needed a plan. Fey were smart, nimble, and I couldn't bulldoze my way through this like I did so many sparring sessions with Ruad.

Looking up at one of the cave walls, I saw three or four of the vine balls I'd made earlier, still stuck to the damp surface. I smiled.

"Adrienn, I'm ready for one more shot whenever you are."

They turned to me and smiled, left fist glowing.

"Whatever you say, Aoife. I hope you're successful."

Only Adrienn is nice enough to root for someone to succeed against them, I thought.

They handed me five more seeds from our supply, and I closed them in my right hand.

"I've got a little plan… for the little Adrienn," I muttered.

That was a stupid rhyme, but probably the best I could come up with after being stuck underground for more than a month, I thought.

"Begin!" Adrienn said, and I threw four of the seeds into my right hand, focusing my magic on the other.

From my enclosed fist sprouted a long vine that snaked up my arm to my elbow and multiplied into smaller vines. I started to sweat, forming them into a shape from an image in my mind.

Vines snaked together tightly to form a solid plant surface. And then ivy leaves sprouted and laid flat against the vines, creating a smooth green disc over my left lower arm. It finished just in time to block a few balls of light. The shield glowed blue and then purple, but the light quickly faded.

"Forming a plant into an object, a shield nonetheless. That's impressive. But can you capture me with a shield?" They asked, throwing a few more balls of light, which I blocked.

I smiled.

Now to drive the cattle home, I thought. *Why all the cowgirl talk tonight?*

I'd deal with my internal Wynonna Earp later. Right now, I focused on making another vine ball and hurled it at Adrienn. They dodged as they had everything else tonight. I made a second ball and threw it, moving Adrienn closer to the cave wall.

My third ball pushed them even closer.

I rushed forward with my last vine ball and leapt into the air. With about ten feet between us, I threw the last ball and seemed to catch Adrienn. But my fey guardian had slid under it with a feat that put Neo to shame.

Before they could say, "Nice try," I opened my left fist and willed the vines to push my shield forward at the fey like a detached flyswatter. Adrienn's eyes grew to the size of dinner plates, but their fists both lit up, and quickly blasted the shield with a bombardment of light orbs that sent it flying to the ground.

My guardian fey was about six inches from the cave wall now and breathing heavily.

"That was the closest you've come yet, Aoife. Really gave me a good workout."

I just smirked and said, "We're not done yet, sweetheart."

My vine balls had all flattened and spread out upon meeting the wall, making a solid patchwork quilt of ivy, several feet tall and wide.

"That was your last seed, Aoife," they said, puzzled.

Closing my eyes, I felt my magic in the quilt of vines I'd grown on the cave wall. Every ball I'd thrown on the surface had unfurled and attached to the others along the wall. They clung tight like a tapestry of vegetation with Adrienn right underneath. I willed the top half of that tapestry to let go of the wall and let gravity take over from there. It fell toward its bottom half, ensnaring Adrienn like a folded piece of bread.

From inside, I heard Adrienn yelling something.

"And that's game," I said, sitting down as Ruad walked over.

"Nicely played, Pup. You want to just leave them in there for a few more minutes?"

I ran my fingers through Ruad's fur and rested my head on her. This scent was one of the only things keeping me sane in this training ground where time stood still.

With another focus of my will, the vines spread apart enough that a green blur of light shot through them and back down to me.

"Well done, Aoife. That was spectacular," Adrienn said before flying into my pendant.

Taking a deep breath and sighing, I walked back over to the spring for a drink. It wasn't that progress was slow. I felt like I'd improved so much in the first month of being in this cave. But my heart was beginning to feel heavy. I missed sunlight, singing birds, and Abi. By the gods I missed my girlfriend. No matter how much stronger I got, it didn't improve my mental standing, and there was still a long road ahead.

Day 71

Ruad was asleep over by a bed of ivy that'd spread down onto the cave floor. I sat over in the spring, dipping my feet in the water. Ruad and I had just finished another endurance session to see how long I could keep my transformation. I'd worked my way up to about 40 minutes.

We'd exhausted ourselves running circles around the cavern, alternating between a full sprint and a jog.

A bead of sweat ran down my forehead, and I stared down into the clear blue water. Thoughts drifted to Abi, and my heart began to ache. Whenever I wasn't training, I had little to distract myself. And I wasn't tired enough to sleep like Ruad was, more so anxious, actually. Sure, it was only a day in Abi's time, but I hoped she's safe.

Ash was being a pal and checking in on her from afar. It was a little stalkerish given that he could literally hide from her sight with an illusion, but it was okay because I texted and asked him to do it. At least, I think that made it okay, even if I didn't tell Abi because I knew she'd object. But given that there's a bloodthirsty necromancer running loose, I think my decisions were more than justified. Yup. Totally okay what I asked Ash to do.

In fact, I took note of how safe I felt with Ash watching over Abi. I carried his deepest secret, his freshest pain. He trusted me with each. So, of course, asking him to protect that which I held most dear came easily enough.

I sat there, just wanting to hear her walk into the cave and call for her sweet cinnamon. A solitary tear ran down my cheek and dipped into the water, causing a few small ripples around my legs.

What time is it? God, I'm so lost, I thought.

With a flash of green light, Adrienn flew out of my necklace, holding something.

"Aoife?"

I looked over at them, not even having the cheer to fake a smile.

"I know you're having a rough time down here. So I brought out something to cheer you up," they said.

Taking a closer look in their arms, I noticed they held a seed.

"Do you have enough energy left to grow this?"

They placed the seed into my right palm. Digging deep, I found I still had enough magic to grow it. Sighing and closing my eyes, I pushed energy into the seed and willed it to grow.

A large bush began to take form and sprout up. When it became too awkward to hold, I held it next to the dirt, and it grew downward. The bush sprouted up until it was about six feet tall and had these long thin twig-like branches that started to weigh some parts of the plant down. Little berry clusters formed where the twigs drooped.

When it finally finished growing, I marveled at what Adrienn had snuck into the cave. We'd brought a big-ass satchel full of all kinds of different seeds to practice, but it seemed like they had brought this seed in via my pendant.

I held my palm out flat as Adrienn flew down into it, smiling. I lightly kissed their head and said, "Thank you." During the summer I loved fresh blueberries. They were my favorite fruit to eat.

Picking a handful, I popped some into my mouth and enjoyed the sweet taste immediately.

I handed one to Adrienn. It took both of their hands to hold the berry and eat it, a splotch of juice dangling from their chin.

I laughed, and we just sat there eating berries for a little bit. There were a few patches left I decided to save for another pity party. Then I went over to my pack of things I'd brought down and fetched my violin.

Bringing it back over to the water, I stood and said, "Adrienn, you're so sweet and thoughtful. I appreciate all you do for me."

They blushed and pretended to kick a can with their foot looking bashful.

"I know this isn't easy on you," they said. "But if anyone can get through it, you can. And we'll help."

Smiling, I closed my eyes and began to play. The acoustics weren't the best, but I didn't care. I wanted to thank Adrienn in a way they'd truly appreciate.

So I played through one of Lindsey Stirling's songs called "Master of Tides." Slowly, I slid the pitch up to where the song started.

Adrienn just smiled and bobbed their head as I got into the main melody. About a minute into the song, Ruad finally stirred. "I thought I smelled fruit. You thought you could sneak food into the training cave without paying the wolf tax, Pup? Nice try."

She slowly rose from her bed of overgrown ivy vines and stretched.

"Some of those berries are mine," she said, but before she could take a step, I remembered what happened last time I played the violin in my old room.

Smiling, I focused my attention to the vines and faced them while playing the song, tapping my left foot. Ruad was almost off the bed of vines, but several of them snaked around her hind legs and rear half of her body. Before she could turn her head and wonder what was happening, the vines dragged her back to the wall and restrained her.

She started a growl that worked its way into a deep laugh and said, "Oh, Pup. That's really cute."

As she tried to free herself, I used my song to keep focus and tangle her further. For every vine she snapped with her fangs, two more wrapped around her.

And when I finished my song and put the violin back in its case, I turned back to see my captive. It felt good to have turned the tables on her for once. I was giggling.

Looking back, I saw a big chunk of ice where she'd previously been and several snapped frozen vines.

"Uh oh" was all I had time to say before Ruad body-slammed me into the frigid spring water.

I just laid there horizontal in the water for a moment replaying my decisions of the last few seconds, wondering if plotting further retaliation would be worth it. Deciding against it, I climbed out of the water and shook myself dry.

Looking over, Ruad was smiling as she munched on the last of the blueberries.

"Well Pup. You're getting better at aggravating me. Or at least, the quality of your aggravations is rising. Of course, as you just saw, I will return whatever you dish out three times over. Remember that next time."

She plopped down to finish her blueberries, and I walked over pouting. I curled up into a ball and nuzzled close to her fur.

"Hey, you're all wet!" she protested.

"Deal with it," I said, knowing full well she could grab my arm and hurl me back into the spring. She chose not to, and I drifted off into sleep.

Day 150

I'd successfully maintained my wolf form for an hour a couple days ago, which seemed to please Ruad, but there was always a new milestone to hit in this stupid cave. Today she was finally going to teach me how to access that ice magic.

I sat in the middle of the cavern cross legged like a pretzel while Ruad circled around me. It was so strange for my familiar to be giving me a one-on-one lecture. But she insisted it was necessary to learn about this particular form of magic.

Behind me, the wolf started her lecture.

"Nine types of elemental magic in the world, one you're already familiar with as a druid... nature. The others are storm, ice, water, wind, earth, flame, light and darkness."

I turned to face her and asked, "So... you're going to teach me all of them? I'll be able to manipulate fire? And ice?"

"Elemental magic is something you're born with, Pup. You can't teach it," Ruad said.

I started to stand up.

"Well, good talk. I wasn't born like Elsa, so I'll just get back to growing plants."

Ruad barked at me and said, "Sit down, Pup. No, you weren't born with ice magic inside of you. But that doesn't mean you lack the ability to use it."

I raised an eyebrow and kept myself seated on the cave floor. "If I wasn't born with ice magic, and you can't teach it, how am I going to use it?"

My familiar moved to face me and said, "How do you take a wolf form?"

I thought for a minute and said, "Our souls and magic are linked, and since mine intertwines with your own, it changes my body."

"Basically. You're borrowing some of my essence, and it transforms you. So if I can use ice magic, then you can borrow that ability as well. Basically, everything good in your life comes from me, your instincts, your form, some of your magic, the works," Ruad said, smiling.

Rolling my eyes, I sighed. This wolf. My wolf.

"So, how are we going to get this ice magic transferred to me?"

Ruad walked directly in front of me and sat down.

"I can give you energy from across our internal bridge with ease, Pup. But elemental magic isn't a baton that can be passed off so easily. You're going to have to travel inside of my mind forest and retrieve it. Once you find it, it'll mark you, and you'll be able to call my ice magic over our bridge."

I flinched a little bit, and Ruad noticed it.

"What's bothering you, Pup?"

Raising my eyes to meet her amber gaze, I said, "My own mind forest is unpredictable enough, Ruad. You want me to wander around in yours for, what? A few hours? Days? Weeks?"

Ruad did not smile this time.

"Every druid's mind forest is different. I can't say what you'll encounter in mine or how long this will take..."

Taking a deep breath, I looked at my familiar and tried not to show any more fear.

Fat lot of good that would do me. She was a magical wolf. No doubt Ruad could smell my fear from five miles away.

She licked my cheek and brought me out of my thoughts.

"You'll be fine, Pup. You're strong, the daughter of Tristan and Iris and now the alpha of the O'Connell pack. Now head into your own mind forest, work your way to our bridge, and then cross into mine. There you'll find the source of my ice magic. But I will warn you, attuning to it isn't something you can just conquer. Like our bond, you must attune through faith, trust and…"

"Pixie dust?" I added, clearly nervous about the task ahead of me.

"And the conviction of our unspoken or spoken promises to each other," Ruad said as she shot me a scowl.

"Right…" I said, taking a deep breath.

Nodding, I thought of my father. He'd done this before, right? And if I was determined to become a great leader like him and Iris, I had to do this.

Okay, let's go get some ice magic, I thought. Then I nodded to Ruad, closed my eyes, and focused. Taking a deep breath, I felt everything go black, and then I opened my eyes, standing in a misty forest.

"Hello forest my old friend…" I muttered, trying to break the eerie silence.

The mist was cool, which was no change from the cave I'd been staying in over the last several months. What I'd wished would come through in my mind forest was a little bit of sunlight. But I guess inner Aoife wasn't a sunshine kind of gal.

The trees I walked through were varied, pine, sycamore, oak, lots of oak. The bark was jagged in places and looked like it'd been clawed through.

Yeah yeah, I know. Inner and emotional trauma. Fun stuff, I thought.

I had no idea where I was going, so I paused to smell the air around me. Humidity carried its own odor, as did freshly-fallen rain and decaying leaves. But the scent of a vermillion wolf stood apart from the rest, a wet canine that smelled like she'd been rolling around in cedar chips. I could thank my enhanced senses for pulling Ruad's scent apart like separating a single thread from a knitted scarf.

Walking for who knows how long, I heard a rustling in the bushes behind me. I turned and crossed my arms.

"Come on out. I know I'm not alone in here," I said.

And out walked… me. Well, a rougher version of me, with a truly messy tangled mane of red bushy hair and wild eyes.

"Hey feral me. How's it going?"

She leaned against a tree and smirked.

"I just came by to thank you, my other half." She said, her voice raspy.

I raised an eyebrow.

"Did I send you a fruit basket by mistake? Because that was meant for something I actually appreciate inside of me, like one of the trees or maybe a patch of moss that you sliced up with your claws for no reason. So if you could go ahead and give that fruit basket back to the patch of moss and apologize, I'd appreciate it. You wouldn't want to make moss sad, would you?"

Feral Aoife did not snarl at my remark as I anticipated. She was wild, but restrained herself a bit, which was a first for me.

"Don't try to mask your fear with false bravado. I can smell it blanketing you in ways you cannot disguise. Remember, Aoife, I am you. I'm your terror, your anger, your sadness, your guilt, your regrets and your deepest fears," she said.

When I simply responded with a scowl, my feral half continued.

"I just wanted to thank you for doing all the hard work and training this body for me. It shouldn't take too much longer, and eventually it'll be mine. And I'll just let you roam around the mind forest all day with nothing to do, just like me."

She glanced at her claws. There, on her finger, scurried a red and purple beetle, jittering from her knuckle to her nail. Without a second thought, she flicked the beetle away.

Her words sent a shiver down my spine. What she described wasn't really possible, was it? Feral Aoife was just like the shadow of my conscience, right? If I had a moral dilemma, and Adrienn appeared on one shoulder, this bitch would show up on the other. Her taking control of my body would be like a headache becoming sentient and seizing my autonomy. That had to be impossible... right?

Taking a deep breath, I turned to leave and said, "I don't have time to mess with you right now. Go back into the trees, and leave me alone."

"Just this once. The line is thinning between you and I. Remember, Aoife... I am you."

Walking onward, I kept trying to shake worrisome thoughts, but I've never met anyone, human or wolf, who was actually capable of ditching doubt. What if my feral side did take control and left me to wander my mind forest? Had I already gotten a taste of what it would be like?

I'd been in this godforsaken cave for months now. I've cried out for sunlight and my friends more times than I could count, only to be continually stuck under those glowing blue rocks in the ceiling. Perhaps this is what insanity felt like, reaching the boundaries of what your psyche can handle before snapping. The isolation and darkness in this cave was pushing me ever closer to the thin membrane separating sane from insane, and my feral half was out here with a razor blade, shaving that boundary away, layer by layer.

If feral Aoife took over, would I just swap the cave for these limitless misty trees? I'd do my crying here, away from even Ruad and Adrienn? And what would even happen to Ruad and our bond if feral Aoife took control?

A whimper of fear escaped my throat, so I closed my eyes and willed these worries away with everything I had. It worked about as well as off brand headache pills. Then I remembered I wasn't here for me, but for Ruad and suddenly some of the worry seemed to diminish.

A little further, the trees began to thin out, and I saw a giant stone bridge about 30-40 feet across and 15 feet high. It was an impressive structure.

"Strong…" I muttered, as the scent of Ruad grew with each step I took closer to our bridge.

My familiar's smell wrapped around me like a rope, pulling me closer to the other side, where all the leafless trees were covered in a thick layer of snow.

Taking a step onto the bridge, I began to feel a tingling energy all over my body. I was crossing over from my inner self to Ruad's. Her own magic was feeling me out, making sure I wasn't a threat.

A deep chasm beneath me descended to a lightless bottom. I couldn't see where the chasm ended. So I just focused on crossing and putting one foot in front of the other.

When my foot hit Ruad's side, I immediately transformed into my wolf form.

Looking down at my claws, I muttered, "Well that sure wasn't me. I guess if I'm going to be in a wolf's mind forest, I'd best be a wolf."

For a moment, my body hesitated. Ruad's energy actually seemed to push me back. I hesitated, wondering if I'd done something wrong in my walk over. But eventually, that resistance gave way, and I took another step in. Pausing, I wondered what could have caused that pushback. Then I realized.

It's the smell of Tristan's blood, which flows through my veins, I thought. *Ruad trusts me but instinctively remembers her pain and scars from my father.*

I walked into my familiar's forest and looked around as the bridge left my view behind me. Ruad's mind forest was hyper charged with an intense energy. She was strong, and she was mine.

None of the energy threatened me now. I knew I was welcome here, the only one. I doubt even Adrienn would be allowed to tread here.

Walking into the wintry woods, I suddenly realized I had no idea which direction to go in. I mean, distance was all relative in a space like this, right? It wasn't like I could measure this out in miles.

Smelling the air, I took notice of evergreens, shrubs, boulders, and… it was starting to snow.

"Okay, Ruad. Which way do I go?" I yelled into the forest. I waited a few minutes, but there was no response.

"How about you Adrienn?" I asked, but they didn't appear. Looking down, I realized my necklace was gone.

Only me, I thought.

Sighing, I muttered, "Well, guess I'll just start walking and hope to find something."

So, I wandered, aimless. There really wasn't anything for me to track. What was I even looking for? What did ice magic look like inside a mind forest?

Walking deeper into the forest, I noticed the snow falling heavier and growing colder. I started to rub my arms in hopes of warming myself up, but it was useless. No matter what I did, the icy wind kept nipping at my bare skin. Soon, I was downright miserable. Mt. Everest was probably warmer than this! Okay, probably not. But when you're in the moment, you know how it is.

After a bit of pained exploring, the cold started to sting. My knees and arms radiated pain, a kind of blunt ache.

Another few steps, and I didn't know what caused me to turn, but I did. Something was coming. I didn't smell it, so much as I felt the ache in me grow stronger.

Then she stepped out from behind a tree, a mahogany-colored wolf. Her fur was patched with dried blood and grime. Some parts of the flesh almost looked rotten to me. And was that bone I saw on the hind legs?

I gasped when I realized this darker wolf looked like a scraggly Ruad. She was in even rougher shape than feral Aoife.

"Geez, Ruad. Who dug you out of the Pet Sematary?" I asked as my words almost got choked up in my throat. I had to try and make light of the situation with humor, or I was going to start crying. Seeing a Ruad, any Ruad, that looked like this reminded me how much she had suffered, and how much she might still be suffering. My heart was starting to splinter, and I didn't even know if this was some kind of illusion.

The darker Ruad snarled and revealed a chipped canine on the left side. The right canine was intact but it seemed practically seconds from rotting away at any moment. Her tongue, when I saw it hanging loose, was covered in holes.

"Oh my God, Ruad. What happened to you?" I asked, my hands coming up to cover my mouth. I felt hot tears welling in my eyes.

My dark familiar kneeled low and started to growl.

"It's me, Aoife. You sent me in here, remember? I'm supposed to find the ice magic."

The wolf didn't look like it understood me. And then it lunged, and I ducked in time to avoid a jaw around the throat. I had a feeling that unlike regular Ruad, this one wasn't going to just leave a bruise.

Before I could spin around, the darker Ruad rebounded and tore into my right thigh. Her fangs went down to the bone. I screamed and raised a claw to strike back but when I caught another glimpse of her wounds, I couldn't bring myself to defend my body and hurt her in the process. No matter how much pain the wolf caused me, no matter how many times she might bite into me, she already looked like she'd suffered enough for a lifetime, and I just couldn't add to that.

But this Ruad had no qualms about hurting me. She flung me into a nearby tree, and my back hit the trunk hard enough that I cried out in pain.

"Another druid, come to abandon me," she hissed in a dark voice that was both my familiar and not. The voice felt like sandpaper rubbed against my eardrums.

"Ruad... it's me, Aoife. You know me!"

"What I know is abandonment... pain... separation... isolation. Your kind never keeps their oath. Druids always cast me aside, just like Tristan!"

I held a hand to my mouth and almost choked on the realization. Looking down at the chest, I saw a deep stab wound where Ruad's heart should have been. Where Tristan had stabbed himself with dark magic to sever their tie.

213

"You're not Ruad. You're a manifestation of her fear of abandonment and rage of betrayal," I choked, starting to cry.

My father did this to her. And this thing... has been roaming her mind forest all these years gnawing at and haunting her like some lurking ghost, I thought.

"Tristan..." I muttered, and even saying that name brought a whole new level of ferocity to feral Ruad. The wolf rushed forward, gnashing at my throat.

A few months ago, she might have gotten to my throat. But I'd been training nonstop since then. I threw up my left arm, playing sacrificial limb again, and her fangs sank around it. Her teeth went all the way down to my radius bone, and I felt a terrible crack. What could I do? I screamed. At least my throat was still intact so I *could* scream.

I managed to claw the side of dark Ruad's neck, and she let go, backing up a few feet.

"How dare you say that name? He broke his sworn oath!"

I'd never felt such a hateful presence. Even Barb with all her spit and vinegar never came close to this level of despising me.

Years of solitary mournful wandering through the Ozarks without purpose had spawned this toxic despair, made it stronger. How could I even begin to help heal it? Even if Ruad and I spent the rest of our lives together, would I be able to make this beast vanish?

Looking into the bloodshot amber eyes of a stained Ruad, I knew right then I had to fix this. My best friend. My familiar. The one I'd bonded my soul to. I couldn't leave this beast roaming around in here, causing her who knows how much torment.

I stood, my left arm dangling near useless. Raising my right arm, I placed a hand on the tree behind me, feeling for a presence.

Wait a second... will I even be able to manipulate the plants here? This is a mind forest, and it's not even mine, I thought, my fingers twitching for a moment.

Eventually, I resolved to try my luck. I needed the help.

Sending magic into the tree, I felt something stir to my will.

"Please help me," I begged.

Feral Ruad lunged again, but I watched the tree branch above me extend toward the ground.

Ruad's doppelganger crashed into a wall of tree limbs, inches from my face. The branches formed a giant birdcage around feral Ruad. And the wood grew thicker, narrowing the spaces between limbs.

Patting the tree and sighing I said, "Thank you."

"I will not be abandoned again!" the screeching wolf said.

I flinched at her words but then turned and said, "One day you won't plague my familiar anymore. I will heal her heart, and I promise you I will never make the same mistake my father did."

Then I turned and limped further into the woods, leaving a trail of blood behind me. After wandering for a bit, I came to a clearing, at least 100 feet around. In the center stood an evergreen tree entirely encased in several feet of ice, a giant glacier. The tree rose about 40 feet, but the glacier stood even taller, made of a jagged and cruel chilled crystal.

A freezing gale rose from the glacier and raced toward me. As the cold raked over my skin, I noticed its origin. This was the same ice magic I'd been blasted with in the cave when I sparred with Ruad.

This is it, I thought.

As I walked toward the glacier, an even larger gust of wind kicked up. The closer I got, the deeper the wind dug into me, like knives burrowing under my skin.

"No wonder Ruad couldn't send you over the bridge," I hissed.

The temperature plunged as the glacier began to glow blue. My limbs were all aching again, and a blizzard raged around the clearing as snow whirled every which way.

Son of a bitch, I thought, hissing again.

I squinted and closed my eyes, the wind stinging them. I fell to my knees as the snow started to bury me in real time.

All I could hear was the howling wind as the snow piled up to my knees.

What I wanted to do was lie down and pass out from the chilling touch of this raw, deadly power. Ruad wanted me to have the ice magic, right? Then why the fuck was it fighting me so hard?

Then I realized something. It wasn't Ruad trying to keep me from the ice magic. I was struggling with her subconscious, something Ruad had lost some grip on through the years of wandering in the woods alone.

The pain was too much for her, I thought. *So she tried to push it down and out of sight. Where have I seen this strategy before?*

When she did this, Ruad lost sight of her trauma, at least a little bit. And this was the result, a neglected subconscious where feral emotions and terrorizing trauma festered for years on end. Ruad wasn't fighting me like I was some bacterial invader being attacked by white blood cells. My familiar turned me loose in a land she was too afraid to look back on.

"It was easier to put the pain aside and try to move forward. I can relate to that," I muttered. But if this was too much for her to handle, how was I supposed to face Ruad's inner demons?

Maybe if I passed out, I would wake up back in the cave. I could explain to Ruad that I tried, but it wasn't meant to be. I didn't need ice magic to fight Malachos and maybe this was a weapon my arsenal could do without.

The snow came up to my waist now. My bones felt like groaning glass as they froze into place.

Ruad... I'm sorry. I couldn't take it. I'm so sorry, I thought.

When listening was about all I could still do, I started hearing echoing voices once more, swirling around in the snow and wind. Was the cavern calling more scenes from the past for me to experience?

A man's grunts and hisses of pain cut through the other noise of the past, and I even heard Tristan swear. His joints and muscles were pulled tight, compressed by the same frigid air I felt now. He'd been here before.

I closed my eyes and listened for some hint of how he succeeded, some advice in the scenes I was seeing. For a few moments I heard nothing but his groaning, but with a deeper level of concentration, I heard something whisper. Was it talking to my father? "Use meeeee," it muttered. I wasn't sure what spoke to Tristan. "My power is yoursssss," the tiny voice whispered to my father.

With a growl of my own, I drowned out the past noise, unsure of what became of Tristan. One thought filled my mind. "He did this." My father was responsible for the pain coursing through my familiar's mind forest. And part of me hated him for it, as I'm sure Ruad did.

The mind forest probably wasn't this intense when Tristan visited the first time, I realized. I'd wager the mind forest greeted my father as a dear friend. He wasn't chased down by a feral version of Ruad. And he likely didn't meet an ounce of resistance when he came to access Ruad's ice magic. Hell, I bet he strolled right up and grabbed it.

But inevitably his actions led to this moment. His choices led to Ruad's torment and the subsequent environment I was facing now, one hostile to myself because of the father who'd come before me and fucked everything up for my familiar. Realizing all this made me angry with him all the more.

I clung to that anger as warmth flooded back into my limbs. My magic kicked into high gear and built around me.

As heat returned to my body, I heard feral Ruad's howl mixed in with the icy wind whipping around me. "No," I growled.

I pictured feral Ruad with that gaping chest wound my father had caused when he severed their bond. It was the greatest pain of Ruad's life, and I was going to heal it. I had to.

My knees buckled from exhaustion, but I screamed, "We don't have a choice. Get up, and get to it!" Sometimes yelling at myself was good motivation. I hoped now was one of those times.

Slowly rising, I lifted my arms and pushed away the powdery snow that'd been piling on me. I climbed free in what felt like slow motion.

Then I took a small step, perhaps the smallest step ever taken in the history of womankind. It couldn't have been more than a few millimeters. But it was a start. And a start was all I needed right at that moment.

Somehow the wind grew stronger, more violent, and ice began to creep up my arms as I raised them to shield my face from the vicious storm.

"I'm coming for you, glacier. So throw everything you've got at me because when I get there, I want you to know I earned this power!" I yelled.

Somewhere behind me, feral Ruad's howl also grew, letting me know the wolf was closing in.

Calling forward every bit of strength I had, I pushed, pushed like I'd never pushed before. Wind raged, and ice creeped, trying to shove me back from the glacier. But I was a goddamn unstoppable wolf, determined to capture this energy so that I can restore my clan and defeat Malachos.

"If that's all you've got, you'd best stop now. It's not enough," I said.

The earth quaked. Trees bent over to the ground from the glacier's wind. I heard branches shattering around me, but it couldn't stop me.

Just a few more steps, and I'd be there.

My left arm was entirely covered in ice, and I couldn't feel it anymore. My right arm was almost there, with just my wrist and hand free. My eyes were bleeding, my ears too. I was pretty sure all the flesh I had exposed was turning blue or purple from the cold. But inside… inside I only felt my determination growing.

"She's my familiar, goddammit. And I'll save her. I'll make sure the rest of her days are filled with joy and laughter at my side. I swear."

217

Advancing on the glacier, my movement took every ounce of strength with each step. I'd put a foot down and spend my remaining strength. Then I'd do it again. And again. How many times could I spend my remaining strength? As many times as it took. As many times as I needed.

A red aura started to glow bright over my skin, piercing the blue light in front of me. Slamming a foot down in front of the glacier, I pushed forward with one last great blast of strength and slapped my claw on the glacier. I wasn't sure if that's how the magic worked, but I prayed a connection would build what I needed.

"Come on!" I yelled and felt the ice magic enter me through my right claw. The energy was frigid and shook me to my innermost joints. But I also knew it was mine now. Ruad had agreed to grant me access, and I wouldn't let her down.

As the wind died down, I felt this new power settle at my core. The ice covering me receded, and I was free to move around once more.

Looking down at my arms, I saw my red aura had turned to blue to match the glacier. A pale blue triangle marking appeared on my right arm, just below the shoulder. That's when I heard a snarl at the edge of the clearing.

Turning, I saw feral Ruad there, glaring at me.

"You're not worthy of that magic. No O'Connell is," she hissed.

"This ends now," I said, taking a step toward the manifestation of isolation Ruad had felt over the last several years. "She has me now, and I'll never leave her side. Your time of haunting these woods is over."

Feral Ruad launched forward with a renewed hatred and barked, "You will die in this mind forest, druid!"

A cold wind flew over my body as I extended my hand toward the wolf, the bastard image of my familiar. And I felt a chilled magic growing in my chest.

"My name is Pup, you bitch!" I yelled.

Then I let it all loose, every bit of determination I had to save my familiar's heart and mend it whole once more.

"Freeze," I whispered, and a crackling beam of blue energy raced from my hand and slammed into feral Ruad, ending her momentum.

I poured everything I had left into the icy blast, gritting my teeth the entire time, assured of my promise to fix that damage Tristan caused.

When the beam finally faded, I saw a new glacier had formed, this one around a snarling feral Ruad. The beast was encased in ice so thick, I prayed she'd never escape to harm Ruad again. This new glacier was about a quarter of the size I'd touched earlier. Limping by it, I looked into feral Ruad's eyes and said, "Haunt my familiar no more."

Then, holding my damaged arm, I limped all the way back to my bridge and into my own mind forest, feeling the cold leave me as I came into my own space. I collapsed not too far off the bridge and felt everything fade to black.

I gradually woke to a warm weight over my stomach and chest, making it a little hard to breathe. When my eyes opened and cleared, I saw Ruad parked on top of me like she had been when Ash was in the greenhouse. Her head was on my chest, amber eyes looking down into my own like they'd been watching and waiting for my own pupils to reappear.

Ruad raised her head a bit when I woke up.

"You got really cold there for a bit," she said.

"You're telling me," I whispered. My hands were shaking, and the cave was a little jarring. I still felt exhausted from the inner voyage.

For a minute, we just sat there staring into each other's eyes. And I saw she was different now. There was a renewed light in her amber glare.

I couldn't put into words exactly what I'd done, and she couldn't put into words how grateful she was for the burden I silenced. So I just ran my hands through her fur and smiled. She brought her nose to mine, and we stayed there like that for a few minutes, just grateful to have each other and knowing nothing could ever separate us.

Day 270

We all sat around the spring, munching on some strawberries I'd grown from a seed Adrienn smuggled in with them. These were the last fruits we'd get until leaving the cave. I'd just pushed my wolf transformation to two hours and was thoroughly exhausted.

Sighing and taking a bite of another strawberry, I let the sweet, mildly acidic juice drip down my chin. I didn't even care anymore. I was beyond caring about a lot of things at this point. Being underground for months on end will do that to you.

Adrienn sat on my left knee finishing off their own strawberry.

"So what's the first thing you're going to do when we get out of here?" they asked Ruad.

Waiting for Ruad to answer, I smiled and thought of Abi for the 1,000,000th time. There was no shame left. I was picturing her in her matching white bra and panties lying on the bed, just waiting for me to come back.

"I'm going to take Pup here and go running after some deer. Just because I don't have to eat here doesn't mean I don't miss the taste of meat in my jaws. And I could use a good long run with some changing scenery."

I smiled. Yeah, a good long run through the mountains. That sounded amazing, under the pale moonlight and stars all around. No more blue growing crystals. No more biting isolation. No more eating only fruit. No more damp cavern air filling my lungs with every breath.

"You two forget, this isn't my first time in this cavern. I trained down here with Tristan as well, a few months before he married Iris. I never dreamed about coming down here again," my familiar said, finishing her last strawberry.

I lightly patted her head.

"Yeah, yeah. You're more badass than Adrienn and me," I chuckled.

"Well I don't know about that. Back before I was a few inches tall in the human world, I was a fierce bandit. I've fought some pretty tough battles myself," they said, in perhaps the first brag I'd ever heard from them.

I smiled, and Ruad scoffed.

"In your last battle, you fled from a monster into the Mortal Realm and had to be rescued by Iris and Tristan."

"Yeah, after I'd killed five other monsters just like it in the Fey Realm," Adrienn said. "Bit off a little more than I could chew."

My familiar didn't have a comeback or retort for that one.

I popped the last strawberry into my mouth and looked longingly at the now-empty bush.

"How about you, Aoife? What's the first thing you're going to do when you get out of here?" they asked.

I pictured Abi on her bed again, just sitting there waiting for me.

"I dunno. Probably text Abi or something," I said, trying to play it cool.

Ruad and I exchanged glances, and she grinned. I had a sneaking suspicion she knew exactly what I was thinking about with Abi.

Day 364

Ruad stood to my left.

"Okay, Pup. Show me something impressive," she said.

I was already in my wolf form and holding a seed in my right claw. I tossed it about 20 feet in front of me, keeping my focus tight on the seed.

"I can feel your magic attached to the seed. You can manipulate plants from a distance now, right?" Ruad asked.

"You ain't seen nothing yet," I said, raising my right hand toward the seed as it hit the cave floor and sprouted into roots.

I throttled my energy into the seed without limit, summoning forth new life at a faster speed than I ever had before.

"What are you planting today, Pup?" Ruad asked.

I was really going to blow her away this time.

"Grow," I commanded, willing it to jet up into the air.

A mighty tree expanded rapidly from sapling into a thick trunk with widening branches. Higher and higher the tree shot up, thickening with rich foliage until it slammed into the top of the cavern. I stood there, sweating profusely. It dripped off my forehead and chin. Adrienn and Ruad just looked on with their jaws open.

"And that… is a white ash tree," I said.

"Masterfully done," Adrienn whispered.

Ruad had no words for me.

Then I lowered the temperature around me and dug into my core, pulling forth frigid magic from deep inside Ruad.

I pushed the energy into both of my hands and raised my flattened palms upward as the droplets of sweat collecting on my forehead turned into a dripping stream. As I raised my hands, a giant sheet of ice covered the tree, growing thicker the further it crept up the bark, until it, too, met the cavern ceiling.

Collapsing to my knees, I sighed.

"What gave you this idea?" Ruad asked.

"You… sort of," I said, still looking at the cavern floor while heavily breathing. My head was light from such a heavy use of magic.

"It's been a long year," I muttered.

"Mmmhhmm. But you're so much stronger because of it, Pup." Ruad said, nuzzling my cheek. "I'm proud of you."

Adrienn stood on top of my head. "Me too," they said.

I just smiled.

"Thank you both. I love you," I said slightly out of breath, but not tremendously like I would have on the first day of training. I was incredibly proud of that and the alpha I'd grown into. I hoped somewhere in the afterlife my mother and father were proud. "Let's get out of here and rebuild the O'Connell clan."

Day 365

Ruad and I walked up to the cave entrance. It was a good hike, but with every step we ascended, so did my heart. We were finally leaving this damp and dark prison—sorry, training ground.

It took about 20 minutes, but we came up to the entrance where a thin yellow field of energy stood, with tiny cracks growing in it.

We stood there watching it for a second as the cracks grew like tiny tree branches extending into the sky.

You'd never know a mystic cavern where time freezes for a year existed in the Ozarks. And it was a pain in the ass to access.

At last, the field of yellow energy shattered and dissipated. A chilly early morning air rushed into us, and I took a deep breath. A few badgers were nearby, as well as a black bear.

I didn't wait. I rushed out of the cavern and stretched under a 4:00 a.m. night sky.

The excitement overtook me, and I let out a blissful howl up at the stars above. I was finally free, and nothing could make me happier. Ruad joined me in the howl as our noise echoed off nearby hills.

When I was finished, I walked over to a tree stump I'd set my phone on and prepared to call Abi and let her know I'd exited the cave. It had only been 24 hours to her, but I was underground for a full year.

As the phone started to ring, I heard Ariana Grande's "7 Rings" start up in the trees behind me. It was a familiar ringtone. And only then did I pick up on a certain coconut lotion. It was one of Abi's favorites.

Turning, I saw my girlfriend standing there in the woods wearing a gray reindeer hoodie and blue jeans. She was holding her phone up and smiling.

I looked over at Ruad with my jaw nearly on the ground.

"Figured you'd want to see her first thing, so I had Adrienn use your phone to tell her the time we'd emerge before we even entered the cave," my smiling familiar said.

Turning around, I looked at Adrienn standing on top of Ruad's head. They both were breathing in the fresh air, same as me. And as my eyes met theirs, a small cry escaped my throat. I leaned down to kiss Adrienn on the head and hold my familiar close.

They'd put me through the wringer while trapped in the same prison I was. And the only thing that got me through it all was knowing Adrienn and Ruad had my back.

Afterward, I bolted over to my girlfriend and hugged her tight. I actually picked her up off the ground and spun her around as she wrapped her legs around my waist. We both laughed together.

I squeezed so tight, but she didn't complain once.

"Oh my Abi, I've missed you so damn much," I said, laughing with tears in my eyes.

I set her down, and we kissed. A deep need cried out in me like I would never be able to satisfy it. I desired Abi, wanted her more than anything. Our kissing grew more passionate as Adrienn began to blush and turned to look away.

Before they could say anything, Ruad tossed her head back. Adrienn flew up and back down before Ruad snatched them by a leg and said, "Come on. Let's give these mates a little privacy."

Abi and I fell to a patch of leaves on the ground, still kissing. I pulled her hoodie up as she slid her hands up under my shirt and ran them over my skin.

"Twice in two days? Lucky me," she giggled.

"More like twice in two years," I said, undoing her bra.

In between kisses, she said "I missed you, my sweet cinnamon."

I was too happy to roll my eyes hearing the nickname after so long, but I couldn't complain.

"I'm back, my fair bird. I'm back."

And we made love under the stars, happily reunited and committing what I'm sure was a misdemeanor in a national park, partially owned by my pack. And in a way, a very strange way, Abi was going to be a part of all that, along with Ruad, Adrienn, and Ash. For the first time in a long time I didn't feel completely alone. Things felt right.

Chapter Fifteen

Abi, Ruad, Adrienn and I were lying in her mother's little fenced-in side yard. It was a little after 1:00 p.m. on a sunny Tuesday. The temperature was 68 degrees, which we do tend to get a few of in Arkansas during December.

True winter doesn't really seem to start until late January or early February. The Boston Mountains give the northwest corner of the state cooler temperatures than the rest of Arkansas, but it wasn't a huge difference.

If it was 68 degrees up here today, it was probably 78 down in Little Rock. Climate change sucks, which I believe even more now that I'm an awakened druid. In a strange way, even with the limited power I have now, things *definitely* felt out of whack, but damn me for enjoying the beautiful afternoon. I was wearing a yellow tank top and red shorts, lying on an old quilt in grass that I may have used magic to resurrect and soften quite a bit.

And sure, houses would use less water if they'd give up the modern concept of lawns and go back to naturalized plants in the yard.

But climate change is a fight for another day, I thought, stretching out on the quilt and taking in every ounce of sunshine I possibly could. Abi rolled over my right arm and onto her side until she was lying right on me.

Adrienn was lying on my hair, which was spread out behind me on the grass. Ruad was curled in a circle with her head resting on my thigh. I yawned and stretched out my left arm as a gentle breeze picked up, bringing me scents of the neighbor's grilling and two or three outdoor cats a couple yards over.

"So… that new tattoo you got on your right shoulder? You were going to tell me what it means," Abi said.

"Oh right. It's a marking from the ice magic in Ruad. It basically means I can access her ice magic and call it forth to wield," I said.

"Wicked cool," she said, chuckling.

I groaned at the pun, but couldn't stop a smile.

Life is good, I thought, thankful to finally be out of that wretched cave.

My cell phone alarm went off a little later, and everyone groaned.

"You still have that corny Uverworld ringtone?" Abi teased.

I rolled my eyes.

"You don't get to judge me," I muttered, moving to get up.

"Goddamn weeb," Abi said, poking one of my boobs.

"Such language! And in the presence of a lady," I said.

Now she rolled her eyes. We all stood up, and I stretched. The alarm meant it was time to head to work.

"You'd better get used to language if I'm giving you a ride to work," she said, pointing a finger at me with a smirk.

I crossed my arms and looked over near the fence posts. A single milk cap mushroom was growing.

"I'll have you know I can teleport through mushrooms," I said with a smug look on my face.

Abi looked skeptical but glanced over at the mushroom.

"Can you now?" she asked.

I looked down at Adrienn who had flown up behind Abi's line of sight and was crossing their arms while shaking their head.

I frowned and said, "Actually, scratch that. Adrienn informs me that I lack that ability."

"Really? A full year down in that cave, and you didn't cover mushroom teleportation magic?" Abi said, her smirk growing.

I didn't dignify that with a response and instead started for her vehicle in the driveway.

"I can understand why you'd want to avoid my car, though. It's a tight squeeze with Ruad in the back seat. There's not mushroom," she said, and I groaned loud enough for the grilling neighbor to hear me.

Looking back at my girlfriend, I saw her flash me a grin I knew had to be fake. Nobody could laugh at a joke that terrible.

She skipped over, not letting me ruin her joking mood and kissed me on the cheek.

"Gay," I muttered. So, she kissed me on the lips.

"You are gay, sweetheart."

Then she grabbed my hand and started toward the car with Ruad behind us. Adrienn vanished back into my locket.

225

A few kids were riding their bicycles on the street in front of Abi's house, and when they saw Ruad, they ran over, one screaming, "So cool! Is that a real wolf?"

Shit... crotch goblins, I thought, my first instinct being to toss a seed in their path and tangle them in vines. That, or just punt them as hard and as far as I could.

I instead hopped over Ruad and threw my arms up yelling, "Whoa! Stop!"

They stopped a few feet short of me and looked disappointed and frustrated. Who was this girl stopping them from petting the pretty wolf?

"My wolf," I growled too low for them to hear. "Don't you dare touch her."

One of the kids, a boy with short blond hair and a Minecraft T-shirt, crossed his arms and looked like he was about to demand an explanation for why he couldn't touch my familiar. I bet his mother's name was Karen.

"You guys see the service vest, right?" I asked, pointing to Ruad. I was glad I'd finally ordered her one online and had it delivered to Abi's house. Somehow I didn't think Amazon would deliver to the "greenhouse in the middle of a Fayetteville city park." And with what they paid their delivery drivers, I'd feel bad for making them come all the way out to the greenhouse anyway.

Ruad's new vest was a little bigger than the one we initially borrowed, all black, and had a sign on it that said, "Service dog at work. Do not touch."

The kids seemed unimpressed with the vest, particularly Karen's son.

"In case they haven't taught you numbnuts to read yet, I'll just go ahead and tell y'all it says 'do not touch.'"

They looked at each other and then frowned at me collectively, like I'd ruined their whole day.

"Piss off," I said, flipping them the bird. They left, sticking their tongues out. One actually said, "Fuck you, bitch." That kid couldn't have been more than eight.

We got in Abi's car as I resisted the urge to transform and beat their asses.

"It's a real shame the way kids these days are raised by violent media. Such filthy language. And in the presence of two ladies," I said.

Abi started her car and laughed, saying, "I'm pretty sure you started it."

I reached into the back seat and stroked Ruad's fur.

"No, that was all on them," I said.

Ruad spoke up, "I agree with Pup. Those kids clearly erred first."

And Abi took me to Petal and Stem.

When we got there, Sabrina was helping an older gentleman carry out a potted fern to his pickup truck. The man eyed Ruad, stared at the service vest, and then turned back on his way without so much as a word.

"Well I'll be," I heard him say under his breath.

I had already clocked in by the time Sabrina returned. She was wearing a blue and white sundress with a white ribbon in her long brown hair. She smiled when she saw me, and I fought the urge to give her a hug. My boss didn't know it'd been a year since I'd seen her. Well... to me anyway.

"Hey Aoife, how are you doing today?" she asked, walking over to the counter and taking a drink of her Coke. I enjoyed the ease with which she used my name, my *real* name.

I smiled and walked into the back room, saying, "You know what? It's been a pretty solid day so far."

I still have no idea who Malachos is or what he wants, but I can't tell you that, I thought.

"That's good to hear. Oh, I brought you these," I said, reaching into a pocket and pulling out a fun-size pack of peanut M&Ms. I tossed them to Sabrina, and she smiled.

"You're bad for my weight, you know that?"

"Oh hush. You look great. But if you don't want them, I can eat them for you," I said, fake reaching for them.

She took a step back and bumped into the counter.

"I didn't say that. Back away!" She said, laughing.

Sabrina didn't waste any time tearing into the package and pulling out a blue one.

"I haven't had time to finish the Sanchez order. Would you get that one for me?"

Nodding, I walked over to the cooler and grabbed a half-finished arrangement. I carried it into the back room, set it down, and grabbed the order clipboard.

"I can probably have this done in half an hour. When are they coming to pick it up?" I asked.

"In about half an hour," Sabrina said, smiling as the door opened again. A new customer walked into the store. I didn't have time to chide my boss for giving me such a tight deadline.

I sat down at the table and got to work.

When Sabrina finished helping the current customer, she came back and leaned against the wall.

"So, I saw your dad on Facebook last night. He was doing a concert over in Phoenix, sounded great," she said.

That absentee dick isn't my father, I thought. But that wasn't fair to Sabrina. She didn't know they'd adopted me and lied about my past. So I tried to put on my best neutral expression.

"Oh yeah?"

"Yeah. How are you and your mother?" Sabrina asked.

I couldn't hide my flinch. But I did manage to conceal my snarl, and even that was a miracle. Ruad just looked up at me, and said nothing. Barb wasn't my mother. The bitch was, at best, a bare-minimum care-taker.

Again, though, Sabrina didn't know that. She knew we didn't get along, but I think I successfully hid most of my spite toward Barb. Or as much as I possibly could.

"That bad, huh?" Sabrina asked, putting a hand on my shoulder. Her tone was sympathetic, not mocking.

"I... moved out," I said.

"Oh wow! Really? You're so young to be living on your own," she said.

I turned to face her with a smile and said, "Oh come on now. You moved to California when you were my age. I'm still in my hometown at least."

Sort of, I thought, trying to remember if Lake Sequoyah was technically in city limits.

Sabrina just smiled and shook her head.

"You're right. Got me there. Still, I wouldn't recommend your life path be exactly like mine," she said.

Oh don't worry. I'm sure our paths will be plenty different, what with all the magic, fey, talking wolves, and everything, I thought.

"Can I ask if you moved out on good terms?" Sabrina asked.

Did I dare tell her the truth? I didn't want her worrying about me. She'd probably offer me the guest room at her house up in Rogers if I asked. Fortunately, I didn't need it. Still, I'd lied enough to my boss over the last couple weeks.

"Not really. Barb found out about Abi and me and said I couldn't see her anymore. So I used some foul language, and Barb kicked me out. But don't worry. I've found a place to stay. I have a roof over my head, food to eat, and I'm safe," I said, holding my hands up.

Sabrina put a hand on her forehead and sighed.

"What am I going to do with that mother of yours? She's such a... mean lady sometimes."

That was as close as my boss was going to get to saying something ugly about Barb. I called her a bitch on a regular basis, but Sabrina was a good Catholic girl. She didn't use salty language... at other people, anyway. Now if her laptop starts acting up, or she's running late on an order, Sabrina can drop a solid dammit as good as the rest of us. But my boss made it a point not to curse at *people*.

She had a polite demeanor when it came to the good folks of Fayetteville. Unless her nephew Nate came to drop off flowers from his nursery. She'd tease him to no end about his mustache or how things were with his girlfriend. Sometimes I felt like he got all her saltiness. Oh well. He could take it. He wasn't much older than me.

"Yeah, Barb's a bitch. But I'm really better off. I've got Ruad to watch my back, remember?"

"Oh yeah! How have your seizures been? Have you had any more problems since you got her?"

Damn lies always get more complicated, I thought.

I just shook my head. Sometimes it was easier to lie without words.

"I just can't believe John cared enough to get you a service dog and then turned around and let Barb kick you out like that," Sabrina said, shaking her head.

"Well, it's not like he's here that often. You said it yourself, he's in Phoenix playing music. He sent me a postcard, and the gist was I should have listened to Barb," I said, crossing my arms.

That was like... mostly the truth.

Sabrina hugged me and said, "If you ever need anything, you know you can call me, right? Anything."

I hugged her back. "Thanks, Sabrina. I really appreciate it."

She let me go, and I went back to work on the arrangement.

"I'm going to run to Sonic and get us some ice cream. What flavor do you want?"

229

"Oh, you don't need to do that," I said.

But she gave me that look that said she was going to, whether I wanted her to or not. So I just said, "Vanilla, please. Oh! Can I get Oreo in it?"

She nodded and left.

As Ruad and I sat there while I worked, she said, "You may have had shit luck with the adopted guardians, Aoife, but everyone else in your life is solid. Especially me."

"Well I agree with all but the last two words of that statement," I said, grinning.

Ruad flashed a fang, and I leaned down close to her face. Dangerous decision.

"Everyone else is solid. But honey, you're damn perfect," I said, lightly kissing her nose. My familiar's fang disappeared pretty quickly after that. A stupid grin captured her face.

"You're not so bad yourself, Pup."

I rolled my eyes.

I continued to work, and my thoughts went back to what Sabrina said about John. I hadn't spoken to him since before all this druid business began. He'd just sent me a letter. I began to ponder what I would say to him if I ever saw him again. And then an idea popped into my head.

"Hey Ruad. I just had a stupid idea."

"So... in other words, a normal Tuesday?"

I scowled at my familiar.

"Har har. Listen, we still don't know what Malachos wants, right? Why he's been after you and me? Ash doesn't know, but what if we could speak to someone who did know?"

"Like who?"

"I know he's dead, but what if there was a way to speak to Tristan? Surely Dad would know what Malachos is after," I said.

Ruad looked into my eyes, and I could feel a mixture of nerves and pain at the mention of the idea. There was still a lot of hurt where my father was concerned after what he did to her.

Still, my familiar put a lid on all that and said, "How do you propose we speak with the dead, Pup?"

I shook my head.

"I was really just spit-balling. I'm honestly not sure. But if we could do it, don't you think he'd be able to fill us in?"

My familiar was silent for a moment and said, "Dark magic is dangerous, Aoife. It's forbidden by the clan rules. And I can't think of another way to speak with him."

Rubbing my chin, I tried to think of a solution. I figured a Ouija board was probably useless. Besides, I didn't even know where to get one. Actually—scratch that. Abi has one in her closet, I'm pretty sure, but I don't think those are really *magic* magic. And if they are, I might have to have a word with whoever's in charge of just giving out generic, factory printed Ouija boards with real magic. I guess there really is no ethical consumption of capitalism, even in the real world.

While I was thinking, Adrienn flew out of my pendant and said, "Why don't you ask Odessa?"

I exchanged glances with Ruad. Then I looked back up my fey guardian and held out my hand flat for them to land on.

"That's not a bad idea," I said.

"Odessa the witch?" Ruad asked.

"You know her?" I asked.

The wolf nodded and said, "The O'Connell pack has dealt with witches in the area before. Odessa was the one we dealt with most often, but we also had dealings with one named Gina over in Eureka Springs from time to time."

"You're going to have to introduce me to all these people that had dealings with the O'Connells at some point. But for now, I say we head back over to Odessa's shop."

Ruad didn't voice any opposition. So that was the plan. After work, we'd walk downtown, and I'd have my second meeting with Odessa. What did you do with a witch? Did I need to call ahead and schedule an appointment? I guess I'd just show up. Could she see the future? Would she know I was coming?

I finished the Sanchez order, and they came to pick it up not long after. Sabrina brought our ice cream back, and customers mysteriously chose that time to give us a break. Afterward, we got back to it and stayed busy the rest of the afternoon.

Around 6:00 p.m., Sabrina let me off after cleaning the shop, and Ruad and I walked downtown. It was after dark, but I was armed with a wolf and druidic magic. I felt safe.

We arrived at Odessa's shop. I stared at the reddish purple letters that said "Odessa's Psychic Center" on the window and thought back to the first night I came here. It felt like forever ago. I had stood out here, a girl without a home or family. When I left, I had family, and they pointed me to a home.

Odessa had granted my greatest wish, and I only hoped she could help once more.

Walking into the shop, I was greeted with red curtains decorating the front windows, same as last time. The thin garnet carpet silenced our footsteps.

My gaze fell upon the couch I'd sat crying on before when I met Adrienn. And right on cue, the fey guardian launched themselves right out of my necklace and over to the opposite couch, where Odessa sat with her right leg over her left.

She was wearing a long black dress with a slit up to her knees. Her shoulders were uncovered. The witch's makeup was minimal but dark and her face had a contemplative and serious stillness to it.

And yet, when Adrienn flew up to hug her cheek, the witch was all smiles.

"Adrienn! I'm so glad to see you," she said, holding out a hand for them to stand on.

They zipped around her head a little bit and then landed gracefully. The fey sure seemed excited to be here. I wasn't unhappy, but Adrienn looked ready to party. I guess it makes sense. They hung out with Odessa for more than a decade waiting to be reunited with me.

"Hey there, wolf girl. And Ruad, you certainly look better than last I saw you," Odessa said, standing up and coming over to us.

"It's good to see you, Odessa," I said.

I shook her hand awkwardly. What else did you do when meeting a witch? I didn't feel like I knew her well enough to hug her. Or even if she wanted to be hugged, by anyone other than Adrienn.

Odessa nodded down at Ruad, and the wolf made a little bow, barely noticeable.

"You certainly look happier with your family," Odessa said, turning her attention to me.

I nodded.

"Yeah, having these two at my side has made me happier than I think I've ever been, at least since I was a baby being held by Tristan or Iris."

Odessa motioned for us to come sit down, and I did, plopping down on the same couch I'd sat on before when I had come here angry and confused. Now I felt mature, maybe even a little older than the girl who walked in here a few weeks ago. I looked over the round pine table between the couches and noted the candles I'd seen last time were gone.

Ruad sat next to me, and I leaned on the couch arm so I could be as close to her as possible. Adrienn stood on my lap.

The witch went upstairs and returned a couple minutes later with a tray. On it was a bowl, a tiny Barbie-sized teacup, and two normal-sized ones. They all had a pink liquid in them and were steaming.

Odessa set the tray down and brought each of us a drink. It turned out to be peach-mint tea. It was delicious. I definitely wanted to know what herbs I needed to grow back home to make it. I finished half the cup almost immediately.

The witch took a seat across from me after setting the bowl in front of Ruad and giving the small cup to Adrienn. They each took a drink and seemed to like it almost as much as I did.

"So," Odessa said, taking a sip of her drink. "What brings you back to my shop, Aoife?"

I finished my tea because I have no self control and set it back down on the table.

"Um. Right. So, I don't know how exactly to make this request," I said, looking down at Ruad. "I was wondering if you could help us speak to the dead?"

Odessa kept a neutral smile. I didn't know what to expect from her. I mean, what abilities did she even have? I couldn't really feel much magical energy from the shop around me like I did when I was around Malachos before. Maybe she was keeping it hidden.

"Can I ask why you want to speak with the dead?" Odessa asked, taking another sip. Her curiosity seemed so nonchalant, like someone didn't just ask her to speak to someone in the great beyond and more like someone asked her where they could get fresh baked pastries, instead.

I cleared my throat and looked down at Ruad who had finished her bowl of tea.

"We've learned the identity of the necromancer that killed my clan. His name is Malachos, and aside from that, we're not really sure what he's after. We want to speak with Tristan and see if he has some insight into Malachos and maybe how to stop him."

"What about the raven that served Malachos?"

Ruad growled a little at the mention of Ash.

"His name is Ash. He was only serving the necromancer to pay off a debt to Morrigu. He's actually on our side now," I said.

Now Odessa's smile widened a little.

"Something tells me you won't be the first girl I encounter who convinces their opponent to switch teams," she said.

I raised an eyebrow, but she didn't offer an explanation for her words.

"Either way, I'm afraid I can't help you, Aoife. Speaking with the dead isn't an ability I possess," Odessa said. "Nor do most people."

Ruad and I exchanged glances, and Adrienn looked disappointed as well. No one said a thing.

"But I know someone who can assist," Odessa said.

We all locked eyes with the witch immediately and waited to hear who she was going to send us to. Our crazy plan wasn't dead yet, just the person we wanted to speak with. Heh. My sense of humor could use work. I saw Ruad look over to me and give me a "are you serious face" as much as a wolf can, as if she sensed the corny joke I was thinking about. I'd eventually have to find a way to hide that from her now and again. You know, private personal feelings. Like one's you do behind locked doors, under the sheets and with your clothes off with the most amazing girlfriend somebody could ever ask for.

Odessa finished her tea and said, "You should head to the shop next door. It's called Funky Dan's. You should find what you're looking for in there. People always do."

"So... is the shop like this one?" I asked.

"Not quite. Dan is a little different, but he works for me. His services are varied, but he mainly deals in enchanted items," Odessa said.

I nodded and stood up.

"Odessa, thanks for pointing us in the right direction. You don't happen to know anything about Malachos, do you?"

Ruad stood as well, and Adrienn flew up into my hair.

"I just know he showed up a little before your clan was killed, Aoife. I don't know where he came from or what he wants. Whenever I've tried to investigate him or read him in some way, it's just a blank, black hole. A dead end if you will. However, I do have a suspicion Tristan will be able to give you that information. He and Malachos are likely connected," Odessa said. "I can sense that much."

Ruad snapped her head up. "What do you mean by that?"

Odessa's eyes moved down to my familiar. They showed no fear for the wolf's sudden aggression at the mention of my father and Malachos being connected.

"Tristan was the last one killed by Malachos that day, Ruad. Surely you remember that. Iris died just before him after putting up the fight of her life and without magic to boot," Odessa said. "That couldn't have been a coincidence."

Ruad started to shake as I felt her heart racing and blood heating with… rage? Fear? I noticed it radiating from her then, a poison seeping into my bones. Toxicity. It was almost like a form of PTSD, and I didn't blame her for feeling what she felt. She was the only survivor that day, but she didn't leave unscathed. The scars ran deeper than the ones on the outside. I saw as much back when I ventured into her mind forest.

I knelt down and wrapped my arms around her slowly.

"I'm here," I whispered softly in her ear as I lightly ran my hands over her coat, trying to ground her in the present moment. "And you're not there anymore. You're my familiar now, and I won't let Malachos hurt you. I promised, remember?"

Slowly, her body relaxed. If she could sense the way I felt and have it affect her, surely the opposite was possible? I started to cautiously send my magical energy across our bridge into her body, trying to give her a sense of place, bringing her out from her tragic memories and back into the present.

At last, her eyes turned to mine. Ruad looked like she was slowly coming back from a distant time and place. So I pushed a little more of my emotions into her, trying to be a reassuring breeze on an easy day. She wasn't alone.

"Go raibh maith agat, Pup," she said.

I'm going to learn to speak proper Irish one day, I thought.

Ruad licked my cheek, and I smiled, kissing my nose. Standing up, I popped my neck and sighed.

"Thanks for all your help, Odessa. We're going to head next door and see Dan," I said.

"Best of luck, wolf girl. One last piece of advice. Speaking with the dead for any real length of time comes at a great cost. So try not to get distracted when talking to Tristan. Stay focused on exactly what you need to know. I'm afraid the longer you talk to him, the more it'll hurt," she said.

Ruad growled, but I nodded, and we left her shop. I was grateful to be putting distance between Ruad and Odessa as we headed back out into the chilly night air. Fayetteville cooled quickly once the sun vanished, and I felt it.

Wait... she said to go next door. But isn't next door just that pizza place? I thought. *I don't remember seeing another shop when we came in.*

Turning to the right, I saw a shop between Odessa's Physic Center and Toppings. It was housed in a long and narrow green brick building with two stories.

Why didn't I notice that before? I thought.

A glass door had "Funky Dan's" written in simple white letters at the top. I grabbed the metal handle and cautiously opened the door, unsure of what I'd find inside. Ruad came with me. Adrienn flew back into my pendant.

Inside, I heard a piano playing and a man singing. Not usually the type of music I listened to, but I think it was Billy Joel. Dan must have had it playing on vinyl toward the back of the store.

A small bell jingled as I entered. I stepped onto a thick green carpet. Ruad stared at it as if to say, "What in Satan's crotch is this abomination?"

In front of me, I saw three long shelves crammed full with random items. The shelf closest to me had an orange bandana with a duck pattern on it trapped underneath a flower pot shaped like a tuba. There was a strange energy flowing from the shop. Were all of these items enchanted in some way?

A man's voice from the back of the shop said, "Welcome to Funky Dan's! I'm... well, Dan. Feel free to look around. I'm back here by the register if you have any questions."

Stepping further into the somewhat musty shop, I smelled pizza, with onions and peppers.

I walked past what appeared to be a cello made of ice and continued toward where the voice had come from, Ruad behind me.

The man I assumed to be Dan stood behind a glass container with more items stuffed inside. Looking into the container, I saw what appeared to be some kind of dagger with a dragon's claw on the hilt. There were other items in the case, too, a book of some sort. I couldn't quite see the title from my angle due to a glare on the glass. Next to the book was a folded purple scarf that had a lightning bolt embroidered on

236

the end, and hanging above that? A small glass orb with some kind of flickering spark on the inside, pulsing to its own machinations and rhythm. On the other side of the book sat a black wooden ring with runes carved into it. And after staring at that, I turned my attention elsewhere. The amount of magic from the items in this case was overwhelming me. I wiped some sweat off my forehead.

"Can I help you?" Dan asked, bringing my attention back to him.

He was bald but had a dark shaggy beard. The shop keep was wearing a red fuzzy robe and sweatpants underneath it.

There was a weariness to his eyes I recognized. Abi told me my eyes looked the same after coming out of the cave. This man had been here a long time. But… he also didn't look to be older than 45.

It was then that I detected a new odor. A fox maybe? But it smelled different than any other fox I'd encountered here in Arkansas. One hopped up onto the glass counter and moved over to a brown Toppings pizza box, where a lone breadstick sat.

"Hold it, Eely. We split the breadsticks evenly. I got four, and you got four. That last one is mine," Dan said, giving the eggshell fox side eye.

I blinked and rubbed my eyes. Did this fox have multiple tails? It was small, white with black tips on its ears, and had nine tails. My eyes weren't deceiving me. And then, to top off all the surprises, it spoke back to Dan.

"By my count, I only had three breadsticks. You had four already, Dan."

His eyes stayed locked on to the fox.

"I don't think so. I counted out four and put them in front of your bed first thing, Eely. That last breadstick is mine. And if you touch it, I'll make sure you don't get pizza again for the next 50 years," Dan said.

The fox rolled over on its back and said, "Oh come on. Can you really deprive a cute animal like me of my fourth breadstick?"

Dan scoffed.

"*Fifth* breadstick! And yes, yes I would Don't touch it, or I'll shave your fur with cursed clippers."

Now Eely scoffed.

"You don't have cursed clippers in the shop."

Dan said nothing but continued to stare. Eely's tone shifted, "Right?" She seemed a little more nervous now.

"Is Eely your familiar?" I asked.

Dan turned his attention back to me and looked at Ruad for a second.

"Familiar? Ha! No. The only thing that furball is familiar with is overeating. Oh, and naps."

I watched as the fox slowly crept toward the pizza box, and I tried not to smirk. Dan was about to look back, but I blurted out a question at him, "Uh, so what are you then? If she's not your familiar, I mean."

"What am I? Kind of a shop wizard. I sell magic items from this place," Dan said, as Eely slowly picked up the last breadstick with her mouth and hopped off the counter without a noise. "Customers come here when they need one of these items. It's just my job to help them find it and give it to them for a price. So, what do you need today?"

Now Dan finally did look back at the pizza box and noticed the missing breadstick.

"You furry glutton! Bring back my breadstick!" he yelled, looking for Eely. She was over on her bed, curled up around some torn newspaper.

"I have no idea what you mean," Eely said, some garlic flakes around her whiskers.

"You ate my breadstick!"

"Did you see me eat it?" Eely asked.

Dan turned to me, and I threw up my hands. Then he looked down at Ruad.

"Did you see her eat my last breadstick?" he asked, putting his hands on his hips and staring intently at my familiar.

"What's a breadstick? I have never heard of such a thing before in my life," Ruad said. I could feel a little bit of snarky joy coming from inside her.

Furs before entrepreneurs, I thought, smirking.

"You're all in a conspiracy against me and my dinner!" Dan yelled, before pointing a finger at Eely. "And I'm shaving your fur tonight with the cursed clippers!"

Eely belched a little fire.

"You go ahead and try it, honey," the fox said, playfully.

Displaying a little bit of wisdom, the shop wizard decided to drop it. He was outnumbered since Ruad and I were clearly on the side of his cute little fox. I didn't get the sense that he bullied her, but I also felt like she could use an ally once in a while if he got grumpy like this often.

Dan closed his pizza box rather sadly and turned to us.

238

"So… druid. O'Connell at that, huh?"

I just blinked at him, trying to figure out how he knew all that.

"The talking wolf gave you away. That, and the O'Connells are the only druids in this part of the country. Or at least… they were. I'd heard they all perished," Dan said.

"All but us. That's what we're here about," I said, crossing my arms.

He smiled. "What do you need?"

"I need a way to speak with the dead, specifically, my deceased father."

Dan rubbed his beard for a moment thinking.

"There's a pretty tough barrier between the world of the dead and living. Necromancy seeks to chisel away at that barrier. But I don't specialize in that kind of magic."

Ruad sighed and looked at the shelves again. I couldn't tell what she was focusing on, maybe a pair of boots covered in red and brown feathers next to the wall.

"I think I know something that'll help," Dan finally said after about 30 seconds of silence. He walked over to the middle aisle and came back with what looked like an old square Cortelco landline phone, with the receiver that sits on top and 12 square buttons on an inclined surface below. The receiver was connected to the body by a short curly cord.

The device was black, and the earpiece and mouthpiece looked like jagged skulls with opened mouths. The buttons were all blood red.

"I think I've seen this before at Hot Topic," I muttered.

The shop keep set it on the glass counter by an antique cash register that looked like it hadn't been opened in years. It was covered in dust.

Dan walked over and leaned on the counter next to the phone. He stood about five feet from us.

"This phone will allow you to contact one person in the afterlife. You can then ask them five questions. After that, the device will literally dissolve into dust," Dan said. "Just pick up the receiver, say the name of the person you want to speak to, wait a second, and they should answer on the other side."

I stared at the item and then looked back at Dan.

"Why only five questions?"

He shrugged.

"This was given to me by a reaper looking for a way into another world. They tend to frown on that barrier thinning in any way, and it makes sense with each question you'd ask, that barrier between the living world and afterlife would thin a hair more, exchange of knowledge from the great beyond and all that. I suppose the reaper equated five questions was as thin as they'd allow that barrier to go. Seems generous enough since the dead hold so many secrets," Dan said.

"I heard dead men tell no tales," Eely snickered.

Sighing, I looked back at the shopkeeper and asked, "So... what's the price for this deadly phone call?"

Dan closed his eyes for a second and cocked his head a bit to the side, like he was thinking really hard or trying to listen for something.

It was slight, but I could almost hear a groaning noise from the building around me, walls, ceiling, and foundation. The noise grew the longer Dan had his eyes closed, and even Ruad was looking around, trying to find the source. I was going to speak up when a thought occurred to me. I bet we were sensing the shop's own calculations on a price for this magical item. It was as though all the magic in the air around us was swirling around Dan's consciousness, some wizardly equation only he could comprehend.

When he opened his eyes again, he said, "The price will be your wolf."

I didn't even hesitate, saying the words and transforming. I shoved him into a wall by the shelf and bared my fangs. I dug one claw into his shoulder and held the other to his throat, ready to tear it out.

"Nobody. Takes. Ruad," I growled so deep the nearest shelf began to rattle.

Eely walked over to Ruad and said, "Your human is really attached to you. Must be nice to have someone you know would kill for you."

My familiar looked down at the little eggshell fox and smiled.

"Yeah, Pup is alright."

Dan looked stunned by what had just happened. His eyes had grown at least twice their normal size, and the weariness glazed over them seemed to have vanished. He coughed and looked me in the eyes before slowly putting up his palms.

"I was... joking," he said.

"He wasn't serious, Pup. You can let the poor shop wizard down now," Ruad said with a chuckle.

Slowly, I took a breath and then let it out, stepping away from Dan and resuming my human form.

He rubbed his throat and coughed some more.

"Damn, you druids sure are touchy about your animals," he managed to choke out. "I guess I should have learned when I tried the same joke with Markus O'Connell several years back. Though he didn't slam me into the wall."

I turned to him and said, "Markus?"

Dan nodded.

"He was another member of your clan. His wolf's name was Liath, a little bigger than yours," the shop wizard said.

Ruad said, "I remember Liath. I called him lazybones. That canine sure did like to nap. Beautiful howl, though. Best in the pack."

"Anyway, sorry if I touched a sore point with my joke. I should have known better," Dan said.

I looked down at the carpet.

Dammit I was jumpy, I thought. But the thought of someone trying to take Ruad away... I'd die if that happened, even if I hadn't made my oath and promises to Ruad. She was more than a familiar now. She was a friend, a family member and maybe even a little bit like a parent... I'm still not sure how Tristan brought himself to cutting his bond with Ruad. I mean, I know he used dark magic. I just don't know how he brought himself to do it. A familiar was meant to be a lifelong companion, a guardian and an advisor.

"I apologize as well. What's the actual price?" I asked.

He hesitated for a moment, rubbing his throat as if it were sore. Ah, who am I kidding? It was definitely sore.

"Costs in this shop are usually heavy, druid. And speaking with the dead doesn't come cheap. For you to take this device, it'll cost you a piece of your humanity," Dan said.

I raised an eyebrow.

"What does that mean exactly?"

Dan sighed.

"You took a wolf form to attack me just moments ago, right?"

I nodded.

"Your magic being so intertwined with your familiar's own energy alters your body quite a bit. But at the end of the day, you still remain mostly human when outside of battle."

Looking down at Ruad I thought about where this was going.

"So to take this phone and speak to your deceased father, it'll cost about half of your humanity, leaving you more wolf than human. In

241

practical terms, that'll affect your behavior even more, but you'll also lose your ability to look 100 percent like a normal person. You'll have wolf-like features all the time."

I was trying to process his words.

"The ears, fangs, claws, tail, etc. won't disappear like they do when I'm done fighting?" I asked.

Dan shook his head.

"That'll be your permanent form from now on. In a way, you'll be bound even tighter to your wolf because you'll share pieces of her appearance 24/7. But as I said, it'll also have an impact on your psychology, your thoughts, your emotions, your behavior, etc."

Taking a deep breath, I asked, "You really don't take debit, do you?"

The shopkeeper shook his head.

"You don't have to take the phone. But if you decide you really do need it, that's the price you pay. The shop itself is magical and sets the prices. I just process the transaction," Dan said.

Nodding and glancing at Ruad again, I smiled.

If Ash has to walk around with those wings and talons every day, I imagine this'll at the very least show him some solidarity, I thought. *And being closer to Ruad isn't the worst thing in the world.*

"Okay. How do you want to take my humanity, shop wizard?" I asked.

"Are you sure, Pup?" Ruad asked behind me. "Maybe we can find another way."

I shook my head.

"I'm not ashamed to bear your appearances all of the time. We're joined at the soul, Ruad. There's no tighter bond than that. Sharing forms isn't any different than that as far as I'm concerned," I said, turning and smiling at her.

My familiar nodded.

Dan walked into the back section of his shop behind the glass counter and came back a couple minutes later with a golden bowl and lid.

"I'm going to open this bowl, and it'll begin capturing pieces of your humanity. When you hit half-way, I'll close the lid, sealing those pieces inside."

"What'll happen to them?" I asked.

"Like the phone, it'll become an item I offer in the store. Humanity is a valuable thing to some people. If you didn't have Ruad and were a normal human, taking half of your humanity would risk leaving you a somewhat blank slate mentally. But since you're bonded to a wolf familiar, when your humanity recedes, wolf will creep in to fill the gaps."

I weighed Dan's words carefully, scratching my head and considering what giving up half of my humanity would ultimately do to me. This was life changing stuff. We were talking about my own essence, after all. What would I be like with just half of my humanity? I started to picture my feral self and shivered.

Is my humanity what holds her in check? I thought. *Would I risk losing control over myself if I paid this price?*

And then I considered Abi. There was no way in hell she'd be okay with me making this decision. But she didn't have the same burden I did in facing Malachos, the same price to pay for learning about him. Ultimately, when I considered Abi, my heart fluttered, and I felt a warmth grow there.

She will keep my humanity intact, I thought. *My love for her will ensure I remain human enough to continue making her happy.*

That was that. This was something that had to be done, and I was merely wasting time delaying the bargain with each minute I stood here pondering.

So, I nodded.

"Let's do it," I said.

Dan took a deep breath and said a few words in a language I didn't recognize. Then he slowly lifted the lid on the golden bowl. My skin began to glow silver and then lightly smoke.

The energy felt like sandpaper rushing over my flesh and down toward the bowl. My vision swam as the smoke thickened and flew down into the bowl. My breathing slowed, and I felt my chest rising and falling at a more gradual pace. Noise and other sensory details entered my brain in delayed wave after wave, lag growing with each second. Taking a step to the right, my dizziness dialed to 11, and I felt myself growing numb, both emotionally and mentally. A thick fog filled my mind.

"Son of a... bitch," I muttered, as the smoke continued to siphon out of my body and into the golden bowl.

"Quarter of your humanity captured," Dan said.

It was then I felt warmth creeping back into me. He said wolf would fill in the cracks. I glanced back at Ruad. Turning my head felt like I was doing it in slow motion and staring through a fish bowl to boot.

When I finally saw Ruad, she was glowing red, and I felt her energy, her raw essence coming across the bridge and replacing the humanity I was spending.

"I've got you, Pup," she said.

I sighed, starting to sweat in addition to the smoke.

Grabbing onto the counter to steady myself, I also felt Ruad pushing against my left thigh to provide further support.

My essence was now a scale. On the left, my humanity being captured into a bowl, the scale rising and taking with it concerns about work tomorrow, my dreams of being a mythology teacher, and those mortal hopes people assume will make up their future. And while this should have alarmed me, I felt numb to it all, unable to rise to a level of caring. On the right, my inner wolf filling in the cracks, the scale sinking, growing heavier with impatience and worry. There was fear and uncertainty over what this process was doing to my Pup. Er—wait. I was the Pup. So that meant these feelings were from Ruad, right? I feel sensing her instincts in the moment as her essence added to mine.

When I was about two seconds from passing out, I heard a clink. Dan closed the bowl.

"Now what?" I whispered, still trying to catch my breath after my transaction.

"Your price is paid. It'll probably take a night before that new wolf self you've taken on settles into all those cracks. I'd imagine it'll happen while you sleep," Dan said.

Looking down in the glass case, I saw my reflection staring back at me as the smoke cleared. My ears were there, along with fangs, claws, and a tail. My hair was thick and bushy. I was a little more muscular.

My jaw sat differently to accommodate the larger canines, and I ran my fingers over the claws that would need to be filed down to avoid extra attention in public. I could smell Eely better now, the kitsune carried the scent of cinders and garlic from her lunch. I listened to Dan's heartbeat, which seemed to have remained unphased through this entire transaction.

I touched the sides of my head to feel human ears under my shaggy red hair, and none greeted me. So I felt the top of my head where two pointed fuzzy triangles stood at alert.

Craning my neck, I turned to see my red bushy tail that kept bumping into the glass case of dangerous items.

Long term, that's going to be the biggest pain in the ass of all, I thought.

This was me now, Aoife Fey O'Connell, payer of prices, caller of canine souls.

So long, humanity, I thought.

Sighing again, I picked up the phone. It was cold and heavy.

"Are we done here?" I asked, sleepily.

Dan nodded and reached under the glass case.

"This blew into my back yard the other day. I think it came from someone walking by, but I never found them. You might as well take it," he said, tossing me a ballcap.

The design was simple, with a black crown and red bill. There was a small green circle on the front, the only design element I could see. Flipping it over, I noticed a few long silver hairs inside. It smelled kind of like dog, though what kind I couldn't place.

"Does this come with a price? The remaining half of my humanity, perhaps? Hey, maybe you can fill the other half of my soul with Adrienne's essence. Fey is in my name, you know."

Dan, appearing unamused at my joke, shook his head.

"Since it blew into my back yard, it's more of a freebie, not part of the shop. All yours. Lord knows that name is going to get you into trouble one day," Dan muttered, and I noticed Adrienn flinch.

Whatever, I'm too tired to worry about this cryptic bullshit, I thought.

I put it on and made sure my ears were tucked inside. Then I made sure my tail was tucked inside my shirt, pressed against my back.

"Guess I'm never wearing my hair short again," I muttered.

We turned to go, and I wished Dan had given me a bag for this thing. It felt awkward to carry. And I had to ride the bus home with it. Awesome.

Turning back to Dan, I said, "Any chance I return to repurchase my humanity back someday?"

He shook his head.

"Shop rules. One stop per customer. Once you leave this shop, you'll never be able to enter it again," he said.

I nodded.

Happy to be outside with a way forward, part of me wanted to laugh or at least smile. But thinking more about the price I just paid and what I still had to do, I just felt unsettled.

Chapter Sixteen

I walked toward the greenhouse, phone in tow. Swaying left a little as I approached the door, Ruad had to steady me at the hip. Gods all I wanted was to close my eyes and let this soul shit settle. But I had a phone call to make.

And really, should I be a little more concerned at how numb I feel about this entire experience? I thought, reaching for the door.

Was it exhaustion keeping me from being more scared? Would that numbness to the lack of humanity remain a permanent feature, or would it resolve once things settled as I slept? I guess, time would tell.

I sat down in one of the green metal folding chairs and put the phone on top of the glass tabletop.

"Okay, are you ready?" I asked, looking at Ruad.

The wolf nodded, and I asked Adrienn to come out as well. I sat down on the floor and pulled up the receiver to my ear. Adrienn flew close to the earpiece and hovered. Ruad's head was next to mine.

The lack of a dial tone surprised me, though I couldn't think of why a phone line to the afterlife would have one. I also noted how calm I was about speaking with my deceased father. Before, I woulda been a giddy, nervous wreck. But now? I felt nothing.

I spoke into the mouthpiece, "Tristan O'Connell, my father."

And the phone began to rattle like a bunch of tiny bones bouncing around inside. The phone continued to rattle for about another 30 seconds until finally it went still.

An airy man's voice answered.

"Hello?"

For a moment, nobody knew what to say. So, I started with the basics.

"Dad, it's me, Aoife," I said.

There was a gasp on the other side of the line. How was this even working? Did he have a cell phone in the afterlife? Was it as simple as some form of telepathy from him? I had no idea. I didn't care. I needed to keep focus on the task at hand: Malachos.

"Aoife? Oh my god," he said, choking up.

Finally, some emotion found its way into my heart with a light gasp. Four words from my deceased father, who I hadn't seen in 16 years. How could that not have an impact on a girl? Ruad was stoically silent.

"Yeah, Dad. It's me. And I have Ruad and Adrienn here with me, too," I said. Adrienn said hello as cheerily as they could for a moment like this, but Ruad stayed silent. I felt a bitterness in her. I didn't blame my familiar for that.

He didn't say anything for a moment. I heard him trying to pull it together on the other side, a couple sniffles and a few breaths.

"I'm so glad you're all still alive," he said. "How... how are you?"

"Still wounded," Ruad finally growled.

Tristan didn't say anything for a moment. He knew exactly what she was referring to. I patted her head lightly with my free hand.

"I'm here," I whispered to her, kissing her fur.

"Ruad... there are no words. I'm just so sorry for what I did. It was unforgivable. And I'm just... sorry," he said, tearing up.

Something in Ruad broke as well. She was in terrible pain, torn between letting him have it and running away. I stroked her fur softly.

"Dad, listen. We only get five questions before the line dies. And we need information," I said. The words stung even as I said them. There was so much more than just five questions that needed to be asked, things to be said.

I pictured my father reading stories to baby me sitting in his robe with my mother on the couch. This was the same man crying now. Another needle of sorrow pricked my heart, and my mind shook off some fuzziness to propose a million different questions I wanted to ask.

Why didn't you keep your oath to Ruad? Don't you realize how badly you hurt her? Didn't you take into account the pain your familiar experienced as you severed that tie, shredding the bond between your souls like cutting a rope with a butter knife?

I understand why Ruad was pissed, and part of me was, too. But I had to be careful here and not waste one of my five questions.

He probably wanted someone to watch over me, care for me in the way they did. But he knew how hurt Ruad would be if he severed their bond. And how could someone find space to love after hurting so much?

Sighing, I tried to put all that aside.

When Tristan didn't say anything, I spoke up, "Who is Malachos?"

A deep sigh came from the other end, like there was a terrible weariness I couldn't even begin to grasp.

"Malachos. Of course it's still alive."

I didn't say anything, fear of repeating the question would count against my limit. All I could do was wait. Slowly, Tristan steadied himself.

"Malachos is… a sort of shadow version of me, my inner darkness."

I just closed my eyes. Of course Malachos was another inner shadow. For fuck's sake. I just couldn't catch a break from dealing with dark versions of my loved ones.

He continued, "Aoife, the questions I imagine you're going to ask will lead to painful answers and confessions. I'm sure it'll hurt to hear them from your old man. But I would never lie to you, my daughter."

That sparked a tear to my left eye. Maybe I wasn't completely numb. My emotions just had to wade through mud for me to feel them.

"I understand," I muttered.

"Malachos is every dark emotion, thought, and temptation I ever had in life, rolled into one corrupted entity. It uh… grew too strong for me to hold and manifested outside of my body. The result was a terribly powerful necromancer that sought the end of the O'Connell clan because that was what I cared most about in this world."

I swallowed and felt my pulse shoot off like a rocket at my father's words. Then I just had to sit there with the reality he painted for me and shiver.

"What does he want?" I asked.

Another sigh on Tristan's end.

"Malachos wants the Siol Eolais, Aoife. It's a… seed from the Fey Realm handed down through generations of O'Connells. Over the last couple centuries, O'Connell druids have stored their wisdom, knowledge, and even a piece of their own magic into the seed. It serves as a living archive detailing the history and abilities of our clan. But all that knowledge… it's corrupting, and very powerful. Every alpha in the clan has been entrusted with protecting the seed and adding their own contributions to it, dating all the way back to our Irish ancestors," he explained.

I took a deep breath. We were finally getting somewhere. My family had something Malachos wanted, and he killed to get it. Obviously, this means he didn't have it yet, or he wouldn't be after Ruad and I.

"The seed is trapped in a crystal, but it mustn't be released into the world. It's our clan's duty to protect it. Keep it hidden and sealed."

Great, another duty to remember, I thought, sighing. *So… keep balance between mythical creatures, nature, and human lives. Also, protect the seed. Got it.*

"As for Malachos himself. The seed… it whispers to every alpha O'Connell, trying to be freed. It wants to be planted and to sprout, Aoife. We've prevented that for hundreds of years. But I grew weak from having to guard the seed. It started a corruption in me, and I began to experiment with dark magic. I just wanted to be free from the burden of protecting the seed. I wanted my family to be free from it. I knew you would one day be alpha and forced to carry the burden as well, my daughter."

That made my throat close up. My hand clenched the bone phone tightly.

"Learning more about dark magic, I eventually enchanted a dagger, with the idea that I would use it to sever the seed from my clan forever. I wasn't thinking straight. And I regret every moment of it," Tristan said.

At the mention of the dagger, I felt Ruad's chest tighten. She knew this dagger… intimately. And I wish she didn't. She let loose a low growl.

"Yeah, Ruad. That dagger," Tristan said with enough regret in his voice to fill the greenhouse. "The dagger was powerful. I used it to hide the darkness inside me from your detection. I knew you'd try to stop me, and you'd have been right too. The night I went to sever our clan's connection with the seed, I raised the dagger high. My body shook with anticipation of freedom from the burden. But before I could do it, the forest around me came to life and restrained me. It was almost as if… the land itself was trying to prevent me from making a terrible mistake. Reminding me of my responsibility and duty, a task you would one day carry, whether we wanted it or not."

Now I sighed. It did all come back to me. Parents will do the worst things to their children sometimes. But a few parents will do the worst things for their children.

"When the forest brought me back to my senses, I stopped. But all that darkness inside of me the seed inspired, that had been craving use of the dagger, broke free from me and manifested. With sheer force of will, it became Malachos, and it sought that seed. I fought it off as best I could, trying to recapture Malachos and protect our treasure. In the end, I only succeeded in the latter. Malachos fled, vowing to return for the seed, as well as the power and knowledge it holds."

Looking at the ground, I said, "He returned when the entire clan was at that wake, mourning one of their own."

Tristan's silence confirmed that to me.

"What happened to the Siol Eolais, Dad?"

"I knew that I couldn't be trusted with it anymore. So I gave the seed to Epona, the horse goddess, until such a time that Malachos could be dealt with."

I made a mental note to ask about the horse goddess, but Ruad could probably answer the question later.

Ruad took the last question without warning me, asking, "Why did you use the dagger to sever our connection?"

A deep fury I'd never witnessed in her rose to the surface, and I had no right to keep her from it.

I pictured Tristan crying and looking at the ground, ashamed of what he'd done. And plenty of shame came through in his answer, along with an uneasy shakiness to his voice.

"That damn lunar eclipse. I thought it'd be a perfect and beautiful night to celebrate Duncan's memory, but Malachos took advantage of the celestial event and slaughtered us all. He'd just killed Iris. She was the last to fall aside from me. I knew you could still run, Ruad, and Aoife would need protection, so I severed us. Malachos was going to kill me one way or another. I didn't want you to die when that happened. That's why I ordered you to flee and protect Aoife."

"You took a goddamned oath, Tristan! When our souls were bonded, you swore to be by my side forever! We would fight as one, and if need be, die together. That's what it means for a familiar and human to share a bond! You broke that oath," she barked.

"I had to ensure my daughter was protected, that the clan lived on," he said.

Ruad choked up a little, "You chose... you chose Aoife over me. You put me through the greatest pain I'm capable of feeling all in the name of your daughter. I was your familiar, Tristan. Your. Familiar. Nothing is supposed to trump that bond."

Tristan didn't say anything for a moment while he wept. Slowly, his voice came back.

"She's my daughter, Ruad. If you had pups of your own, you'd understand."

Her voice was harsh as Ruad uttered, "I have a Pup now. And I won't throw her away like you did to me. And I know for a fact that if Aoife had to choose between a loved one and myself, she'd choose her familiar."

I gasped. Would I really choose Ruad over Abi if such a terrible choice was forced upon me? I loved Abi with all my heart. But my familiar could access and anticipate my instincts well by now. In this case, it seemed like Ruad knew this truth before I did.

Son of a bitch, I thought, realizing her truth.

Abi had my heart, but I loved Ruad with all my heart AND soul, my very being. It would destroy me, but I would choose her over Abi if it came down to it. She was right.

"Goddamnit," I muttered, clenching the phone tighter.

There was silence for a few seconds, and Tristan said, "Adrienn?"

The fey cleared their throat and said, "Yes?"

"Can I just ask... will you please do everything you can in your power to protect them? Don't let them make the same mistakes I did. Don't let them die with as much regret as I did," he said.

"Yes sir," Adrienn said, a small tear forming in their right eye.

And that's when I started to sob.

"Dad... you did something terrible, but I don't wish for your death for a second! I wish you were still here, with Mom and the rest of us. I wish you were alive to help me, because rebuilding the clan is so scary. And now I have to find and protect the Siol Eolais on top of that. Daddy, I'm so scared of failing," I said, collapsing into tears.

To his credit, Tristan seemed to understand better than I did that our time was short, and we were officially out of questions. I realized this as he quickly pulled himself together to relay one last message.

He finally managed to choke out, "Listen to me, Aoife. If you're scared of failing your mission, instead of fearing the burden itself and trying to run away from it, then you're already a better alpha than I was in life. You have a brilliant fey guardian at one side. And on the other... is the greatest familiar to ever walk the earth, the most loyal creature that will crawl through Hell and back to ensure your safety. She will love you, guide you, and protect you from even yourself. You just have to let her, like I couldn't."

Even Ruad had a few tears in her eyes now.

"I'm sorry, Ruad. I love you, and I regret everything I did to hurt you. I'm sorry."

And then, without warning, the phone literally dissolved into dust, falling right through my fingers. There was nothing remaining but a little pile of black and red powder on my floor with a few wolf tears mixed in.

"I'm sorry, too," Ruad finally muttered and walked over to our bedding corner to curl up. Her emotions radiated a thick blanket of everything from regret to sorrow. It washed over me in a way I'd never felt before as I started to shake, and my vision blurred from an overabundance of tears. Now I wasn't just crying for me. I was crying for her too. For Tristan. For Adrienn. For the pack.

I knew we had to find Epona and reclaim the seed before Malachos found it.

But that would have to wait until we spent every last tear in our collective wallet of grief. It was just one more cost on this goddamn day.

I walked over and curled up with Ruad, a morose ball of red fur, the two of us. Adrienn floated down into my hair, and the three of us just laid there sobbing.

Chapter Seventeen

The next day as I was still moping around the greenhouse, Ruad came over, and I buried my face in her fur for the 500th time.

She really was becoming, if not a service animal, then an emotional support wolf.

While I continued my moping, the vermillion wolf nuzzled me and said, "Hey, I have an idea. There's something I've been meaning to show you."

It took a few more seconds of nuzzling before I got up, sighing.

"You're gonna love this, Aoife. Tristan and I used to do it all the time," Ruad said, with a bit of giddiness I'd not seen in her eyes before.

She really thinks this will cheer us up, I thought.

We went out to the fairy circle, and she had Adrienne warp us somewhere. Traveling via mushroom was still disorienting, but the gas mileage was nice. Ruad had waited until sundown for this plan of hers, and even in daylight I wasn't sure I'd know our location.

The three of us appeared on the side of a mountain in some part of the forest I'd never seen before. There really wasn't any noise to speak of. I didn't hear any cars nearby.

"Where are we, Ruad?"

"This is a little east of a town called Winslow, or as your father called it, the middle of nowhere," Ruad said.

"Okay… what are we doing here?" I asked.

Ruad certainly seemed to have a new spring in her step out here, and I had to admit, the breeze blowing through the trees was nice. Dots of light in the evening sky looked down on two she-wolves and a fey getting ready to—well, I guess I had to wait for my familiar to reveal that last part to me.

And while Ruad was giddy on the outside, it didn't take a hard push toward our bridge for me to sense she was close to shaking from the mix of emotions in her heart. I closed my eyes and searched deeper to sense what my familiar was going through out here.

Ruad's emotions hit me in waves. The first was sadness upon seeing these hills and trees again, almost weep-worthy memories of better times when Tristan was still her partner and came here with his wolf to blow off steam.

The second wave filled me with joy, knowing my familiar had a second chance, of sorts, to run through this grass again under the night sky with no humans around us for a mile or two. And the final wave was… relief. I had to really focus to figure out this emotion and what caused it. But at last I understood. Ruad didn't think she'd be able to handle being here again after Tristan's death. Even in her years of wandering the Ozarks, she avoided this patch of land.

Still, she was here now, and Ruad hadn't shattered into a million pieces. There was good reason for relief.

"This is where Tristan and I came to run, Pup. It was his favorite way to blow off steam. We'd wait until sundown and then come out here. It's nothing but woods and mountains east of here. Just dozens of square miles of Ozark National Forest."

I looked down at my clawed feet standing on the chilled earth. It only took me about an hour to realize I'd stopped wearing shoes and socks unless I was around other people, courtesy of a certain bargain.

Definitely one step closer to fulfilling the Arkansas stereotype, I thought, rolling my eyes.

"You want to run?" I asked, not really understanding.

"Just shut up and follow me. You'll feel it almost instantly," Ruad said, darting through the trees and down a mountainside at speeds I didn't think I could match even in this wolf form of mine.

But I shrugged and did my best as Adrienn flew back into my locket. Before I knew it, Ruad and I were rushing through trees and bushes, over creeks and around caverns.

"Come on, Pup! You can do better. Really cut loose and throw your self restraint to the wind! Let the wolf take over," she yelled ahead.

I could smell her, but I couldn't see Ruad. So I did as she suggested as a small smirk formed on the right side of my lips.

Plunging all my strength into my legs and arms, I darted forward faster than I'd ever moved before. Olympian sprinters had nothing on me. Wolves were capable of moving at around 35 miles per hour in short bursts. But wolves with magic inside of them? That's another story.

I felt adrenaline course through me as Ruad and I raced down the mountainside. A normal human moving half this fast would have fallen and broken every bone in their legs. But I wasn't a normal human. I was a wolf girl.

The night air chilled once the sun went down. It was probably about 31 or 32 degrees out. Still, Ruad and I were plenty warm. We leapt over a small pond and broke out into a full sprint east across the valley we'd reached at the bottom of the mountain.

"No trees to slow me down anymore, Ruad. So show me how fast you can really move," I said, laughing. Wait, was I laughing? I was, wasn't I?

"Oh Pup, you have no idea," Ruad said, rushing forward at an instant speed that would put any sports car to shame. Zero to 60 in seven seconds for a Mustang? Ruad hit that in half the time for a short burst.

And somewhere inside of me, I knew I could, too.

So I crouched low and kicked forward with all my strength in my legs. I was close to Ruad's tail, but not quite on it. As we raced across the valley, two flashes of red fur, I smelled something.

"Deer," I yelled.

"Was wondering when you'd pick that up," Ruad said.

And we darted toward a group of doe. They sensed us coming all too late as we leapt forward and found the sole buck in the group. Ruad had her jaws around his neck, and I dug my claws into his right legs as we slammed the deer to the ground and killed it pretty quick.

We tore into the animal like… well, animals. And suddenly, human Aoife seemed very far away. Human Aoife that had given away half of her very essence seemed so distant to wolf Aoife.

Wolf Aoife had a fresh kill she'd just helped slaughter beneath the stars in a valley miles away from any people.

In fact, Aoife felt pretty damn good. She and Ruad finished their meal and washed the blood off them in a nearby pond.

"You ready to run some more?"

"The night is young, Ruad. Show me everything," I said.

And we bolted up another mountainside heading further east at top speed. We were in the moment, and that was all I wanted right now. Wolf Aoife, human Aoife, feral Aoife, whoever I was right this second. I just wanted this moment with speed, blood, trees, and mountains. And that's exactly what I got.

When I looked down at Ruad, I knew this is what she wanted at this very moment as well—something she has been waiting years for. Her Pup, her hunt, and O'Connell territory spread before us, just waiting to be sprinted across.

As we raced, I felt the steady beating of my heart, the warmth in my soul, and the surety of my decisions up to this point. Ruad and I were closer than ever before. And that made me pretty damn happy.

Chapter Eighteen

"So run Epona by me one more time, please. I mean… she's an actual goddess? THE goddess of horses?" I asked, sipping my hot chocolate.

Everything is so upside down, I thought. *On one level I'm starting to make some semblance of peace with being followed by a talking canine and becoming half wolf myself. But gods? Literal deities? That's just a whole new headache for a former normie to wrap her head around.*

Ruad sighed.

"Yes, Pup. The goddess of horses. As in, their protector and guardian. The O'Connells have made Epona their patron goddess for centuries now. A few clan members even had horse familiars."

I raised an eyebrow and smirked.

"Trying to get those horses into grocery stores and sleeping in the same bed must have been a pain in the ass."

My familiar rolled her eyes and said, "Look, not all clan members had familiars. And the ones that did… they're all different from you and I."

Turning my head a little sideways, I asked, "How so?"

Ruad sighed again. She looked around the room and then back at me before responding.

"Occasionally when my attachment to Tristan would agitate Iris, your mother called me clingy," Ruad said. "Some familiars are perfectly fine only being near their mortal partner once or twice a day. But Iris was accurate to call me clingy, Pup. Let's just say the two things that have increased steadily throughout my life are bitterness and abandonment issues."

"And ultimately, what does all that mean?" I asked, taking a rare moment to respect Ruad's vulnerability that she so rarely displayed.

My familiar's amber eyes locked with my own, and I saw a little bit of grumpiness building. The next sentence wasn't one she wanted to speak.

"That… I need you, Pup. I need you to be near me at all times, or I'll risk freaking the fuck out. There. Is that what you wanted to hear?"

Holding up my hands, I showed her I wasn't poking fun… for once. Ruad sneezed and looked down at the floor before returning my gaze.

"Okay, let's just… get back to Epona. I'm never going to part with you, Ruad. I'll kick you out of the room when Abi and I want to do stuff, but that's about it. Can you tell me more about this goddess?"

"Epona is the patron goddess of the O'Connell Clan. Our whole family, everyone in the clan, swears fealty to her. And that includes every O'Connell going back to the founder of the clan, Avalon O'Connell. Legend has it she was on the run from Christian missionaries centuries ago, an entire gang of them running her down for refusal to renounce her druidic beliefs. With nowhere to hide and nowhere to run, she prayed to the gods for help, and Epona took pity on her. The goddess appeared in her moment of need and carried Avalon to safety.

"Afterward, Avalon made regular offerings to Epona and dedicated herself to the goddess. In return, Epona blessed her, and she established the O'Connell clan with those blessings. It's been tradition every member of the pack continued to share in those blessings since, so long as regular offerings were made and pack members dedicated themselves to her with their belief.

"Big picture: Epona protects and nurtures horses all over the world. Little picture: the O'Connells named her their patron deity centuries ago and have regularly shared in blessings since."

Looking across the parking lot, I saw Abi coming over toward us. She skirted around a red pickup truck parked crooked. She was wearing a black puffy coat with red jeans.

The announcer came back over the muffled speaker system. It would sound a little better once we were closer to the show.

"So… we have to track down Epona to find the seed our clan has been protecting for generations. Any idea where to start? Maybe we can summon her?" I asked.

Ruad shook her head.

"I tried that. Whenever I caught a break from Malachos or Ash chasing me, I tried to summon Epona once or twice through prayer and asking for her blessings. She didn't show."

Something subtle fluttered in my chest, a rogue emotion, not my own, but one from my familiar. And it felt like a feeling she was trying desperately to bury. Closing my eyes, I dove after that feeling, trying to figure out what Ruad was keeping from me. After a few seconds of flailing through our connection, I finally grasped it. Now an intense loneliness raked across my heart, and I flinched, hissing a little.

This isn't my pain, I reminded myself and closed my eyes again to make sense of this emotion.

I felt… alone, at the end of my rope, and like every step was another fruitless pawing at straws. Remembering to breathe, I took in air and realized what this meant. Ruad had tried to summon Epona multiple times after the clan's extermination. And what she didn't want me to know, likely for reasons of pride, was she'd wanted guidance, maybe even some semblance of friendship from our patron goddess. Any crumb of light and warmth to chase away that numbing ache in her chest would have been a welcome relief. But she got nothing.

I wanted to cry for her, cry with her, try to make these memories go away. But if Ruad knew what I'd sensed just now, it would likely cause even more pain by cracking her image of a sterling and stoic wolf, one above petty worries like loneliness. And I wasn't going to do that to my familiar. I'd leave her ego intact.

Even if I wanted to say something to help Ruad, there were no words capable of doing that.

During my lowest moments of living under Barb's heel, I wanted what Ruad wanted, a little help, a sign that things would eventually get better. And back then, if someone had just offered me words, I would have slapped them.

So, I resolved to do whatever I could to give my familiar as much light and warmth as possible.

"What then? You think something prevented her from appearing?" I asked.

"It's possible."

"What would be strong enough to prevent a goddess from showing up when summoned?"

Ruad looked me in the eyes and said, "Another deity."

I shrugged.

"Sure. Why not? Why wouldn't we also have to deal with a potential hostile deity in addition to Malachos?" I asked.

Abi came over and kissed me on the cheek.

"Hey there. Ready to head in?" she asked.

"Just waiting on you. Remind me why we're at the Springdale Holiday Rodeo again?" I asked. This was pretty damn far from my usual scene. Too many denim vests and cowboy boots for my tastes.

"They've got a local band playing tonight called Nighttime Whispers. One of my friends recommended them to me. I listened to some of their songs online, and they're really good. Plus, the drummer is a trans girl, and I want her to have as much support from the stands as possible. So a group of Fayetteville High School students and alumni showed up to support the band," Abi said, starting to drag me toward the ticket booth.

As long as I'd known her, Abi was always trying to support people who probably didn't have enough support in their hobbies and dreams. In fact, I'd say my girlfriend was relentlessly optimistic.

There was a guy named Thomas who crashed his truck last year and wound up in a wheelchair. He was already pretty shy, but the accident seemed to rob him of what confidence he had left. But somewhere Thomas found the guts to enter a standup comedy night on Dickson Street. Abi made sure he had plenty of friends from FHS in the audience to laugh at his jokes. That's just the way she was. It's part of what I loved about her, that giant heart beating in her chest.

A lady wearing a blue scarf with the words Springdale Chamber of Commerce embroidered on them sold us some red paper tickets for $5 a piece. She eyed Ruad carefully, but when my familiar didn't immediately tear open her throat and behaved as a normal service animal would, she handed me my ticket.

It had the words "admit one" on the back in black letters.

We walked past an older couple and found some seats in the first section of bleachers we could. There were hundreds of people out on this chilly night.

Next to a municipal airport and community center, the Old Ozark Rodeo sat on the eastern outskirts of Springdale, the next city up north of Fayetteville. Follow the interstate up, and you hit Rogers next, and then Bentonville. The way Northwest Arkansas is growing, some folks expect the four cities will just merge into a large metropolis one day.

But I could tell most of the folks here at the Springdale Holiday Rodeo would fight that tooth and nail. Individualism reigned king in the hearts of some folks. I didn't really care one way or another. As a druid, most of my concern was now relegated to the Ozark Mountains and National Forest.

Another college student wearing a black leather jacket saw Ruad and started to approach with that stupid "Whoa! Is that a real wolf?" expression. At this point, I figured I could copyright that glance since I'd seen it so much.

He got about five feet away before I glared at him and flashed my own canines, just enough to scare him and make him wonder what he'd really seen. Taking a few steps back, he turned and stumbled around some spilled popcorn.

"Better run," I muttered, checking my knit beanie to make sure it was still hiding my ears.

Some feedback on the speaker system caused me to cover my ears in pain. Ruad didn't look all that happy, either.

"You okay?" Abi asked.

I shook my head.

"It's just too noisy, and I'm not used to having this enhanced hearing all the time yet. Can we move please? Further from the speakers?"

Abi nodded and took my hand. I'd done my best to file down my claws to where they didn't cut Abi's palm open when we held hands, but even shortened I could still get a good slash in if I wasn't careful. I could file them down to about an inch above my actual finger before they started to really hurt.

Combine that with the fact that it was annoying keeping my tail tucked upward into a shirt all day, and I was a little grumpier than normal. This form had some major disadvantages. However, the fangs gave me a good excuse to never visit the dentist again, so there was at least one upside.

I appreciated Abi being more graceful with me since I'd taken on my wolf form permanently. But Dan had been right about psychological changes. Some things I was increasingly indifferent to now more than ever before. Abi and I had gone shopping earlier today to find her a new coat. Before, when we went shopping together, Abi would make a little show out of modeling new clothes for me. She'd walk down the dressing room hall with an exaggerated swagger, and my reaction would be used to decide which items she purchased. The bigger my smile, the faster she pulled out her debit card.

But today? Not so much.

Today, Abi put on a brown peacoat and did a little spin. And all I wanted to do was be out in the woods, away from all these people and their strange smells. The perfumes, the deodorants, the hairspray, the lotions, god, it was annoying.

I spent half my time in each store just immediately darting away from people, my nostrils burning, and my eyes watering. Fat lot of good it did me since most stores in the mall were the size of a small apartment. It left me with a severe headache and irritability. I definitely growled at two or three customers with the most offensive odors, ones that human Aoife would have enjoyed just a week ago. These were scents like vanilla, coconut, and cherry blossom. My prior scent sanctuary had been turned against me overnight.

And when I wasn't running from odors, I was trying to pretend I wasn't bored, but Abi could tell. She could always tell, even without a familiar's link to my emotions. My acting was terrible. This is why I wasn't majoring in drama like Abi.

At one point, she put on one of those rubber yellow raincoats just to get a reaction out of me. Internally, I sighed. Were we almost done yet? But on the outside, I put all my energy into laughing and asking if she was looking for a little curious monkey to accompany her.

But she saw through that performance, too.

Going to the food court and splitting a pizza didn't go much better. Abi was talking excitedly about the upcoming spring semester and how she'd be taking fundamentals of theatrical design.

She was just gobbling down a slice of cheese pizza, and I... just kept staring at the pepperoni in front of me, wishing it was on the run so I could chase it and slam it to the ground. Tear my teeth into its throat and feel the warm life drain from it.

I ate a piece half-heartedly. Ruad looked up at me. She knew. Or rather, I knew. I knew how she felt when I dragged her around town with me during work or other errands.

When Abi dropped me off at the greenhouse, I kissed her and apologized for being so aloof. She just put a hand on my face and said, "You're going through a lot of changes, but I'm staying right here, okay? We'll get through this, too."

I had nodded and then went into the greenhouse to cry. Was it going to be like this from now on? Was I only going to be happy in the woods, running wild, or hunting prey? And we hadn't even tried being intimate since I'd given up a portion of my humanity. Surely that would be different.

"It's always going to be like this, isn't it, Ruad?" I had asked, as she walked over and nuzzled my cheek.

"It'll get easier, Pup. But I think you're also realizing there are some fine elements that separate humans, and even druids, from animals," my familiar said.

I sighed.

Goddammit.

Abi's voice brought me back to the present.

"How about here?" she asked.

She pointed to a couple seats on the opposite side of the ring from where we'd been sitting previously. There weren't as many people on this side, and the speakers were more spread out.

I nodded at Abi and smiled, muttering, "Thanks."

She lightly kissed me on the cheek, and I saw an older couple staring at us. They were both shaking their heads, so I flipped them off. They scowled and went back to watching kids in the dirt trying to see how long they could ride sheep before falling off. What was it called? Mutton busting? That seemed a tad cruel. The animals didn't seem to be in pain, but they sure weren't thrilled to be here.

God, I hate being here, I thought, growing more agitated. But Abi seemed determined to stay until the band finished playing. In the theater community, Abi was exposed to all manner of folks. Gender, sexuality, skin color, disability, the drama folks around here were pretty accepting of anyone who wandered into a production.

The result was my girlfriend growing up in an environment that fostered her exploration, that encouraged her to be true to herself when she realized she liked girls instead of boys.

When I realized I liked both, I knew there was no way I could tell Barb or John. They'd never even come close to understanding. I'd have been shipped off to a conversion therapy camp and locked in a room with sermons being pumped in on speakers until I was so far back into the closet that my diet consisted solely of clothes hangers and shoes.

But Abi, I understood why she wanted to be here. Not only was the local creative scene important to her, but someone that was taking the stage had a hard lot in life, and she wanted to offer support to a complete stranger. Her heart was too good. That made me smile.

When the rodeo really got started, I looked around. Three military members in full regalia walked down into the dirt with flags.

The dirt center was surrounded by a round metal fence. The risers we sat in weren't covered, but the other side we'd been on had a big metal roof.

American flags hung everywhere inside. One of the gray pickup trucks outside had a Confederate battle flag proudly erected on a pole in the bed. I made a mental note to stay away from that vehicle. I didn't want to meet its owner. And they didn't want to meet me.

They went through the national anthem, an opening prayer, and before long, events were underway. I smelled horses, bulls, pigs, cows, chickens, sheep, and other animals I was tempted to leap onto and eat. I wiped my mouth and decided I needed something to keep my instincts from overtaking me.

So Ruad and I went to the concession stand and got nachos. I was about as thrilled eating them as I was the pizza earlier, but it put something warm in my belly, which dulled my animalistic needs a tad.

I checked my phone and saw I had a text from Ash. He was asking for a little more information about joining the clan and what all that would entail. I sent back a little more information, but honestly, I didn't know much more than him. Most of that information was in Ruad's mind, and I still wasn't sure she'd be cool with her previously sworn enemy joining.

Then again, it wasn't like we had a bunch of prospective applicants ready to become O'Connells. If I intended to rebuild the clan, I had to look at Ash seriously as a member. Where else was he going to find people who would accept him, wings, talons, and all, besides a secret government lab where they'd want to dissect him? My spine shivered a little upon realizing I was now in that same boat.

We could broach the topic of Ash becoming an O'Connell once we figured out what happened to our clan's patron goddess. And that could wait until this date night with Abi was over.

After watching several cowboys get thrown into the dirt by a wild bull, I smiled a little bit. I knew who I was rooting for. The rodeo clowns got a good workout tonight. They saved quite a few riders.

Amateur hour, I thought, laughing.

I smelled a mixture of hay, dirt, dust, sweat, and livestock. I heard boots hitting mud and scrambling over the metal gate trying to get to safety.

The event before the band came on was a flag display with 13 women riding horses. The breeds ranged from appaloosas to mustangs and thoroughbreds. Most horses were black and white, some were all brown, and a few were spotted.

The women, all antebellum ladies with matching red lipstick and white cowgirl hats, carried American flags while riding in different patterns. Everyone in the crowd looked like they were watching the proudest performance of their lives.

I fired off another text to Ash. He was having a tough night with dysphoria and didn't want to take off his binder. I gently reminded him it wasn't meant to be worn for more than eight hours, and he'd been wearing it all day. Any more, and he risked really hurting his chest.

He finally relented and decided to go to bed early. I smiled. Wow. From trying to capture me to taking my health and safety advice. Who was this spiky raven boy?

At last, Nighttime Whispers took the stage. The three girls were wearing matching long sleeve T-shirts with the band's name on the front. They looked to be a little younger than me.

"So the guitar player's name is Jenna. I think the bass player is Tessa. And the drummer's name is Roxie," Abi leaned over and said.

"Are you friends with any of them?" I asked.

"Tessa is dating a friend of mine," Abi said, crossing her arms and waiting for the show to begin.

"Oh, the mayor's kid," I said.

Sometimes Fayetteville was a smaller town than I remembered to give it credit for. It was growing more every year, but at its core, this was still a small Arkansas college town where everyone knew everyone else.

I looked over at Roxie. She wore long chestnut hair and purple jeans. Her makeup was minimalistic, like she was cautious about what she wore, trying not to draw attention to herself.

She's cute, I thought, smirking. *I bet she plays kickass drums.*

A man's voice came over the speakers, "Ladies and gentlemen, please give a warm welcome to tonight's musical guests. They're a local band from Fayetteville called Nighttime Whispers. Please put your hands together for Jenna, Tessa, and Johnny."

Abi clenched her fists. It took me a second to figure out who the announcer was talking about.

That must be her deadname, I thought, sighing.

The audience cheered, but I saw some Fayetteville High School students clustered together down near the rail, maybe about 10-12 of them. They screamed various encouragement, with one girl yelling, "Knock 'em dead, ladies!"

Roxie looked down at her drums. I think she was trying not to cry. She did not look like a Johnny in the least.

Tessa and Jenna looked at each other when the audience grew silent, and then they stepped up to their microphones.

Jenna pointed to the deck where the announcer and a few others sat behind microphones and red, white, and blue flags of their own.

"Sorry, there's been a slight mix-up, folks. We don't have a Johnny in our band, never have. But we do have a Roxie, the best drummer in all of Arkansas. We're just three girls from Fayetteville ready to kick ass and play music. Are y'all ready?" Tessa asked.

The audience cheered, and when they grew silent again, Jenna whispered into her mic, "Someone might want to confiscate the announcer's Bud Light. He's probably had enough for the night."

A few folks around us laughed.

Jenna turned around and winked at Roxie, who looked beyond joyful to have her friends on stage with her. I smiled. Now that was some loyalty.

"This song is called Glistening Steed. Hope you enjoy it," Tessa said.

And the group went on to play a kickass show. This band really knew how to rock. I swayed back and forth as they played the next few songs. When Roxie sang, she harmonized well with the others.

But as they played what I really noticed were Roxie's drum skills, how her rhythm really set the pace for this group. She was the power and backbone of Nighttime Whispers, and that put the band on a whole new level.

Strange, I caught myself thinking suddenly. *When I watch her play, I feel at ease.*

After a drum solo that went on for a good 15-20 seconds, I realized why that was. She played on her own terms. The way Roxie allowed her true self to flow through this instrument in spite of a world that undoubtedly challenged her very existence left me speechless.

I smiled.

And if I'm honest—I thought. *Roxie makes me feel like when I play the violin at my own pace.*

Nighttime Whispers closed with the Johnny Cash rendition of

"Hurt," and the audience really seemed to like that. Cash fans at a rodeo? Color me shocked.

I turned to Abi, and she seemed to know what I was going to ask.

"Yeah, we can go, after we say something to the girls," she said, smiling.

She'd just finished posting a supportive comment on the band's Instagram page letting them know she was here tonight, and they rocked.

It took a little bit for the band to finish tearing down, but we caught them on their way toward the exit carrying their equipment.

Abi hugged Tessa and told her how much she rocked. I smiled and waved. Roxie looked bashful at all the compliments. I caught her staring at Ruad.

"Your companion is beautiful," she said in a quiet voice.

I smiled. She made no move to pet Ruad, just complimented her. I think I liked this girl. Or maybe someone with manners was just extra refreshing to encounter.

"Thanks. Her name is Ruad. I'm Aoife, by the way," I said.

"I'm Roxie," she said, almost extending a hand and then awkwardly stopping. Like she realized that would have been a little weird, but stopping it mid-way was even more strange.

I chuckled a little.

"I'm guessing wolves are your favorite animal," Roxie said, looking at Ruad again.

Smiling, I nodded.

"They're beautiful creatures. But this one in particular, I'd quite literally die for her," I said. And that was true, both literally and figuratively. "What's your favorite animal?" I asked.

Roxie thought for a moment and finally said, "Probably foxes. They're just so cute, cat software running on dog hardware." I smiled even more at that.

We said our goodbyes to the band and turned to leave, but the announcer spoke up before we were gone.

"And now, the best cowgirls from across Arkansas will see if they can take the best time in this year's barrel racing event," he said.

I'm not sure why I turned. Maybe I was morbidly curious about what barrel racing is.

Barrel rider? I thought in Smaug's voice. I smirked at that.

But maybe there was more to it than morbid curiosity, because I slowly felt the hairs on the back of my neck stand up. It sounded like someone whispering my name on the wind. And I instinctively moved back toward the crowd.

Three water barrels had been set up in a triangle in the center of the ring. Each was draped with sponsorship covering from Coors Light.

The first woman took off racing between the barrels riding between them in a cloverleaf pattern. She was riding a brown and white American paint horse. I wondered if it was her first year doing this because her feet scraped the barrels a couple times, even knocking one over.

After she was done, the announcer spoke up again, "Next is the reigning champion of the Springdale Holiday Rodeo barrel racing event. Miss Leslie Dominson and her fierce Friesian mare, Shade! Each year, Leslie has gotten closer and closer to the world record of 13.46 seconds. Will this be the year she does it?"

Leslie was wearing a denim jacket and brown pants with fringe down the side. The saddle that carried her was a darker shade of brown. She wore a white hat like the girls from the flag ride earlier. Long curly blonde hair bounced as she rode into the ring to a cheering audience. She was apparently a local favorite. Leslie was probably approaching 40, which put her out of the age bracket for most girls competing in barrel racing tonight, but it was her horse that really captured my attention.

I felt a wave of magical energy wash over me. The feeling was like a miniature earthquake only I seemed to sense. And I knew without a doubt the black mare Leslie rode was no normal horse. Shade's sleek coat was so shiny that it practically glowed under the stadium lights. Her mane was long and curly, dark as a night sky accompanied by a new moon.

Shade's legs were strong, but they were strained, not by the weight of Leslie, but by anger. The animal's ears were flattened, and when it stood in place, one hind leg lifted off the ground. This horse was furious. And the more I watched her prance around the ring, the angrier I got.

Hanging throughout Shade's bountiful mane were sky blue feathers, and they radiated with dark magic that left me feeling anxious and nauseous.

It's similar to Malachos' magic, I thought. *Not his exactly, though.*

Each feather was connected to Shade's mane and to each other by a thin golden chain. They bounced with the mane as the horse galloped.

Shade appeared to be close to chewing through her bit. This horse didn't want to be here anymore than I did. And yet, we both were.

When her russet eyes locked with mine, I felt another wave of magic wash over me as goosebumps rose up my arms. This horse was powerful. And yet… restrained. The feathers on her mane were holding back the lion's share of her energy.

Leslie ordered the horse forward toward the barrels to begin her run. And when the horse didn't immediately comply, she roughly squeezed one of the blue feathers into the mane, and Shade let out a pained whinny. I doubt anyone else in the stadium noticed.

I saw a little bit of smoke rising from Shade's mane, and I snarled, revealing my fangs in their full tearing glory.

Shade's eyes locked with mine again, and I felt a wave of sharp and pointed magic race across the dirt and slam into my mind, and not just mine, but Ruad's as well. Our consciousnesses were lassoed from the present moment into a memory of a clear summer night. Looking around, I saw the entire pack had gathered before three large torches, a group of people and familiars I didn't recognize, but nonetheless felt connected to.

Everyone gathered around the horse in this memory. Shade stood tall, moonlight reflecting off her onyx coat. I watched as my parents placed a large basket of flowers before Shade, then bowed in her presence.

Shade's aura filled the entire meadow they stood in with a shimmer of potent magic. I watched as every few feet Easter lilies twisted and sprung out of the Earth, blooming in gradual unison, fed by her energy.

"We swear fealty to you, the great Capall, Epona. Please accept this offering and bless us once more," Iris said.

Our goddess, I thought, mouth agape.

Epona looked over the offering of flowers and appeared satisfied.

"Once more the O'Connell clan calls forth to present offerings. Once more, I accept and bestow my blessings upon you all," she said.

And then, with a sudden rush of wind, she was gone, whinnying into the night with her offering. The meadow filled with the scent of spring squill and clovers.

I felt the same energy Ruad did that night, and when I opened my eyes, I recognized it and the scent of clovers and spring squill present at the rodeo.

My muscles seized, and from the depths of my chest, I let loose a growl that started to rattle the benches around me. And at the same time, my vision grew blurry as tears raced down my cheeks. It wasn't right for rage and sorrow to mix so thoroughly.

This was our patron goddess, and she was ensnared, made to ride for sport between these fucking barrels. Our goddess carried some unworthy bitch upon her back, and every ounce of power in my legs wanted to leap into that ring, while all the power in my claws and fangs longed to shred her apart.

"We let her down," I muttered, stepping toward the railing. "But I swear I'm going to make it right."

I wasn't paying much attention to my peripheral vision, but I saw my familiar standing tense and looking back and forth from me to Epona. She sensed everything I did.

Ruad put her body between myself and the gate. Epona danced between the barrels with a speed much greater than I'd seen any horse pull off. She was so incredibly agile and energetic. But I know she wasn't performing willingly.

"Not yet, Pup. Not here," my familiar said.

Feral Aoife was seething inside. I felt her in every tremor as my body shook, barely able to contain my furor. And I was right there with her for once, my claws tensing.

"That's our goddess," I growled, something primal growing inside of me. This hate didn't feel like a normal human emotion. It was something that rose from my blood. My O'Connell heritage fueled this fire.

It was almost like I was furious for the entire clan, as if all their anger and sorrow were coursing through my veins calling on me to save Epona.

"Our goddess is being ridden for entertainment!" I hissed at Ruad.

I noticed the same anger in her, but she had a tiny shred of control over it.

"I know, Pup. But we can't do anything about it here. Too many eyes. We'll follow them after this is over and free her. I promise," Ruad said.

"Fine," I said, watching Leslie complete a run that fell 0.2 seconds short of the national record. I smiled, as she ground her teeth. I just knew that despite Epona being ensnared by dark magic, she'd had enough strength to cost her rider that record.

"Get ready, bitch. Because I'm coming," I growled.

Abi came over and said, "What are you waiting for? I thought you wanted to go?"

I took a deep breath and looked at my girlfriend before saying, "Change of plans. Druid business to attend to."

Abi raised an eyebrow.

"Tonight?"

I nodded.

"That horse leaving the ring now? She's our clan's patron goddess, Epona. And she's ensnared against her will. Ruad and I are going to free her after she leaves with her captor," I said.

She looked a little nervous but slowly nodded.

"I mean no disrespect, but that looks like a normal horse to me," Abi said.

Ruad sighed and said, "You can't feel the magic she's putting off, but trust us. That's the goddess of horses being ridden away. Our clan has worshiped Epona for centuries. It's our duty to free her."

Abi looked at the horse again and nodded.

"Do you need any help?" she asked.

Ruad and I exchanged glances.

"We'll be fine," I said. "She's going to die tonight for her transgressions."

Abi's face paled, and she grabbed my wrist, pulling me away from Ruad a little bit.

"Baby, I fully support all your druidic history. I'm glad you've found your family and understand how important it is to you. But you just told me without flinching that you were going to murder a woman tonight. That scares me a little—a lot, actually."

I pointed at Epona being led out of the ring.

"That's our goddess, Abi. She's been disrespected and ridden like a show animal for years, all because my clan was decimated. Now I've got a chance to free her, and you can bet the woman who took Epona from us will pay with her life."

Abi shook her head.

"I know you've given up half your humanity. I don't fully understand what that means for your heart, but don't think for a second that I'm going to stand by and let you commit murder tonight. Being magical doesn't give you the right to kill people. And the Aoife I know wouldn't take a life unless it was self defense. Giant spiders from another realm trying to eat a little boy is one thing. Murdering a human woman is another, even if she's done terrible things to your goddess and, by extension, your clan, is another thing."

Looking into Abi's eyes I saw concern, fear, and worry for me. The remaining human part of my mind clicked on and clawed for control. Taking a deep breath, I pushed all that rage and feral Aoife down.

"She's our... goddess," I growled.

Abi nodded.

"And I fully expect you to go rescue Epona. But don't you kill that woman, Aoife."

I shook my head, fighting that rage in my tightening chest.

"She has to answer for her crimes. You know human law won't do anything to her."

My girlfriend sighed and said, "You're probably right. But you don't get to be judge, jury, and executioner."

Abi grabbed my chin and raised my eyes to her own.

"Look at me, Aoife. I see the animalistic side of you is craving blood. But you're human, and humans have laws to follow. I won't let you go until you promise me you aren't going to kill this woman. Figure out some other punishment," Abi said.

I growled and clenched my fists. I wanted this Leslie woman's life to end for what she'd done, for the dishonor she'd brought on Epona and the O'Connells. But I also recognized Abi's voice and what she was saying. I processed it... slowly.

"Fine," I barked. That was all I could manage at this point.

Abi drew me in for a kiss. When we parted, she said, "I love you, all of you. This magic is consuming and redefining you. And you're a big girl who can deal with it. But I won't let it take you away from me, do you understand?"

I nodded, and we kissed again. Then she turned to go.

After she'd gone, a tall man in a plaid shirt and red ballcap walking by muttered, "Fucking dykes."

I used my pent up anger to punch him in the gut so hard all the wind rushed out of his groaning mouth. He sank to his knees.

Ruad and I left him there, wheezing. I didn't break anything, but he would be sore for the next week.

We exited the rodeo, muffled applause and announcements continuing behind us. Following Epona's scent, we came to an area where livestock was loaded and unloaded. Epona was being placed into a blue horse trailer pulled by a brown Ford Bronco. The irony wasn't lost on me.

Leslie hissed at her about not breaking the record. She yanked more mane and feathers, causing Epona to whinny in pain. And then, she hopped in the Bronco and pulled out onto Emma Avenue, heading east out of the city.

Ruad and I built up our energy and took off running in the shadows along the road. She was probably driving about 30-35 mph. We matched that pushing ourselves and followed her Bronco as she headed further east, mostly through fields and past the occasional cookie cutter house neighborhood. More and more of those seemed to be popping up in Northwest Arkansas.

She turned onto a street called Parsons Road, and Ruad and I continued to hound her, never losing sight. We ran for a few miles, moving closer to Blue Springs Village. Eventually, Leslie turned off onto a gravel road toward the south, and we followed her.

The woman drove about a quarter mile toward a tree line. She arrived at a farm consisting of an orange barn, a single-story ranch house painted blue, a small chicken coop, and a large fenced-in pasture that bordered the tree line with a few mustangs.

When her vehicle finally came to a stop, Ruad and I paused to catch our breath. We were about 30 feet back from the trailer, kneeling in a ditch.

There was just one light up by the house, wired to one of the power poles that followed her driveway.

I locked eyes with Epona, and my rage returned. Her stare said she knew who I was and what I was going to do.

Chapter Nineteen

Leslie closed her door, and that's when Ruad and I revealed ourselves. How easy would it have been to just pounce on this woman and end her life? Easier than future me would probably want to admit. But I'd promised Abi that wasn't going to be the end result of this little operation.

The woman jumped and immediately raised her voice.

"Who the fuck are you? This is private land."

I looked down at Ruad and stifled a growl. I would give this woman one chance to release the goddess. One. But part of me hoped she'd pull out a weapon or give me some excuse to claim self defense as I ended her. Abi would understand that, right? If she drew a blade or a gun? Then I had no choice.

I tried to push those thoughts aside and said, "My name is Aoife. This is Ruad. We're here for the horse."

My right arm twitched a little. I knew this was no regular horse. And surely this woman knew it as well. The only question was, would she try to play dumb about it?

"This is my prize horse. I would die before I let you take her," Leslie said. "Now fuck off before I get my gun."

Ruad took a step in front of me.

Cute. As if I'd let you get shot for me, I thought, stepping up beside her.

"Listen to me. That's no normal horse, and you know it. Her name isn't Shade. It's Epona, and she's a goddess, our goddess," I said slowly so she'd understand every word.

Leslie flinched at this, and I saw her reach behind her waste, pulling up a small handgun and pointing it at me. "A goddess? You expect me to believe the horse I just rode on was a goddess?" she asked, wearing a face painted by incredulity.

Okay, so playing dumb it is. I thought, rolling my eyes. *I don't have time for this.*

274

"Put down the gun, Leslie. I'm trying to find a way out of this where we both walk away alive," I said. "Ruad, tell her about the goddess in her trailer."

Leslie had the gun grasped with both hands now, finger on the side of the weapon and off the trigger. That's when my familiar spoke.

"We are wolves of the O'Connell clan. And you've committed a grave error by imprisoning our goddess, Epona, guardian and master of all horses," Ruad said, trying to match my slow and semi-patient tone.

The woman before us flinched as my wolf spoke, and she shook her head, twitching a little now.

"That's bullshit. She said the horse was mine for 10 years," I heard Leslie mutter, her heart rate hitting the gas pedal. I watched her skin pale, and she took a second to look back at Epona. The goddess' glare washed over Leslie as though it was enough to trample Leslie into the ground.

Ruad and I exchanged glances. My own heart skipped a beat when Leslie said "she." Had someone given this woman our goddess like some kind of twisted present? Who had the power to do that?

The wind picked up, and a new scent reached me. There was something familiar about it, and not in a comforting sense. My nose twitched as I struggled to place this odor. It was a strange mix of overripe blackberries and mud, a damp and chilled sensation touching each one of the hundreds of cilia in my nostrils.

The sound of fluttering wings from a tiger owl nearby triggered the final clue. It was a murky and somber magic, the kind I smelled when Ash was around. This curse twisted his very being through a deceitful bargain, preying on desperate desires one would never achieve on their own.

When I realized whose magic puffed through the air, the scent multiplied, or maybe I just became more sensitive to it.

The odor radiated from the chains and feathers in Epona's mane that left her in such torment, and as my eyes returned to Leslie, I smelled it coming from her body as well.

"What did you give Morrigu for the horse, Leslie?" I asked, lowering my hands to my side.

The rider's hands started shaking harder, and I heard each breath coming faster.

"How do you know that name?" Leslie finally whispered. "Did she send you? Because I'm supposed to have 10 years! It's only been nine."

Looking back at Ruad, we each sighed. It was becoming clearer what had happened now. I just needed Leslie to fill in a couple more blanks. I relaxed my legs, knowing I probably wasn't going to kill this woman. In fact, if she was anything like Ash prior to striking his bargain, Leslie was already a broken individual.

"We're not from Morrigu, Leslie, though we've crossed paths with her bargains before. We're a pack of druids. And Epona is our patron goddess. It's an affront to us that you've got her locked up or riding around like some kind of show pony when she's so much more."

Leslie avoided looking back at Epona now, probably feeling the rage building in the trailer behind her under the chains and feathers.

The rider started shaking her head and said, "Morrigu never told me that. It was just… supposed to be a special horse, one that would help me finally get the one thing I've always wanted."

"What did you promise her, Leslie?" I asked, again. But the woman before me was lost in her own memories, darting her eyes around as if putting the pieces together and trying to figure out where she so royally fucked up. I could relate to at least that much.

That owl flew overhead again, searching for supper, and moved into a different tree. Leslie's heart rate only climbed as she got lost in whatever flashback played internally for an audience of one, her face twisting into a mix of sadness, anger, and desperation

"It wasn't supposed to be complicated… she just showed up, gave me those weird feathered chains, and told me where to find the horse. I hid by the river, and… she was supposed to help me get what I wanted," Leslie muttered, looking down at the ground, as if there might be some clue or answer to her impending crisis there.

Do I risk asking a third time? I thought. *She's clearly trapped in her own memories.*

At this point, I saw something black snaking its way up Leslie's neck. A closer look revealed it wasn't something outside her neck, but inside, like a series of dark veins working their way upward.

"It doesn't matter," Leslie muttered. "In the end, I'll get what I want. Next year, it's mine for sure."

And at that point, I figured maybe I'd been asking the wrong question.

"Leslie… what is it you really want?"

This seemed to bring the rider back from her memories, and her glassy eyes renewed their gaze upon me. I didn't feel quite so threatened by the gun anymore. She wasn't mentally present enough to use it for entire minutes at a time.

"Well I want that record, wolf girl. When I started riding as a child, the world record for barrel racing was just over 20 seconds. Year by year, it's been shaved down by riders all over the world to just over 13 seconds. And I want to be a record holder. I'm going to be, next year," she said.

I squinted. Her eyes were fluttering a little, and those black veins were moving further up her neck. Ruad didn't seem to know what to make of them, and I didn't either. For her part, Leslie appeared to be having a harder time breathing, and I smelled sweat forming on her forehead thicker than anywhere else.

A sneaking suspicion grew in my gut, that if I could keep pulling at this thread, what's driving her, I might be able to get Epona free. Nothing about this situation smelled right. A bargain with Morrigu gone wrong, memories that reek of deception, and an unsteadiness that left a chill down my spine the more I witnessed it.

"Why? Why is this record so important to you?" I asked as she kept staring at me…or maybe behind me. I couldn't tell with her awkward gaze, almost as if she were looking through me.

"Why? Why?!" she suddenly screamed, and those veins rose higher on her neck, growing closer to her chin. She gasped for breath after screaming. "Why? Because it's all I have! It's all I'll ever have, so I can't let you take this from me, even if she is some goddess of yours."

Ruad tensed, and I was about to growl again, but I stifled it. Aggression… strange as it sounded coming from me…wasn't the answer here.

Without further prompting, Leslie removed a hand from her gun and lifted up the side of her shirt. I saw two things, more black veins that appeared to be pulsing, and scars in a jagged pattern down her ribs.

"My mother and father weren't exactly great to me, wolf girl. They had issues with drug and alcohol abuse, and when they got going, I was often to blame, not the methamphetamine or the beer. It was always my fault when the mortgage payment was late or a flat tire presented itself. It was my fault when the scratch offs didn't make them rich. Hell, it was my fault when it rained on a day they wanted to mow the lawn. And when things were my fault, they brought out this black leather belt they named Juno. Through the years, I got to spend a lot of time with Juno," Leslie said, putting her shirt down as I flinched.

What could I say to that? What could anyone say to that?

"The one place Juno couldn't reach me was on top of a horse. Seems I had some tiny skill for riding and even won a few small contests. God, you should have seen the way my parents looked at me when I won, how the seemingly-eternal disappointment vanished like dust kicked up behind a horse. You may have guessed it, but my best event was barrel racing, and their favorite part was the prize money," Leslie said, taking her eyes off me again and probably picturing past rodeos she'd competed in.

I know a thing or two about fucked up parents, I thought.

When something breaks you as an adult, you're already pretty well put together, so rebuilding is at least possible. But when something breaks you as a child, that shit never gets fixed. It's like having a cracked foundation, and you just learn to live with it, the unbalance and the uneasiness of it all. That is, until you find those special people who fill in the holes of your heart and become the solid ground you stand on. Then it hits you. They're who you wish were around when you were breaking inside as a child. They could have picked up the pieces when nobody else would.

Better late than never, though, I thought, picturing Ruad and Adrienne in my mind. *Some people are worth the wait.*

"I'm sorry that happened to you, Leslie," I said, grasping for words. "You didn't deserve that childhood. No kid does."

At this, Leslie threw her head back and laughed in an exaggerated hoot. But there wasn't anything funny to be found for miles. This was the laugh you gave when the only alternative was falling to pieces.

Then her head lowered, and she was dead serious again.

"Everybody was sorry. They were all sorry my mother and father were terrible people. But nobody was willing to do anything about it. And what does a child learn from eternally disappointed parents? Hm? They learn, incorrectly, that there has to be something they can do to fix it. And dammit I was sure breaking this world record was the answer. I think they liked to claim some credit for the hours, days, and weeks I put into riding. People always asked them how they knew to put me on a horse as if I didn't climb up there fleeing their wrath on my own."

I took a step toward the rider slowly with my hands up. She was right, of course. There is always something just out of reach for the child of perpetual disappointment, a solution that dances on the edge of one's fingertips. On the rare occasions where I tried to appease Barb, usually through getting better at playing the violin, I was convinced making advanced junior symphony would make her proud and finally get that bitch off my back.

Maybe there was a small part of me, even through all the rebellion, that wanted just an ounce of acknowledgement for my efforts in between being locked in the attic during the summer.

"What happened next?" I asked, taking another slow step forward.

"Pup..." Ruad warned, tensing behind me.

Leslie cocked her head sideways and stifled another laugh. This time a tear flowed down her cheek.

"Well, wolf girl, a few years back, they died in a drunk driving crash, went off 412 into the river by Blue Springs Village. Big fall. Found their bodies a day later. And I... well I just kept trying to beat that goddamn record," she said, her voice growing quieter with each word.

This was something that didn't add up to me. I still wanted to know what she'd given to Morrigu in exchange for this weapon to ensnare Epona. But before that, the piece that didn't seem to fit was why she kept going with this stupid record bullshit.

"I don't understand why you're still so obsessed with this world record if your parents are dead. Why continue to put yourself through all of this?"

Leslie snapped before I could react and yelled, "Because it's what I'm fucking owed! Years of pushing, riding, training, trying to claw my way to that record. And I'm always a fraction of a second over? No! It's my record, and I'm going to break it. I've worked too hard not to. It's not about my parents anymore. It's about achieving this one... singular... goal."

All at once, she was coughing up a lung, and I realized those black veins were at the top of her neck now. Leslie struggled to breathe and fell to her knees.

Suddenly, I understood what she'd sacrificed for Epona and Morrigu's grand scheme. It was horrific.

"You gave Morrigu a meal. She gave you the means to capture a goddess, and in exchange, you fed her for 10 years with this sole obsession. And Morrigu knew each year you'd get a little closer, but never quite over the line, a carrot you were guaranteed to work yourself to death for but never quite grasp," I said.

Leslie was rolling on her left side now, trying to get air into her lungs. I remembered what Ash told me about his bargain. He'd lived for years with dysphoria that ate him alive, an inner hatred of his body that ran so deep, a goddess of fate was able to sense it and twist him into a bargain he had to live with for the rest of his life.

Morrigu fed off his misery and delighted in the knowledge that she was able to use it to her advantage. Looking down on Leslie now, my rage at her actions dissipated into pity. I sighed and realized she was a victim in all of this, her obsession preyed upon by a malevolent force that I seemed to keep bumping up against.

This could have been Ash's fate if we hadn't met. If I'd just let Malachos kill him or finished him myself, that would have been a nice tidy bow for Morrigu. And it's not like a goddess that feeds on war and chaos would have lost any sleep over Ash's demise. I was more determined than ever to make sure I did everything I could to help Ash avoid Leslie's path in life.

Would I have ended up attracting Morrigu for a bargain if I hadn't stumbled into Odessa's shop and found Adrienn? I thought.

Ruad and Adrienn… had they kept me from ending up like Ash? Like Leslie? I shivered as a chill rattled every nook and cranny of my spine on the way down. What would I have needed to bargain, and what would I have received?

If I can save Ash from this fate, maybe Leslie could be freed as well. The sole factor complicating things was how much further along she was in her bargain. Morrigu was undoubtedly near closing out this deal.

Walking over and kneeling down beside Leslie, I looked at the pulsing black veins. The smell of Morrigu's curse was almost over-whelming now. And Leslie's face was turning blue as she struggled to breathe.

"One… more … year," she gasped. "She promised."

I shook my head and said, "I don't think she promised you 10 years with Epona, Leslie. I think she probably used some qualifier you were too eager to hear. Up to a decade or Nearly 10 years, something you'd gloss over in the verbal fine print."

More tears flowed from Leslie, and I sighed. She didn't have long, and I didn't have a way to free her from this bargain. Morrigu was about to take the final bite.

That's when my locket glowed, and Adrienn flew up into the air.

"Aoife! You need to free Epona now!"

"What are you talking about?" I asked, raising an eyebrow. "She goes free when Leslie dies, and the bargain is complete, right?"

Adrienn shook their head.

"If Leslie dies with Epona still ensnared, the goddess will still be trapped under Morrigu's power. No part of this bargain stipulated Epona went free when it was all over. In fact, I'd wager keeping Epona bound permanently was Morrigu's long con," Adrienn said.

I twitched and rose to my feet again. Leslie reached for me, and I pitied her. I really did. But at the end of the day, she made her bed. And while that sounded like a shit response, our goddess was my priority.

"How do I free her?" I yelled, running to the trailer.

"Remove the feathers and chains. But Aoife… it won't be easy. They'll fight you. It could even ki…" I ignored their warning and ripped open the back gate of the trailer. Epona just stood there staring, eyes wide.

I cracked my knuckles and rushed toward the chains. Outside I heard Leslie's heart beating slower and slower. Her body was convulsing now. There were seconds left until she died, and Morrigu showed up to claim her real prize.

It won't happen! I thought, grasping the small gold chains and feathers in each claw.

Instantly, blue flames engulfed my hands, swallowing them whole. Searing pain radiated through each individual joint in my fingers, and I felt my very flesh starting to blister from the heat. I didn't want to look at my hands, so I locked my jaw and growled to stifle the pain. The blue fire hissed and popped across my flesh, as though I'd just stuck my fists into the grease of a deep fryer.

"You're going to be a bitch to remove, aren't you?" I hissed at the chains and feathers.

Smoke filled the trailer, and for a moment, I began to wonder if my very flesh was melting off. When the smoke cleared, would my hands be nothing but bone? Would even bone survive this heat?

I screamed, pushing all of that aside and grabbing tighter with whatever flesh I had left on my hands. It dawned on me then. This was the wrath of a war goddess pushed into a single fixed point, meant to torment my own patron goddess and drive her into submission. For nearly 10 years she'd endured this pain. Every time she failed to obey Leslie, this was her punishment.

And here I was, making all this fuss over the minute or two I had to endure it? I could handle this. I was an O'Connell, dammit.

"Come on you fucker, break!" I yelled, pulling back with every ounce of strength I had in me.

There wasn't much give. The chains really wanted to stay attached to Epona, and I felt that with every degree they burned hotter around my hands. Before long, that fire was inching up to my wrists, and with every piece of new territory it claimed on my flesh, that much more pain found its way into my nerves.

The smell of my own burning skin was enough to churn my stomach, but my goddess wasn't free yet, so I had more to endure.

Epona turned her head and stared deep into my eyes, and I saw splendor in her gaze. Even after a decade of being ensnared, this was still a goddess, her power buried under a cruel and dark magic. Her eyes were white that bled into blue with a dark center, and I could almost hear her speaking to me as we briefly shared a common torment.

"In dreams I've seen you, little wolf. In day, I waited, knowing your potential. You're resilient and steadfast. The power of the O'Connell pack and its members flows through you. Use it," the goddess spoke.

I squeezed the chains harder, bringing a new degree of pain, but also pushing a realization into focus. This was a goddess standing before me, and she'd placed her faith in my ability to rescue her. Should I not also place my faith in Epona during my desperate hour?

So I took a small breath and engaged in something Barb had fought bitterly to drag me into across our years together… prayer. It felt a little like trying to light a campfire with damp twigs. I'd never really prayed and meant it before, not as far I could remember. But my desperation drove something, a new need defined by my given reality.

As I pulled against these chains with all of my might, I began my invocation, "Dear Epona, it is in this hour of need I call upon you for the first time. While my faith is new, and likely insignificant, I hope it helps, somehow, someway."

I bit my tongue to keep from saying "amen," too many Sundays growing up in a First Baptist Church had burned that word into my vocabulary.

Outside the trailer, Ruad screamed, "Pup! Time's almost up!"

I couldn't even hear Leslie's heartbeat over the sizzling of my flesh burning, so I knew the timer was running down to precious seconds.

The blue flames and agony continued their march up my arms halfway to my elbows, and I realized my claws weren't enough.

In for a fucking penny, I thought and opened my jaws wide.

Without hesitation I tore into the chains and feathers with my canines, and suddenly the blues flames had a whole new target.

But I didn't whimper. I was an unstoppable force in these seconds, and I was about to prove this wasn't an immovable object. This was my duty as the last living O'Connell, the alpha, and the daughter of Iris and Tristan. Every fiber of my being screamed at me to get this done.

Saliva evaporated, and my tongue met the sun as I pulled the chains a little looser. They gave a centimeter, then an inch, and as I growled and grasped with every last ounce of power I had, the damned things finally pulled free. The release of Epona came not with a whisper but with a small explosion that blew me out of the trailer in a puff of smoke and down the driveway.

Before the dust even cleared, I sensed the goddess' energy pour out over the ranch like a tidal wave, nearly blowing me further down the driveway.

When I opened my eyes, Epona stepped out of the trailer where Leslie had finally breathed her last breath. Our goddess' power was free and washing over Ruad, Adrienn, and I.

The black mare took a few steps toward me, and I slowly reached into my right pocket, pulling out a lone seed. I planted it into the ground and used some energy I pulled from Ruad to grow a cardinal flower. A few stems bloomed with red flowers on top. I struggled to get to my feet, only making it to my knees.

But then Epona stood over me, and I just kneeled and said with a raspy voice, tears still in my eyes, "I, Aoife Fay O'Connell, swear fealty to you, the great Capall Epona."

Picking the flowers and holding them up to her in my flattened right palm, I realized it was meager, but it was the best I could do given the circumstances.

"Please accept this offering, and bless us once more," I said.

Epona took the flowers in her mouth and ate them slowly, the first offering she'd been given in years.

"I accept your offering and once more acknowledge that I am patron goddess of the O'Connell clan. Furthermore," she said. "I acknowledge you, Aoife Fey O'Connell, daughter of Iris and Tristan O'Connell, to be the true alpha of this renewed pack. I mark you as a sign of that acknowledgement."

The underside of my right wrist began to glow green, and I noticed Epona's energy flowing over me, a galloping sensation of every equine running free over an endless landscape. Goosebumps covered what little unburnt flesh on my arms.

When the glowing faded, I looked and found a small tattoo of a dark horse figure. Draped around the horse and down through its mane were flowers. They looked like little cardinal flowers. This marked my second magical tattoo in as many days. To top things off, Epona had healed my burns and scorch marks without me even noticing until now.

"Thank you, my goddess," I said, bowing.

"No, little wolf. Thank you. You freed me from Morrigu's grasp. To repay this debt, I will allow you one favor from me in the future," she said.

I bowed. Listening to the horse goddess speak was like nothing I'd ever heard before. Her voice was easily understood, but there was a slight wheeze to it. When Epona spoke, it was like the vocalization of rustling trees in the night wind under a starry sky.

I didn't realize it until she was upon me, but Epona was huge. She towered over me as I bowed.

"Rise, Aoife," she commanded.

Slowly, I stood.

"Hold out your hand," she said.

I did as instructed, and she closed her eyes. Her nostrils flared, and her ears fluttered. In front of her snout, a flash of white light appeared. I closed my eyes until I felt something hard fall into my grasp. It was cold to the touch.

Looking down, I saw a chunk of crystal no bigger than my palm. It was clear and had a small brown and red seed encased in the center.

I shivered, feeling a deep and raw power whispering up at me from inside. Quickly, I put it in my pocket.

Then I bowed slightly to Epona and said, "Thank you for keeping that for my clan."

"Think nothing of it. Tristan used the favor I owed him to have me secure it. Now I return the Siol Eolais to you, little wolf. Be careful with it. Don't let it corrupt you like it did your father."

That stung a little. But she was a goddess. What could I do?

With our business concluded, there was a rush of wind, and then the horse goddess vanished. And I didn't realize until then, but Leslie's body was gone as well. Did Epona take it? Or had Morrigu snatched it away?

Either way, the smell of clovers rushed over this little farm.

I bowed and said another prayer to... Epona, I guess? It still felt strange, but this time my faith had grown. I didn't know how long it would take for the act of prayer to lose the taint of what I was forced to do each Sunday morning while living under Barb's roof. But I had to believe my feelings associated with prayer would change, especially now that I had something to believe in, a goddess I'd seen with my own two eyes, who'd marked me as her own and who now actually watches over me.

After tonight, I really had a lot of philosophical things to sort out regarding what I believed in and how I lived my life.

As my thoughts turned to the thing in my pocket, I shivered. I could hear vague whispers coming from it.

"Free me," one whisper said.

I sighed and walked out to the edge of the dirt road with Ruad and Adrienn and called an Uber to take us back to Lake Sequoyah.

My fey guardian flew back into my pendant as a navy Ford Fiesta appeared and pulled into the driveway.

I climbed inside after sliding Ruad's service dog vest on, and after a few quick glances in the rearview mirror, my driver took off down the road, carrying us to our destination with the exhaustion of a completed task marked off my mental clipboard.

More whispers echoed in my mind, and I did my best to ignore them. I suddenly understood how my father could succumb to this over a period of years. Even just a few seconds were starting to agitate me, and it didn't help that I lacked half of my humanity. Either way, I had the seed now. Failure or success rested on my shoulders, a weight that seemed to be growing heavier each day from the consequences of each choice I made.

Chapter Twenty

After all the madness of rescuing my patron goddess, I was relieved to have a few days of normalcy. Ruad and Adrienn certainly didn't complain about a little bit of quiet, either.

Work seemed to fly by today, and before I knew it, I was on my way back home. We didn't take the bus, and instead decided to hike up to Mt. Sequoyah to use the fairy ring to get home.

As Ruad and I walked further up the mountain, I looked over at her. My vermillion companion looked back up at me and asked, "Something on your mind, Pup?"

She probably already knew what was on my mind but was just giving me the space to ask about it.

My familiar had been watching me extra closely ever since I became guardian of the seed. I could sense her eyes on me more than usual. I had to assume she was feeling my inner discomfort that'd been building today. I couldn't hide anything from her. But that also meant I had a friend I could trust.

"I've just been thinking that Malachos could attack at any time if he senses we have the seed," I said.

"Yeah?" Ruad said.

"I was wondering if you could tell me about the day he attacked our clan," I said, quietly. "Minus the parts where Tristan severed you."

My familiar looked at the trees ahead and then stopped. A fox ran through the bushes behind us, but we let it go. In the night sky above us, clouds had covered the moon and stars.

With a deep sigh, Ruad said, "That was the worst day of my life, Pup. And I don't think I'll ever forget it as long as I live."

I nodded and put a hand on her head.

"We had all just gathered for Duncan's wake. His car had crashed during a heavy thunderstorm out near Gentry. Every clan member was there. Everyone was drinking, listening to music, and telling stories about Duncan. The group had built a bonfire out west of Farmington. We were all in the middle of nowhere, and Ciara had a guitar out playing a song in Duncan's memory. Her weasel familiar was in her lap. Honestly, we were having a good time celebrating Duncan's life. And that's when everything went to shit," Ruad said.

The light in her eyes dimmed as she spoke about the coming fight.

"Malachos used dark magic in coordination with the eclipse above us. It was powerful. Whatever spell he used, it sealed everyone's magic inside of them. I couldn't even summon a whiff of ice. But we still fought him. People like Iris were skilled in combat with or without magic. She pulled out a knife and challenged Malachos. One by one, he slaughtered everyone, mostly with his storm magic. Ciara was the first to die that night. Then Patrick. Liam was burned beyond recognition."

I just listened quietly while she continued her tale. But I definitely wanted to revisit the dark magic Malachos had used amplified by the celestial event. If it sealed everyone else's magic inside of them, that put the entire druid clan at a major disadvantage. They would have wiped the floor with Tristan's darker self if he hadn't ambushed them. But he did. There wasn't anything I could do that would undo that, unless Dan had a time machine in his shop. Not that I could enter again, anyway.

"I fought as best I could, mostly defending Tristan, who was somewhat frozen in fear. Malachos wanted the seed, but your father had already passed it off to Epona. To his credit, he took that secret to the grave. Iris was the last remaining warrior aside from Tristan and myself. She continued to fight, even with an arm broken in three places. I'd been put through the wringer, struggling to stay conscious. But then Tristan pulled out that dagger he'd made, and I was awake real fast after that," Ruad said, tears in her eyes.

I felt that sadness wash over us both, the reminder of my father's desperate act. And even though he did it to ensure my protection, it left Ruad with such emotional damage and trust issues.

The seed's corruption hadn't left my father's mental health in a good place after all those years of carrying the burden and listening to its whispers. And these last couple days, I was starting to understand how that could happen.

I was ready to chuck the thing into Lake Fayetteville after a few days of whispers, hours really if I was being entirely honest.

We continued walking and eventually made it back home. I smelled raven as we entered the Lake Sequoyah area, and Ruad did, too. She growled.

"Easy now," I said.

Returning to the greenhouse, I saw Ash lying on the ground ensnared in roots. He did not look pleased. Though when I walked through the bushes and around the corner, he did look relieved.

"That's a nice security system you've got," he said.

I looked down at the mess of black feathers, spiky black hair, and fresh earth. Then I just laughed. I couldn't help it. Ash clearly wasn't having any fun, but I had been serious and gloomy all day. Even Ruad chuckled at the bird's predicament.

"That's it, Aoife. You've yee'd your last haw. When I get out of these things, I'm coming for you," Ash said.

I crossed my arms with a big grin on my face.

"Okay then, partner. Come and get me," I said, with an exaggerated cowgirl accent. Wynonna would have been proud.

Ash made an expression like he was going to struggle and break free for exactly five seconds. And then he sighed.

"Okay, but before I destroy you, could you let me go please?"

I laughed and did as Ash requested, touching the roots and sending my magic into the ground to free him. As the roots sank back into the Earth, I helped Ash up.

He was bent over coughing and stretching his wings.

"I was only like that for half an hour, but no man, no matter how tough, wants centipedes crawling through their feathers," he said, shaking them about. Little bits of dirt and soil flew everywhere. I could immediately smell a damp earth scent all over Ash. He wasn't lying about being down there for half an hour.

He breathed a sigh of relief and then said, "And now, you'll pay!"

Before he could even pretend to lunge at me, Ruad had him tackled to the ground, a claw on each wing and fangs in his face.

"Somehow I figured I'd end up right back on the ground," he sighed.

Now I was laughing again.

"You can let the poor raven up, Ruad. Pretty sure he was just going to sling some of that mud in his hand at me in some petty gesture of revenge for the roots," I said.

Ruad looked down at Ash's muddy hand. She gave one last growl and said, "Next time you look like you're going to take a swipe at my Pup, it'll end much worse for you."

She stepped off, and I helped Ash up for a second time.

"Ruad, you're not one for a practical joke, are you?" he asked, dropping the mud and wiping the muck off his hands on his jeans.

"Yeah, chasing me for months on end, that was a hilarious one," Ruad said, scowling at the raven.

"I've apologized for that at least 5,000 times now. When will it be enough?" Ash asked. "You know I wasn't doing that of my own free will."

"Why don't you go on the run for a few months, and maybe we can talk about when it'll be enough," Ruad said.

I held up my hands between them.

"Enough. Let's just go inside already. Ash. Next time you want to wait for me instead of just texting like a normal person, stay outside the runes on the ground. Pass over them without an O'Connell at your side, and you'll wind up wrapped in roots on the ground every time," I said.

We walked indoors, Ash looking down at the ground the entire time, waiting for something else to tackle him. I didn't blame the guy.

After a few minutes, I was pouring us some tea. Ash and I sat at my green metal and glass table. I hadn't actually had anything to drink since my lunch break at work, so I was thirsty. I took off my skull cap and jacket to get comfy.

I caught Ash looking at my ears, and he said, "Wow, they really are permanent now, aren't they?"

Nodding, I said, "Yup, and I don't have any illusion magic to hide them… or the tail… or the fangs."

He sipped his tea for a minute, and I asked, "What can I do for you, Ash?"

The teen boy looked up into my eyes, maybe shaking just a bit. I saw a nervousness there before he opened his mouth and said, "I want to join your clan, Aoife. I want to become an O'Connell."

On the one hand, this hadn't come as too much of a surprise. We'd been texting back and forth about this for a while now. His interest had only grown. And I had technically offered him an invitation. I was eager to regrow my clan, and Ash was right here asking to sign up. The raven was looking for people that would accept him as their own, and I knew I was capable of providing that. Ruad on the other hand… And speaking of, my familiar bark/scoffed, an unnerving noise.

"You can't be serious," Ruad said.

Ash looked down at his tea, swallowing and trying to stifle a tear. It was apparent now his legs and wrists were shaking under one hell of a frown. The shame of his past actions had probably never been more apparent on his face. While I could forgive him, I wasn't the one he'd chased for months on end working for the man who slaughtered my clan.

I put a hand on Ruad's head and looked up at Ash.

"Why are you interested in becoming an O'Connell, Ash?" I asked.

He looked like he'd been rehearsing an answer to this question for the last several days and was now trying to recall his notes.

After a deep sigh, Ash said, "I think it's pretty clear I'm never going to be a normal human again thanks to my deal with Morrigu. Everything I've done since then has been one mistake after another. Striking a botched bargain with an evil goddess, serving a necromancer, and hunting Ruad ruthlessly."

I nodded. Those were all pretty terrible mistakes.

But he's also a 16-year-old boy, desperate for relief from his emotional and mental torment, I thought. *Gender dysphoria sounds like a bitch.*

"I've done terrible things to you and Ruad in the service of a man who also did terrible things to you both and your clan. But ever since you saved me, and I helped you save that boy from the fey spiders... I feel like maybe I'm capable of making good decisions again. And joining your clan, fighting to help defeat Malachos, and adding my own strength to yours... that feels like a good decision. So I'm begging you to let me join. Let me set my life back on the right track."

Now I knew how the American Idol judges felt during the audition phases. Ash was looking at me praying I was more Paula than Simon.

I looked down at Ruad, who looked less than impressed with the raven's speech. She didn't care that Ash was looking at me like I was his last chance at salvation.

"Adrienn, can you come out here, please?"

The fey popped out of my pendant and flew up into the greenhouse.

"Oh, hey, Ash," they said, waving before turning to me. "What can I do for you, Aoife?"

I smiled and held out my hand for them to land on. Their wings stopped buzzing as their feet touched down in my palm. They looked up at me expectantly.

"Can you tell me about the process Tristan used to bring in new clan members?" I asked. Ruad didn't look happy at this. I felt more anger building in her chest, like she was a few seconds away from snarling at Ash.

Adrienn didn't have the bridge to Ruad but still sensed her hostility. I'm sure it wasn't lost on Ash, who just stood there clenching his hands together.

"It's actually pretty simple. The person who wants to join makes their case before the clan. Then everyone votes. Becoming an O'Connell is a lifelong commitment. We fight together as one. We die for each other if it comes to it. We share power. That's why each person who wants to join must secure a unanimous vote. Just one 'no' would ruin their chances for entry," Adrienn said.

Looking over at Ruad, I asked, "And I'm guessing the clan's alpha can't overturn a vote?"

Adrienn shook their head.

"Since everyone in the clan shares some of their power, it has to be unanimous," the fey said, clasping their hands behind their back.

I nodded.

"If I asked you to vote on Ash joining the clan right now, can you tell me what your vote would be?" I asked.

Adrienn sighed and glanced at Ruad.

"Do I really have to vote?" they asked.

"Did you vote when Iris and Tristan were alive?"

"Yes."

"Are you a member of the O'Connell pack?"

"Yes."

"Then you have to vote. If I'm just being pragmatic, I know how Ruad will already vote. And I know how I'd vote. So Ash's chance of getting in right now is fucked. But depending on how you'd vote, he might have a shot in the future if I can persuade Ruad. If you vote ney, then I'd know better than to try and take you both on in a debate," I said.

I suddenly thought of Abi and knew if she were here, she would have told me Epona should get to cast a ballot so she could vote neigh. I smirked at that. My girlfriend's bad jokes had finally penetrated my mental defenses. My brain was making them for her even when she wasn't present. I suppose that's better than a whispering seed trying to corrupt my soul.

Adrienn looked at Ash for a moment, and I saw him pleading with the fey. He didn't look happy when I said his chance of getting in was fucked now. But Adrienn held Ash's future chance in their hands.

"I don't need to be the 50th person to remind you of what you've done, Ash. But let me tell you what I've seen since Aoife saved your life. You returned the favor and rescued her from fey spiders, taking more than a few beatings in the process. And now you're back, looking for further redemption for your past mistakes," the fey said.

I nodded. Ash had dropped everything to come help me rescue some strange boy he'd never met before, exactly as any other clan member probably would've. And there's no denying we had good fighting chemistry. That was on full display during the battle. Add that to the fact he'd saved my life, and I was willing to let him into the clan.

"I believe in second chances," Adrienn said. "So if you asked me what my vote would be, I'd say let him become an O'Connell, Aoife."

Ruad scoffed again, clearly unsatisfied with Adrienn's answer. But she still held the ability to keep the raven out of the one place he'd be at home.

Ash thanked Adrienn with a little bow and then turned to me again, trying to avoid the intense glare from my familiar.

"Looks like the best answer I can give you is not right now," I said.

The raven just nodded and looked at the ground. I sensed there was some gratitude that I had been able to at least promise him the possibility of joining in the future. But this still clearly hurt him.

I walked over and put a hand on Ash's shoulder as Adrienn flew up in my hair. The raven looked up at me.

"I'm still your friend, Ash. And I promise I'll work on persuading Ruad to change her vote. What I can't promise is that it'll work. No matter what, though, I want you to know you're a strong ally. And I trust you. I've got your back, just like you had mine with the spiders," I said.

That brought a smile to his face.

He looked over my hand and then added his own.

Okay, we're quickly approaching my limit of physical contact tolerance, I thought. Ruad and Abi had all the physical contact they wanted. And though I considered Ash a friend, that came with limits.

"Can I ask a favor as a friend, then?" he asked.

"What do you need?" I asked.

"Freedom," the seed whispered, and I twitched in anger and slapped my left ear. It hurt. Ash raised an eyebrow, but then I moved on, ignoring it.

For a moment, Ash looked like he'd changed his mind about asking me a favor. But then he took a deep breath, his grip tightening on my hand a tad.

"The last few days have been excruciating. And I don't think I can keep my secret from my parents anymore."

I raised an eyebrow.

"You're going to show them your wings?"

Ash frowned and said, "Hell no. I'm going to tell them that I'm trans and want to start transitioning to live as a man. That'll upset them enough without them also finding out about my botched bargain."

That made slightly more sense. What would freak out two normal human parents more, learning their child was assigned the wrong gender at birth or learning their child was now part bird and could use magic? Both would strike out with Barb. I had no clue about Ash's parents.

"Anyway, I was wondering if you'd come with me when I had that conversation with them. I... need a friend there so I don't chicken out and confess to being—I dunno, Catholic... or a Jedi."

"Yeah, there are a lot of those running around," I said, smirking.

He finally let my hand go from his shoulder.

"Ash, I said I had your back, and I meant it. If you want me there when you come out, I'll be there," I said.

Ash looked like he was trying to avoid crying, but then he threw his arms around me and squeaked out a thanks.

Danger. Limit reached. Danger. Limit reached, I thought as I slowly wrapped my arms around him.

"Okay, so how do you want to do this?" I asked, trying to keep myself from sighing. More human interaction. Great. That's just what I wanted. The only thing that had gotten me through the second half of work earlier was the idea that I could go hunting with Ruad tonight. I was practically foaming at the mouth for it.

Pulling out his phone and checking the time, Ash grimaced.

"Um, my dad is actually grilling steaks right now. I can ask Mom if inviting a friend would be okay. We're actually eating out back since dad's been wanting to test out this new outdoor heater he just got," Ash said, sending a quick text.

Steak. I guess I could eat some steak. I'd rather tear into a fresh cow myself, but steak wasn't a terrible choice if I had to eat an animal that had already been killed for me. I looked down at Ruad who sighed. She clearly didn't want to be in her service dog vest for another hour or two. I was eager to be out of my bra as well. But… duty calls.

The raven's phone chimed, and he glanced down at it.

"Mom says you're invited. Dad's cooking way more food than the three of us can eat, as usual," Ash said.

I nodded. Good luck getting leftovers by my appetite. I bet I could eat these folks out of house and home. I might not, though, depending on how they handled Ash's coming out announcement.

"Thank you so much. You have no idea how much this has been eating me alive all week. Every time they called me across the house, yelling "Ashley, dinner's ready" or "Ashley, can you clean out the litter box? I mean, it's not their fault. They don't know. But hearing that name makes me want to claw at the walls with my nails until my fingers bleed," he said.

"Well I guess now's the best time to do it, then, when you just can't take it any longer. Can you tell me a little more about your folks so I'm not going in blind?"

"Mom and Dad run their own computer repair shop out in east Fayetteville. Dad is pretty quiet unless there's a ballgame on. He's got several guns out in the shed, and he loves to shoot them, clean them, and buy and sell them. His name is David.

"Mom's name is Lula. She's really very loving, but that's only because she thinks she has a daughter. She's constantly setting up all these mother/daughter outings, getting manicures, weekly ice cream dates, Friday bookstore trips. Some of it I like. Some of it I want to fake my death to avoid. She's very involved in the parent teacher association and always around for my school events. I have no idea how they'll take the news, and it terrifies me until I think I'm going to puke. But if they call me Ashley one more time… it makes me want to fly as high as I can go and then just stop flapping my wings," Ash said.

I put up my hands.

"Okay, I get it. It's a stressful situation. But if you really do feel that way, then I'd consider asking them to find you a therapist that specializes in gender issues. You clearly have a lot of steam to blow through. And ignoring it won't lead to anything good," I said.

He looked forward and nodded.

"That'll have to come after tonight," he said.

"Sure. But it needs to be one of the first things you ask for once things calm down," I said.

"It will be. I promise."

There wasn't much more to talk about, so I put my beanie back on, we walked back to the road, and called for an Uber. Then we were off for what I was sure would be the most awkward family dinner I'd ever attend. And I'd had plenty with Barb and John.

Our ride to Ash's house was a little long. His parents lived in north Fayetteville in one of those cookie cutter neighborhoods west of the newer movie theater, not far from the mall. Their home was a mix of bricks and siding and had been built way before the new movie theater.

The driver's name was Rebecca. She pulled into the driveway next to a white van that was wrapped with a "Budget Computer Repair" label. The logo was a little mouse with a screwdriver in one hand and a flash drive in the other.

I tipped Rebecca $4, and she resisted the urge to try and pet Ruad as we hopped out of the car.

"Thanks for the ride," I said.

She smiled and pulled her little economy car back out onto Jane Circle Drive. I smelled the steak, and my stomach growled.

Ash turned around and smiled.

"Aw, it's like you have a little wolf inside your guts that makes noises when you're hungry," he said, giggling.

I flashed him some fang and said, "You know I could change my vote instantly, right?"

He paled a little and said, "But you wouldn't, right? Because you've always got my back and stuff?"

I smirked a little and nodded.

"For now, raven. For now."

We walked around the house through crunchy dead grass and past a garden that looked well kept for three seasons of the year.

A sycamore tree grew at the edge of the property as Ash led me around past the porch and up to a wooden privacy fence. I heard sizzling meat on the grill. I smelled Ash's father over seasoning it. And probably overcooking it.

Amateur, I thought.

Ash pulled open a gate entrance to the back yard that was already cracked. It scraped over flattened grass that had the misfortune to be seeded next to a future door.

The raven went in first as I saw his appearance change back to the shorter girl whose parents knew her as Ashley. Ash's hair was longer, but the same shade of black, and he was wearing a long sleeve T-shirt with little pandas on it and a pair of mom jeans.

A small backyard stood before us, with a tan shed in the corner, one of those prebuilt ones that come from a giant hardware chain like Home Depot. It had darker shingles.

The charcoal grill Ash's father was cooking on was round and a faded red color. It'd seen some mileage, but I got the feeling the man cooking on it was one of those "drive it until it dies," kind of people. The stupid grill alone had probably burned enough coal to punch a small hole in the Ozone.

Standing behind the grill singing a Journey song was a large balding man wearing a Dallas Cowboys T-shirt and torn jeans. He saw Ash coming and gave a little salute. Then he took a look at Ruad and I. His eyes widened a little bit, but to his credit, the man didn't say anything. He kept humming that Journey tune and gave me a slight nod as if saying, "Welcome, I guess?"

Ash's mother came out of the house's sliding door with a plate of baked potatoes, setting them on a long wooden picnic table. Next to the table stood that new heater Ash's father seemed so proud of. I smelled the propane and coughed a little. That was going to be a joy to sit next to.

"Set me freeeee," the whisper cried, and I cringed. I didn't need to look like a crazy person in front of these folks who were about to find out they had a son. I clenched my right fist, took a deep breath, and let it out.

Lula was a shorter woman who had her hair long and dyed it auburn. She was wearing a blue blouse and a long matching blue skirt.

"Ashley! You made it back just in time!" she said with a higher-pitched voice than even I expected. She walked over and hugged her child as I saw Ash flinch at the name.

Then she let Ash go and looked at Ruad and I. Her eyes widened even more than David's did when he saw my familiar, but as she read the vest under the plentiful light from their patio, she seemed to be at ease.

"You must be Ashley's friend she told me about. My name is Lula," she said, holding out her hand. I gingerly took it and said, "My name is Aoife. And don't worry about my service animal. She's well trained. I promise."

"Looks like a timber wolf," David said from over by the grill.

"The breeder told me she was mostly Alaskan malamute, but who knows? I didn't exactly check the pedigree, you know?" I said, with a fake laugh.

David grunted in acknowledgement. A man of few words. "Yup, that's certainly a dog breed I've heard of," I imagined him thinking in the same way I would if a mechanic was describing what was wrong with my car.

"Well it's a pleasure to meet you, Aoife. My, that is a unique name," Lula said.

"It's Irish," I said, smiling as she went back to the table.

"Oh! You know, David has some Irish on his father's side. Though it looks like you certainly inherited quite a bit more than he did. My goodness, that is some gorgeous hair," Lula said.

"Thank you," I said, smiling.

Yeah, the hair's great. But you should see how fast I can dart across a field after a deer, I thought, trying not to smile big and reveal my fangs.

Lula went back inside and brought out some boiled corn on the cob and a pan of brownies. We were going to eat well tonight. Really well.

We sat down at the table, with Ruad lying in the grass right behind me. She seemed happy to be out of sight and no longer the topic of conversation.

David gave me the first choice of the steak picks. He had seven of them on a yellow porcelain plate. I asked which one was the most rare, and he pointed to one closer to the bottom. I nodded at that one, and he put it on my plate. I reached for a potato, carefully grasping it with my claws so I didn't burn myself.

I ignored the corn. It was the devil's vegetable as far as I was concerned.

"Didn't expect you to pick the steak that was still mooing," David said, smiling. He had this little nod as he laughed.

I smiled, just millimeters from revealing my fangs.

"What can I say? If you can't take the steak to the vet, have it patched up, and sent back onto the pasture, I don't want it," I said.

That got a snort from David.

"So, how did you meet Ashley?" Lula asked.

There was another twitch from Ash, who hadn't touched his food yet.

"We met when Ash came to tour the college. I was in charge of the group's tour, and we really hit it off," I said, lying through my fangs.

Damn I'm good, I thought.

Ash flashed me a little smile and nod.

"Well, I'm glad you two hit it off. Ashley is a little shy, so new friends are few and far in between. What are you studying at NWAU?" Lula asked, taking a drink of water.

"Freedom," the seed whisper said, rattling my skull.

I grabbed my knife so tight it dented the handle.

Whoops, I thought.

"Um, I'm studying mythology," I said.

"Oh, that's really creative. What do you want to do with that? Are you going to write stories or research or something?"

Well, I'm thinking of dropping out of school to become a full-time druid, earning practically no money, I thought, taking a bite of my steak.

That isn't what I said, though.

"I think I want to teach high school mythology/folklore classes. It'd make a pretty interesting elective," I said.

Lula took a bite of her corn and said, "That would be a fascinating subject to teach. But I wonder where you'd find a high school that would offer it? I don't think Fayetteville's high school offers a mythology class, do they, Ashley?"

Ash slammed his left hand on the table and blurted, "Stop calling me that!"

It froze the chatter. Even David stopped eating and looked over at his kid.

The raven hadn't touched a single bite of his food, and if I looked real hard, I could see feathers starting to reappear. Shit. He was losing his focus on the illusion.

"Is something wrong, dear?" Lula asked, putting a hand on Ash's wrist. He still looked agitated.

She looked back at me.

"I'm sorry, Aoife. She's not usually…"

I cut her off and said, "Um, I think Ash just needs a second is all."

While his parents looked at him and away from me, I locked eyes with the raven and made a motion to breathe deep and slow.

Calm, Ash, calm, I thought.

I mouthed the words, "I'm here."

Ash nodded slowly and seemed to at least get the message. He took a deep breath and slowly pulled his hands away from Lula.

"Mom… dad… there's something I need to tell you," he said, taking another deep breath and sighing.

Lula and David both gave him their undivided attention. David looked fairly stoic, though I suspect that's how he looked most of the time unless he was laughing or pissed stupid. And Lula had a slight expression of worry.

"I'm… transgender. It's been eating me alive for the last few weeks, but I've known for a year now. I… should have been born a boy. And it hurts when you treat me like a girl and call me Ashley," he said matter of fact.

His parents exchanged expressions. The table grew silent enough that all I could hear was everyone's heartbeats and Ruad snoring.

Then, David sneezed, and I'm pretty sure three of the neighboring houses were rattled down to their foundation. Maybe a car alarm went off. Maybe this is what killed the dinosaurs. Maybe I over exaggerated.

Nobody knew quite what to say. I didn't want to be the first one to speak. Hell, I didn't actually want to speak at all.

That's when Ash started to cry. He finally got it off his chest, and now the lava was flooding out of the volcano. No putting the magma back underground now.

"Well honey, that's… I don't think either of us saw that coming," Lula said. "But it was never our intention to hurt you."

Ash looked down at the plate of food he hadn't started on and said, "I know, Mom. I'm sorry I yelled. I just, waking up in the wrong body every day is the hardest thing. I can't even begin to describe the toll it takes on me. I feel like a prisoner in my own body or the victim of some cruel cosmic joke. I know what I should be, what I want to be, but nobody else sees that."

His parents exchanged glances again. I saw a slight shrug from David like he didn't know what was going on.

"Okay sweetie. Let's start with the basics. What do you want from us?" Lula asked.

Ash looked up at her and wiped his nose on a napkin.

"Wh-what?" he stammered.

"What can we do to help you with this?" Lula asked.

"Y-you want to help me?" Ash said, his face in shock. I guess he expected them to put him on the grill next and have fried raven.

"Well yeah... what else would we do? You're our child, and we love you," Lula said, smiling and wiping a tear from Ash's face. This just made him cry more. We sat there for a second, and I wondered if it would be rude to keep eating my steak. They were all pretty distracted. And I didn't want it to get cold.

Nah, better not, I thought. I was still hungry, though.

When Ash could finally talk again, he said, "Well, I don't want to be called Ashley ever again. I want to go by Ash from now on."

"Done," Lula said. David said nothing.

"I also want you to use he and him as my pronouns, please," Ash said, with an even quieter voice.

Lula nodded.

"That one might... take a little bit of time. But if you'll be patient with us, I know we can get that, too," she said.

I smiled. Holy shit this was going so well. Lula was like anti-Barb.

"And um... I guess I want to start transitioning to living as a boy. That's a bunch of stuff. Therapy, hormones, name and document changes. But maybe... maybe for now I can start small? Some new clothes and a haircut?" he almost squeaked that last part out.

His mother slowly nodded and said, "There's going to be a lot to talk about. And... I need to go to the library and start getting some books on this stuff. But we'll do our best because we love you and want you to be happy, Ash."

Now he was crying again. He had exactly what he wanted. Well... almost. He looked nervously over at David. This was the wildcard. I took David for a man's man. I wouldn't be surprised if he had a red ball cap in his garage somewhere. That wouldn't automatically make him a bad person, but it drastically decreased the odds of him being accepting of this latest news.

David locked eyes with Lula, and then he looked down at his child.

Everyone at the table was holding their breath, except me. I was stealing glances at my steak. Had my training made me fast enough to steal a bite without them noticing?

Slowly, I picked up my fork, and there was this intense feeling of shame that grasped my chest, paralyzing me. The source felt external, like someone was reaching inside me, forcing me to stop eating as If I could sense a deep mixture of embarrassment and scolding.

Who is doing this? I thought, before looking at my familiar and seeing her glare.

I scowled and put down the fork.

"Always wanted a son," David muttered and shrugged, and that was the extent of his words.

Ash's smile was so big he could fit his entire steak in his mouth. He jumped up and hugged his father so fast even I was surprised.

"Can… I start coming with you to the shooting range?" Ash asked.

David just nodded, lightly returned the hug, and went back to his steak. Then Ash went over and kissed his mother on the cheek.

"I was so scared of how you would both react," he said, sitting down and eating his corn.

Lula smiled and rubbed his shoulder.

"We were just worried something was wrong these past few weeks. But your mental and emotional health is important. So, of course, we'll deal with this. Just try to be patient with us. We're old fogies," Lula said.

I smiled at that. Lula was probably pushing 50, and Dave was a little older than her. They'd apparently had Ash late in life.

"As long as you're both trying, I'll be happy. I promise," Ash said, taking a bite of his steak and washing it down with a Coke.

We ate in silence for another moment. I cleaned my plate, even eating the fat old Aoife would have just tossed into the trash. Potato skin, too.

David suddenly froze and then turned to me.

"Are you… his girlfriend?" he asked, raising an eyebrow.

I put up my hands and said, "Oh no. I'm already spoken for. Ash and I are just friends. He just invited me for moral support."

With a quick nod of understanding, David went back to eating.

"So… does this mean you don't want to do our manicures anymore?" Lula asked. There wasn't any guilt tripping in her tone. She was just trying to get a feel for what Ash wanted.

Bashfully, he said, "Yes please. But! I still want to go get ice cream every week and visit the bookstore. And maybe we can replace manicures with something else. How about we go bike riding?"

Now Lula looked like she was going to cry. She just smiled and said, "I'd like that very much."

The rest of dinner was uneventful. I thanked both David and Lula for hosting me and finished eating a brownie. I'd had enough emotion from the knapsack for one night. This meal had been taxing, and I wasn't even the one coming out. Though I would have given just about anything for my own coming out with Barb to have gone half as smooth as Ash's.

It was then I started to wonder what Tristan and Iris would have said when they found out I was bi. If they'd caught me making out with Abi on the couch, they probably wouldn't have thrown me out. And that thought made me angry at Barb all over again. The bitch.

Perhaps it was immature of me. Scratch that. I knew it was. But part of me resented how well things had gone for Ash. Not only had his parents accepted him at a crucial moment in his life. But he still had them.

The whisper came again, but unlike before, now it was accompanied by an emotional gut-punch.

"If he'd just freed me then, your father would still be around today to accept you as you are," the seed said. I growled loudly at that.

Everyone stopped and, fortunately for me, stared at Ruad who was asleep again. I mean, it made sense logically. What human would growl at random?

Leaning over, I stroked her fur and gave a fake little laugh.

"She must be dreaming about that rabbit escaping again," I said.

David shrugged and went back to cleaning the grill. Lula offered me leftovers and asked where I lived.

"Oh, over by… Lake Sequoyah," I said. Technically accurate.

She nodded, and I politely accepted a steak and potato wrapped in foil. Then Ash said, "Hey, can I have your keys to drive Aoife and Ruad home please?"

Lula nodded and went inside. She came back out and tossed a set of car keys at her son. I raised an eyebrow.

"You have your license?" I asked.

"Yeah."

"Ironic," I said, thinking of the wings. Why use a car when you could fly anywhere?

"Why's that?" Lula asked.

I gasped and choked a little. Ash gave me a frown. So I fired up the lie generator and said, "Well it's just… you know, most kids these days don't get their license. They aren't usually interested."

Lula seemed to buy that and said, "Well Ash has always been a bit motivated."

Ash backed a gray Honda Accord out of the garage, and I opened the back door for Ruad. After she was in, I climbed in. The interior of the car smelled like coconut.

Before putting the car in gear, Ash looked over and said, "Thanks for your help tonight, Aoife. I'm not sure I would have been able to do all that without you."

"No problem," I said. "That's what an alpha does for her future clan members."

That brought another smile to Ash's face. We didn't talk much on the ride back to my greenhouse, which gave the seed more opportunities to whisper to me.

"Tristan was right. Free meeeee," it said, and I had to do my best not to dig my claws into the seat. Sweat started to form on my forehead.

"This ends when I'm released. Unbind me, daughter of the wolf," the seed hissed.

I started to grit my teeth. We hopped on Highway 16 heading southeast out of Fayetteville, not that I was overly aware. I had my eyes closed, trying to drown out the noise. But the seed did not stop.

"Let me go, Pup. I'm not the darkness you've been told of," it said.

"You don't get to call me that," I yelled to a surprised Ash. We had pulled off the road by where I usually walked into the park. I was sweating like crazy.

"Are you okay?" he asked.

I nodded.

"Haven't been sleeping well. Must have dozed off," I said. "Sorry about that. Thanks for the ride."

I hopped out of the car and let Ruad out.

"Pup, it's the seed, isn't it?" she asked. I gave a slight nod.

That was when Ash got out of the car and came over to us as we crossed the road toward the woods.

"What are you doing?" I asked.

"I'm going to walk you back and make sure you're okay. If you pass out or something, I can help Ruad carry you," he said.

"That's not necessary," I muttered.

"Clan members support their alpha," he said, falling in behind us. Ruad said nothing, just giving him a blank stare. Then she looked back at me. I felt her concern rising. The Siol Eolais was almost vibrating with a strange energy in my pocket, and I began to sway left and right. Ruad and Ash took my flanks to keep me steady.

About 20 minutes later, we finally made it back to the greenhouse when a familiar couple odors came through my nostrils.

I heard Ruad growling before I put two and two together.

"You've finally returned. And here I was beginning to worry I wasn't going to get the Siol Eolais tonight, Aoife," a voice said. I must have been delirious because the voice sounded a bit like Tristan's, except raspier, grittier, and angrier, and it carried within it all manner of threats.

Chapter Twenty-One

I bolted awake and saw Malachos standing next to the border of my greenhouse, just out of range of the roots. Ash stood in front of me, his wings reappearing and moving to shield me. Ruad also took a step forward.

With my eyes focused on the man that killed my clan and my parents, I saw him clearly for the first time. He was wearing a black cloak and dark pants. Malachos' hood was down this time.

His face was almost exactly like Tristan's, except his forehead was covered diagonally with a huge scar, and the flesh was gray as if slowly decaying by the hour. One eye was solid black, and the other solid white. When he spoke, I saw his teeth were rotted, some even chipped. Around his neck hung a long beaded charm with a smooth black orb at the end. The orb appeared to have a hog carved into it.

All at once I recognized a second scent, separate from Malachos. He jerked an older woman into view, his gray fingers wrapped around her neck.

"Barb," I whispered. She looked terrified and disheveled.

"Eve!" she yelled. "I should have known you were behind this."

I rolled my eyes.

He couldn't have found a better hostage? I thought. *I guess I'm lucky he didn't go after Abi.*

"I thought something felt strange the other night. A very specific magic returned to the world, and I knew at once you'd retrieved the seed. So I started working extra hard to track you down. I learned this old bag is your adopted mother. Then I decided to check out some old clan hideaways. Imagine how surprised I was to find Tristan's greenhouse looking relatively fresh, like someone had just moved in. I don't know why I didn't ever think to look here before. It seems like such an obvious location. Then again, I thought the daughter of Tristan might have been a little smarter than to paint such an obvious target on her back. I suppose I should have expected less," he said.

The seed started to vibrate even more now that Malachos was near. And why not? The seed created him in a way. It recognized him as its best chance at getting free.

"So how do you see this playing out, Malachos?" I asked.

He held up his other hand, the one not wrapped around Barb's neck, and said, "Simple enough. You hand over the Siol Eolais, and I give you back your mother. I mean, it would just be cruel to steal two mothers from you, wouldn't it?"

I snarled.

"That bitch is not my mother."

Barb tried to speak, but Malachos tightened his grip on her throat until her voice was nothing more than a few choked squeaks. The one thing we had in common was a lack of patience for Barb's shit.

"Adopted mother. Whatever. Semantics I don't have time for. Hand over the seed, young O'Connell. My journey is nearing completion," he said, smiling and showing off those rotted teeth.

"Not gonna happen," I said. "What are you even going to do with it? You're already a pretty capable necromancer. Are you really one of those cliché people just wanting more power for power's sake?"

"You don't even know what that seed is, do you?" Malachos asked, chuckling.

"Release me!" the whispering voice came close to shrieking in my head.

I closed an eye and held my head for a moment.

"Oh you poor girl. You're succumbing to it even faster than Tristan did. Best hand it over now and be done with it," Malachos said.

I raised an eyebrow. Something wasn't adding up. I'd just asked Malachos what he wanted the seed for, and he dodged my question. I wasn't expecting a monologue, but he'd been pretty direct with revealing information to me so far. I was the only thing standing between him and the seed. Why not go ahead and reveal his ultimate plan?

My jaw dropped a little when something finally clicked in my head. *He doesn't have a plan,* I thought.

Looking down at my pocket and then back up at Malachos, I decided to approach him with this theory, maybe even try a little psychological warfare.

306

"You can't tell me why you want the seed, can you? It's too embarrassing for you to admit," I said.

Ruad and Ash exchanged glances.

"What are you going on about?" Malachos said, but I caught him gritting his teeth just a bit. He also squeezed Barb's throat just a little tighter, nearly making it impossible for her to breathe.

"I have a theory. You grew inside my father's heart, fed by his desperation and exasperated by the seed. When Tristan failed to sever his connection to it, you finally had enough power of your own to break free of him during his greatest moment of weakness," I said, watching Malachos closely. "But I suspect you quickly realized power alone isn't enough to create an entire existence. You are, after all, just pieces of negative emotion and dark magic contained in a poorly-borrowed image. There's an emptiness in you, a longing to feel all those gaps in your existence solidified."

He wasn't even making an attempt to hide his disgust anymore, clenching his free fist so hard it looked like the ligaments would snap. Malachos' eyes narrowed, a snarl curled into his lips.

"I'd wager you want this seed because you know it's filled with generations of memories and magic from O'Connell alphas. And you're banking on it finally making you a real boy," I said.

Somewhere, Malachos got ahold of himself. He appeared to remember that necromancy and inner darkness were his specialties. And while I was playing at psychological warfare, he'd mastered it in the years since killing my clan.

"Oh, little wolf cub. You speak as though you're untouched by Tristan's darkness. But that's just ignorance. You and I both know you have that same darkness inside of you, Aoife."

I shook my head, swallowing and telling myself it wasn't true. Malachos was full of shit.

"The seed grew Tristan's darkness. And you were born of it," I said, my voice quivering as I struggled to breathe. I was sweating again.

At this point, it dawned on me; my nerves weren't just from facing Malachos, but from the dark magic polluting the entire area we stood in. Once more, it felt like a thick sludge was washing over my skin, even if there was nothing present. Looking down at my pocket, I realized the one common denominator. the Siol Eolais.

It's resonating between Malachos and I, driving a fever pitch in

307

hopes it'll escape confinement, I thought. And somewhere within my mind forest, I heard a resonant whisper say, "The seed isn't the only thing fighting to be free, Aoife."

I shivered and started to feel a fever coming on.

"The dark magic is driving my feral self crazy, too. We're all subject to its influence," I whispered as Ruad looked at me, clearly worried. "This burden is not yours to bear alone like Tristan thought."

Malachos, it seemed, was ready to continue his mind games.

"The Siol Eolais just fostered what was already in Tristan's heart. As it will do to you, unless I take it. I'll free you from this burden, the one your father sought release from," he said, turning to Ruad, "The burden he kept hidden from you, Ruad. Driven by a madness that caused him to rip you away."

I felt a familiar darkness stirring in Ruad. In fact, I felt the ice magic stirring. And at once, I knew Malachos was fueling that dark wolf I'd frozen inside of Ruad, as well as feral Aoife inside me.

I have to keep him focused on me, I thought, feeling a growing shadow stirring in my familiar.

"Don't talk to her, you bastard," I said, stepping forward. We were about 15 feet apart.

Ash kept looking from me to Malachos, his face paling more each time. I saw his lips pressed tight and fists ready to rumble. He would back me up in any skirmish we started, but he wouldn't be happy about it. I sure wasn't happy about any of this.

"My... freedom!" the seed rattled in my head.

I clutched my skull with both hands.

"You see, Aoife? You're filled with the same darkness as Tristan. You can claim I'm born of nothing but negative emotions and shadows, but those same ingredients fill your heart all the same. They press upon your shoddy boundaries, pushing for freedom as I did years ago. I broke free. I killed Duncan. I manipulated your father to plan Duncan's wake around the celestial event so that my powers would be amplified, taking down everyone he loved and feeding from their fear. Now here we all are, full circle. And you're about to crack, just like he did, Aoife."

I shook my head, trying not to think of feral Aoife. That was different, though, right? She wasn't the same. Feral Aoife was just a collection of wolf instincts and aggression that had formed when I bonded with Ruad's soul. It wasn't the same as my father's corruption fueled by the seed. Or at least, that was what I was desperate to believe.

My chest tightened as more sweat poured down my face.

"Just give the seed to me, Aoife. I'll release your mother, and when I free the Siol Eolais, you will be free of the burden that broke your father."

I couldn't even try to focus enough on what he was saying to get mad. I felt like I was on a raft trying not to sink with the Titanic as it submerged under the ocean, dragging anything around it down with it. Just a swirling void of darkness threatening to swallow me and everyone around me whole.

"Let. Me. Go." My head rattled again. I clutched it even tighter.

"Give me the seed, or I'll snap your mother's neck. I'm done waiting, Aoife."

He's bluffing. He knows I don't care about the hostage. I think I've made that pretty damn clear, I thought.

Cracks formed in my subconscious as I clawed desperately for any remaining shred of sanity. When I closed my eyes, I saw feral Aoife crouched and waiting inside my mind forest. Drool dripped from her chipped and crooked fangs as she hungered for freedom. More splintering glass as pressure mounted on all sides of my psyche driven by an alter-ego's fury, the righteous anger of my familiar, and a seed of unknowable power.

The combination formed an unbearable weight on my shoulders, and all noise fell around me as I continued to hold my head. My psyche couldn't bear the load any more, and I snapped.

"Just do it and shut the fuck up already!" I screamed, my head feeling like it was about to burst. And yet, for all the stress I was under, I heard the snap of bone and ligaments clear as a bell.

My heart sank. *No. There's no way.*

Opening my eyes, I saw Barb's lifeless corpse falling in slow motion. The son of a bitch had actually done it. Her eyes were wide with shock and desperation, red from a lack of oxygen. Barb's mouth carried a plea for help. And maybe, just maybe in the final moments she'd cried out to her disappointing adoptee, pleading for any shred of aid I could dole out.

"No!" I yelled, reaching out, as if I could suddenly catch her and make it all okay. If I could just keep her from hitting the ground, she'd start breathing again.

When Barb hit the earth like a lifeless, limp puppet, splattering mud up into the air, I sank to my knees.

"You see, Aoife? Same darkness as your father. And now perhaps even worse. For all of Tristan's inner demons, he never wished death upon anyone. Not even his worst enemies," Malachos said, laughing.

The whole forest spun as I felt a split forming in my chest. I screamed and dug my claws into my arms until they drew blood. I was just as bad as Tristan had been. No, I was worse. Malachos was spot on.

My heart tore right down the center as guilt crippled one side over the death I'd caused, and the other, to my shock, laughed, a mad cacophony of years of pain, abuse, and repression.

She deserved it, the bitch! One half of my heart cheered as memories of being locked in the attic during summer sprang forth from nowhere. It was a toxic mixture twisting in my chest, and I was already at the end of my rope.

I'd spent most of my life hating the woman who had just died, but I never wished for her death, not really. Now that blood was on my hands. I'd given her over to Malachos and just told him to kill her, end her like stepping on a beetle crossing the sidewalk.

Between the seed shaking and shrieking for freedom and my stained consciousness, I was losing my grip on reality fast. The next few seconds were a blur.

"Thanks for everything, Aoife," my feral voice said, coming out of the mind forest.

Two forests flashed before my eyes, one with Adrienn and Ruad turning toward me, yelling things I couldn't comprehend, and one filled with mist, gray skies, and a feral version of myself grinning like she'd just eaten the canary right out of the birdcage. These two images rotated before my eyes faster and faster until I could barely tell which I stood in.

I let out a bloodcurdling scream as guilt and bittersweet rapture tore through me like lightning, my consciousness shattering into several bite-sized pieces as I sunk into my mind forest and watched what happened next. Feral Aoife was in control now.

The last thing I heard was Ruad and Ash screaming my name as I sank into darkness. Suddenly, it wasn't Lake Sequoyah I was seeing anymore, but quiet trees filled with mist and endless clouds. I hit the dirt in those woods and didn't struggle to get up.

Chapter Twenty-Two

I didn't stir for a while. And I'm not sure how much time passed. Somehow, I woke up despite the exhaustion I felt. My eyes were sluggish, and the arms and legs attached to my body felt heavy, as if they'd take years to move. God, I was so tired. Where was I? I looked around and felt a clammy damp air crawling over my skin. My human skin. My claws, my fangs, my tail, they were gone.

Tall Douglas fir trees and alder trees surrounded me, as did a misty canopy. I pushed myself up from the ground and leaned against a nearby tree with claw markings in the bark as I struggled to stand. The world was spinning, and then the memories hit. I shook. Barb was dead. Feral Aoife had used my grief and mental instability to take control and force me back into the mind forest, and to be entirely honest, I wasn't quite sure I had the will to fight her and retake control.

She'd seized all my wolf abilities, every drop of magic, and left me here.

What does that leave me with? Just… half of my humanity, right? I thought. Man, did I feel numb upon that realization. And alone on top of it. Where was Ruad? Not that I felt like I deserved her company at this particular moment, but I did want to know she was okay.

"Ruad?" I called out. But there was nothing. Just a quiet mind forest… and me. I suppose it would be like that for the rest of my life. That's probably better than I deserved. "She got exactly what she wanted," I muttered, and sat back down to cry. The dirt on my feet was moist. It stuck to me as did my guilt. It was then I noticed for the first time I couldn't hear the seed whispering. Maybe this wasn't such a bad punishment after all. Here there was some sort of peace. Maybe at least the absence of conflict.

Apathy continued to wash over me, but I tried my best to stand, to keep moving forward somehow. And then I began to wander

Did everything in this place stay the same? No matter how long or how far I walked, I never seemed to get anywhere new. These trees all looked alike and yet different and strange at the same time. Once in a while there would be a little variety, an evergreen or a bush would show up. Maybe if I walked long enough, I would just magically end up back at the beginning, like a forested labyrinth?

I wonder if feral Aoife will show up to taunt me now and again, I thought. *That seemed like something she would do. Or would she leave me alone knowing that would hurt me more? The loneliness of it all.*

Then I heard something zipping through the trees above me. Was my feral self already showing up for her first visit? Would she just kill me? Branches above me rustled, and normally I would have been a little startled. But now, what was the point? Out of the trees dropped a little man with shaggy green hair that hung down past their shoulders. Their eyes were of a matching shade.

"Aoife!" they said and hugged my cheek. This was weird. I knew who this was, but I wasn't necessarily excited to see them. In fact, I felt myself getting a bit annoyed at their presence.

When I didn't return the gesture, they flew up slowly and looked me in the eyes. Then they seemed to scan me for a second. Or five. Who knows? Who cares?

"Aoife... you're human again. What happened?"

I shrugged, "Feral Aoife took it all, I guess. Even the wolf half that filled the cracks. I'm just half of Aoife now."

They raised an eyebrow.

"Have you been looking for feral Aoife so we can fix this?"

I shook my head.

Shock filled the fey's face, and they said, "Aoife... I don't understand. What's happened to you?"

Not even shrugging this time, I turned to go. This conversation bored me. Unfortunately, Adrienn followed, zooming in front of my face.

"Where are you going?"

"Who knows?" I said.

"Aoife, do you have any idea what's happening right now?" they asked.

I did not.

Good ole apathy wasn't letting me down.

My fey guardian, for once, seemed angered. I'd never seen them like that before. Their brows furrowed, and they gritted their teeth.

"They're fighting for you. And what are you doing?" they asked.

"Just, wandering around I guess."

They scowled and hovered closer to my face.

"Ruad and Ash are out there battling your feral side, trying to recapture her so you can return, Aoife! On top of that, Malachos is still fighting to take the seed from feral Aoife. It's free-for-all chaos. They need you back right now!"

I turned to leave again, hoping they wouldn't follow.

Adrienn wasn't having it. They flew up and slapped me with surprising force for their size. I gasped, a bit surprised.

"They're out there bleeding for you, Aoife. And getting torn to pieces in the process because they don't want to hurt your body," Adrienn yelled.

I shrugged, apparently the only gesture I knew. The apathy wasn't going away. I could acknowledge Adrienn's desperation without moving an emotional muscle to match it within myself.

"Those fools are fighting for a lost cause, fey. I'm not worth bleeding for. Hell, maybe things would have been better if Malachos had killed everyone at the wake, myself included. Then we wouldn't be here fighting over—whatever this is," I said. Maybe now they'd leave me alone.

Again, Adrienn slapped me with all of their strength. To the little guy's credit, my head actually turned from the force.

"Those people are your family! And I know you're only operating with half of your humanity right now. But even so, you have a responsibility to them. Aoife Fey O'Connell is their alpha. They'll die for you, but it's your job to defend them so that it never comes down to that. Fight for them! I, Adrienn of the Emerald Cutlass, call upon you to fulfill your duty as leader of the O'Connell clan!"

While my cheek was still tingling, I did feel a little bit of something flutter in my chest. It was faint and didn't immediately dissipate. What the hell was it?

That's annoying, I thought, scowling.

There was another rustle from the trees above, and out of the foliage leapt someone who carried an uncanny resemblance to me, a very disheveled me that looked like they'd been living in a cave full of bones for the last several years. Feral Aoife.

Adrienn never had a chance. Feral Aoife snatched the fey out of the air and held them in her claws.

"That's enough out of you, you little cockroach," she growled, landing on the ground like grace was a foreign concept.

I stared over at the two, that faint flutter in my chest still there. I tried to drown it out.

Shut up! You're bothering me. Go away, I thought, scowling.

Adrienn struggled to free themselves from feral Aoife, but she had both claws wrapped tightly around them.

"You were literally the only one who could come in here after her, you know that? She trusts you with her whole soul, allowing you in her mind forest whenever you please. And that's a problem."

Her claws squeezed tighter together, and Adrienn screamed. Still, they turned to me, eyes full of grace. I could see their pain, even a bit of anger. And despite it all, Adrienn tried their best not to cry or yell or call for help, but the pain was worsening. It was then I realized, they didn't want me to see them cry out for help.

Even now they protect my heart, I thought.

"The human you swore to protect is going to watch as I end your life here and now, fey. Then she can wander the mind forest with another death on her hands."

As she squeezed tighter, Adrienn cried even louder. I heard little bones begin to crack. Their face turned purple

They slowly turned to me and said, "You're a good person, Aoife... but even good people make mistakes. The difference between good and evil is what you do... after the mistakes."

More screams filled the forest.

"Someday you'll smile again. I promise," they said, coughing up green blood.

I just stood there. Should I help? I mean... why would I? But they were going to die. That was something I didn't want, right?

A memory flashed into my head.

I saw Iris lying in a bed with Tristan leaning against the wall looking down at her arms. She was holding a baby with a tiny bit of red fuzz on her head. The child was wrapped in a small green blanket embroidered with leaves.

Ruad sat nearby, sniffing toward the baby but not saying a word.

A familiar green-haired fey flew around the bed and landed softly on Iris' shoulder. They looked down upon the newborn with deep affection.

"So... have you two picked out a name?" Adrienn asked.

Tristan and Iris exchanged glances. They both smiled. Then Tristan said, "Her name is Aoife."

The fey smiled now.

"Aoife O'Connell. That's a gorgeous name. She's going to grow up to be strong just like her parents," Adrienn said, not taking their eyes off the child as if she were their own.

Slowly the child looked up at the fey, staring in wonder. Adrienn waved and giggled.

"She's so beautiful and precious. Mortal newborns just have such an amazing energy to them," Adrienn said.

Tristan cleared his throat and said, "We actually wanted to ask you a question."

Adrienn looked up and said, "Sure. Anything."

Iris locked eyes with the fey and said, "You once swore to serve our family for the rest of your days. We accepted your oath, and you've faithfully executed it, becoming part of our family. You have a valuable spot in our hearts." Adrienn teared up at that.

"You both are most of my heart," they said.

Tristan smiled again and asked, "Would you save some room in your heart for our daughter? In fact, we'd like you to consider letting her fill up your entire heart. We want you to become her guardian for all of her days."

Adrienn looked stunned. The fey didn't know what to say. Outside, a bumblebee hit the bedroom window, bounced off, and flew somewhere else. The ceiling fan above squeaked as it slowly spun.

"You want me to be her guardian? You'd trust me with such a responsibility?" they said, eyes wide.

Tristan nodded, and Iris spoke up, saying, "Adrienn, she's going to be the alpha one day. That position comes with so much joy and sorrow. It's heavy. And our little girl is going to need all the allies she can muster. But you... we want you to always be close to her, never leaving her alone. Be there to cry with her on her worst days. Be there to laugh on her brightest days."

Adrienn slowly nodded, crying more now and said, "I solemnly swear it. The rest of my days, I'll serve as your daughter's guardian."

Tristan pulled a pendant of Celtic knotwork off his neck and fastened it to his daughter's own neck. It was big on her, but she'd grow into it. And she'd grow with a lifelong friend.

Her body glowed a faint green, and she held up a tiny hand toward the fey.

Adrienn hovered up and placed their own hand in the baby's. Even at this age, Aoife's was bigger. Her hand was warm, full of promise.

"Oh, we forgot to tell you we finally decided on her middle name," Iris said.

Adrienn looked over in surprise, asking, "Oh yeah? It's about time! What did you pick?"

"Her full name is Aoife Fey O'Connell," Tristan said.

The fey's face went straight to ugly crying after hearing that. Their tears fell upon the little green blanket wrapped around the baby they'd protect for the rest of their days.

"I won't let her down. I promise."

More tiny cracking bones brought me out of the memory and back to the present. Adrienn didn't even have the strength left to cry out anymore.

Tears started streaming down my face as that flutter in my chest grew into a great and powerful rage. I roared and suddenly appeared in front of my feral self.

I punched her in the throat with everything I had, and while she did spit up a little, my feral self then sank her fangs into my left wrist. I grimaced. Both of her claws still held onto my fey guardian who seemed unresponsive.

"What do you think you're doing?"

"I'm taking back my fey guardian and *my* body, you bitch!"

"With what? I've taken all your magic!"

Thrusting my hand into the air, I said, "My life has been far from perfect. And I've made plenty of mistakes. But Adrienn reminded me that I have friends who are counting on me. And they accept me for all that I am, every ray of light and every crease and shadow in my heart. I won't give up on them ever again. I'll do whatever I can to protect the ones I love because I know they'd do the same. Ruad! Please lend me your strength, and let's end this once and for all, together!"

With a boom in the distance, I sensed Ruad's bridge with a corresponding pulse in my heart. Her magic roared across the connector. It surged through my mind forest until it met my body with a crash of energy. I shuddered and gradually became whole again, feeling wolf energy filling the cracks in my being.

Wind swirled around the two of us as leaves, twigs, and dust flew up in the air, spinning around me until my transformation had taken place, returning me to my wolf form.

"You're too late, Aoife! I've taken your body, your magic, and now your fey guardian."

I plunged my right claw into her belly and tore into gooey flesh. Feral Aoife let go of my bleeding wrist to scream. When she did that, I hollered, "Give Adrienn back, you bitch! I'm done letting you take from me!"

Grabbing her left wrist with my claws, I snapped it, and she howled, stumbling backward and loosening her grip on Adrienn. I inverted her right elbow with a solid punch, and then I snatched my fey guardian as they were tossed up in the air.

Holding Adrienn, I spun and kicked my feral self through a tree. Then I kneeled and cradled Adrienn's broken body in my arms.

Tears leaked down my cheeks as I squeaked out, "I'm so sorry, Adrienn. I'm so, so sorry. I never should have let any of this happen. And I need you. I need you in my life so desperately. Please don't leave me now. Please just be okay."

I whimpered some more as they stirred and opened one eye.

"Hey… Aoife. I knew you'd come back," they said with a weak voice.

I smiled as more tears dripped down my chin.

"Listen, I fucked up, fucked up bad. And you paid the price to get me back. But I need you to know how much I love you and need you in my life. I would give anything for you to just be okay. Say you'll be okay," I whimpered.

They slowly smiled and said, "Don't worry… if you can get your magic back and lend me some, I can heal myself a bit."

I nodded and stood up. Reaching behind me, I held Adrienn up to my hair. They climbed in slowly, and I said, "Hang on tight. I'm going to finish this."

Feral Aoife was also standing up and popping her elbow back into place with a grunt.

"I finally have everything I want. And I won't let you take it from me!" she screamed.

I snarled and said, "My name is Aoife FEY O'Connell. You may be a part of me, but my failures and mistakes do not control me. You've

317

caused me enough trouble this night. But it's over. I'm taking everything back in the name of my guardian, in the name of my pack."

I started to glow green, the exact same shade as Adrienn. I could feel their own energy getting weaker with each passing second, so I darted forward to meet my feral self head on.

We crashed through the trees of my mind forest like they were popsicle sticks, blow after blow, swipe after swipe. I'd gotten a couple good hits on her trying to free Adrienn, but my feral half was up to speed now.

As Adrienn's energy reached its weakest point, I knew it was time to end this.

"Ruad, I'm taking more!" I yelled. And though I couldn't hear her, I sensed my familiar yell, "End it already! Take whatever you need."

My body rattled with cold as a layer of icy wind filled the area around us. Feral Aoife noticed this as well.

"I got Barb killed, and I almost let Adrienn die, too. Ash and Ruad are out there getting banged up because of me. But here's where I turn things around. This is my life, my story, and I'm taking it all back!"

Raising my right hand, I aimed for feral Aoife and summoned a blue glowing orb of icy magic.

"You'll never hit me with that" she taunted, moving between trees. But then I closed my left fist and a tree branch whipped down, wrapping around her. Three more did the same thing.

"What the fuck is this?" she yelled.

"I'm more than you, more than the worst parts of myself. I am Ruad's strength, Adrienn's love, Ash's bravery, and the daughter of Tristan and Iris O'Connell. But most of all, I'm a survivor. These are my woods, my body, and my fucking magic," I yelled, before blasting half of her body with a thick wave of ice and freezing her to the ground.

I darted to her side, and she snarled at me with her teeth. But I grabbed feral Aoife's hair and jerked her whole head to the right before sinking my fangs into the space where her neck and shoulder met.

She screamed, and I pulled back everything she'd taken from me. I sent Ruad's energy back across the bridge and breathed my own magic in deep. There was something about not knowing what I had until it was gone, and I felt that entirely here as peace returned to my existence. This was right. It was who I was meant to be. Who I *deserved* to be. I was whole once more.

With blood dripping down my jaw, I stepped away a little and backhanded her, knocking my feral side out cold.

Then I gently pulled Adrienn out of my hair and cradled them again.

"Okay, I've got my magic back. What's next?" I asked.

They sighed and slowly placed their hands flat on my fingers.

"I'm going to borrow some to heal myself if that's okay," they said.

Tearing up again, I nodded and said, "Take every ounce of energy I have. Whatever it takes to save your life, you brilliant little fey. I'm so sorry all this happened."

"Not to worry, Aoife. It all worked out," they said and closed their eyes.

I felt Adrienn's energy probing my own, and I fully opened up to it, allowing their body to take in a solid chunk of my magic. Before my eyes, Adrienn began to look healthy again as they glowed a bright green. Bruises and purple splotches on their skin faded as muscles and bone mended themselves. Fey were truly something.

"Can all fey do that?" I asked.

"What? Exchange magic? Only if they share a deep and profound bond with another individual," Adrienn said.

When they were halfway back to normal, the glowing stopped, and they slowly sat up.

"There. I should be fine now," they said.

I didn't wait to kiss them on the head and then hug them tight to my chest.

"Owowow, still sore," they said, and I flinched, letting go.

"I'm sorry!" I shouted, my heart skipping a beat.

They smiled and hovered up in front of my face.

"It's okay. Let's get back to reality, shall we, alpha?"

I nodded and closed my eyes, feeling control return to me again. With a repaired psyche, I prepared to return to whatever state of battle waited for me. When I opened my eyes again, I was in a real forest, trees snapped around me and holes blown in the ground like little craters.

All I had time to do was mutter, "Shit."

Chapter Twenty-Three

New pain surged through me, and I suddenly realized I was seated at the base of a tree, one that had been snapped in half. My right arm was torn in several places and bleeding. Looking down, I saw my shirt had been obliterated on the right side, with burns covering the flesh over my ribcage. It smelled rancid. I gagged.

My hair was filled with dried blood, dirt, twigs, and grass. And one of my eyes was swollen shut.

"What the fuck happened while I was away?" I muttered, trying to stand but finding my body slow to respond.

Apparently feral Aoife hadn't been able to fight on two fronts, both in real life against Malachos, Ruad, and Ash and in my mind forest against me. I assumed Malachos got the drop on her with a lightning bolt and blasted her, now me, into Kingdom Come.

The fight must have turned into a chase at some point, because I didn't recognize where I was. It seemed so far out into the woods surrounded by pines and oaks I'd never walked under before.

A splitting headache rattled my noggin, and I moaned.

Fuck. Did she at least do me a favor and kill Malachos? I thought.

Ruad's whimper brought my attention forward through the pain.

The world went sideways as I looked up and spotted Malachos. He was grinning and holding a very familiar dagger.

Fucking hell, I thought, sensing my familiar once more. Fear and pain were most of her consciousness at this point.

"Yes, this is the one Tristan made, the one he severed Ruad's connection with. Now tell me, girl, whichever one you are, your familiar survived that traumatic event the first time. What do you think will happen if I sever her connection with another human partner?" Malachos asked.

I shook, trying to stand up. My body was exhausted. It felt like my joints and ligaments had endured a war while my mind was away. Things weren't looking or feeling great.

"Your fight is with me, Malachos. Bring that knife over here, and see what happens," I growled.

"My fight is with your entire clan. You've proven hard to kill tonight. But how about your wolf? I've chased her down for years, beaten her ragged. She's growing weak, and I can sense it. How long can she keep up her little charade of pretending to still be so strong?" he asked.

I looked over, and four reanimated corpses, three men and one woman, in various states of decomposition, had Ruad pinned to the ground. She looked battered and beaten, fur covered in blood, cedar chips, and mud. We exchanged glances, about 30 feet apart, and I heard her growl. I felt her pain and exhaustion radiating from a body that had endured so much already. Separation from a human partner, years on the run, and battle after battle with me.

"Hold her still," Malachos commanded, walking toward Ruad.

I struggled to get up, groaning, but a gash in my leg prevented me from really going anywhere. I hadn't noticed it until I tried to put weight on my legs and it stung like hell.

Looking around, I hollered for Ash, but he was being held down by another three corpses, pinned to a tree with a blade to his throat. These three were mostly bone, with glowing gray eyes, all locked on the raven. I knew on a good day Ash could kick the shit out of those three, no problem. But after going toe-to-toe with Malachos while chasing me down? He was probably too exhausted to even lift a finger.

"Ruad!" I screamed, turning back to my familiar.

Malachos moved in on her and held out the dagger. My familiar knew what was coming. I felt fear transition to outright terror radiating from every fiber of her being. She didn't want to endure this pain again. She'd do anything to avoid it. She must have been picturing the last time this happened, reliving the worst memory of her life over and over again.

I could almost hear her screams in my head from the last time that dagger had been used to sever her tie to Tristan.

She won't survive, I thought, my stomach sinking into my lower intestines.

Paralyzed in horror at the fate that awaited her, Ruad locked eyes with me one last time. Malachos drew closer.

"Aoife… I don't want this," she whimpered.

I promised her I would protect her. I promised her I wouldn't let her feel this pain again, and I would do anything to keep my word.

I screamed and started to crawl forward, blood pouring out into the mud around me. Things were getting hazy. I tried whipping together a spell, any spell. But I found my feral half had spent nearly all of my magical energy during her attempts to escape Malachos, Ruad, and Ash. It felt like I was lowering a bucket into a well and hearing it bang into dry rock.

"Time to die, wolf, the last O'Connell familiar," Malachos said, raising the blade high.

"Ruad!" I screamed.

What can I do? I have no magic, and I'm down for the count. I'm going to lose my wolf, my familiar, my very heart. Mother... father... what do I do? I thought, crying in the dirt.

And then I heard Iris' voice pop into my head, and she said two simple words, "Something stupid."

My eyes snapped open, and I rammed my hand down into my pocket, grabbing the Siol Eolais. Pulling it out, I roared and squeezed the crystal with everything I had. It started to crack, and I finally shattered the damn thing.

I'll pay the bill when it comes due. But now... just for now, let me save my wolf! I thought.

And then I did something stupid, but quite possibly the only thing I *could* do. I mashed the seed into my open wound on my thigh. It took everything I had to keep from screaming as pain shot up and down my leg like a lightning bolt smacked between two ping pong paddles.

In terms of magic, I didn't feel anything, but as I watched Malachos' dagger start to sink toward Ruad, I yelled, "Wake the fuck up, seed! You want your freedom, take it! Just give me the power to save Ruad!"

Apparently that was all it took, because the seed germinated, and roots snaked up my leg between veins and muscles up into my chest. The roots multiplied and crawled all throughout my body, down arms, up my neck, under my skin. I shivered and tried not to go into shock over these changes, a living plant literally taking root in my body.

But the plant came with advantages, as I felt its magic, a deep pool of power for me to tap into washing over every nerve in my body. I shivered at its potential, then turned my thoughts back toward Ruad.

Without hesitating, I slammed a palm into the earth and spawned roots to race through the ground at rocket speed. Those roots crossed a creek separating me from my familiar. They closed the gap between Ruad and me like nothing. In a split second they'd leapt the earth and formed a thick covering for my wolf, inches above her fur and just before the dagger made contact.

The blade slammed into those roots shielding Ruad, and even against the full force of Malachos, they held firm. It was almost as if they were slowly absorbing the dark energy radiating from the dagger. The necromancer growled and turned to me.

"What did you do?" he yelled.

"I protected the most important person in my life. You can't fucking have her. Ruad is mine, mine until these lungs no longer breathe," I said, standing up. "Ash! Save my wolf."

The raven seemed to find renewed strength in a command from his alpha and shattered the corpses pinning him with his wings. With renewed speed, I saw him race across the forest floor and snatch Ruad, landing about 50 feet away and nearly crashing.

With Ruad and Ash safe, I looked down at my leg, drawn by the lessening pain. The torn flesh on my thigh turned green like the stem of a plant and slowly fused back together, closing the gash. A child's voice spoke in my head.

Of all the possibilities for my freedom, this was the one I hadn't anticipated, it said.

I paused for a moment as the necromancer planned his next move.

"Yeah well… let's just focus on killing Malachos right now. After that, you can exact your price," I grunted, feeling my magic racing to new peaks I had never charted before. An incredible and archaic energy pushed me to new heights.

I checked "bill me later" on the form for unlimited power and threw it behind me. All that mattered now was Malachos' death.

"What did you do, Pup?" Ruad asked, looking over at me as the ground continued to quake. The trees around me seemed to be vibrating. Each one started to sprout leaves and flower at a rapid pace, making like spring had arrived.

"Impossible. You shouldn't have any magic left," Malachos said.

Malachos looked closely at my body, at the leaves and twigs now sticking out of a small slit in my thigh, the very wound he'd opened on feral Aoife.

"You actually sewed the seed into your own body? You're insane!" Malachos yelled.

Ruad looked at me with renewed fear.

"You took my pack. You took my family. And then you tried to take my wolf. Fuck you, Malachos. There's only one more thing to take tonight, and it's your sad, pathetic imitation of a life," I said.

Can you make this? I thought, picturing a plant in my mind.

Easily, the Siol Eolais said in my mind.

Then do it, I thought.

I threw back my head and howled as magic shot out of me and into the earth. A blinding green light emerged as the ground parted, and a magnificent plant arose. Ruad and Ash shielded their eyes, but Malachos stared straight ahead, trying to see what fate awaited him.

The light split into different stems, between 15 and 20 in total. The stems rose higher and higher until they were each about 20 feet long. Heads formed on the end of each, and as the green light faded, the heads took on a more visible form. They were shaped like clam shells and had jagged yellow "teeth" around the edges.

The outside of the shells was green, and the inside was blood red. They began to shake and shriek as they finished growing.

"What the hell is that?" Ash yelled.

"Giant ass Venus fly traps," I said, taking a deep breath and focusing my will into the plant.

Malachos was holding his dagger tight, eyeing the plants with apprehension.

"Get it, Malachos? You and your skeletons? They're the flies," I said. "And these babies track movement, so if I were you, I'd stand still."

The plants shrieked, and a bit of acid began to leak from some of the heads, melting stones and earth beneath them with a mighty hiss.

"Do you have any idea what you've done?" Malachos asked.

"I've signed your death warrant, Malachos. In the name of the O'Connell clan, I demand your life this night."

Malachos flinched and then shot his hand up, sending energy into the sky and building up storm magic. The plants gave him no quarter, racing across the earth for their next meal.

He blasted one with lightning, and it burst into flame, shrieking. But two more raced through the fire for his position.

Ruad and Ash stayed still, watching in awe. But the reanimated corpses all rushed to Malachos' side to back him up. One of the Venus heads snatched a skeleton up and clamped down on it, melting the bones in seconds with acid and sending a few crumpled bits of cartilage to the ground below.

Malachos was dodging the plant heads left and right, but they were getting closer and closer, smashing into trees and boulders where he previously stood seconds prior. He darted across the battlefield like a little rabbit, blasting a head with thunder magic when he had to, but mostly trying to conserve his strength.

"Destroy the plant, now!" he screamed at his little undead army, and they rushed forth to do that. My babies made quick work of them, their weapons maybe piercing the occasional head, but doing little damage.

Within another minute or two, the reanimated army was no more, and Malachos was sweating furiously, tired of dodging and blasting plant heads. He'd only taken out about five or six of them. The others filled the forest with their giant screeching bodies and raced after him.

He must have lost his sense of the battlefield, because he retreated right toward me, and I snatched his throat with one of my claws.

The dark wizard's eyes, one black and one white locked with my own glowing green eyes.

"Enough of this. If you keep going, that seed will devour you whole!" he said.

"Your life is the only one you need to worry about," I said.

In desperation, he slammed the dagger into my stomach. I didn't even flinch, just glanced down at it as though I were an outsider observing this happen to me.

A purple ooze leaked from the blade and started to gum up on my new injury. Malachos grinned as his dark magic seemed to poison the wound. I made no movement.

Within seconds, the ooze fell to the ground as Malachos flinched. Green blood poured out of my stomach, washing the poison clear. I didn't really feel the pain. And I had a guess as to why that was. Just another thing Siol Eolais could tack onto my bill.

When Malachos saw the dagger wasn't working, he pulled it out and shivered. We both watched my skin where the wound was. My flesh turned green and began sewing itself up, like watching a torn leaf repair itself in sped up motion.

"What have you become?" he gasped.

325

"I'm your death, Malachos," I said.

He shrieked as I haphazardly tossed him into the air.

"Wait!" he yelled, but that was all he got out before one of the heads snatched him, an arm and his head dangling from the mouth of the Venus fly trap. He used the dagger to try and stab the head, but that only made my babies more furious. Another head latched onto the arm. A third took his leg. The rest piled onto him, forming a giant ball of plant matter and acid.

From somewhere inside, I heard his muffled screams until there was nothing other than the tearing of skin and crunching of bone.

All that remained was his dark magic, which leaked down onto the earth with a sickening splat from the plant. Without my direction, roots sprouted from the remaining tear in my leg and crawled across the ground to that puddle of negatively-charged sludge. Within seconds, they'd absorbed it and taken what started as Malachos back into the Siol Eolais. All I could think was, *Disgusting, but I guess that really does bring this full circle.*

Popping my knuckles, I relaxed my shoulders and felt a wind blowing through the trees and shrubs around me, leaves rattling in the breeze.

"We got him, Mom and Dad. He's done," I whispered.

I took a deep breath and fell to my knees, dizzy from all the energy it took to grow each and every plant from pure energy alone.

Any chance you can shove that thing back into the earth so it doesn't hurt random hikers that come this way? I thought.

Of course, the Siol Eolais said in my head.

"Add it to my tab," I muttered, falling over to the cool earth on my side. Snow had started to fall, and I felt flakes melting on my cheek. The forest was spinning again.

"Pup!" I heard Ruad yell. Ash hollered something, too, racing over. But I couldn't make it out. The last thing I saw was my giant Venus fly trap sliding back into the earth. And everything faded from sight.

When I opened my eyes, I was surrounded by tall Douglas fir trees and alder trees once more. Clammy air moved over my skin as my focus bounced through the mist above.

Rolling over in the dirt, I slowly got up and realized I was back in my mind forest. Taking a deep breath, I rose. I felt dizzy and exhausted. Though it didn't take me long to smell vegetation I was unfamiliar with, one that didn't belong in my mind forest.

I turned around to see the source and spotted a young girl, perhaps eight or nine years old. Her skin was olive, and she had long pink hair. Her eyes were a shade of green much darker than my own.

She wore a dress made of maple leaves and danced between the trees.

"Free, I'm free. No more imprisonment for me," she sang.

I looked at her and said, "You must be the Siol Eolais."

She stopped dancing and came over to stand before me. She was maybe a little more than half my height and had to look up to see me.

"I'm what the Siol Eloais you planted within yourself gave birth to. And you can call me Brea," she said with a sing-song voice.

"Brea?"

"It's the name I've chosen for myself," she said.

"Right… so what happens now? Do you take over? Enslave me to pay my debt for defeating Malachos?"

The girl laughed and grabbed her belly, doubling over.

"You people are so funny. Debt? Were you not the one who freed me?" Brea asked.

I raised an eyebrow.

"Well… yeah. But then you gave me the power to defeat Malachos. So I figured I owe you a debt," I said.

She laughed again.

"You silly wolf. Do you think trees have a concept of debt? Or do they merely live? The seed you planted in your body came from a forest older than the human concept of bartering. I'm not here to take anything from you. I'm just here to share your body and live. I do not wish to seize control," Brea said, resuming her dancing. "Just experiencing."

Taking a deep breath, I tried to wrap my head around what she was saying. There was no way I got the power to defeat Malachos free and easy. The bill would come due. Brea was just going to be sneaky about it.

"So… since you have no concept of debt. If I asked you to leave my body, would you?" I asked.

That stopped her dancing, and Brea frowned at me, sending a chill down my spine all the way to my knees.

"Once a tree is planted in fertile soil, you don't uproot it. Removing me from your body by force would kill one or both of us. I've got a powerful druid host to live in. And you've got unparalleled magical abilities now like no druid has ever known. I can give you access to so much knowledge, plants you've never even dreamed of can spring forth from your fingertips. I'll repair any damage to our body and slow your aging to a crawl. My power is limitless. Why would you want to be rid of me?"

I flinched as I spoke.

"Don't take this the wrong way. I'm grateful for your help, but I don't trust that all these gifts would just be mine for free. We have a saying in Arkansas. 'That dog won't hunt.' It means, that doesn't make sense. So, I'm suspicious of your true intentions," I said.

A slow grin worked its way over her little pink lips.

"Silly wolf. You were the one that planted me here instead of the soil. And I'm not leaving, not now, not ever. So, you might as well be my friend," she said, with a stare that caused my heart to quiver.

I said nothing, and she took off, dancing between the trees of my mind forest again. Sighing, I wandered away to find the site where I fought feral Aoife. I located it and the ice shards where she'd broken free, fleeing into the mind forest once more.

"Great... another loose thread," I muttered.

Closing my eyes, I felt myself returning to the real world. When I opened them, I saw sunlight peeking in through the greenhouse roof.

Well, I guess she meant what she said about not wanting to take me over... for now, I thought, rising and realizing Ruad was asleep with her head on my chest. Her eyes opened, and she licked my cheek.

"About time you woke up, Pup," she said, getting up and stretching.

"How long was I out?"

"Two days," she said.

My eyes grew to the size of dinner plates and twice as white. I'd been unconscious for two days?

"You've got to be kidding me," I said, my stomach growling.

"Not even a little bit. Abi stopped by a couple times. She got real mad when the roots wrapped around her, and I laughed, eventually going out and letting her free," Ruad said.

"Ruad!" I scolded my familiar.

"Hey, you've been unconscious for two days, and I can only play checkers with Adrienn so many times before I get bored," Ruad said.

I was puzzled at that visual.

"You... played checkers? Do you... push the little pieces forward with your nose?" I asked, smirking.

"Yeah. What of it?" she asked.

I shook my head.

"Nothing, it's just… that's really cute," I said, giggling.

"Shut up. You wanna go hunt?"

"Yes please," I said, standing up and stretching.

Nothing felt too different about having Brea buried inside of me. I pictured little vines moving around under my flesh and grimaced. That was definitely weird.

As we hunted, I filled Ruad in about Brea and our conversation. She scolded me for trying something so stupid. And we both had suspicions about the seed's ultimate goals. Still, for now, things seemed calm.

We destroyed a deer and ate heartily.

I smiled and enjoyed my first meal in two days. Then we returned and washed up in the lake.

After texting Abi to say I was awake, I asked Adrienn to come out, and we discussed removing Brea. They didn't really see any way to do it.

"We're really in uncharted territory here, Aoife. That seed isn't from this world. And the means to remove it… I don't know."

"Who would?" I asked.

Ruad and Adrienn looked at each other for a moment. Then Adrienn glanced back at me and said, "Maybe some older druids would know… back in the homeland."

I turned slowly at that.

"And by homeland, you mean… Ireland?"

They nodded.

"What do you think, Ruad?" I asked.

She thought for a moment and said, "The O'Connell clan left Ireland back in the 1700s, arriving in America and eventually moving here. I guess it wouldn't be outside the realm of possibility for some O'Connell ancestors to have stayed behind. Perhaps their descendants would have knowledge of how to remove the seed."

Sighing, I realized I wasn't going back to school next semester. I had a new mission to undertake. I had a pack to rebuild, yes. But I also had a magical problem to solve with Brea. I didn't trust her. And the answers I needed to get rid of her weren't on this side of the pond.

"How do you feel about flying, Ruad?" I asked.

She grimaced.

"Unless you want to take a ship across the Atlantic," I muttered.

My familiar liked that even less.

329

Epilogue

Abi scolded me even more than Ruad did for planting the seed in my body, but when I asked what she would have done differently, she couldn't think of anything. Then she scolded me for pointing that out.

"Yes ma'am," I eventually sighed, admitting defeat.

We spent the rest of December patching up our relationship and trying to get back to some resemblance of normal. I made some very tiny progress on having fun with her doing normal human stuff again. We could eat meals together, and it held my interest once more. That seemed a relief for Abi. And with my grand enemy defeated, boy did we spend a lot of time rolling in the grass, as it were. That was more intense and passionate than it ever had been before.

The police found Barb's body buried in a grave next to her sister. They questioned me about it, but I had an alibi, spending the last several nights at Abi's house. Both Abi and her mother told them I'd been there for quite some time.

Some folks from the Arkansas State Crime Lab gave me a sideways glance as I left the interview, as though I just didn't look right to them. But since I wasn't a suspect, I left before they could take my hat off and figure out I wasn't 100 percent human. Hell, with Brea inside of me, I didn't know what percentage of human I remained anymore.

They set out to find the person who snapped Barb's neck, but I knew any remains of Malachos were deep underground in the Ozark National Forest. It would be a cold case before long.

I left John a postcard taped to the front door saying sorry for his loss and telling him I wasn't interested in any contact. So far, he hasn't even sent me a text. I don't even know if he cried about losing his wife. And I didn't want to spend any time thinking about the absentee adopted father or what he would do now.

Maybe he'd just sell the house and go right back to playing music like nothing had changed. Perhaps he'd meet someone he actually did love on the road and get remarried. I didn't care.

We finally got around to making Ash's entrance into the clan official. Ruad and Adrienn just said there had to be some sort of ceremony for the magic to enjoin him into the clan. They didn't specify what kind. I didn't think it really mattered.

So I did a little research and dug up an old Celtic friendship ceremony. We chose a sunny December afternoon and went hiking up by Beaver Lake. We packed a picnic, made flower crowns, and vowed to be friends forever. He really seemed to like that bit.

With Ash now officially an O'Connell, I told him I had to leave for a while with Ruad and Adrienn. He frowned but nodded in understanding.

"I'll watch things for you until you get back. You will be back, right?" he asked.

I smiled and ruffled his hair.

"Of course, silly. I just need to go dig up a little information on getting this seed out of me. Then I'll come right back. I promise," I said.

Abi told me she was coming with. She didn't ask for permission. God I loved this girl. There was a reason she was the top in our relationship.

With some frantic overnight mailing and applications, Abi told Jen she intended to spend a semester studying abroad and taking classes at a university in Dublin. She was accepted a few days before classes began.

Abi's mother scrounged up a couple one-way tickets for us and drove us to the airport up in Bentonville. I'd said goodbye to Sabrina the day before during my final shift at Petal and Stem.

We got out of the car, and I grabbed our bags. There were cars zooming in and out of the drop off point. It was a busy day, apparently. Ruad nearly got hit by a green Ford Explorer, so I yanked her back. She was wearing her service dog vest and barked loudly at the vehicle that almost hit her, cracking its rear window.

"Come on…" I said, chuckling and pulling her toward the sidewalk.

Jen hugged us tight and said, "You text me when you touch down in Chicago and again when you get to Dublin, okay? If you don't, I will fly after you and scold you myself!"

We hugged her tight again and said our goodbyes. Abi tried not to cry.

"You gave me the address to your new flat, right?" her mother asked.

"It's at home on a sticky note on the fridge," Abi said.

They kissed each other on the cheek, and then Jen turned to me.

"Watch her close, and keep her safe, will ya?"

"I promise," I said.

A guard started giving us a look saying that we were overstaying our welcome in the drop off zone, so Abi's mother drove off, waving at us.

We went inside and up an escalator toward the security lines. I could smell pretzels from an Auntie Anne's stand on the other side of the TSA booths.

Just before we got in line, an announcer spoke over the intercom system, saying, "Would Aoife O'Connell please go to the nearest phone? You have a courtesy call on line three. Aoife O'Connell to the nearest phone at your convenience, please."

Abi gave me a look, but I told her I'd catch her at the gate.

Ruad and I walked over to a black phone on the wall with two thin plexiglass guards on either side. Several people eyed Ruad nervously, but they generally left her alone when they saw the vest.

"I don't like it here," Ruad said, nerves in her voice.

"I know. I'm sorry. At least you get to ride on the plane with us instead of in the cargo bin," I said, patting her head.

"The cargo WHAT?" she hissed, but I ignored her and picked up the phone, pushing a button for line three.

"This is Aoife," I said.

A rich voice on the other end said, "I'm glad I caught you, little wolf."

"Oh, hey Odessa," I said, blinking.

"I wanted to give you a parting gift for defeating Malachos. Some of the local witches are glad to have that toxicity cleared from the region. His energy interfered with a number of their spells. But they certainly didn't have the power to take him down," she explained.

"Glad to help," I said, looking at my phone to see what time it was. "You guys going to be okay with me gone? If a new threat arises, you can ask Ash for help."

"That shouldn't be your concern right now. There's sure to be some trouble while you're gone, and tears will fall, but someone else will handle it," Odessa said.

I didn't know how to respond to that, nor did I have any clue what she was talking about.

"Anyway, I know you're in a hurry. So I just wanted to give you a name to look for in Ireland. Try to find Sinead Murphy," she said.

I gasped.

"Odessa... Murphy was Iris' maiden name," I said, my claw tightening on the phone.

"Good luck, little wolf. Ta ta," she said, and the line went dead.

Hanging up the phone, I looked at Ruad. She'd listened in.

"Sinead, huh?"

"It's a start," I said.

"American Airlines flight 2365 to Chicago is now boarding first class at gate A2," a voice over the intercom said.

"Crap, we'd better head over to security," I said. "Ready to set off on a new adventure?"

"I'm by your side until the day we die, Pup."

I smiled at that. She was worth fighting for, and I was overjoyed to have her. I was also glad to have Adrienn.

We'll figure this out, I thought. *I swear it.*

Excerpt from
A Pixie's Promise

Book Three in the Boston Mountain Magic Series

The polished floor mixed with precious stones still left me flabbergasted, even after living here for a month. With a silly grin, I caught myself looking at my image in the reflective floor of my new quarters. I stuck out my tongue.

"Neeeehhhhhh," I said, before laughing.

Pixies are probably supposed to take their responsibilities a little more seriously, but being melodramatic wasn't what got me through everything for the past month...

My smile only grew when I remembered that tomorrow I'd get to see my mother and friends again. And then next week I'll start my senior year of high school. Sure, I'd be doing battle against nightmares while everyone else was asleep, but I'd have some resemblance of my old life again.

Not that getting a crash course in all things pixie was torture, but it was hard work. Between tutoring sessions on pixie history, introduction to dream magic, and nightmare combat sessions, it was almost like I'd bypassed my last year in high school and started as a freshman at Pixie University.

All that's missing is a pixie sorority for me to join, I thought, laughing to myself again.

The first few nights without being in the same house as Mom were rough. To her credit, my tutor immediately sensed my internal distress at being disconnected from the people I loved, and how it was distracting my studies. She then had the mirror in my room enchanted so I could call home. The mirror in my quarters connected to one Mom had in her bedroom. And then it became obvious I wasn't the one having trouble being with the move.

Since I took Selene's spot serving in the Dream Court, that meant I got to live in the palace, study and train with royal staff, and generally had an easier time transitioning into this pixie stuff. The flip side to that is if Selene had just been some normal pixie off the street who had convinced me to start the Dreamwalker trials, and I had become a pixie outside of the queen's service, I wouldn't have nearly as many responsibilities as I do now.

I sat down on a cushioned bench next to my wardrobe and looked around my room for about the 100th time, still trying to wrap my head around the fact that I lived in a royal palace.

"I just wish I had a bed," I muttered. "I know pixies don't sleep, but beds are useful for lying on your belly and reading a book."

Across from me was a desk with some pencils and a few scattered pieces of paper, notes I'd taken, a few doodles when I got bored.

Large windows with a nook and a second bench with cushions overlooked the castle's courtyard. Beyond the nook was a door leading to the bathroom, complete with a large tub.

My bedroom walls were covered in some kind of enchanted paint that would change scenes at my command. There were four in total, a luscious forest with a crystal-clear pond, the open sea, gigantic mountain peaks and a hidden desert oasis.

When I first moved in, my tutor played a trick on me, changing the wallpaper when I wasn't looking and then pretending nothing looked different when I asked about it. I was nearly in tears before she finally let on to her little ruse. And I didn't speak to her for a solid 30 minutes afterward. I can't really hold a grudge or whatever even if I tried.

It was my fourth day living in the palace before I learned the walls changed according to a little dial beside the wardrobe. It looked like a color wheel about the size of my palm and cut into four pieces. Four colors on the wheel, one for each setting, green for forest, blue for ocean, white for mountains, and brown for desert.

A simple spin of the dial would change the walls. And the coolest part? The scenes moved, water rippled, waves crashed, leaves fell. It was amazing, and I never grew tired of watching it. My tutor seemed amused that I watched the walls every time she came to my quarters for study.

That's when a knock came at my door. I looked over at the source of the noise, my long silver hair bouncing around me.

If we'd been back home in the human world, I'd have just said,

335

"Come in," if I suspected it was a friend. That must have been a southern thing. I might have also said, "It's unlocked," if I knew it was Jenna or Tessa. God, I missed those two.

But in pixie culture, I learned, boundaries were sacred. You did not enter someone else's space without that person actively bringing you into it. So, I couldn't just say my door was unlocked (which it was). I had to go open the door and invite the individual into my quarters, even if I'd done it 1,000 times before.

The only exception to the rule of boundaries was for an emergency or if the person seeking to pass your boundary was someone extremely close to your heart. If Jenna and Tessa were pixies, they could pass any boundary I put up for others.

I hovered over the floor, floating to the door with my wings beating rapidly behind me. Opening the door, I saw my tutor standing there with a weathered brown book under her left arm.

"Kesi Saffrin, please come in," I said with a smile.

It had taken me about a week to fully adjust to terms of respect like Kesi for a female instructor or Kesa for a male instructor. And if the teacher didn't identify as either? Keso. A human college could probably start an entire degree program on pixie linguistics, or any other language in the vast amount of realms out there. Fortunately, they'd been patient enough with me to try and cut out as much jargon as possible.

The tall pixie kept her silver hair cut in a bob and wore a blue dress with a few Lapis lazuli stones sewn into her sleeves. Around her neck hung a string of pearls. Large, rounded silver frames rested on her nose.

She walked barefoot, which I learned in pixie culture meant a sign of comfort. Pixies walked without shoes in places where they felt safe and secure, no matter how cold the floor. And yet, there was no expectation for newcomers to feel comfortable in the castle so soon. So, nobody pressured me to ditch my sandals. I would remove them when this truly felt like a home, instead of a royal palace I had no business being in because I was just a drummer in a garage band with two other girls, girls I'd give my right arm to hug again.

They'd just call me Ricki Allen.

Saffrin came into my room and held out the book. I could see the title, *The Dreamwalker Mission* by Raine Cozythistle.

"That author's name is a real mouthful," I said, smiling.

"You should see some of the other doozies we have in the royal library. There's an author by the name of Tarragon Sunweb," Saffrin said.

"Oh, you're joking," I said, laughing.

"It looks like the criteria for foolishly naming a human baby and pixies taking on a new identity once they transform is about the same," Saffrin said, smiling, her pink glowing eyes a little brighter than mine.

I thought back to some of the most terrible baby names I'd heard of, like when folks tried to name their kids Optimus Prime or Voldemort.

"So, are you ready for your last lesson with me before heading back to the Mortal Realm?" Saffrin asked.

"Sure. What are we covering today?" I asked.

"Today we'll be going over why pixies fight nightmares, the real grand purpose, you know?" Saffrin said.

I couldn't believe I'd never thought about this before. It seemed like such an obvious question. Why? Why had a high school girl given up her mortal life to become a pixie and turn nightmares into dreams for humanity?

Then again, I guess I'd stopped asking the big questions once I figured out how Selene had used me. Just thinking back on how everything unfurled with the Queen of Tears sent an ache through my heart again. So yeah, maybe it wasn't surprising I'd refused to think about any big question stuff.

"Where do we start?" I asked.

"Why don't we head down into the garden for this lesson?" Saffrin suggested, and I nodded. We walked down a long hallway full of other quarters for members of the Dream Court and some servants.

Not all members of the Dream Court lived in the royal palace. Saffrin had told me once one had spent enough time in the queen's service, they were granted their own property and homestead. Selene had her own place, after all. It's where she died right before my eyes.

We walked down a stone spiral staircase and came to the first floor in the east wing of the palace. The first floor contained a large dining hall where everyone ate when there wasn't any kind of grand event being held.

I could smell pastries being baked and made ready for dinner, along with several kinds of stews. Pixies had their own meats, fruits, and vegetables I'd been slowly picking up. But they also had some foods from the mortal realm. Apparently, the queen had pixies bring groceries back through the portal with them when their month in the pixie realm was about to begin.

Could I go into the dining hall and grab a paija fruit? Sure. Could I ask for a Pepsi at the bar and have the kitchen chef bring me one? You bet. It never surprised me just how many human products I could find here in the pixie realm.

It really shouldn't have been that much of a surprise, though. We're beings that infiltrate human dreams on the regular and live in the mortal realm every other month. On top of that, we're all former humans. When we get here, we're bound to want something from home. For me, it was a huge relief to find Crunch bars. I sometimes helped Talos the head cook scrub pots after dinner to earn a few.

Pixies don't really use currency in their world. Everything is bartered for goods or services. Sometimes I wonder if human life would be simpler like that, but then I realized I'd hate to walk into Target to buy a pair of leggings and have the cashier say, "Sure. Take out 30 bags of trash to our dumpster, mop the entire store, and they're yours."

Was that what the free market was? I have no idea. I elected not to take AP Economics this year.

Saffrin led me out a pair of glass French doors and into the castle's garden, which sat on an acre of land. The garden was divided into four sections, each in a corner. One was a cluster of trees for migratory native birds of the pixie realm. Another produced fruits and vegetables for castle dining. In another corner sat a sort of hedge maze and walking paths. The last corner consisted of all varieties of flowers.

My tutor took me to a spot under some fruit trees where two blue cushions sat.

"It looks like they're still damp from this morning's rain," I said.

"Can you take care of it, please?" Saffrin asked.

I nodded.

Since my arrival, I'd been taught that the pixie realm is like a giant dreamworld of sorts. In that, we can manipulate small pieces of it with magic like a human dream. It just took a lot of focus for newbies like me. Manipulating the pixie realm felt like trying to grab a piece of the ocean with one hand. There was just so much, as opposed to one self-contained human dream.

I placed my right hand on the damp fabric and closed my eyes, picturing a desert, one dry and parched. Sighing, I felt the moisture in the cushion disappear.

When I still had my soul kite, I gave all my dream magic to my wrist, because that's where the bracelet that held my pixie magic sat. But now that I was a full-blown pixie, my whole body was the bracelet. And I didn't have a battery on my wrist to draw from. I had me. And me got tired a lot sooner than the bracelet ever did. It took days of rest after saving Fayetteville from Hiawatha's nightmare before I could even feel my magic again.

After I dried the cushion for Saffrin, I repeated the action for myself. We stood there, and I motioned to Saffrin's cushion.

"After you, Kesi Saffrin."

"Thank you, Roxie," she said, taking her seat.

I sat after she had placed her book on the grass. She looked over at me and said, "Roxie, why do you think pixies do what we do?"

"You mean, turn nightmares into dreams?" I asked.

She nodded.

"I honestly have no idea. Is it not to provide emotional and mental help to those in need?" I asked, cocking my head to the left a little.

Saffrin smiled and said, "That's certainly a motivator for some pixies. Your heart shines bright for a newly turned pixie, Roxie. I have no trouble believing you will use the happiness of others to motivate your efforts. But if we're being realistic, there's a more pragmatic reason for our actions as a whole."

I suppose it would be ignorant of me to think pixies fought nightmares out of the generosity of our hearts.

As if she could read my mind, Saffrin gave me another smile and said, "Humans are fascinating creatures. They're imaginative, passionate, with a great capacity for both good and evil. Their lives are short compared to ours. You know the saying about the candle burning twice as bright?"

"Half as long," I said.

"Correct. Humans have a very potent life force. And many mythical creatures and beings interact with it, whether feeding on it, protecting it, nurturing it, or simply snuffing it out. Humans typically don't possess great strength or abilities, but the tradeoff for that is their life force itself."

I clasped my hands together and nodded.

"Another fascinating aspect of humans is they're all linked to one another. Their minds connect and form relationships from across the globe. Billions of strands forming between each human's thoughts and emotions. These strands together form a great collective unconscious, a giant web of memories, perceptions, and shared experiences that people cannot see or comprehend. But it's there all the same," Saffrin said.

I nodded again, though much slower this time. Trying to wrap my head around it all.

"Here. Picture your friends, Tessa and Jenna."

A smile formed on my face as I did so.

"Imagine one back in your home city of Fayetteville. Then place the other on the other side of the Mortal Realm… let's say Moscow. Now while they're separated, each friend will likely think of the other, communicate via their phones, and maintain a connection. Now imagine that connection between their minds as a long piece of string. No matter where they go, that string stays connected."

"Okay."

"Multiply that string eight billion times to represent connections for the entire populace. And then multiply that number by five to represent people's loved ones. All those strings together, those connections, would form a giant ball. And with their life force passing through the strings, that giant ball would be a massive pool of energy. Well, that ball is what I called the collective unconscious earlier, the mental connection each human shares. And the life force within that ball… it's insanely powerful," Saffrin said.

A bird that looked like a cross between a blue jay and a starling landed in the tree above us and started to sing.

"Okay. I think I get most of that. But where do the dreams come in?" I asked.

Saffrin held up a finger and said, "That's a great question."

Thanks, I made it myself, I thought, trying not to smirk.

"The collective unconscious of humanity is a force to be reckoned with, but it's also a bit like a seesaw. If humanity as a whole starts generating too many dark thoughts and negative emotions, that reflects on the collective unconscious, making it unstable and dangerous, which feeds back onto humanity in a terrible loop. It's why things like plagues and wars are so hard to pull out of. But when humanity sees the light and is united together in harmony, that energy is at peace. Think of it as manifesting.

Dreams are another facet of the unconscious mind, and they can have a wide impact on a dreamer, both emotionally and physically. Too many nightmares, and a person's health and life force start to dwindle. Multiply that effect by billions, and you start to see a growing shadow in the collective unconscious.

So, it's our mission to do battle against nightmares, whether internally or externally influenced, in an effort to stabilize emotions and thoughts on a wide scale," Saffrin said, showing me diagrams from the book on this collective unconscious of humanity.

It took everything I had to keep my jaw from the grass beneath me.

"When you... when you consider all of that, it just seems too big, Kesi Saffrin. Way too big for me to influence. Billions of dreams and nightmares to process? And how many pixies are there working on all of this?" I asked, feeling my head about to explode. Sure, I saw many pixies passing in and out of the Pixie palace, but each and everyone was a different face. I rarely saw one Pixie twice, unless we had some business together of sorts.

"There are about half a million pixies in existence, Roxie. We are a small rudder, not an overwhelming force. All we can do is try to steer humanity toward the light," Saffrin said, her smile returning.

Sighing, I shook my head and then looked back at the pixie before me. My left arm wasn't far from hers, with both our hands sitting next to the book. Saffrin's brown skin was a contrast to my ghostly complexion.

The sky here is filled with a variety of colors, streaks of ultramarine, indigo to violet. It's beautiful, but the one thing it seemingly couldn't do was give me a healthy tan. I'd spent hours down here walking the garden since my arrival, and I was just as pale as when I got to this world.

Saffrin continued her lesson and further instilled the foundation of my ultimate pixie mission inside of me.

We sat on those cushions for a couple hours before Saffrin finally asked if I had any questions. The whole collective unconscious responsibility I now shared part of felt like it was smothering me. I figured as time went on through the lesson that feeling would subside. But it didn't.

Each layer of responsibility Saffrin wove about our magic and the worlds all around us just added more weight to my chest. What had Selene roped me into? Sure, the whole "manipulating dreams" thing was a bit much, but hey, it's magic. If a pixie shows up in your therapist's office one day, heals some of your trauma, and gives you a magical item to manipulate dreams, that's easy enough. But hearing about the

341

 ̴ollective unconsciousness of humanity and how it factors into things like wars, diseases, progress, and more just expanded it all to a level my brain had trouble wrapping around.

It's all too big for one high school girl to deal with, I thought.

I hadn't felt this lost since I'd first set foot in her garden, and she dumped her truth on me.

Sweat formed on my forehead and dripped down my cheek.

I can't do this, I thought. *Just let me go back to being a human again. Somebody let me off of this train!*

My heart rate sped up. An entire world of connected human minds. Entire worlds connected together. And we… we were a rudder. But faced with such a violent storm, what hope did we have? What hope did I have of fulfilling the mission? And what if I screwed up? That could really hurt a person.

Clenching my fist next to the book and grabbing up a handful of dirt and grass, my breathing grew shallower. And my eyes started to dart from side to side, the images around me becoming a blur.

Suddenly I felt like I weighed 1,000 pounds and the garden was swallowing me whole.

"I can't," I muttered, as my shoulders buckled. I shook my head.

About the Author

Courtney Lanning is a writer and journalist from Arkansas. Because *The Ozarks Druid* didn't wear her out enough, she's busy trying to get its sequel, *A Pixie's Promise*, to readers by Halloween.

When she's not writing, Lanning is probably playing Dungeons and Dragons next to her wife, reading, or watching a movie. But through all of it, she's daydreaming about fae, magic, and talking animals.

Her debut novel, *Funky Dan and the Pixie Dream Girl*, the first book in the Boston Mountain Magic fantasy series, was published in 2021.

She can be found on Twitter under @CourtneyMovies or on Facebook under Courtney Lanning - Author

Other Riverdale Avenue Books You Might Enjoy

Magic University: The Complete Series
By Cecilia Tan

The Macroglint Trilogy
by John Patrick Kavanagh
Sixers
Weekend at Prism
Sanctuary Creek

Venomoid
by J.A. Kossler

An Outcast State
by Scott D. Smith

Made in the USA
Middletown, DE
19 April 2023